Dance with the Harem

D.P. Scott

DEDICATION

For my daughters, Brittney and Alexandra

CHAPTER ONE

Davon Marshall adjusted her position and contemplated taking an Ativan to help her fall asleep. She wanted to be fresh and alert when she reached her destination, but recognized that was most likely impossible. Although she was surprisingly comfortable in the business class seat, now turned sleeping pod, she couldn't help but keep wondering if she'd made a huge mistake. It had all happened so fast, and with only forty-eight hours to make her decision she had thrown caution to the wind by agreeing to accept an extremely high-paying, but unusual job in another country. Her parents who were always so supportive had actually yelled when she told them, suggesting she needed psychiatric counseling. That had really hurt, especially when her mother said she must be completely insane to give up her current position. Davon knew they had good intentions, but they just didn't understand what she was going through. She had to get away, from Boston, from Matt, from everything.

Whatever, she thought, attempting to reassure herself. If worse comes to worst, I'll quit and go home. She snuggled deeper into the pod trying to relax, and as she turned her head the soft cabin lighting settled on her flawless features. Davon had inherited her father's aristocratic nose, her mother's pouty lips and high cheek bones, and a silky ivory complexion from her paternal grandmother. People often remarked that she certainly must burn when out in the sun, but when exposed to sunlight, Davon's winter, snowy white complexion quickly changed to a glimmering golden brown.

Davon pulled her arm out from under the navy blue woolen blanket, glanced at her watch, and sighed. There were still eight hours until arrival. It was her first time flying business class and she was impressed. If it had been up to her to purchase the ticket, she would have been at the very back of the plane trying to find the room to stretch out her long legs. Excited about reaching her destination and unable to control her racing thoughts, she discreetly lifted herself up on one elbow and peeked over the partition at her sleeping neighbors. The layout of the cabin was definitely clever. The seats were angled so when they turned into pods, it was a quick and simple procedure of reclining the back and lifting up the base of the seat to create a full-length sleeping compartment. Each chamber had its own TV hosting a multitude of movies and shows, deluxe over-sized earphones, and a window, which seemed just a little bit larger than the ones in economy. "Business class is amazing and the food…" she murmured, reminiscing about dinner. They had been served cold deviled shrimp, rice pilaf, lamb with dill, honey nut cake with rum sauce, and Turkish coffee presented on gold trimmed china placed upon a crisp white tablecloth. It was dining at its finest, in a five star restaurant with a thirty thousand foot view.

But now she needed to sleep! Reaching into her briefcase, she grabbed her iPod. She straightened the wires from the ear pieces and thought of Matt and the unpleasant memory of her twenty-sixth birthday when he had given it to her as a present. He had handed her the small gilded gift box and she'd been thrilled, positive she was going to find an engagement ring nestled in the rumpled gold tissue paper. It had been extremely difficult to hide her disappointment.

She still couldn't believe he had ended their relationship three days later! And the reasons he'd given--they were ridiculous! He had said he loved her, but with his job and family situation, their paths were heading in entirely different directions. He seemed to believe that with his current obligations he could no longer measure up to her expectations. According to him, she was better off without him. It didn't seem to matter when she said they were perfect for each other, reminding him that in three years they had never really had an argument, except for this one. They thought alike, loved to be active together, and laughed at the same things. They were both ambitious and responsible. And she would be more than happy to be the main bread-winner until his family obligations were met, and then of course when he resumed schooling. He was going to go back, wasn't he? Surely he would finish his architecture degree? She loved the fact that he felt his responsibilities so deeply, but he'd go back so they could get on with their own lives, wouldn't he?

Matt had replied that taking care of the family was the man's responsibility and he wasn't the type of person who could allow her to assume the role. Things had changed with the death of his father and brother in the plane crash, and now he couldn't possibly consider anything else but taking care of the family business, and his mother, sister-in-law and young nephews, who were all dependent on him. It was an awful twist of fate, but it was his problem, and she certainly didn't need his burdens to complicate her life. And then he stood and walked out! It had been almost a month to the day, and there had been no communication since. Davon couldn't count the number of times she had picked up her cell phone wanting so desperately to call him, if only to hear his voice on the answering machine, but she had never completed the call. After all he had been the one who left, and she wasn't going to sink so low as to beg him to reconsider.

"This is crazy. You're going to be a mess if you keep rehashing this!" she said, reprimanding herself. Turning over Davon pulled the thick blue blanket over her head and began a series of deep yoga breathing.

Pushing her long, thick, blond hair out of her eyes, Davon blinked a few times and sat up. The light in her section was becoming brighter and brighter as the lights were gradually turned up to gently wake the sleeping passengers. She must have slept and was extremely surprised to see that it was 7:00 am local time. Still three hours until arrival, but all the same she had enjoyed a couple of hours of shuteye. Flying business class did have its perks! Davon pulled out her cosmetic bag with her toiletries and wiggled down to the end of her pod. Scooting into the washroom to beat the predictable lineup of other passengers, who would want to freshen up, she splashed water on her face, applied a bit of makeup, and brushed her teeth.

By the time she returned to her section, someone had already transformed the pod back into a seat and straightened the area. Davon sat down and smiled; she could get used to this type of service. As she settled in and switched on the news, she caught a wonderful scent and then noticed the food trolley approaching her seat.

"Can I interest you in coffee and a spinach mushroom omelet with marble rye toast?" asked a cheerful flight attendant.

"That'd be great, thanks," replied Davon, accepting a large cup filled with the most amazing smelling coffee.

When her meal was placed before her, she smiled at the detail. Her omelet was in the shape of a flower and some of the spinach had been pulled to one side to form a stem and leaf. The toast was round with six alternating dark brown and white rye pie-like sections. The whole eating experience was delightful, and Davon was convinced there had to be a chef onboard.

She was engrossed in the *Boston Herald* crossword when an overhead announcement asked the passengers to secure their belongings for landing. Looking out the window she could now see land below the low lying cloud and was positive that she caught a glimpse of the tallest building in the world. As they approached the city, Davon was in awe; it was much more beautiful than the pictures she had down-loaded.

The landing was easy and as they taxied in Davon could see an enormous, modern terminal with numerous public and private jets pulled into the various gates. She could also see several emergency vehicles with lights flashing, followed by two black limousines heading towards them on the tarmac. "That's odd," she whispered, as the plane braked hard. Her body was propelled forward and hung on the seatbelt for a few seconds before she was slammed back into her seat. The plane then came to a screeching stop. Her first thought after the ordeal was that they were lucky to be on the ground if something was wrong with the aircraft. As she sat listening intently for information and instructions from the pilot, Davon was startled when a hand touched her shoulder.

"Miss Marshall?" A flight attendant she hadn't seen before was looking at her for confirmation.

"Yes?" she replied, somewhat puzzled.

"It's been requested that you exit the plane here, on the tarmac. Could you please gather your belongings? A staircase is being placed in position for you," he told her.

"Pardon me? I'm sorry, but I don't understand. Is something wrong?" asked Davon, trying to remain calm. She felt her heart pounding.

"Please follow me," he said, ignoring her question. He assisted her with her briefcase and jacket.

Davon stood up, her legs somewhat wobbly. She was conscious of the curious stares from the other passengers and wished she had listened to her mother. What had she been thinking? This is the problem when you act on impulse, she yelled at herself! The night Matt left her, she found the job on the internet, applied for it, and got it. In truth, she hadn't planned to take it; she had just hoped that when Matt found out she was thinking of leaving the country he would beg her to stay. Well that sure back-fired, she thought, anxiously approaching the front of the plane and two attendants who were in the process of opening the door. I'm probably going to prison for not having the proper work visa. Why did I trust these people from the internet?

When the door was finally opened, the flight attendants stood to the side allowing Davon to pass. She took a step forward and made her way to the top of the mobile staircase. There she could see several military personnel with submachine guns slung over their shoulders. It was a frightening sight. Davon could almost make out a driver in each one of the limousines, but because the rear glass was darkly tinted, she couldn't see if anyone was in the back. As she hesitated on the landing trying to decide if she should run back into the plane and demand to see a representative from the American Embassy, the flight attendant motioned her forward.

"Please, Ms. Marshall, could you deplane? We have a schedule to maintain for our other passengers," he said politely.

"Of course." Davon took a deep breath, lifted her head high and proceeded down the staircase as though nothing was wrong. Clutching her cell phone, she berated herself for not entering some emergency contact numbers. She could see the heat waves rising from the tarmac and it suddenly seemed incredibly hot. Tiny beads of sweat started to form on her forehead and she could feel her nylon stockings sticking to her legs. Her mind was awhirl. She had rights as an American citizen, didn't she? They can't just yank anyone off a plane here, or can they? Before her foot touched the bottom rung, the back door of the nearest limousine opened and an older man dressed in an impeccable black suit stepped out and approached her.

"Welcome to Dubai, Dr. Marshall. Your helicopter has been arranged. Please come with me," he said, indicating to the second vehicle.

Pretending this was an everyday occurrence, Davon did as she was told, but still eyed him suspiciously. At least he knows my name, she said to herself, glancing nervously at the ten or more soldiers. By the time they reached the second car, the driver was out of the vehicle and opening the rear door.

"Dr. Marshall, please have a seat inside the air conditioned limousine. You will be much more comfortable out of the heat. If you would be so kind as to give me your passport, I shall make all of the arrangements to expedite you through customs. The driver here will be taking you to the helipad where you will board a helicopter. It will take you directly to the palace. The prince felt that after such a long plane ride, you would not be happy about a four hour car journey through the desert."

Although her greeter attempted a smile, it was rather forced. It didn't reach his eyes, which were dark and cold. And his expression, one of disinterest and irritation was not at all welcoming! Against her better judgment she bent her head and ducked inside. Rummaging around in her purse, she pulled out her passport. "Thank you, Mister???" when he didn't respond, she carried on. "I appreciate your assistance, but really, I am very capable of going through customs on my own. I truly believe one should always keep their passport on their person. So, if you could just have the driver take me to…"

"I am afraid the Prince would not allow it. You are his honored guest, and he will not have you mingling with commoners. Please, if you will give me your documents I will deal with the authorities. Things are done a little differently in this part of the world."

"What about my luggage? I can't arrive at the palace without my luggage, Sir. I'm sorry I don't know your name." Davon begrudgingly placed the passport and work visa into his hand.

"I am Mr. Bedon, and I will be personally responsible for your luggage. You don't need to concern yourself."

Before Davon could reply, she saw Mr. Bedon make a small hand signal to the driver. The rear door to the limousine was immediately shut. The driver slid behind the wheel of the idling car, and quickly moved in between the three escorting military vehicles. Two were in front and one was behind the limousine.

Davon nervously took one last look at the plane, and for the first time noticed that every window had a face crammed into it. "Take a good look people, I may need you as witnesses," she mumbled, feeling new beads of sweat forming on her forehead as she watched her last place of refuge shrink into the distance .

Trying to convince herself that everything would be alright, Davon looked around the inside of the limo. The luxury was unbelievable. Wide, plush, black leather seats, with enough room for six or seven passengers let her comfortably stretch out her legs in utter decadence. There was even a mini-fridge, where a glass door revealed its contents of chilled bottled water and fresh fruit. She took one bottle, opened it, and reveled in a long cool drink, then casually reached for two more and snuck them into her purse while looking through the opening in the partition to see if the driver noticed. She assumed the drinks were free, but rationalized that even if they weren't she'd need water to survive in the heat, in case for some unknown reason she was abandoned in the desert. The email had said she would be met at the airport, not taken off the plane in the middle of the tarmac. And there was no way she trusted the shifty looking guy behind the wheel or the smooth talking Mr. Bedon.

"Where the heck are you taking me?" she said under her breath, when they entered an industrial looking area. "You'd think the helipad would be somewhere near the terminal, not in the middle of a bunch of buildings. Oh dear God, what if they are planning to interrogate me?" she moaned, dramatically.

The partition between the driver and the back seat was only slightly open, but suddenly thinking about why it was open, Davon quickly stopped talking. She wondered if the driver understood English and then thought about her horrible habit of talking out loud. Frowning, she glanced around the interior of the car speculating that there might be some type of recording device. She noticed an intercom on the ceiling and saw the green light was on. A green light in the operating room in Boston meant the intercom was active so that everyone in the viewing theater could hear what was being said during the operation.

"Maybe the driver doesn't understand English, but I bet I'm being taped…even filmed!" she mouthed the words quietly, reminding herself again to stop vocalizing all her concerns. I need to shut up, keep my wits, and memorize the passing landmarks, she told herself. Then, I can make my way back to the terminal if the driver does anything weird. Twisting back and forth, she looked out both side windows and started counting buildings. The black interior of the limousine smelled like new leather, and had extremely comfortable down-filled seats, yet she took no further notice, and instead poured all of her energy into her task. But by the time she had counted twenty-nine corrugated metal warehouses, her hopes faded. She was lost in a maze of identical looking hangers and industrial buildings, and had no idea where she was in relationship to the airport.

When they were well entrenched in the middle of the industrial area, the two head military vehicles pulled over, allowing the limousine to move into first position. Protected by the tinted windows, Davon stared at the serious faces of the military personnel and the manned, green machine guns on the top of the Humvees. Never in her life had she seen anything so menacing. She turned around and looked out the rear window and noticed that the third escort vehicle was still behind them. It raced to catch up as the limousine continued to speed past a series of connected warehouses. Feeling extremely warm, Davon leaned into the air conditioning unit. She let the cool air refresh her and prayed it was the Middle Eastern heat causing the sweating and rapid heart rate, not an anxiety attack. Please let this be okay, she thought, grabbing her cell phone from her bag. Opening it she saw the words 'no signal'.

"Figures," she whispered, drumming the keyboard.

Before putting the phone away, Davon snapped a few photos of her surroundings and then contemplated taking a picture of the driver. It's always better to be safe than sorry, she told herself, determined to have a picture of everyone she was in contact with in case of problems. After all, when she'd applied for the job, she had to send them three head shots. Wedging herself between the door and the back of the seat, Davon knelt and practiced positioning her phone in the middle of the driver-passenger partition. Her plan was to take a snapshot of the rearview mirror and catch the reflection of the man at the wheel. The partition was only open about three inches, but this was enough space for a photo buff like Davon, who was usually in charge of the fiber-optic camera during surgery.

Suddenly becoming aware of his passenger's odd behavior, the driver found his eyes glued to the mirror. He was mesmerized with the antics of the extremely beautiful passenger in the back seat, and although he knew better than to look at her, he found that he couldn't tear his eyes away. Davon who was totally occupied at getting the best picture didn't realize until she looked into the lens, that his eyes were on her, not the road. Letting the phone fall into her lap, she knew they were in trouble when she felt the car swerve hard to the right. Following the momentum, she fell and plowed into the door. The driver had lost control of the speeding vehicle, and now was fighting to keep the limo on the road by clutching the shaking steering wheel with all his might.

Barely managing to grab onto the padded door handle, Davon braced herself as the vehicle began to vibrate so intensely, she thought it was going to break in two. She could hear the hot tires squeal as they skidded sideways across the scorching pavement, out of the industrial area, and into an open space of narrow road flanked by desert. She could see nothing but a blur of yellow zooming by as the car fishtailed. Instead of letting the car slow on its own accord, the driver suddenly decided to slam on the brakes. Davon's body lurched forward in response and smashed into the mini-fridge. The driver held the brake firmly down, locking them, which caused the car to spin. Now the back of the vehicle was pulling the front towards the edge of the pavement.

As she hysterically searched for something to grab onto, she realized the car was going to flip. "Get your foot off the brake!" she cried, holding back the profanities she really wanted to say as the car continued to turn and forcefully shudder.

Ignoring Davon, the driver held his foot hard to the brake, choosing to fight the steering column in his attempts to right the vehicle. The limousine's low center of gravity and the perfectly flat road helped to stop the car from flipping over, but it was still skidding backwards and sideways. For a split second it seemed as though they were suspended in time, and Davon realized she only had moments to prepare for the crash. Seizing a leather strap from behind the top of the rear facing seat, Davon pulled herself up and wedged her feet under the door handle in an attempted to brace for impact. As she did this she fleetingly glanced at the rear view mirror. The driver had his eyes closed.

"What the hell are you doing?" she screamed, "Open your bloody eyes!"

The driver's eyes blinked open, but rather then concentrating on the road he glared back at her through the mirror, as though their predicament was her fault. If Davon had had more access to him she would have slapped his face, but instead she was abruptly thrown to the floor and pelted with flying objects. She was going to die, and there was nothing she could do about it!

Without warning, the intervals of shuddering and swerving slowed, and Davon sensed the driver was beginning to gain some control. "Thank God," she kept repeating as the vehicle slowly came to a quivering stop. The smell of burning tires was unpleasantly strong, and when she pushed herself up, Davon noticed the contents of her purse strewn about along with bottles of water, and various pieces of fruit from the now empty mini-fridge. Before she even had a chance to get properly back onto her seat, military guards surrounded the limousine, their weapons drawn. Yanking open the driver's door, the driver was roughly pulled out and thrown to the ground. Staring, mouth agape, Davon watched as four of them kicked and butted him with the ends of their rifles. "Stop it!" she called out, suddenly empathetic for the man. Reaching for the door handle, she pushed down the square lever and threw her weight into it shoving with all her strength, but the door wouldn't budge. She looked up and back and saw a soldier blocking her exit. Quickly thinking, she got onto the seat and slid across to the opposite door. Another soldier secured that exit as well. Furious, she wiggled the door handle and pounded at the window. "Let me out! I demand to speak to whoever is in charge! Do you hear me!" she cried angrily. The soldiers remained rigidly at attention and ignored her pleads.

Two more Humvees pulled up on either side of the limo creating a blanket of dust, and although Davon temporarily lost sight of the driver, she could still hear loud shouting. As the sandy film gradually settled, she saw the driver with his head bleeding being dragged away. There was nothing she could do. Closing her eyes, she pressed her hands over her ears, and cowered in the back seat trying to make the madness vanish. What am I doing in this place, she asked herself? I was supposed to have a perfect life in Boston, marry Matt, and have lots of beautiful children. I've got to tell them I made a mistake. I'm going back home. Being here is just wrong, totally wrong.

She heard the driver's door being wrenched open and looked up to see one of the military personnel getting into the car. The engine roared to life and as the car spun around to face the right direction, the tires kicked up dust obstructing her view until they were well on their way. They traveled for about ten minutes and she became aware that the pavement was coming to an end. There was no building, no helicopter, just hot dry sand.

She felt the bump when the back tires left the road, and looked behind to see another trail of dust. They were now on hard packed sand heading, as far as she could see, towards nothing. But, not more than five minutes later the vehicle stopped, and the rear door was opened. The new driver held the vehicle door, looking straight ahead. He gave no instructions. Feeling her compact clenched tightly in her hand, Davon casually opened it. A tiny bruise was beginning to form above her right eye. Snapping the compact closed, she gathered her things, and pulling her skirt down discreetly, she exited. She could hear the sound of whirling blades and saw a lone, shiny black helicopter waiting, presumably for her. The heels of her shoes immediately sunk into the sand, and she cursed the driver as she struggled to walk to the helipad tarmac, and her next mode of transportation.

It seemed to be even hotter than it was at the airport, and Davon felt as though there wasn't enough oxygen in the dry air as she made her way towards the helicopter. There were two pilots sitting inside the cockpit, but no one else in the vicinity. As she came closer, one of the pilots jumped to the ground beside the portable step-ladder and stood at attention. He didn't attempt to speak to Davon, which would have been difficult with the noise from the blades. Yet, what was more disturbing to her was that he didn't greet, instruct or even acknowledge her. He acted in a similar fashion as the driver, looking above or around her as though she was invisible.

Rolling her eyes, she climbed into the back of the copter. It was at that moment that she caught him taking a sideways glance at her legs. "Oh brother," she whispered, shaking her head. Once she was seated, the pilot on the ground quickly scooped up the step-ladder, jumped into the bird and then in a roundabout way indicated the seatbelt and ear protectors that she was to use. He did all of this without helping or really looking at her, which again made her feel incredibly uneasy.

"Yeah, don't worry about me buddy, I fly in helicopters all the time," she said, sarcastically under her breath.

Within minutes they were airborne, and Davon was looking down on one of the most beautiful cities in the world, totally forgetting her concerns. It was hard to believe this amazing place had been built in fifteen years. As she attempted to identify some of the buildings she had seen on-line, the helicopter banked and began to head straight towards the desert. It would have been nice to fly over the city, she thought, so that she could see some of the landmarks. Oh well, she told herself, as the scenery began to fade into the distance, these guys wouldn't exactly be my first choice as tour-guides anyway. Sighing, she took in the golden sand and barren landscape, and hoped the pilots were more competent than her driver. The beating she had witnessed was ugly, and she was definitely going to report it to Mr. Bedon when she resigned. Although she felt terrible about breaking her contract, it couldn't be helped. The job just wasn't going to be a fit.

A sense of serenity and peacefulness began to overtake her. The rolling dunes, which played in the afternoon sunlight glistened and reflected colors not just of beige, but of orange, yellow and red. Somehow the exoticness of it all created a feeling of freedom and adventure, which called to her. Caught up in a dream of wandering the desert with Bedouin nomads, Davon didn't see the large reflection ahead of them, until it was so bright in the cockpit she had to retrieve her sunglasses from her bag. Wondering if she was seeing a mirage or optical illusion, something she heard was common in the desert, Davon quickly realized the reflection was in fact a lake. She could now see hundreds of tall, gently swaying palm trees surrounding the water and beyond the trees, grasslands, which tumbled softly towards a turquoise sea.

A very large whitish stone structure was now coming into view. It was built in the exotic Middle Eastern fashion she'd imagined when she found out she would be working at a palace. Feeling excited, Davon hoped this was the place of her employment. The building was rectangular in shape with a large dome in the center of the roof, and had four domed towers, one on each side. An open porch with key-hole archways surrounded the front side of the building. There were forty or more gigantic white pillars supporting the archways, and when she looked at them, she realized they were topped with gold.

Davon felt a rush of excitement. The palace reminded her a little bit of the Taj Mahal, so enchanting and mystical. Although she had never been to India her sister had and Davon, a poor student at the time remembered how envious she'd been when she had looked at Meg's incredible pictures. She thought now of Meg's easy disposition and infectious laugh, and missed her already. Meg had been the only one who had supported her decision to take this job. "Go for it, Sis. It's an adventure you can't afford to miss," she had said. Lost in her thoughts for a moment, Davon came back to reality as she felt the helicopter beginning to descend. Beneath them she could see a landing pad and a shiny white golf cart in close range.

The copter touched down gently and Davon could hear the blades slowing. As she removed her seatbelt and ear protectors, she noticed a woman leaving the golf cart approaching them. She was dressed in a light green kandoura or full-length dress of local design, and her head was covered with a long matching scarf artistically draped around her neck and over one shoulder.

The pilot, who had originally attended the door, did so again, placing the step ladder in position. Davon now used to his lack of interest, gathered her things and exited, cautious of the blade still whirling above her head.

"Welcome, Dr. Marshall. I trust you had a comfortable flight?" asked the woman in perfect English.

"Yes thank you. The flight was most comfortable." She didn't mention the limo ride. "The palace is stunning," said Davon, with a smile. "You live in paradise."

"Please come," said the greeter, returning her smile and pointing to the golf cart, "We'll be taking the cart to your residence because it is some distance from here. My name is Raja, and I will be your contact and translator while you're employed by Prince Abdul." Once they were seated, Raja pulled a white silk scarf out from behind her seat. "This is a gift from the Prince and according to custom it's used to cover the hair. We believe in modesty, and you will observe here at the palace all men and women dress like this," she said, indicating to the garment she was wearing as she stepped on the gas and started them on their way.

Davon nodded, but didn't reply. The scarf was extremely beautiful, and although Raja had not exactly come out and told her to cover her head, Davon knew it was implied. She unfolded the pure white scarf and placed it over her long blond curls. Crisscrossing the ends she let them fall naturally back over her shoulders. The scarf actually enhanced her looks, and with her dark navy suit, four inch, newly purchased pumps, gorgeous long legs, and stylish sunglasses, Davon Marshall except for the small bump on her forehead, could easily have been on the front page of *Vogue Magazine*.

"The palace grounds cover over ten thousand acres of cultivated lands including the lake, however the Prince owns another seventy thousand acres of the surrounding desert. As you can see we are on the golf course and will proceed past the stables, aquatic center and guest villas on our way to the palace. The large building to your left is the desalination plant," said Raja proudly.

"So you make all of your fresh water from seawater?" asked Davon, thoroughly impressed.

"Yes, in fact the lake you saw flying in is completely man-made."

"Wow, so you're quite self sufficient. When was the palace built?"

"Originally it was constructed in 1930, but over the years there have been many additions. Here to your right are the stables, which house over three hundred Arabian racing horses and the Prince's many falcons," said Raja, pointing to a vast one story white washed structure. "This building is the breeding farm for the birds. People come from around the world to buy the falcons we raise."

Davon grinned. It was hard to believe this oasis had been created from the inhospitable desert. The pathway they traveled crisscrossed many exquisitely groomed and very lush gardens. Flower beds planted beside a shallow meandering stream exploded with brightly colored blossoms. And ahead, a beautiful old stone bridge, which looked as though it had been built centuries ago, arched gracefully across a deep pond. Davon looked in the pool of water and saw it was filled with glimmering, orange, long finned Koi. Noticing her interest, Raja slowed the vehicle and explained the Prince had designed the bridge and pond to resemble one he had seen in the Orient. Must be nice, thought Davon, to have anything your heart desires.

"There are the guest villas, and next to it the aquatic center and…"

"Will I be staying in the guest villas?" interrupted Davon, feeling thrilled about cooling off with a swim when she gazed upon the huge, empty swimming pool through the plate glass windows.

"No Dr. Marshall. The Prince felt that you would be more comfortable closer to the medical clinic. He has just finished renovating your suite, and I'm sure you'll be delighted with it. Your apartment is over there," replied Raja, indicating with her index finger towards the left side of the palace.

Seconds later they pulled up in front of a wide staircase that had an exquisitely carved herringbone design imbedded into the rise of each step.

"This way please," Raja said.

Delicately stepping out onto the hot paving stones Raja lifted her skirt slightly to take the first stair and as she did so, Davon caught a glimpse of her gorgeous jeweled slippers, which sparkled in the sunlight. Considering the surroundings, Davon thought, I wouldn't be surprised if the stones are real!

As Davon pivoted to exit the vehicle, she gasped. At the edge of the red clay paving stones, the immaculate garden and grass sloped gently for about one hundred yards before it was abruptly interrupted by a wide band of red sand in front of an endless turquoise sea.

"Dr. Marshall, if you please."

"Sorry Raja," answered Davon. "I'm just trying to take it all in. Unbelievable, I had no idea it would be so beautiful." As she stood up, Davon felt her shirt and nylons clinging as though they were glued to her skin. Such beauty and yet such heat, I can hardly wait to cool off with a swim, she said to herself, making her way quickly up the staircase.

"This is the east side of the palace, where the women and most of the children live," said Raja, the second Davon caught up to her on the spacious landing. "There are nine enclosed gardens and five pools." She pointed to several walled courtyards with tall ionic columns, inviting alcoves, swimming pools, and oversized black glazed pots filled with long leafy palms and exotic flowering plants. "Your suite is here, on the second floor, and the medical clinic," she stood on tippy-toes and waved to the other side of an out building, "is over there. The clinic is brand new and has been completely out-fitted with the latest equipment. However, if there's something you require, please let me know and it will be purchased for you. Right now, I'll to take you to your suite and give you the rest of the evening to settle in," she paused and looked at Davon, "if that's suitable?"

"Of course I'm overly excited to see the clinic, but I'm also a bit jetlagged and need to freshen up. I'm happy to have some down time, thanks," replied Davon, completely forgetting about her plans to resign from the job.

As they walked towards the apartment, Raja indicated areas of interest. The place was mind-boggling, pure opulent luxury. Who lives like this, thought Davon, completely enthralled. They proceeded from the covered landing through two large French doors with elaborately carved brass handles into a wide hallway with creamy off-white walls, and under a vaulted archway that seemed to float beneath the ceiling's intricate moldings. Davon looked from the delicate Venetian glass chandeliers, to the rich dark brown hardwood accented by a thick colorful Persian carpet runner.

"Here we are, Dr. Marshall," said Raja, opening a massive wooden door.

Standing aside so Davon could enter her new home, Raja waited. Davon paused for a few seconds in disbelief; it was as if she had suddenly found herself on the movie set of *Aladdin*. The room was absolutely huge with high coved ceilings, columns and enormous windows. The decorative lattice work in front of the windows, and choice of furniture gave it a definite Middle Eastern feel. The walls were soft ivory white and had large pieces of gorgeous abstract art. Dark hardwood floors, similar to the hallway, were adorned with massive Persian carpets. And centered on the silk rugs were ornate groupings of plush white furniture and heavy glass tables. Vases of fresh flowers sat on each table, making the room look more like a hotel lobby than living quarters.

When Davon stepped into the suite she noticed a petite woman with large questioning eyes standing behind one of the chaise lounges. "Hello," said Davon, presuming they had disturbed the cleaning lady, "Have I arrived too early?"

"She doesn't speak English," replied Raja, with an air of arrogance. "This is Bin, your servant."

"My servant?" exclaimed Davon, turning to look at Raja.

"Yes, her job is to cook, clean, and care for you."

"Thank you so much, but I don't need a…a…any help." She couldn't bring herself to belittle the woman by calling her a servant. "I've always cooked and cleaned for myself," added Davon, feeling uncomfortable at the very prospect.

"In our country we employ the needy. Bin was chosen out of two hundred women who desperately want to serve in the palace. If you're not satisfied with her Dr. Marshall, I'll select another," said Raja, her lips pursed in obvious annoyance.

"No, no, I'm very satisfied with…with Bin," blubbered on Davon, who had taken a second glance at the woman. Bin, who stood quietly behind the sofa with her head bowed low, looked as though she was terrified of rejection. Davon knew she had to protect her. "If this is the way things are done here, I'm totally happy," she continued, not wanting to be responsible for putting anyone out of a job.

"Fine, then I shall leave. If you require any assistance, please pick up the phone and you'll find a direct link to me. Now, before I go, is there something in particular you would like for dinner? I'll translate."

"Chicken, vegetables, rice anything really."

Raja spoke in rapid Farsi and Bin quickly turned to do her bidding. After a brief goodbye and promise of a meeting in the morning, Raja left Davon alone. Standing in silence, she wished she could share the experience with Matt. Davon couldn't believe this was where she was going to live for the next twelve months. As she slowly made her way around the room looking at the art work, Davon yawned. It was already after five in the evening. Where had the day gone? Even though she'd slept for several hours on the plane, jetlag was beginning to take its toll. At a time like this she'd normally have a shower and power nap, but she didn't exactly feel comfortable in the apartment yet, everything was too new and perfect. Besides, if she could tough it out until nine or ten, she would have a better night's rest.

Removing the scarf from her head, Davon carefully folded and placed it on the white couch before she sat. The sofa was incredibly soft and comfortable. Soon, she was melting into the down cushions letting her head fall and relax on the high back. "Maybe, I'll just sit here and close my eyes for a minute before dinner," she whispered. But before she had a chance to think about what might happen, Davon Marshall was fast asleep.

CHAPTER TWO

Stretching her arms and legs, Davon turned over and opened her eyes trying to focus on the person standing beside her head.   She couldn't quite remember lying down, but had had the most marvelous sleep on the sofa. She lifted up the light blue duvet and looked at it, assuming Bin must have tucked it around her. Then she made eye contact. Bin was grinning from ear to ear and holding a large box of Raisin Bran cereal.

"Sorry, I guess I was more tired than I thought! The United States is very far from this place. Very far away," she said, as she stood up using elaborate hand and arm movements to explain her words.

It was obvious Bin didn't understand what Davon was telling her, but she smiled and nodded and vigorously began to shake the box of cereal.

"I guess that means breakfast." Davon smiled back at her. Is it possible I slept the whole night on the couch, she wondered, looking down at her wrinkled suit. Davon's first clue had been the box of cereal, but with her watch saying 6:45 she couldn't quite believe she'd actually slept for more than thirteen hours.

"One moment please," Davon said, using her hand as a stop sign when Bin tried to give her the Raisin Bran box. "I'd like to have a shower before breakfast. Shower…water…clean," she said, pretending to wash herself.

Bin laughed and nodded, and then taking Davon's hand, she attempted to pull her along towards what Davon hoped would be a bathroom. Now we're communicating, thought Davon, as she allowed herself to be dragged down a wide hallway. At about four and a half feet tall Bin was extremely cute and motherly. She had silky short dark brown hair with only a touch of gray, beautiful smooth skin, and a pixy face. Tiny wrinkles crinkled around her large dark brown eyes when she laughed, and Davon immediately found herself liking her. Although Bin's uniform was immaculate, Davon could tell it was made from cheap material, and she found this peculiar considering the elegant surroundings.

As they walked by the kitchen entrance, Davon smiled at the classy black brown, almost ebony colored wooden cabinets and spotless beige granite countertops. She had always enjoyed cooking and was excited to see what type of appliances she had. As she attempted to pause and look at the range, Bin turned around and shook her head. Davon wasn't positive what Bin was trying to tell her, was she not allowed to cook, or not allowed in the kitchen? I guess it's her territory, Davon figured, as they passed the kitchen and continued down the hall halting in front of an exquisite set of carved doors. When Bin opened them, Davon smiled. It was Shangri-La, a dream bedroom with high ceilings, dark wood floors, plush Persian carpets, and a king-size canopy bed with white mosquito netting tied creatively to each of the four posts. She giggled ruefully at the fact that she'd spent the night on the sofa, and hoped Bin wouldn't tell Raja. As she stood admiring the surroundings, she felt a small hand pulling her towards the large walk-in closet. Here she saw all her clothes had been unpacked and pressed, and now were hanging perfectly straight above her five pairs of shoes.

"Thank you Bin," she said gratefully, as she was nudged in the direction of the bathroom.

Her small apartment in Boston could have almost fit inside this one room alone. The colors were predominately black and white, with polished black marble tiles on the floor, and white marble sinks and countertops. Beveled mirrors stylishly covered every wall reflecting the enormous sunken bathtub, which was positioned slightly off-center, but directly under a colossal gold and crystal chandelier with a diameter of at least five feet. The large white marble walk-in shower with a heavy tempered glass door had six shower heads. The gold faucets and decorative handles sparkled regally, adding to the elegant ambience. To the side of the shower Davon found a linen closet filled to the brim with towels, a second vanity with a sink, and built-in makeup area. She stood mesmerized. Scanning the room in admiration, she was positive it had cost at least a hundred thousand dollars to construct.

Bin said something in Farsi and placed two thick white towels into her arms before leaving and closing the door. Davon giggled, "I can't believe this is really happening to me." As she caught a glimpse of her reflection in the mirror, she could see she was long overdue for a shower. Stripping quickly, she kicked her clothes out of the way and stepped into the shower area, turning the nozzles away from her body before reaching to turn on the tap. She didn't want to get a blast of cold water, which was the norm with her shower in Boston. However, much to her surprise the initial spray was warm and inviting. Adjusting three of the shower heads towards her tight shoulder muscles she let the hot pulsing water massage her back. It felt like heaven. Seeing a multi shampoo, conditioner and soap dispenser on the corner shelf, she reached out and took a sample. The shampoo smelt exactly like her brand from home. It's got to be a fluke, she told herself, as she lathered up.

With her dressing gown on and a towel wrapped around her head, Davon strolled into the kitchen. She was famished. "I haven't eaten since...breakfast, yesterday on the plane!" she told the uncomprehending Bin. The kitchen although stunning, was the smallest room in the apartment. The cabinets were exquisite, and the over-sized stove looked as though it belonged in a restaurant. Davon walked towards the stainless steel fridge, which took up one wall, and opened it. But before she even had a chance to peek inside, Bin gently shooed her into the elegant dining room. Once there, Davon quickly found herself seated at an eight person table in front of the most sumptuous breakfast.

The amount of food on the table could have fed fifty people. Davon always liked to eat a hearty breakfast, but this was outrageous. Picking out several pieces of fresh fruit from a colorful platter, Davon placed them on her plate with a dollop of yogurt. She hesitated for a fraction of a moment wondering about the water sanitation in the palace. She had forgotten to ask Raja last night if there was a water purification unit in her apartment. If there wasn't, she risked getting a water-borne disease like giardiasis, a type of traveler's diarrhea, or something more life-threatening like typhoid fever or cholera. Davon had seen enough cases of dysentery in vacationers returning from five star resorts in Mexico to know you should always use bottled water, even to brush your teeth when traveling in a third world country, and that you should never eat raw vegetables or cut fruit. Was this part of the Middle East considered a third world country? She wished she'd spent more time gathering information about the area before taking the job. Pushing the untouched plate to the side, Davon took a bowl and filled it with yogurt. Granola with yogurt instead of milk was one of her favorite breakfast foods.

As her stomach growled, her thoughts now turned to Louis Pasteur and pasteurization, bovine tuberculosis and brucellosis, diseases of raw milk. Convinced she had read somewhere that Arab countries do not pasteurize milk products, she took the bowl of yogurt and placed it beside the plate. "Sometimes having a medical background can be detrimental to your diet," she sighed. Biting her lip, she rubbed her hungry stomach. Spying the box of Raisin Bran, she filled up a bowl and began to eat it dry just as Bin came into the room holding a tray with two steaming cups, one with coffee and the other with tea.

"Kalloog," Bin said, with a big smile.

"Oh you mean Kelloggs, yes thank you, very good," lied Davon, as she munched a dry spoonful.

Davon could hear Matt laughing at her. He always said she was too cautious and paranoid about what she ate, forever analyzing everything that went into her mouth. As far as she could remember, she'd even done this as a child, but admitted the problem had gotten far worse after her honors course in Microbiology. Matt, of course, was the exact opposite, and Davon would tease him back, saying he'd eat dog food if it was garnished nicely with parsley. That's why he was so perfect for me, she thought, he kept me in balance. With him she was more of a free spirit. "Take a chance Davon," he'd say, "it may change your life."

"Well Matt," she said, as she dipped her spoon into the yogurt and put it in her mouth. "This one's for you!" She sat there missing him intensely as Bin quizzically watched her talking to the spoon. "If I don't have you, the man of my dreams, what does it matter if I die of brucellosis in a foreign land?"

The yogurt was unexpectedly creamy and smooth with a slight hint of honey. It was the best yogurt Davon had ever tasted. Switching bowls, Davon put the rest of the Raisin Bran on top of the yogurt and added a banana, one she peeled herself. Taking a sip of the aromatic coffee, which had a wonderful nutty flavor, Davon began to eat heartily. She tried not to think about where the food originated, turning her attention to the taste experience.

Satisfied her charge was eating Bin disappeared back into the kitchen then reappeared with more coffee. She pointed to the clock on the wall and said something in Farsi. Davon saw it was 8:10. Walking over to the clock Davon pointed to it and said, "Go medical clinic?"

Bin repeated what she'd said in Farsi again, and when Davon realized they weren't getting anywhere in understanding each other, she thanked Bin for breakfast, and then headed off to the bedroom to get ready. She selected a sleeveless summer dress with an appropriate neckline and below the knee skirt length. Drying her hair quickly and applying minimal makeup, Davon pulled the white scarf out of the closet where Bin had so neatly hung it, and wrapped it around her neck. She wasn't quite sure if she had to cover her head while on route to the clinic, but decided to play it safe. At 8:27 am with her blond hair covered, Davon Marshall found herself wandering up and down the corridor trying to find a way down to the inner courtyard.

"Dr. Marshall, good morning," said Raja pleasantly, walking towards her.

"Good morning to you Raja," said Davon, looking relieved. "I'm so glad you found me, every corridor looks similar. I think I've lost my way. I was trying to get down to the courtyard you pointed out yesterday afternoon, but I couldn't find the stairs."

"The palace complex is large and it will take some time to learn your way around. I must apologize because I came to your apartment to escort you, but you had already left. I asked Bin to let you know I would be there at 8:30 am."

Davon noted her non-verbal clues, and could see that Raja was embarrassed and angry. It was her job to show Davon the palace and medical clinic, and frankly in Davon's view, Raja had screwed up. She had forgotten to tell Davon what time she was coming in the morning and had relied on a Farsi-only speaking individual to give her the message. Davon really didn't care, but was concerned Raja might take out her anger on Bin. "It is entirely my fault Raja. Bin did point to the clock, but I misunderstood and thought you'd be meeting me at the clinic. I'm going to have to brush up on my Farsi," Davon added with a forced laugh. "And thanks for selecting Bin, she is more than wonderful."

Raja's expression softened at Davon's thank you. "So, shall I show you around?" she asked.

Their first stop was the gym. It was close to Davon's apartment and unbelievable. The equipment was brand new and the weight machines were the exact type Davon had used at her gym back home. When she commented on this, Raja let it slip that the Prince had had the room built specifically for her.

"My goodness, he knows what type of gym equipment I like?"

"The Prince wants all of his employees to be happy. It must have been in your background check," said Raja, nonchalantly.

In one way Davon was flattered because she liked to work out on a daily basis, but she felt a little apprehensive about what else the Prince had found out about her. It wasn't because she had anything to hide, it was just unsettling to think of being spied on, or checked out without knowing about it. In this situation, the Prince definitely had the upper hand. She was in a country where she couldn't speak the language, had not researched the culture, and actually had no idea as to her exact whereabouts. She didn't even know anything about the incredibly wealthy Prince Abdul. Her mother's last words about insanity echoed in her head, and Davon shivered when she thought about how she had ended up here in less than thirty-two days, start to finish.

Noticing the involuntary shudder, Raja piped up, "Dr. Marshall, I apologize, the room is too cool. I'll have the temperature adjusted immediately. Now if you please, I'd like to show you the dance studio." Opening a mirrored door next to the window, they walked into a connecting room, which had ballet bars, floor to ceiling mirrors, polished hardwood flooring and an extensive sound system against one wall. "Once a week the women have a three hour dance class instructed by the famous Gege, I'm sure you've heard of her," said Raja proudly.

Not wanting to insult Raja and admit she'd never heard of Gege, Davon nodded, and when Raja looked like she wanted more from her, she said, "I believe I've read something about her special techniques in teaching."

Raja smiled. "If you would be interested in joining the class, it could be arranged."

Davon wondered if they knew she had taken ballet as a child. Most likely, she thought, again feeling violated. "Once I get settled that would be nice. Thank you Raja."

From the dance studio, Raja took her outside to look at the walking gardens, swimming pools, and common areas. Although it was still early in the day, it was hot. Only 39 degrees Celsius, Raja reassured her, much cooler than yesterday. Coming from the air conditioned palace, Davon wasn't convinced. She felt the first trickle of perspiration between her breasts and knew she'd need some acclimatization before she would call this temperature cool. The tour had already taken close to an hour, and Davon had seen only a small percentage of the palace. She found it strange that they hadn't run into one other person, even though there were approximately two hundred and seventy-two people who lived and worked here. It wasn't until they began to approach one of the swimming pools that they heard voices and laughter. Sitting around the edge of the pool were some of the most beautiful women Davon had ever seen. They all wore stylish western bathing suits and dangled their long, well-toned legs in the cool water while conversing with one another. Children darted in and among the many legs, some seeking protection from their mothers, while others played on bright floating balls and pool tubes.

The clicking sound of Davon's high-heeled pumps alerted the group to the presence of intruders, and the happy party sounds quickly silenced. All of the women instantly looked towards the water seemingly to avoid eye contact with Davon and Raja, and quietly instructed their children to stop staring. Davon hadn't expected a grand celebration, but had hoped her future patients would be a little friendlier. She could feel a growing uneasiness, as Raja continued with her rant about rules and hours of operation completely ignoring the twenty or so people sitting and swimming in front of them. When a small boy broke away from the group and came to stand beside Davon, she squatted down and spoke to him. He was adorable, between five and six years of age and although it was obvious he didn't understand what Davon was saying, he smiled, and then suddenly reached up and touched her hair. There was an immediate groan from the women around the pool, and one of them jumped up, a gorgeous young woman whom Davon assumed was the mother. Before she even had an opportunity to reach her son, Davon was stunned to see Raja grab the boy and pull him away. Roughly gripping his wrist and twisting it, she then proceeded to leer at the approaching mother, turning the physical into a verbal attack, oblivious to the loud cries of the youngster.

"Stop, stop it Raja. The child did no harm!" Davon's voice suddenly rose up even though she had no idea what the excitement was about. However, the second the words left her mouth Davon realized she had made a mistake in interfering. The silence, which ensued, was deafening, and Raja, the women, and even the children stared at her in astonishment. Davon spoke first. "I'm sorry. I think we started off on the wrong foot." When there was no response, she tried again, wondering why she was the one apologizing. "Please, could you introduce me to these women and children whom I assume are to be my future patients?"

Raja narrowed her eyes and glared, and in that split second Davon realized she had humiliated the interpreter in front of the others. However, to her credit, Raja quickly regained her composure and complied with the requested introduction in Arabic. The women smiled at Davon, and gently bowed their heads together in a gesture of welcome.

The second Raja finished speaking she took a step back, leaving Davon alone in front of the group. Davon felt compelled to say something. "Hello Everyone, I'm Dr. Davon and I've been hired by the Prince to take care of your health needs. Please come to the clinic if you have any medical issues. I'm looking forward to getting to know you all."

"They do not speak English, Dr. Marshall," said Raja under her breath, dramatically emphasizing the word 'not'.

"Then I'll learn to speak Farsi, Arabic, or whatever I need to do to communicate with my patients," whispered Davon between clenched teeth, still facing forward.

She refused to take part in Raja's mind games. Raja did not respond, but turned abruptly, and Davon hesitated for just a moment, and then followed her towards an iron gate in the brick wall surrounding the pool. Before she walked through the gate, Davon stopped and gave a little wave to the kids. It was upsetting that Raja viewed her as a threat. But what was I supposed to do, let her abuse a child and scream at his mother because he touched my hair? Come on!

When the gate clicked firmly shut behind them, Davon heard the pool suddenly became boisterous once more. It was unfortunate she had made such a bad first impression. As a physician, it was extremely important to create a trusting relationship with these people, her patients, and she vowed to learn more about the language, and culture.

On the other side of the wall, Raja led her to a separate building constructed out of the same stone as the palace. It was a decent size, and had a large welcoming wooden porch, which wrapped protectively around the middle. Polished multi-colored stained glass windows, two on either side of the bright green door sparkled behind several pieces of white wicker furniture. As they made their way up the stairs and onto the porch, Davon spotted her name in bold gold lettering on a plaque.

"Your clinic, Dr. Marshall," said Raja with pursed lips, as she pushed open the door.

Davon ignored the tone and stepped inside. There was an adequate waiting area with comfortable looking chairs, two fully equipped examining rooms and an office at the back of the space. The patient rooms had new examining tables, with an excellent supply of equipment: blood pressure and temperature monitors, stethoscopes and otoscopes, fetal and ultrasound monitors, laryngoscopes, IV pumps, and defibrillators. In the office there was even a small laboratory space with a beautiful new microscope.

"It's very impressive Raja. I know I'm going to enjoy working here. Please thank Prince Abdul."

Raja appeared slightly mollified, but said nothing.

The clinic felt familiar, and Davon realized the Prince had most likely copied an American design so she would be more comfortable. She was beginning to like this Prince Abdul. It was too bad she would probably never meet him. Raja on the other hand was a concern. After the swimming pool incident she had remained cool, only speaking when absolutely necessary.

As Raja was preparing to leave Davon at the clinic, she handed her a pager. "Dr. Marshall, please feel free to organize the clinic to your liking. If we've forgotten any equipment, it will be immediately ordered for you. This is the pager we would like you to have on your person at all times. By using it you'll have the full run of the women's quarters and won't be restricted to the clinic. If it beeps, you're requested to phone me first, and then come here immediately. Do you have any questions?" she asked, robotically.

"Thanks, and yes, I do have a few questions. I didn't see any patient charts, and was wondering how many patients I have?"

"There are nineteen women in the harem, and seventeen children, although you will see only sixteen of the children, as one male is of age. You will also be responsible for the mother-in-laws, aunts and cousins who live in the women's quarters."

"I see," said Davon, trying not to react at the number of women sleeping with the Prince. She knew she wasn't allowed to treat male children over the age of thirteen because it had been in her contract. "I'd also like to request some native language instruction, and to call my parents to let them know I arrived safely. Is there a phone I can use to call the States?"

Raja smirked, "You have no need for language instruction. I am the translator and will assist with any patient that comes to the clinic. In regards to your question about calling home, Mr. Bedon already left a message with your parents that you arrived."

"You can thank him, but I'd still like to call them myself," Davon said firmly.

"I will make the arrangements through the communications department. An appointment time will be set up for you as soon as possible. Are there any other questions?" asked Raja, brusquely.

"No. You've been most helpful," lied Davon, trying to hide her frustration at the awkward tension. An empty silence filled the room. As Raja turned towards the door Davon called out. "Raja…about the incident at the pool…I apologize if I misspoke." And that, was the extent of what she could truthfully say. She despised Raja's unjustified abuse of the boy and her cool arrogance, but she needed to make amends, to make the job she had flown half way around the world for succeed.

Raja eyed her for a long moment. "You're young and a foreigner Dr. Marshall, please remind yourself!" Turning she walked out.

Davon watched her leave the clinic and noticed she skirted the pool area. "You're young and a foreigner and have no need for language instruction," she said, imitating Raja's accent. "I'll learn Farsi and Arabic whether you like it or not!" Plopping down in one of the waiting room chairs, Davon felt exhausted. Not a great way to start a new job! The conflict brought back a rush of memories of the night Matt left. She placed her elbows on her knees and rested her head in her hands. Sighing heavily she whispered, "Maybe it's me?"

After twenty minutes of soul searching, Davon came to her senses. "I'm a good person and I try to stand up for what is right. The truth is things don't always work out the way you want them to," she told herself, her spirits brightening. "I've been given this amazing opportunity and I'm going to make the best of it!" Getting up, she walked into her office, looked out the window at the magnificent ocean view, ran her fingers gently over her exquisite handmade mahogany desk, and then started exploring the clinic. She opened every drawer and cabinet in the office, examination, and storage room, and found each of the rooms well stocked and organized. Noticing the empty bookshelves in the office, Davon decided to go back to her suite and bring over her medical books. Anatomy, physiology, pediatrics, obstetrics, and tropical disease textbooks, that she had packed with care when she had accepted the position. Grabbing the pager from the table, Davon wondered how busy the clinic would be. She felt excited about getting started.

On the way back to her suite, Davon remembered she had again forgotten to ask Raja about the water purification and pasteurization methods. She felt perfectly fine after the yogurt, and dreaded the thought of having to converse with Raja again so soon, but decided she'd better call when she got back to the apartment. Weaving her way back by identifying land marks, Davon smiled. She knew how she would learn Farsi. Bin would be the key.

The swimming pool was now vacant. It was the hottest part of the day, and Davon fought the urge to jump in with her clothes on. She'd done that once on a dare. She and Matt had been together for about six months when he had called her rigid, inflexible, and too perfect, and then said, "I dare you to do something out of the ordinary because you just can't. You have to do everything properly Davon, everything!" They were in evening clothes, coming home from a dinner party and had just started to walk by the clubhouse swimming pool when Davon, determined to prove him wrong, climbed onto the diving board. Standing at the edge of the board in her one and only long gown, she removed her shoes and dove in. Two minutes later, Matt was in the water hugging her. That was the real start to their relationship. She'd ruined her dress that night, but it had been worth it. They had fallen in love. Not only had she shown Matt she could be spontaneous, she'd found the crazy part of her personality she had lost doing medicine.

When the door to the suite opened, Davon was hit with a blast of cool air. She stood for a moment enjoying the air conditioning and the wonderful aromas originating from the kitchen. Bin heard her come in and bounded into the living room offering greetings. Grinning, she took the wooden spoon she was carrying, and used it to make eating gestures. Davon laughed at her antics and grasped that lunch was ready, as if she couldn't already tell from the magnificent smells, which gnawed at her hungry stomach. Smiling, she raised her hands to show Bin she wanted to clean up.

When she returned to the dining room a few minutes later, the table was laden with food. Platters of rice, beans, vegetables and chicken, and wafting scents of cinnamon and ginger surrounded the single place setting. Although Davon was starving, she decided to call Raja before she forgot. "Raja, yes it's Davon Marshall. I have a question regarding the water and dairy products at the palace. Is the tap water safe to drink, and are the dairy products pasteurized?"

It was quickly explained that as the palace made its own fresh water, it was filtered and therefore extremely safe to drink. In regards to dairy products, there were none; the creamy yogurt Davon had so thoroughly enjoyed that morning had been made from camel's milk. With Raja making her feel extremely ignorant, Davon didn't dare ask if the camel's milk was pasteurized, and chose instead to end the conversation with a simple thank you.

Davon brought a notepad and pen with her to the table, and during lunch began to draw pictures of human activity: eating, showering, walking and sleeping. She then drew a variety of common objects and foods.

Beside each picture she wrote the English name. It took several attempts for Bin to understand that Davon was looking for the Farsi word for each drawing, but once she understood what Davon was after, it was an easy process. With much glee, the two of them filled three pages of diagrams with phonetically spelled Farsi. Davon was determined to learn the language one way or another, and Bin was proving to be an excellent teacher.

CHAPTER THREE

Every day at precisely 8:30 am, Raja came to the suite to escort Davon to the medical clinic. They would walk to the clinic making small talk and once there, Raja would leave Davon sitting at her desk reading medical journals. There was no internet, except at the communications department, which Davon had no access to, no patient histories or charts, and really nothing for her to do except wait for someone with a health concern to come and see her. Days off were supposed to be Friday and Saturday, but as she was still on call for emergencies, her job was basically 24/7.

By week three, having still not seen one patient, Davon summoned the courage to tell Raja she knew the way to the clinic and could walk there herself. She began a new routine where she would workout in the gym doing weights for about an hour, cool off with a quick swim in the pool, and then end up at the clinic by 10:00 am. At first she felt guilty as though she was goofing off, but rationalized that she had a beeper and could be at the clinic within minutes if she was called.

The weather remained hot although it was only March, and when she made a comment about this Raja warned her to prepare for the temperatures of July and August. Davon was aware those were the hottest months in this part of the world, however with air conditioning and the cool ocean breeze, which blew inland each evening, she assumed she'd be just fine. She was already acclimating. As far as she was concerned the weather and temperature weren't the problem. It was whether or not she would ever be called upon for her medical expertise.

After a month of working out daily, Davon was feeling amazingly fit and healthy. Her body was toned, her hair was a touch blonder and her complexion had a rosy glow. She was learning words in Farsi at a rapid pace and had even learned some of the anatomical names of parts of the body. But she was extremely lonely. At breakfast, lunch and dinner she sat eating by herself in silence, and although she had asked Bin to sit and eat with her, Bin refused, preferring to eat while standing in the kitchen.

Davon had passed a handful of women on her way to and from the clinic. However each time, despite her attempts at a greeting in Farsi, all of them had just given her a smile and a nod. I have got to learn Arabic, she thought, as she struggled into her one piece swimsuit. This morning, she decided to change her routine and go for a swim in the ocean. The small swimming pools in the women's quarters were wonderful for a quick dip, but today feeling invigorated from her workout she wanted to swim laps. She had initially thought to ask if she could use the Olympic sized pool at the aquatic center, but figured Raja would forbid it, so grabbing her goggles, she headed off to the beach directly in front of the women's section. It was paradise. The u-shaped bay had two groves of healthy, fully grown date palms offering shade on either side of the water with the most unusual red sand, which created a perfectly flawless band that dipped invitingly into the turquoise sea. The sand was piping hot when Davon removed her sandals at the ocean's edge, so she put her flip-flops back on and waded into the sparkling, clear water, diving quickly under the surf. It was bathtub warm, and when she rose to the surface, she found herself extremely buoyant, floating without effort as the gentle waves pushed her and her floating shoes towards the shore. Rescuing her sandals, Davon threw them onto dry land, and turned back to admire her surroundings.

The bay was much larger than she had realized, and although she was only several feet from the shoreline, the water was quite deep. She swam out a little farther and let herself float. Below she could see the smooth sandy bottom ending abruptly at a coral covered ridge that plummeted down at least twenty feet. Treading water, she pulled her tinted goggles over her eyes and dove, excitedly finding herself in the middle of a school of white and black angelfish. As they darted away, she could see swaying sea grass, red and yellow sponges, pink sea anemones, and swimming along the bottom just ahead of her, a beautiful green turtle. Coming up for a breath of air, Davon dove once more and swam hard to catch up to the graceful reptile. By combining different swimming strokes, Davon was able to follow the turtle as he swam along the ridge to the opposite side of the bay. The water was crystal clear and she could see him well although he was more than ten feet in front of her. Undisturbed by her presence, the reptile suddenly turned towards the shallow water and made his way out onto the red sand. Davon watched as he selected a nicely shaded place beneath one of the towering palms, and began to dig.

"I thought you were a boy turtle, and now I find out you're a girl, getting ready to lay eggs!" laughed Davon, as she watched the procedure. She quietly inched her way closer to get the best view, enjoying the peaceful serenity. Knowing it took several hours for a turtle to lay and bury eggs, she eventually left the mother to her task, and swam back in the direction of her towel and shoes. I'd love to come back and see those babies make their mad dash to the ocean, she thought. Sixty days incubation or something like that, if she had use of the internet she could check, but since that wasn't the case...the isolation of the place was really beginning to get to her. Think positive, she reminded herself, you're in paradise!

Happily exhausted from her swim Davon ran to her possessions, jumping the second her feet hit the dry sand. "Ouch!" she cried, grabbing her flip-flops and towel. Jogging back into the cool ocean water, she toweled off, standing ankle deep in the teasing surf. She lifted each foot, and balanced precariously on one leg, to examine the sole before slipping on her bright pink flip-flops. The heat had evaporated the water on her back and arms, and left small white blotches of salt residue. As she licked her dry lips, she could taste the salty brine.

While Davon was putting on her flimsy blue bathing suit wrap, she noticed a group of workers leaning on their garden rakes, watching her from the far side of the palace grounds. Nervously wrapping her towel around her almost dry hair, and pulling her wrap tightly around her chest, she power walked to the staircase that led to her apartment and tried not to look at them. This was her first encounter with the male workers, and they'd seen her in a bathing suit. As far as this culture was concerned, they might as well have seen her naked! Worried about the ramifications, she prayed Raja wouldn't find out.

As she proceeded towards the protective corner of the stone wall, she let out a huge sigh of relief, and then one of surprise, as she felt her pager vibrating. Running to her apartment, she sailed through the door and to the phone. "It's Davon Marshall," she said, when Raja answered.

"Dr. Marshall, you have a woman in labor at the medical clinic."

"I'm on my way," replied Davon.

Sprinting to the shower, Davon was in and out, in less than four minutes. She brushed her hair back off her face, and yanked on clean pair of sweat pants and a T-shirt. As she passed the dining room, she downed a glass of water and then went out the door yelling "medical clinic," to Bin who had peeked out of the kitchen. Running down the inner hallways, she approached the staircase that led to the courtyard and jumped down five of the eight stairs onto the hot paving stones, and without missing a beat continued to sprint around the pool arriving at the clinic in record time. When she entered, Davon could hear loud wailing coming from the largest patient room. Dashing to the door, she saw a very beautiful, very pregnant woman squatting on the floor hanging on to, and almost pulling over a rather small servant woman. Clear fluid pooled around their feet, indicating that the woman's membranes had ruptured.

"We must get her onto the birthing bed," Davon said, using several words of Farsi. Trying to not slip in the amniotic fluid, she went to the woman's side and attempted to pull her up. Resisting, the woman continued to squat, screaming with each contraction. "You must get on the bed so I can examine you," said Davon very slowly, wondering where in the hell was Raja.

In broken English, the woman responded between groans. "It is painful…to stand…I cannot."

"Ask your assistant to help me get you on the bed," said Davon softly, "I must examine you. Please try."

Although it took several minutes, the woman, who Davon discovered was called Nisha, was finally positioned on the examination table with her knees pulled towards her abdomen. Davon quickly draped sheets over and under her, and pulling on sterile gloves she explained, as simply as possible, the technique of the vaginal exam which determined how quickly the birth would happen.

"Is this your first pregnancy?" asked Davon, noting the birth canal was seven centimeters dilated. When Nisha gave her a puzzled look, Davon added, "Do you have other children?"

"No other children," screamed Nisha, as a strong contraction overwhelmed her.

At ten centimeters, Nisha would be fully dilated and ready to push, but there was something not quite right. Her abdomen was too large for one child, and the head, which was already in position, seemed small. Davon grabbed her stethoscope, and after listening to the abdominal wall, began to panic. She could clearly hear two heartbeats.

"Nisha, you are having twins," said Davon slowly, and calmly.

"I do not understand," she gasped, sweat dripping off her forehead.

"Two babies," said Davon, holding up two fingers, "Did your doctor not tell you, you are having two babies?"

"You only doctor I see," answered Nisha, not comprehending what Davon was saying.

Oh God help me, thought Davon. This woman's had no prenatal care, no ultrasound, and I'm expected to deliver two healthy babies in the middle of nowhere with one helper who doesn't speak English! When another contraction came, Davon showed her how to pant, and told Nisha she couldn't push no matter how desperately she wanted to. The patient seemed to understand and rapidly exhaled the way Davon had demonstrated. Using the few minutes she had left by plugging in and organizing the one incubator with two sterile sheets, Davon removed the bottom half of the birthing table, and quickly put on a sterile gown over her clothes. Kicking a stool towards the end of the bed, she sat down and waited.

When the next contraction came, Nisha was unable to control the urge to bear down, and Davon watched as the first baby's head crowned. Although she had delivered over ninety babies, Davon had never delivered a set of twins. The complications with multiple births were huge, and for that reason alone Nisha should have been having her babies in a hospital, not a one hour flight away from one. Ignoring the bead of sweat that was trickling down between her breasts, Davon began to manipulate the baby's shoulder through the birth canal. Seconds later she was holding a baby boy. As she cleared his mouth and nose of mucus, a loud healthy wail was heard. The mother quietly asked if the child was male.

"Yes, a baby boy," said Davon, as she wrapped and placed him in the warm incubator. "We need to concentrate now on baby number two," she added, noticing that the second baby's head was already starting to make its way into position. The mother not understanding she was about to have another child started to get off the table, and Davon realizing this, jumped up and pushed her back down with her elbows, so as not to contaminate her gloves. "No Nisha, stay on the table, please. Wait, wait," she cried, as she assisted the second child into the world.

The minute she announced the birth of a second boy, Nisha began to cry out loudly, giving thanks to her God. Ignoring the commotion from the mother, the servant, and the two infants, Davon did the routine checks on the five pound and five pound, one ounce babies, and found them both to be healthy. Placing them one at a time into the mother's arms, she now waited for the birth of the placenta. It was at that exact moment that Raja came bursting into the room with three servants in tow. Rambling on quickly in Farsi, she started to take over, organizing the servants to take the babies from Nisha.

"Please, hang on a minute Raja," Davon called, "and let me finish up with the mother. I don't want this many people in the room. Go to the waiting area until I call." Obviously irritated, Raja did as she was told, and Davon returned her attention to Nisha, delivering a healthy placenta. Afterwards, Nisha was thoroughly examined, and taking one last check of the boy's vital signs, Davon gave the okay to move them all back to the palace apartment, emphasizing to Raja to let the mother know she would do a home visit in one hour. She watched them exit. Two servants cradled the tightly wrapped infants in blue blankets, and walked cautiously one behind the other with the mother trailing behind the procession in a wheelchair. As Raja was about to follow them, Davon called out to her. "Raja, before you leave I'd like to have a word with you."

Raja returned to the porch with a blank stare, "Yes, Dr. Marshall?"

"First of all, why was I not told that there was a pregnant woman in the harem? I did ask about pregnancy and health concerns when I arrived a month ago."

"Nisha was not at the palace when you arrived. She just returned home three days ago."

"Well, I would ask that in the future, I'm immediately informed about any pregnancy. Nisha didn't have any prenatal care, and wasn't even aware she was having twins. We are lucky there were no complications. In fact, Nisha really should have had her twins at the hospital in Dubai, and could still need to be flown there if she develops any problems," informed Davon.

Raja shook her head, "Giving birth is a natural process, and women have done it successfully over the course of thousands of years without any medical intervention."

"That may be so, but giving birth to twins is not always simple. And my recommendation is that any woman having a multiple birth will be flown to the hospital," retorted Davon, placing her hands on her hips in frustration.

"I will have your recommendations noted, Dr. Marshall." Raja huffed and began to walk away.

"Another thing," called Davon after her, "I'm still waiting to call my parents. It's been over a month and the telecommunications department hasn't contacted me about an appointment!"

"Oh yes," said Raja, turning back momentarily, "I forgot to mention the communications system is not functioning properly. But your call has top priority the minute the repairs are done."

"I bet!" said Davon under her breath, as she watched Raja walk away.

CHAPTER FOUR

Davon returned to her suite exhausted. It was well past two o'clock and she hadn't had anything to eat. She could smell a delicious curry scent filling the air. As she made her way into the dining room, Bin came from the kitchen and handed her a cup of coffee. She couldn't help but smile at the way Bin took care of her, anticipating her every need. Davon still couldn't apply the term servant because the reality of having one made her feel extremely guilty. After eating a filling meal of lentils and rice, she went into the bedroom planning to have a have a shower and short nap before checking on the new mother and babes. When she stepped into the room she stopped in mid-motion, noticing two elaborately wrapped boxes, one large, and one small on the bed. Intrigued, she carefully opened the largest box and was perplexed at a white garment she found gently folded between layers of tissue paper. Removing it so that she could have a closer look, still left her puzzled. It seemed to be some sort of outerwear with an attached hood, made of plain, heavy, cotton material.

"Humm, what would this be for?" she asked.

Dropping the garment back into the box, Davon tackled the smaller gift and audibly gasped when she discovered a Rolex watch inside. Not quite believing it was real, she pulled it out of the box. It definitely was a Rolex; an eighteen carat platinum and gold Rolex with twelve diamonds on the watch face. Davon was speechless. She couldn't possibly accept a twenty thousand dollar watch, it was unethical! There was no card and she had no idea who the gifts were from. When she approached Bin and asked about them, Bin, in their elaborate action-minimal-word method of communicating, indicated the boxes had been delivered by a servant minutes before she had arrived home.

"Oh great!" sighed Davon. The only way she was going to find out the reason for the gifts was to call Raja.

The power struggle, which had started the day she had challenged Raja's authority at the pool had to stop. As much as she hated to admit it, Davon needed Raja on her side. That had been evident this morning when Nisha and her servant had not seemed to understand the few words in Farsi she had spoken to them. If Nisha hadn't been able to understand English, there would have been real trouble, and both of the twins would have probably been born on the floor. Was Raja lying when she said none of the harem women spoke English? Or was Nisha an exception. It was hard to believe Raja would lie about something like that, yet Davon wouldn't put it past her. Raja definitely liked to be in control, and Davon would just have to bite the bullet, and let her. She needed to make amends with Raja not only for her translating skills, but as a go-between.

The women's quarters took up a third of the palace, and although Davon had explored a bit by taking different routes to the medical clinic, she had no idea where to go to find Nisha's suite. She was beginning to figure she was lost, and was wandering down an unfamiliar hallway when a little girl carrying an exquisite porcelain doll appeared out of nowhere. Davon knelt down to the child's eye level and greeted her in Farsi. She racked her brain for the Farsi words to ask about Nisha's apartment, but unfortunately her vocabulary wasn't that advanced.

"I am looking for Nisha," she said slowly in English.

The young child was absolutely gorgeous with huge brown eyes and long curly brown hair, and looked as perfect as the doll she was tenderly cradling. Reaching out to Davon, the girl took her hand and pulled her around the corner towards an open door. Davon could hear talking and laughter. She held back, not wanting to intrude. When the child realized that Davon wanted to wait in the doorway instead of coming in the apartment, she ran into the living space calling out. An attractive older woman quickly approached her.

"Dr. Marshall," the woman said, smiling warmly, "Welcome, we are honored by your visit. Please come in."

"I'm so sorry to bother you, but I appear to be lost. I'm looking for Nisha. She gave birth today and I need to do a medical check on her and the babies. Would it be possible for you to help me find her suite?" asked Davon.

"Of course, I will take you to her. May I offer you a cup of tea before we go?"

Not wanting to offend, Davon agreed to tea, rationalizing Nisha would be fine for a few more minutes. "Thank you. That would be very kind." She was surprised she had uncovered another person who spoke perfect English.

"I am Mirum." The woman offered her hand. "Come in and make yourself comfortable. I shall return in a moment."

The living room was huge, at least twice the size of Davon's, but the furnishings were different. Instead of several formal sitting areas with sofas and chairs, there was only one--an enormous white leather sectional flanked by two matching arm chairs. A long elegant dining room table, which could seat at least forty people, had been placed in front of the windows. Although there was only one formal seating area, there were two groupings of multi-colored silk cushions arranged on the floor. One set was in front of the enormous fireplace, and the other beside the entertainment unit, both centered on magnificent Persian carpets.

Feeling a touch out of place, Davon settled on the sectional and crossed her legs. When Mirum disappeared into the kitchen, she looked down at her pretty summer dress and felt pleased she had decided to change and put on some makeup. Her hostess was clearly a woman of class and culture.

Mirum was dressed in a pink heavily embroidered silk kandoura, which was obviously very expensive. It looked stunning on her petite, slim figure. She had accented the dress with diamond embedded gold filigree earrings and jeweled encrusted gold bangles, which tinkled softly as she moved. The jewelry, which would have been over the top on Davon, was perfectly elegant on Mirum.

"So Dr. Marshall, how do you like living in our humble country?" Mirum asked, gliding gracefully into the room and settling beside her.

"Please, call me Davon. Although I flew into Dubai, I haven't had a chance to see the city yet, but the palace is simply stunning. I've never seen a more beautiful place," replied Davon, smiling.

"Yes, we are blessed to live in such beauty. There are many opportunities to go into the city, so you will be able to see some of the amazing buildings and attractions of Dubai," said Mirum, as two servants placed tea, fruit, and small cakes on the coffee table. "Please forgive me, I would have prepared more food if I had known you were coming," she added, pouring Davon a cup of steaming jasmine tea.

Davon laughed, realizing that to be polite, she was going to have to eat something from the delightful display on the table, even though she was still stuffed from lunch. "This is wonderful, thank you for inviting me in. Mirum, you speak English so well, where did you learn the language?"

"I went to school in Britain. My father did business in London, and my family lived there for fourteen years. Although most of the educated people living here understand and speak some degree of English, we converse in Arabic. It is very nice to be able to practice with a true English speaking foreigner. The few foreigners who come here are usually male and short-term guests, and because of this, the women are not allowed to have any contact with them."

"Interesting," said Davon. "Is that because they are foreigners or male?"

"Both, our culture protects and segregates women. The women in the harem belong to Prince Abdul and we must always remember our place."

Davon wasn't sure if the last comment was just conversation, or a type of warning. She was still feeling awful about the workers seeing her in her bathing suit. Changing the subject Davon asked, "Your daughter is very sweet. How old is she?"

"Oh," laughed Mirum. "That's my granddaughter Ismil, she's four years old. When my husband died, I came here to live with my daughter. My daughter Lamna is one of the Prince's favorites."

"And Ismil is the Prince's daughter?" asked Davon, trying to figure out who was related to who. She took a sip of tea and selected a small piece of fruit cake.

"Of course," replied Mirum. "She is the thirteenth child and seventh daughter. Including the twin boys born today, the Prince now has nine sons, and ten daughters."

"How wonderful," said Davon, trying not to be judgmental of the situation, "Speaking of the twins, I hope you understand I can't stay for too long, because I need to assess the new babies and mother. But I'd love to come back at a later date when I have more time," she said, quickly glancing at her watch.

"It's nice to see a woman who takes her job so seriously. So another time?" replied Mirum, standing.

"Thank you Mirum for your hospitality, I'm honored to have met you."

One of Mirum's servants escorted Davon to Nisha's suite taking her deeper into the hallway's maze and closer to the center of the palace. How fortunate she had been to run into little Ismil, because she realized she would have never found the place on her own. The palace seemed like a giant hotel, albeit a five star luxury hotel, but one where every floor and hallway looked absolutely identical.

When Davon arrived at Nisha's suite, she noticed its close proximity to a pair of heavily embossed brass doors at the end of the hallway. Curious about where they led, she asked the servant in her limited Farsi. After some confusion with the language, Davon finally grasped these doors connected to the main part of the palace, and that she was not to go there. She remembered Mirum saying the closer a woman's suite was to the Prince's quarters, the higher in favor she was. I guess that suggests Nisha's right up there with the Main Man, she thought. But what does that mean anyway? More presents, more attention, more sleepovers? Upon entering Nisha's chambers, Davon could see this woman was certainly in the Prince's favor! The suite was utterly mind-boggling and fifty times more ostentatious than anything Davon had yet seen in the palace. The ceiling in the living room was at minimum twenty feet high, and held up by eleven large white and black marble pillars. The columns were stunning and looked Egyptian or

African as they rose in alternating bands of white and black from the dark hardwood floors to the carved, off-white herringbone ceiling. Giant mosaic urns stuffed with exotic flowers, and fully grown palm trees, their boughs spreading upwards and outward, separated various seating areas. Priceless antique tables, cabinets, mirrors, and art filled the room complimenting the room's exquisite grandeur. The furnishings, in white or black linen, fit in with the general color scheme of zebra, and the whole effect was one of elegance and total sophistication.

Davon was welcomed by Nisha's servant, and understood she was to follow her upstairs to the bedroom, but suddenly found herself lost in the breathtaking surroundings once inside the suite. Drawn to one of the sunken seating areas, Davon stood looking at the panoramic view of the gardens that flowed into the greenish-blue sea. She could clearly see the bay where she had gone swimming that morning, and smiled ruefully when she realized there may have been more onlookers than just the gardeners she had encountered.

"Dokter," said the servant, trying to get her attention.

"Of course, forgive me," replied Davon, following her up a magnificent wide staircase.

The master bedroom was enormous with high ornamental ceilings, gold walls, beautiful furniture, and large gilded mirrors. Davon found Nisha sitting in the middle of a round king-sized bed propped up by mounds of silk pillows looking absolutely gorgeous. There was no way anyone would have guessed she had given birth just hours ago. Her makeup was perfect, and her curled hair gracefully flowed over one shoulder. She wore a flimsy white satin nightgown, and was fully engrossed in a golden colored bound book. Wow, thought Davon clearing her throat.

"Dr. Marshall, thank you for coming," Nisha said, putting the book on the night table.

Davon smiled, "How are you feeling?"

"Wonderful, I am so blessed. Not one, but two healthy boys. The Prince, he will be pleased."

"I'm sure he will. Now I'd like to check your blood pressure and do a quick physical assessment," said Davon, as she removed the blood pressure cuff and stethoscope from her bag. Gently placing the cuff around Nisha's arm, Davon checked her pressure, then her pulse and respirations, and finally listened to her heart.

"Everything is good. Now, I need to have a quick look at your vaginal flow," she said, removing the covers, "Perfectly normal." Davon jotted down the information. "After having a baby, you need to have daily salt water baths until the bleeding stops. We don't recommend sex for several weeks. Do you understand what I'm telling you Nisha?"

"Yes, I think so." She paused, searching for the right words in English.

"What if the Prince calls for me?"

"The Prince has had other children, and I'm sure he is aware that a new mother needs to heal from childbirth. I wouldn't worry. Do you plan to nurse the boys?"

"Nurse them?" asked Nisha, with a puzzled look.

"Nurse means to breastfeed. Will you breastfeed the twins?"

"Oh!" She shook her head. "No, a woman is hired. She is with them now," said Nisha.

"Alright, if you have no intention of nursing the twins, I will give you some medicine to stop your breasts from making milk. If I don't give you this drug, you will start to produce breast milk in three days and it will take time for it to go away."

When Nisha looked puzzled again, Davon said, "I'll tell Raja. She will explain. Now, I'm going to go and check on the twins. Do you have any questions?"

"When will I be able to get up...be...normal?" asked Nisha.

"You will be feeling more like your usual self in a few days. But you have to remember that you just had twins Nisha, and you need to give your body some time to rest and heal. You did an amazing job," said Davon, patting her shoulder reassuringly. "I will come and see you again later today."

The twins were in good hands with three servants and a wet-nurse fussing about them when Davon walked into the nursery. She checked the boys, and was pleased to see both of their assessments were close to perfect. It had been a routine delivery with no complications and Davon was thankful, especially now that she knew how much the Prince favored Nisha. As she was gathering her things to leave, Raja burst into the room.

"Dr. Marshall, I hope you are finished because you must leave at once," she said rapidly.

"I'm almost done. I'd like to make sure the woman chosen to feed the twins has enough milk for three children. I assume she is also feeding her own child," said Davon, irritated at Raja's tone.

"The woman who is nursing the twins lost her child. You do not need to be concerned." Raja began waving her hands. "Prince Abdul is on his way to see Nisha and the children, and guests are not permitted!"

"I hardly see myself as a guest, however I am leaving Raja," said Davon, heading towards the door. "But I do have a few instructions I need you to relay to Nisha. I don't think she quite understood everything I told her."

"Later!" said Raja, practically pushing her out of the nursery.

When Davon stepped out into the hallway, she saw Mr. Bedon and another man heading up the stairs towards Nisha's room. Davon froze and pressed her back into the wall, hoping that they wouldn't notice her. She assumed the man with Mr. Bedon was the Prince. He had the look of

'Prince' written all over him. Extremely handsome, about six-three and somewhere between thirty-five and forty, he exuded power and wealth. He was smartly dressed and took the stairs two at a time, anxious and excited, Davon assumed, to see the love of his life and new sons.

When the men reached the top of the landing, Mr. Bedon stepped aside so the Prince could enter the bedroom, but suddenly, as if sensing her presence, the Prince stopped, and abruptly turned to look at her. For one split second their eyes locked. Davon had never had such a jolting physical response to a man in her life. In that one searing glance, she felt ravaged! The look lasted only a second, but Davon was left weak at the knees, her heart pounding. "My God," Davon said audibly, as the Prince turned and entered the bedroom. He was drop-dead gorgeous, and utterly the most attractive male Davon had ever laid eyes upon. Sighing, she leaned her head momentarily against the wall. *I can't believe I'm having this kind of reaction to a man I've seen for five seconds, especially one with umpteen wives and nineteen children. Yet, I'd like to bear him one!*

As a physician she understood only too well what had happened to her body. She'd just experienced a primitive and innate mating response, something to do with hormones and pheromones. But these strong sexual feelings were something new. She had never experienced this with anyone, not even Matt. "It doesn't mean anything. I'm still in love with Matt, I am," she whispered, trying to convince herself. "It's got to be rebound effect." *Matt* was who she wanted, not Prince Bedroom Eyes with his multitude of wives. Anyway, she assured herself, *I'm only the hired help. The chances of ever seeing him again, let alone talking with him are extremely remote.*

"Dr. Marshall, if you please!" Raja came out of the nursery and snapped Davon back into reality. "You must leave immediately. Come."

Clutching her medical bag, Davon followed Raja down the stairs, past Mr. Bedon, who pretended not to see them tip-toe to the front door. She felt like some sort of criminal or pathetic untouchable. *Really, this is ridiculous,* she thought. *Just because the Prince was born with a silver spoon in his mouth doesn't give him the right to treat people like they're pariah. This is such a peculiar culture!*

Once they were in the outer hallway Raja glared at her. "You had no right to make your way to Nisha's suite on your own. I may lose my position because of your arrogance, Dr. Marshall!"

"I'm sorry Raja. I'm just trying to do my job. I needed to check on Nisha and the babies. In America, new moms and twins are hospitalized for days, and monitored around the clock. You have to understand the boys are small, and need to be checked often."

"I am sorry, I am sorry, that's all you say," replied Raja, rigidly crossing her arms.

Taking a deep breath, Davon started over. "I don't know how to make you understand. I'm only trying to do a good job and be a good doctor. I'm not trying to make you angry. I know I've offended you, but I feel you are purposely making my job more difficult, Raja. I met Mirum this afternoon and she was the one who graciously helped me find Nisha's suite."

"Mirum had no right to help you. I'm in charge here, not Mirum, who is an interfering mother-in-law with no position. If you wish to see your patients, or your patients wish to see you, it will happen through me. I'm to take you to them, or they will go to the clinic. You must never go again on your own," snapped Raja.

"I'll try to remember that," said Davon, realizing there wasn't to be a truce. She felt quite angry, yet managed to control her emotions. "I received two packages today. I have no idea who they were from or why I received them, but please give them back. I'm being paid very well for my services and cannot accept gifts."

"You would be wise to accept both, Dr. Marshall. The watch was from the Prince as a thank you for the safe delivery of his sons, and the swimming burka was from me, so you will not cause further humiliation of the harem by swimming almost naked in the sea!"

Covering her embarrassment, Davon redirected the conversation. "I'll need to check on Nisha and the twins again tonight before bedtime. Please make the arrangements. Thank you." With that, Davon turned her back to Raja and proceeded confidently down the hallway, secretly hoping she wouldn't get lost trying to find her way back to her suite.

CHAPTER FIVE

Suddenly, the medical clinic was quite busy. Davon assumed word of the successful delivery of the twins had something to do with it. Every morning when she arrived, there were at least three or four patients waiting to be seen. She was now so swamped the days seemed to fly by. Treating the typical childhood and adult diseases she had expected to see from day one, Davon wondered where these patients had gone before. In regards to the 8:30 am pickup, it started up again. Raja would accompany Davon to Nisha's apartment to check on the new mother and twins, and then leave her to do the assessment, and make her own way to the clinic afterwards. The two of them usually walked in silence, and if Davon did ask a question, Raja would answer the question, nothing more. On occasion, Raja would drop into the clinic, but she was doing little translating. Mirum had told the truth when she had said that most of the women had basic English skills.

One Wednesday after much deliberation, Davon made a difficult decision to send a teenage girl to Dubai for an emergency pelvic ultrasound. The thirteen year old had presented with right-sided abdominal pain, and Davon thought she palpated a mass near her ovary. To avoid dealing with Raja, she considered doing the ultrasound herself, but changed her mind because it was in the child's best interest to have the skill and expertise of a radiologist. And so, the child was flown to Dubai hospital.

The next morning just as Davon was about to enter Nisha's suite, Raja touched her shoulder. "How long do you need to examine the twins this morning?" she inquired.

"About twenty minutes unless there are issues. They're doing beautifully, so I expect twenty, maybe thirty minutes," replied Davon, hoping the reason for the question was because the Prince was paying a visit.

"I'll be here in thirty minutes to take you to the communications department. The hospital in Dubai needs to speak with you," said Raja. She turned abruptly, leaving Davon puzzled and alone at the door.

When Davon came down the expansive stairway, Raja was waiting for her with a green silk scarf.

"You must cover your hair, Dr. Marshall, if you please. There are many men in the main part of the palace."

Davon was grateful the color of the scarf was the type of green she could wear. The lime green scarf Raja had wrapped around her head wouldn't have suited her skin tone. Carefully trying to emulate the way Raja had done her head covering, Davon placed the scarf over her hair, pulled it forward, crisscrossed the ends, and threw them back over her shoulders. She was wearing navy pants and a white long sleeved linen shirt, and half expected Raja to ask her to change into a kandoura. But without any comment, Raja left the suite expecting Davon to follow her through the mysterious brass doors. Davon followed, and walking about ten paces behind stepped into a completely different world. This was the working part of the palace with many people, mostly men, going about their business.

The room they entered was a gigantic lobby, which looked as though it belonged in a hotel or museum. It had an open design with white marble floors and an immense staircase at least twenty feet in width, rising grandly in the center of the room. Like the floor, the staircase was also made of white marble, with beautifully curved railings held up by carved marble newel posts. The outer walls of the room were not square, but round, with key-hole shaped arches dramatically supporting large windows and doorways. Looking up, Davon could see a spectacular rotund ceiling with intricate mosaic tiles, and suddenly realized this was the dome she had seen from the helicopter when she had arrived. Small stained glass windows circled the perimeter of the dome and created colored speckles that dotted the back wall. It took Davon's breath away. The whole effect was grandeur at its absolute finest.

As they passed the staircase, Davon noticed several people cautiously glancing in her direction. She considered stopping to introduce herself, but there didn't seem to be any time as Raja was making a bee line across the lobby. Quickly taking her into a private room, where there was a small desk, telephone, intercom, and tiny window over-looking a huge room of computer equipment, Raja picked up the phone.

She spoke in Arabic, and then handed the receiver to Davon. "The hospital is on the line. I'll wait outside for you."

Davon heard the door click closed. "Yes, this is Dr. Marshall speaking. That is correct. You have a patient of mine, Anish, the daughter of Prince Abdul."

"Dr. Marshall, I'm Dr. Tassame, Anish was referred to me yesterday. She has been seen, and I'm sorry to inform you that she has a large tumor on her right ovary. I recommend immediate surgery and removal of the ovary and fallopian tube. Her mother has given her consent, but the Prince must also give his consent to the operation."

"I see. Considering her age, would you do a biopsy first? If it's not cancer, all attempts I feel should be made to save any part of the ovary and the fallopian tube," replied Davon, sitting down.

"We will do a biopsy during the surgery, but I think saving any part of the ovary or tube is out of the question. It looks like the tumor is embedded in the fallopian tube," he answered.

"That may be so, but I'd like the results of the biopsy called to me before you remove the complete ovary and fallopian tube. In fact, if possible, I would like to come to Dubai and assist you with the surgery. Gynecology was one of my specialties."

There was a long pause on the other end of the phone. "As time is of the essence, I'm afraid that would be impossible. If you could get the written consent from Prince Abdul and fax it to me, we will proceed with the operation. Thank you for your help, Dr. Marshall. Goodbye."

Davon heard a click and then silence. "I guess that means no, you won't be calling about the biopsy!" Biting her lip she pressed the button to the intercom. "Hello, this is Dr. Marshall. Can someone please help me?"

"Yes, Dr. Marshall," said a male voice.

"I'd like to call Boston, Massachusetts, right now please," said Davon, nervously giving him her parent's phone number. She prayed Raja couldn't hear her, and turned around to check that the door was firmly shut.

The phone rang until the answering machine connected giving the usual pleasant greeting. Hearing her mother's cheerful voice on the recording made her feel homesick. "Mom, Dad, it's Davon. I don't know what time it is there. I just want to let you know I'm doing well. The place is amazing and I have an incredible apartment and medical clinic. We're totally surrounded by desert about four hours out of Dubai on the ocean. There's no internet and limited telephone service so that's why I haven't called, but I'll try to figure something out. Anyway, I hope you're all well. Say hi to Meg. If you could give Matt a call and let him know I miss him, I'd be grateful. No wait a minute, that may be weird, just say hi from me if you run into him. I love and miss you." Gently placing the phone in its cradle, Davon frowned. That wasn't hard, she thought. What a liar Raja is! There's no way she set up an appointment for me at the telecommunications department to call home. Opening the door quietly, Davon expected to find Raja's ear glued to it, and was shocked to see her politely sitting on a bench nearby.

Approaching her, Davon knew the next conversation was going to be a difficult one. "Raja, I need to speak with the Prince immediately."

"I don't understand," she replied, looking confused.

"The hospital in Dubai called about Anish, and I need to speak with Prince Abdul," repeated Davon, enunciating slowly.

"You cannot talk with Prince Abdul. We have procedures. Tell me what the emergency is and I'll take the problem to Mr. Bedon."

"As a physician I can't discuss medical issues with you or Mr. Bedon. The Prince is the father of Anish, and I need to speak with him about his child." She strongly emphasized the last three words. "Take me to him or get him on the phone please," said Davon, with as much authority as she could muster. She was tired of dealing with Raja's antics!

"One moment," replied Raja, walking quickly into the room Davon had just vacated.

Returning minutes later, Raja demanded that Davon follow her. They proceeded up the white marble staircase to the second floor, and down an exotic looking hallway, which was decorated with ornate carvings. Approaching a massive, wooden door engraved with Persian writing, Raja knocked twice and unconsciously sighed as they waited for someone to answer. After some time, the door was opened, and Mr. Bedon dressed in an immaculate grey suit, exited. Not even acknowledging Davon, he spoke to Raja and then dismissed the translator by a wave of his hand. Raja skirted around Davon and respectfully turned her gaze to the floor.

Bedon's black beady eyes slowly shifted towards Davon. "What's the emergency Dr. Marshall?" he asked curtly.

"The hospital in Dubai called about Anish, and I need to discuss the problem with the child's father," said Davon, calmly meeting his glare.

"You have five minutes!" he replied rudely, pushing the door open.

Davon cleared her throat as she walked past the dreaded Mr. Bedon. She attempted to say thank you, but the words just stuck. Anyway, she rationalized, why should I be grateful for a five minute audience with the Prince? The arrogant attitudes of Raja and Bedon were really beginning to irritate her.

Once through the doorway, Davon entered a circular foyer. The room had a dome ceiling similar to the one in the main lobby of the palace, but on a much smaller scale. Identical inlayed mosaic tiles completely covered the archway forming a geometric pattern, which extended down to the window sills. The rich colors of dark blue, green, and red tiles interlaced with gold made a grand impression.

Mr. Bedon asked her to wait, and as she did so, she paused to smell the sweet bouquet of fresh flowers on the round antique table in the center of the room. She had just reached out to touch the flawless white orchids, when she was summoned. Suddenly, the anticipation of coming face to face with the Prince made her feel giddy. Be serious, she told herself, as she walked around the table and down a short hallway. Davon found the Prince working at his desk, and her heart began to pound as she stood waiting for him to notice her. Although it seemed much longer, it wasn't more than a few seconds before he looked up.

"Dr. Marshall," he said abruptly, standing and extending his hand. "How wonderful to finally have the opportunity to meet you, I want to thank you for my two healthy boys." They shook hands firmly, and then the Prince placed his other hand over top of hers, holding it tenderly.

Davon looked into his dark brown eyes and melted. He was even better looking than she remembered. Her body tingled, and for a moment she was lost for words. "You're most welcome, please call me Davon."

"And you must call me Abdul. Sit, sit, I hear you have some news," said the Prince. He gently let go of her hand and sat back down behind his desk at the exact same time Davon gracefully sat in one of the two plush, silk, upholstered chairs offered.

"Yes, yesterday I saw Anish in the clinic. She was complaining of right-sided abdominal pain. At first I was concerned it was her appendix, but when I examined her, I realized there was a problem with her right ovary. I sent her to Dubai for an ultrasound and unfortunately they have found a large tumor around her right fallopian tube. Dr. Tassame at the hospital is recommending immediate surgery." Davon paused to let him process the information. His smile faded and became a frown, and Davon realized he feared the worst. "Now at her age it is unlikely cancer, but we will need to do a biopsy to make sure."

The Prince leaned back into his chair. "And if it is cancer?" he asked softly.

"The odds of it being cancer are very low, but if it is, we will fight it aggressively."

"I was informed you sent Anish to Dubai, but I never expected this. She is so young, what would have caused it?" he asked, shaking his head.

"All I can tell you is that we'll know more once we get the biopsy results. Dr. Tassame asked me to explain the situation, and let you know the hospital requires your consent for the operation. They would like to do the surgery as soon as possible."

"Of course I'll give my consent. Do you recommend surgery, Davon?"

"Yes, I do," she said, wishing she could have met him under more pleasant circumstances. "I've asked Dr. Tassame to call and discuss the biopsy results before they proceed with the total removal of the ovary and fallopian tube, because in the United States if the tumor is benign we try to save as much of the reproductive unit as possible. Although Anish will have a perfectly normal life with one ovary, it could affect her chances of becoming pregnant when she does decide to have children."

"I understand," he said, as he quietly picked up the gold pen from his desk and fiddled with it.

For a moment both of them sat in silence. Davon noticed how beautifully shaped his hands were as he flicked the pen back and forth. He really was a perfect male specimen, tall, dark and handsome. It was hard to believe he was also rich beyond belief, and had been born with a title. Yet surprisingly he seemed to be a caring person. For some reason, she had expected a spoiled, unreasonable, Casanova.

Lost for a few seconds in her own thoughts, Davon wondered about his upbringing. Was he like Anish, a harem child with a multitude of brothers and sisters? She bit the side of her cheek as the strong feelings of attraction again surfaced, and had to fight to be professional. What is wrong with me? I'm giving the poor man bad news, and I want to jump him. "I'm sick!" she whispered under her breath, thinking about the 007 complex, and women who are attracted to dangerous and powerful men. The Prince certainly fit the requirement of powerful, and when she thought about it, there was a sense of danger lingering in the air.

"Pardon?" asked the Prince, coming to his senses, "Did you say something?"

"Excuse me, I didn't mean to interrupt. Will you be calling the hospital or would you like me to draw up a consent form?" asked Davon, determined to be completely business-like. Concerned she might inadvertently say something inappropriate she tried to avoid looking into his dark sexy eyes. She felt drawn to him, and the uncomfortable interludes of silence were making it difficult for her to stifle the overpowering feelings of lust. As she waited for him to respond, she nervously adjusted her position on the chair, accidentally sitting on one of the long loose ends of her scarf. Before she could stop it, the scarf slipped off her head exposing her blond, sun-kissed hair, which tumbled seductively down her back instantly attracting the complete attention of the Prince.

"Oh no!" gasped Davon in embarrassment. Grabbing the scarf she apologized several times as she began to retie it.

The Prince laughed in amusement. "Please," he said, "don't cover your beautiful hair, Davon. It's one of your best features."

"But Raja said I must." She let the green scarf fall into her lap and self-consciously clutched it.

"That's not true. We are a very progressive nation," replied the Prince, as he stared openly at her delicate Grecian features and mass of white blond curls. His eyes lingered for a moment on her face and then moved downward towards her cleavage. He grinned sheepishly and started to say something when the phone rang.

They were both startled. The Prince reached for the receiver, and Davon stood thinking she should leave and give him privacy, but he covered the mouthpiece and asked her to wait. As she repositioned herself, she was astonished to hear him speaking in French. She knew some Arab countries like Morocco and Algeria had French as an official language, but she was unaware of French being spoken here. It must not have been in her background check, because the Prince obviously didn't realize Davon was fluent, or that French had been her mother tongue. The conversation he was having was something she absolutely shouldn't have been privy to.

Davon's mother, although now proudly American, had been born and raised in a small town in rural Quebec, a French speaking province of Canada. She had dutifully taught both of her daughters the French language. Every summer vacation for as far back as Davon could remember she and Meg had been placed on the express train to Canada to spend six weeks on their grandparent's farm, practicing their language skills.

Feeling like an interloper, Davon tried to show no expression or clue that she understood what was being said. The Prince was cancelling an important meeting in Cairo, and the caller was extremely agitated and unhappy. Although Davon couldn't hear everything the caller was saying, she could hear his inflection, and his shouting. The interesting point about the conversation was the tone; it appeared as though the caller had equal status to the Prince in the world of the rich and famous. The Prince repeatedly told the caller he was cancelling because of a personal matter, which Davon assumed to be Anish's surgery. And when the caller screamed that millions of dollars were at risk, the Prince nonchalantly replied he didn't care because the human problem was about to be eliminated. She didn't understand the complete meaning, but the thought of eliminating a human problem made her feel more than a little uncomfortable. Had she mistranslated?

"Pardon me Davon," the Prince said, as he placed the receiver down, "I had to postpone a business meeting in Cairo."

"Oh dear," she responded, not wanting to give herself away. "I hope to see Cairo one day." She gripped the scarf nervously. As if on cue, Davon heard someone clear their throat. She knew instinctively it was Mr. Bedon, and standing up for a second time she said, "Please, if you could call or fax Dr. Tassame about Anish. The hospital is waiting to hear from you. Thank you for seeing me, Prince Abdul."

"We will speak again," he said, reaching out his hand. This time when Davon took it, the Prince gave her hand a tender squeeze. "It has been more than a pleasure to meet you," he said softly, looking longingly into her blue eyes.

Davon nodded, finding it difficult to let go. There was something captivating about this Prince Abdul. But when she turned around to see the scowling Mr. Bedon, reality quickly returned with a vengeance. At least there's one rose amongst the thorns, she thought. Straightening the scarf, Davon covered her hair before she exited the suite. She assumed she would run into Raja somewhere on her return to the women's quarters. Sure enough, she found Raja fretfully waiting at the top of the staircase.

CHAPTER SIX

By the time Davon reached the medical clinic she was two hours behind schedule. The waiting room was packed, every seat taken. Some of the women had actually moved outside to the wicker furniture on the front porch. Apologizing for being late, Davon quickly put on her freshly starched lab coat and called in her first patient, a twenty-two month old boy with vomiting. After a complete examination, Davon picked up the otoscope to examine the child's ears. As she had suspected, the vomiting was the result of a raging ear infection, which required antibiotics. Administering an intramuscular injection of Penicillin, she assured the mother the boy would be better in a few hours, but stressed the fact that he needed fluids. The mother was asked to give him small amounts of diluted fruit juice every fifteen minutes until he could tolerate a full bottle, and if that didn't happen by dinner, Davon was to be paged. She made arrangements to see the boy the next day and called Raja to go through the instructions again, because she had concerns regarding the mother's English comprehension.

Some of the children at the clinic were waiting for their vaccinations, a program Davon had recently initiated. The first preventable childhood disease Davon had seen four days ago had been a case of mumps, with the typical bilateral swelling of the parotid glands, fever and malaise. When she discovered the children at the palace were not routinely immunized for these common, highly contagious diseases, she had immediately ordered the necessary vaccines. Unsure of how the response to the vaccination program would be, she let it leak out that sterility was a complication of mumps. As she assumed, the word got around quickly, and the women started showing up with their kids in tow. Although she had told the truth, Davon felt a touch guilty because she had discreetly left out the fact that sterility only occurred in rare instances.

Now, it was after lunchtime. Davon poked her head around the corner and saw there was one more patient waiting to be seen, an extremely pretty child. Davon thought she should be accompanied by her mother, and shook her head in frustration. Raja had already left the clinic and she didn't really want to call her back to translate.

"Hi, I'm Dr. Marshall. Are you waiting to see me?" she asked, speaking slowly.

"Yes, my name is Zatum."

Davon was surprised the girl understood English. "It is nice to meet you Zatum. Does your mother know you are at the clinic?"

"My mother is not at the palace," she said in perfect English, refusing to look at Davon. She kept her gaze to the floor.

"Oh, I see," said Davon, puzzled. "Usually when I see one of the children of the harem, they come here with their mother."

"I'm not a child of the harem!" she answered rudely, suddenly looking up.

"Why don't we go into the examining room to talk," said Davon, swallowing her mistake and forcing a smile. "I love your earrings Zatum. They are such delicate gold hoops, very beautiful."

"Thank you," she replied, sitting down in the chair. Davon positioned herself on a stool.

"Now I'm a bit confused, you're not the daughter of the Prince?"

"No, I belong to him," she replied, bitterly.

Zatum was definitely angry, and Davon was now even more baffled about her position at the palace. "So, can you tell me why you have come to the medical clinic?" she asked, standing up to close the door.

"I'm not sure," answered Zatum, as if she was second guessing herself for coming to see the doctor.

Davon sat down again and softened her voice. "Zatum, what did you mean when you said you belong to the Prince?"

"I'm part of the harem. My parents gave me to Prince Abdul!"

Davon tried to hide her concern. So that was why she was angry. "How old are you?"

"Seventeen."

"You speak English very well for seventeen."

"My dream was to become a translator for the United Nations in New York before my parents gave me away. In our culture, beauty is the most important thing…no one cares about a woman's dreams, hopes or intellect."

"Never give up on your dreams Zatum, you still have a long, long life to live," said Davon, trying to gather her thoughts. "You're obviously upset about something, and if you want to talk about it, I'm here. As a doctor anything you say to me will be kept in the strictest confidence, which means

I can't tell anyone what you tell me as a patient."

Zatum didn't say anything for a few seconds, and then burst into tears. "I want to die. Please give me some poison, something that will kill me."

Davon stood up and went over to her. Squatting down she took Zatum's hands and cradled them in hers. "What's upsetting you that you want to end your life?"

"I don't want to be here! I don't want to marry Prince Abdul! He's an old man and I'll kill myself if they force me to marry him. I will!" Zatum looked directly into Davon's eyes and Davon realized she was serious.

"When are you supposed to marry him?"

"In three and a half weeks when I turn eighteen."

"And what happens if you refuse?"

"I'm not allowed to refuse, the only way out is death. You have to help me Dr. Marshall, give me some pills," pleaded Zatum.

Davon handed her a tissue. "I'll speak with the Prince and ask him to let you go back to your family. I'll tell him you're young, that you're very depressed and unhappy here. He is a kind and understanding man, and I'm sure he wouldn't force you to marry him."

"My family will not take me back. I'll be disgraced," Zatum said, crying again.

"Listen to me. You're a perfectly normal young lady who has dreams and aspirations of her own. Being a princess is just not one of them. There must be some special circumstance where you can go back to your parents for a period of time to mature and grow up. And then once you're home, we'll figure out a way so you never have to come back. This could be your opportunity to go to the United States," said Davon reassuringly. "I promise to help you Zatum, but you must promise me you won't try to kill yourself. Deal?" she asked.

Looking at her watch Davon saw it was after three o'clock. Zatum had left the clinic over an hour ago, and she was still sitting at her desk brewing about the child. Her thoughts drifted to her promise to speak to the Prince. How in the world was she ever going to be able to make another appointment to see him, after Raja had given her so much grief about the appointment regarding Anish?

The wind had picked up and Davon suddenly became aware of it when she saw one of the pool's blue and white beach balls blowing past the window. As she stood to investigate, she noticed two men hurrying towards the clinic carrying large pieces of plywood and dragging a short metal ladder. They quickly started to cover one of the clinic's end windows loudly hammering the wooden panel in place. As they completed one window and moved onto the next, Davon wondered what she was missing. No one had said anything to her about a need to board up the windows.

Straightening papers on her desk, she turned to hang up her lab coat in the closet when a piece of plywood was pushed against the office window. It immediately threw the room into semi-darkness. "Hey!" she exclaimed. There was no point in going outside to speak with the men before she headed home. She didn't know the word for window in Farsi, nor could she see her head scarf. Swearing softly, she restocked her medical bag and grabbing it, and her stethoscope, she walked through the reception area towards the door.

The second she turned the knob, the outside door blew open with such intensity that Davon was forced to block it with her foot to prevent it from hitting the back wall. She hiked the strap of her medical bag onto her shoulder, and seized the door handle with both hands, surprised at the amount of effort it took to pull it closed. Her hair whipped back and forth across her eyes obscuring her vision, and she struggled to get it out of her face to see if the door was securely shut. The wind was wickedly strong, yet uncomfortably warm, almost as if she was beside a coal belching furnace. With the clinic's door now properly fastened, she turned around to make a run for her apartment, and halted in mid-step.

There, only meters away from the building was a solid wall of red and brown. It encompassed her whole field of vision, obliterating everything beside and behind the palace. It was miles high and miles wide and was moving with momentum. The sight was terrifying and yet incredible, and although Davon recognized she had little time to cross the courtyard and safely get into the palace, she stood there staring, mesmerized by the sheer enormity of the beast. Tiny bits of sand stung the exposed skin of her hands and face as she tried to shield her eyes from the flying debris. She could hear a deep, eerie groan, and shuddered at the sound that seemed to be growing in volume, even within the few seconds she stood watching.

Davon had correctly identified the turbulence as a sand storm, and intellectually knew she only had minutes before the storm would engulf the palace. But strangely, instead of seeking shelter she found herself rooted to the porch, plastered to the back wall, clutching her medical bag. The only thought that kept racing through her mind was what was the difference between a tornado, a hurricane and a sand storm? She didn't know and this upset her. When a hand reached out to get her attention, she jumped and screamed. It was one of the workers who had been covering the windows, and Davon was embarrassed when she looked into the reddened eyes of a very elderly man.

"I'm sorry," she began to shout, stopping when she realized he wouldn't be able to hear her over the wail of the storm.

The man left her alone on the porch and moved into the open wind. She witnessed him struggling to keep his balance while he frantically pointed at the palace, and then waved at her to follow. His long native gown billowed erratically about him, and he was forced to bend his head several times to prevent the loss of his head covering. Although he was having incredible difficultly maintaining his own balance, he again turned back to Davon urgently indicating she had to come. Without a second thought Davon leapt over the four stairs to the pavement behind him. The brutal force of the wind pushed her over twice as she fought to stand. Placing her medical bag in front of her face, she ducked her head letting the worker bear the brunt of the gale force wind, which was worse than she had imagined. Grains of sand hit her hands and face like bullets, stinging and cutting into her exposed skin as they moved like snails across the open courtyard.

Squinting, she could see nothing through the whirling madness, and had no idea if they were even heading in the right direction. The drone of the howling wind taunted her, sounding almost human as it whipped in and around the stone buildings and walls. Sand was beginning to accumulate on the ground and Davon could feel it sloshing uncomfortably in her open toed shoes. She looked continually downward pressing the bag to the top of her head as she tried to protect her face, while watching for pieces of blowing white robe in front of her. She was worried she would lose sight of her guide and could think of nothing but moving forward, amazed that a normal three minute walk from the clinic to the palace could take so long.

Just as she was convinced he had taken a wrong turn, Davon saw the base of a white marble newel post and reached out to touch the smooth welcoming surface. She could now feel her way up the staircase railing to safety. Making her way quickly to the inner hallway, she bolted through the closed French doors like a frightened animal, and collapsed on the wooden floor breathing heavily. Red sand pooled around her, falling from her clothes, her shoes, her bag and her hair. And when she brushed her cheek, more sand dropped into her lap. She could taste it in her mouth and saw it under her finger nails. She was absolutely worn out and extremely grimy. Too tired to even hold up her head, she leaned it against the wall, thinking how thankful she was that the worker had come to her aid.

When she had gone through the French doors, Davon had caught a glimpse of the worker's white gown heading down the covered balcony. She presumed he had to enter the palace at a different place because he had taken her to the entrance of the women's quarters. "You'd think that during a natural disaster, there'd be an exception to the rule," she said, forcing herself to stand. Davon shook more sand from her clothing and hair as she started to move, and then looked back at the mess on the floor. A trail of sandy footprints followed her on the expensive Persian carpet. She wondered if she should take her shoes off, but thought it was probably too late. The cleaning lady was going to hate her.

Bin greeted Davon enthusiastically and fussed over her, unconcerned about the dirty sand falling on her newly polished floors. She shooed her into the shower, and when Davon reappeared cleanly scrubbed, her skin still tender and raw, it was to a large and delicious table of food. Finally, nestled on the living room sofa reading her book, Davon took another sip of coffee and thought about the two pounds of sand she had left on the bathroom tiles. Being stubborn, Bin wouldn't hear of giving Davon the vacuum cleaner because cleaning and cooking was her job. So there Davon sat like a queen, listening to Bin vacuuming up the mess. Well, at least the power is still on, she told herself, wondering how well the palace was insulated. She could hear the storm wailing outside, and every few minutes the shutters on the windows would shake. When the phone rang, Davon put down her book to answer it.

"Dr. Marshall, I'm glad you made it back to your suite. I trust it was not a problem," said Raja, indifferently.

"Actually, Raja it was. I had no idea that a sand storm was brewing, and by the time I tried to come home it was almost too late. One of the elderly workers putting up shutters on the clinic assisted me and frankly, I owe him my life. I never would have made it back on my own. I'd like you to thank him on my behalf, he was amazingly brave."

"The worker will be taken care of," said Raja, in a completely uninterested tone. "I wanted to inform you that the storm will most likely continue for two or three days. There's a small room in the women's quarters I'll have cleaned and set up as a temporary medical clinic, if you wish."

Davon wasn't about to be blown off. "How will the worker be taken care of? I'd like to give him something, but I don't know what is appropriate."

"I'll deal with the worker, Dr. Marshall," said Raja curtly. "Now, regarding the medical clinic?"

Davon felt like screaming, but gritted her teeth and said, "There's no need to set up a temporary clinic for a few days, if anyone needs to be seen, they can come to my suite or I'll go to them. But...I am expecting a call from the hospital in Dubai, will it get through?"

"All outside communication has been shut down because of the storm. If you have any further questions, don't hesitate to call," replied Raja, hanging up.

Davon put down the phone in disgust. "I'll deal with the worker Dr. Marshall," she said, imitating Raja's tone. "I'm sure you will. You don't care two hoots about anything that doesn't directly affect you!"

Irritated, Davon sat back down on the couch. It would be impossible to check up on Raja's promise, and even crazier to try to find the elderly worker herself. She hoped she might see him tending to the grounds around the clinic, because she wanted to personally thank him.

CHAPTER SEVEN

After dinner, Davon decided to take a little personal time and go to the gym to workout. Since the delivery of the twins, her morning exercise routine had become almost nonexistent. Walking slowly into the darkened room, she found the light switch, flicked it on, and proceeded to the thigh master. As she vigorously exercised, she became aware of music coming from the dance studio. Stopping to listen to the intriguing sounds, she recalled Raja telling her about dance lessons. "There must be a lesson going on tonight," she said to herself. Before moving to the next machine, she went over to the connecting door to sneak a peek. "Damn it," she cried, when the door creaked open. She had drawn attention to herself, and noticed that at least half of the women in the room looked over to see who was interrupting the class.

There were about fifteen ladies dressed in bright colorful costumes. All of them had bare feet, and little bells on their wrists and ankles. It was like a scene from *Arabian Nights*.

"Dr. Marshall, have you come to attend the class?" asked Nisha, looking very beautiful in her orange tight-fitting sequined outfit.

Davon stared at her. It was hard to believe she had just delivered twins. "I was planning to workout in the gym and heard your enchanting music, I didn't mean to interrupt," she replied, feeling embarrassed in her black yoga pants and t-shirt.

"You are not interrupting anything, come in, and join us. I'm teaching the belly dancing class tonight because Gege our real instructor was unable to come. She normally flies in from Dubai to teach the class, and of course with the storm, well..." Nisha turned back to the group. "Everyone if you have not already met her, this is our new doctor, Davon Marshall."

All of the women inclined their heads in unison as Nisha positioned Davon at the very front of the class. Quickly removing her runners and socks, Davon ran and placed them against the side wall. The music was turned up, and they began a series of hip thrusting and swaying. The movements oozed pure sexuality, and Davon laughed to herself. The culture covered women from head to toe and then taught belly dancing, it was crazy. The women, with their tightly fitting tops, bare midriffs, and balloon cinched pants, looked like beautiful, wish granting genies.

When Davon had trouble keeping up, Nisha took her to the side of the room and demonstrated the basic movements over and over again. Although Davon had taken ballet, belly dancing was totally different, and she struggled at first to emulate the flow that seemed to come so easily to the others. However, by the second hour she was beginning to get it. She mastered the art of moving her arms by relaxing and focusing on the rhythmic beat of the music. The arms were held out, perpendicular to the body, with the elbows bent. The hand was held soft, but not limp and the fingers were straight, except for the middle finger, which delicately hung lower than the rest. It wasn't all fun, it was a workout, and that was precisely what Davon liked about it. For three hours they dance, repeating each movement until it was absolutely perfect. When the class was over Davon was tired, but excited.

"Now I understand why you're in such great shape, Nisha. No one would ever guess you had twin boys a few days ago. Thanks for a great class, I enjoyed it," said Davon, using her towel to wipe the sweat from her brow.

"Please come again, Dr. Marshall. It was nice to have a new face. Next week, Gege will be here and you will be amazed to see a real dancer at work. She is unbelievable."

"There's no need to be formal, call me Davon, and I'd love to come to another class, especially if Gege is all you say she is. Is it the same time every week?"

"Yes, unless we have a guest dancer, but I can always let you know if that happens."

"Then we have a date. Tonight was really enjoyable, and it was nice to meet a few more of the women here. Thanks for including me."

As they chatted a gorgeous young woman came up behind Nisha and smiled at Davon. She looked to be in her early twenties, and had highlighted her brown hair with auburn streaks, which nicely accented the dark plum costume she was wearing. She waited until Davon's conversation with Nisha came to an end, and then held out her hand.

"Dr. Marshall, I'm Lamna. You had tea with my mother, Mirum."

"Yes, how wonderful to meet you, Lamna. Your mother was so gracious to me. I had gotten terribly lost when I was on my way to check on Nisha's new babies, and your sweet daughter found me and took me to her."

Lamna laughed, "That's Ismil. How did you like the class?"

"It was great. I noticed that you're a fantastic dancer. How long have you been belly dancing?"

"For years, you see we're selected at a young age to fulfill our purpose. I was always meant to become part of the harem, and so you learn to dance," said Lamna, smiling.

"Oh," replied Davon, trying to hide the fact that she thought it was totally weird to have your fate selected for you. She figured Lamna had to be at least twenty-five or six, although she looked much younger. Lamna had large dark brown eyes with unusual flecks of green, high cheek bones, and a beautiful smile.

"However, that being said, not all of the women in the harem dance. Some of them just don't enjoy it, and prefer to do other things," she added, with a giggle.

"Like what type of things?" asked Davon, intrigued.

"Shopping, shopping and more shopping," laughed Lamna. "The last Thursday of every month, we are allowed to go to Dubai for the day. It's a long four hour drive, but we leave early, shop till we drop, and get home late. During the drive we play games and sing songs. It can be tons of fun depending on who goes. You should come Davon!"

"I'd love too. Ever since I arrived, I've wanted to explore Dubai, and take in some of the touristy things," said Davon, grinning.

"Well," said Lamna, wrinkling her nose, "touristy things might be a problem. I'm not sure if you would be allowed. We're sent with bodyguards and always go to the same shopping districts...and we have to wear a full burka." She paused for a moment. "Do you know what that is?"

Davon frowned, "Yes I do. In fact, I received a swimming burka from Raja to wear in the ocean. Do you think I'd have to wear one in Dubai? I'm not part of the harem."

"I don't know, it's up to Raja, and you never know with Raja," whispered Lamna, leaning closer. "Raja's very strict, too strict if you ask me. So the rumor is true about you swimming in public. And in a bikini! You're my type of woman."

Davon burst out laughing, and Lamna joined her. "It wasn't a bikini. I was wearing a one piece bathing suit and the minute I got out of the water I covered up," she whispered back.

It felt wonderful to find a person who agreed Raja was overbearing. Davon knew Lamna was going to become a good friend. She spoke English as well as her mother, and Davon felt a definite connection. In many ways they were similar: close in age, confident, and unafraid to say what they really thought. But physically they were like night and day. Although they were about the same height and weight, Davon's blond hair and blue eyes dramatically contrasted with Lamna's coloring.

They could have gabbed all night, but when some of the other women came over to introduce themselves, they parted after arranging to get together for tea the next day. Davon was on cloud nine; she had finally made a friend.

A funny humming noise woke Davon up, and for a moment she couldn't identify the source of the sound. Turning over and glancing at the bedside table, she suddenly realized the noise was coming from her pager. It was 3:00 am. Instantly awake, Davon was out of bed and dashing down the hallway to the phone in the living room.

"It's Davon. What is the problem, Raja?"

"One of the children can't breathe. The mother and servant are bringing him to you now. Do you wish me to come also?"

"Does the mother speak English?" asked Davon.

"Yes, Tagette speaks English."

"Fine, I'll call if I need you," said Davon, hanging up.

Returning to her bedroom, Davon grabbed her housecoat and medical bag. She then proceeded back into the living room and tried to locate the wall switch to turn on the lights. She couldn't seem to find one. Although it was ridiculous, she realized she'd never turned on or off the living room lights since she had been there. Panicking that the patient was going to arrive to a dark suite, Davon rushed to Bin's door inside the kitchen. She really hated to wakeup Bin, but she needed help.

"Bin, I have a patient coming to the suite, and need to turn on the lights. Please, can you help me?" called Davon softly, speaking in half English and half Farsi.

She could hear shuffling and then the door opened. A smiling Bin greeted her. She ran quickly past and towards the closet in the main hallway. "So that's where the light switch is," said Davon, under her breath, "I never would have looked in a closet." With the lights now on, Davon glanced into Bin's room. The room was a small cubbyhole with a tiny connecting bathroom. There was no furniture except a small bedside table. Her eyes moved to the mound of ruffled blankets lying on the floor. Davon was horrified. She was living in the most luxurious place in the world, and her servant was living in a windowless closet, and sleeping on the floor!

A loud knock at the door brought her back to reality, and by the time Davon came into the living room, Bin was ushering in two frantic women with a boy in acute respiratory distress. "Bring him to the sofa and sit him down. I need to listen to his chest," said Davon. Even without her stethoscope, she could hear loud whistling sounds with his every expiration.

Davon unbuttoned the child's pajama top, and quickly rubbed the end of the stethoscope to warm it before placing it on his back. She could hear wheezing sounds on both sides, and could see a faint blueness around his lips, meaning his oxygen levels were low.

"Has he ever had an attack like this before?" asked Davon, as she reached into her bag for an inhaler.

"Yes," said Tagette, "It comes with sand storms."

"He is having an asthma attack, which means the tubes to the lungs have become narrow or small. The whistling sound he is making is because of this narrowing, and he needs medicine to open up these breathing tubes. How old is he?"

"Memen is eleven years, in three weeks," she anxiously replied.

Davon pulled out a bronchodilator canister and a corticosteroid inhaler. The steroid was indicated in children age twelve and up, yet this was all she had. Close enough, thought Davon putting the inhalers on the table. "Please tell Memen to watch what I do. This will open up his breathing tubes," said Davon, as she demonstrated how to take a puff. The drug gave an immediate and positive response, and within minutes the boy's wheezing slowed. Tagette thanked Davon and Memen looked up at her, and smiled sweetly. "In twenty minutes, I'm going to give him another drug, and after that you can go back to your suite. With this second drug," Davon showed Tagette the container, "he will need to rinse his mouth with water after every dose. If he complains of a sore throat, headache or stomach upset, let me know. Do you have any questions?"

The mother shook her head as she stroked her child's face. Davon listened to the boy's chest again, and could hear only slight wheezing in the right lower lobe. She checked her watch and then instructed him how to take the corticosteroid. The blueness around his lips was gone and he was breathing more easily. Memen had responded well.

"You can go home, but I want to see Memen in the morning, around 9:00 am. If he has any problems before then, call me right away. I will come to your suite," said Davon, as she escorted them to the door making a mental note to call Raja to accompany them to the next appointment. The mother had not said much, and Davon wasn't sure how well she understood English.

When she climbed back into her comfortable king-sized bed, Davon tossed and turned, her thoughts racing. It wasn't concern about Memen that kept her awake. She knew the child would be fine the rest of the night. The reason she struggled to fall back to sleep was because Bin was sleeping on the floor.

Morning light streamed into the bedroom. At first, the brightness of the sunlight didn't register, but as Davon turned over, stretched and extended one leg out of the bed, she realized the storm had blown over. Going to the window she peeked through the lattice work and saw blue sky. Relieved that she would be able to see patients at the clinic, she headed for the shower. Her thoughts turned to Bin, then Anish, and then Memen. It was going to be a busy day.

When Raja arrived at precisely 8:30, Davon had already been waiting for five minutes.

"Good morning Raja," she said, cheerfully.

"Good morning Dr. Marshall."

"Today after I check on the twins, I'd like to see Memen in his suite, and then I want to go to the communications center to call about Anish. I trust the phone lines will be up and running now that the storm has abated," said Davon, in an authoritative tone.

Not waiting for a reply, Davon marched confidently towards Nisha's quarters with Raja trailing two steps behind. She was dressed in her only pantsuit, made from a chocolate colored, light-weight cotton. A silky gold sleeveless shirt peeked out from under the jacket, complimenting the color of her sun-lightened hair. The new sandals she had purchased three days before she left Boston to go with the shirt, the only gold sandals that she had been able to find, had wedge-heels and ankle ties. For a conservative dresser like Davon, the metallic gold straps were much too gaudy, but she had purchased them, and now she was glad. Just before they left the suite, she had noticed Raja looking at them, and for some horrible reason this made her feel giddy. It wasn't that Davon felt she had to compete with Raja; it was a matter of the woman's unrelenting arrogant, "I'm better than you" attitude. Raja always had to have the upper hand, and Davon had had enough.

A light beige scarf, almost the same color as her hair, hung about her neck in preparation to cover her head when they entered the lobby on route to the communications department. Davon didn't want to give Raja any excuse not to take her there. When they arrived at Nisha's apartment door, Davon knocked briskly. She was anxious to get inside the suite before Raja could ramble off a list of objections.

"Dr Marshall, before…" started Raja.

Her gut reaction had been right. Davon grimaced. The door opened, and she put up one hand and interrupted the translator. "Hold that thought Raja; we're in a hurry this morning. I'll check on the twins and then we need to see Memen. He was a sick little boy last night," she called back, taking two stairs at a time up the grand staircase.

Both babies were sleeping peacefully when Davon entered the nursery. Whispering to the three nannies and one wet-nurse in her limited Farsi, Davon tried to ask about the time of the next feeding. She didn't want to wake the boys for vital checks if they had just been fed and put down. It wasn't until she pointed to the babies, her mouth and her breast that they seemed to understand. The smiling senior nanny explained by using her hands that the twins had slept through the night. She implied by counting on her fingers that they had been sleeping for seven hours.

Davon was instantly concerned. The babies were little and needed to be fed every three to four hours, not allowed to sleep seven. Just as she turned to get Raja to translate, Nisha walked into the nursery. "Nisha, thank goodness you're here. I think the nanny told me the twins didn't wake up last night for a feed. Could you ask them about this for me please?" Davon unconsciously bit her lip as she waited.

Nisha asked the nanny what she said, and then laughed. "Not to worry Davon, both of the boys were fed at 7:00 am. The servant thought you were asking for the last time they had breast milk."

"That was sort of what I was asking," said Davon, shaking her head. "Bin's taught me many words, but I'm still a bit lost as to how to put them together. It's a difficult language. While I'm here, could you tell the servants the boys need to be fed every three to four hours? If the babies don't wake on their own, they are to be awakened."

"They understand," said Nisha, after translating.

"Thanks. How are you feeling?"

"Wonderful. I'm sleeping well, and I have been blessed with two perfect sons."

"That you have," said Davon. "How about if I do your assessment first, and then check the babies. If everything looks good today, I'll be able to start decreasing my daily visits to every second or third day."

As she ran down the stairs towards Raja, Davon was mentally preparing herself. Although she told Raja that her next patient visit would be Memen, she had lied. Secretly, she planned to go directly to the communications department after visiting the twins. The minute they stepped out of Nisha's quarters into the hall, Davon pulled her scarf over her hair and turned toward the polished brass doors. She pushed one open quickly and began to walk as fast as she could to her destination--the telephone room.

"Dr. Marshall, you're going the wrong way!" Raja called after her.

"Oh, I figured I might as well contact the hospital since we're here." She heard the door swing closed, and the patter of Raja's jeweled slippers on the marble floor. Davon increased her gait, making it to the communications room only seconds before the translator. Opening the door, Davon stepped inside and said, "I won't be long." She shut the door firmly, taking the time to quietly lock it. She didn't think Raja would try to come into the room, but didn't want to risk it. Placing her bag on the table, she took out her recently charged computer. "Yes, this is Dr. Marshall," she said to the operator, "I'd like to place a call to Dubai Hospital and speak with Dr. Tassame, and I'd also like to hook up to the internet. Can you help me?"

"Of course, Dr. Marshall. I will place the call to the hospital. Because we do not have wireless, you will need to plug your computer into the phone line next to the receiver, which I will activate. Please hang up the phone and it will ring when the call to Dr. Tassame goes through."

"Thank you," said Davon, feeling pleased with herself.

Well that was easy, she thought, as she turned on her computer and connected it to the land-line. Within minutes she was on the internet and accessing her email. Eighty-four new emails, most group messages from the hospital in Boston, some junk, and several personal. Right now, anything from home was wonderful. The first email was from her parents, saying they had gotten a voice mail from a man confirming she had arrived. They wrote that they missed her already, and were waiting patiently for her phone call. The second, also from her parents, said they listened to her voice message, and wished they had woken up when she had called. They were now sleeping with the phone at the bedside.

An email from the Bank of America caught her eye. Davon groaned. When she had taken the job, she had asked that a portion of her pay be put in her Boston, Bank of America account to pay her monthly student loan payment of $2532 US. This had been a make or break part of her contract, as all of the employees of the palace were directly paid through an account at the Bank of Dubai. She had been told there would be no exceptions. However, after many back and forth emails, she finally was assured that arrangements to pay her monthly payment would be allowed. Davon's heart sunk, she had left Boston with just over one thousand dollars in her account, and now she was positive that the money had not been transferred. She was probably overdrawn and facing penalties. Opening the email she sat stunned at what she read:

Dear Dr. Marshall,

Thank you for your payment of $93,021.00. Your student loan #494647 has been paid in full. Should you require any further funding for your practice, or for a mortgage, please do not hesitate to call or come into the branch. We would be more than happy to do business with you again.

Yours truly,

Brad Smitt, Bank of America

Before she had a chance to read the next email, the phone rang. Almost speechless, she picked up the receiver and managed to squeak out a "Hello."

"Dr. Marshall? This is Dr. Tassame."

"Dr. Tassame, thank you for taking my call. I wanted to follow-up on Prince Abdul's daughter Anish. I'm sorry I was unable to call earlier, we had a sand storm yesterday."

"We had one also, but I understand it gathered strength when it made its way inland. In regards to Anish, the operation went well, the tumor was benign, but large, almost two pounds. Unfortunately, she lost her right ovary, but I was able to save the fallopian tube. She is resting comfortably, and will be able to return to the palace in two to three weeks."

"Is that really necessary? I'm more than happy to come to Dubai and escort her home."

"Considering she is the Prince's daughter, I want her to stay here until her stitches are out, and make sure she is well-healed before she is flown back. A nurse will be accompanying her home, it has already been arranged."

"So I can expect her around the beginning of May?"

"I think we are looking at May 10th."

"Thank you Dr. Tassame. I will expect Anish on the tenth," said Davon, hanging up the phone. Glancing at her watch, she realized she had been in the room for fifteen minutes. Raja was going to be mad one way or another, so she decided to finish reading her emails, and then try to call her parents.

The next few emails were from friends with personal updates, one was a wedding announcement. Davon sent quick replies, not going into detail about her whereabouts. She had left the United States in such a rush, many of her friends had no idea she was out of the country. The last email was from Matt.

Hi Davon,

I phoned your parents when I discovered your phone was disconnected. Imagine my surprise when they told me you were in the Middle East. In my wildest dreams, I never thought you would even be capable of doing something like this. I'm still in shock, and just hope you are safe. Honestly Davon, I don't know what happened. After one month without you, I knew I had made a big mistake and now I hope it's not too late. If you still want to be with me, please come home.

Love Matt

p.s. I can't talk about marriage right now, but if that is what you need to get on the plane, I'll consider it. Please let me know what you are thinking.

Davon was instantly angry. "You can't talk about marriage but if that's what I need, you'll consider it! Give me a break! I wouldn't come home if you were the last man on the planet! Besides, I've changed...that's right, now I take lots of risks buddy. My new life motto is living on the edge!" She deleted the email, pounded the table, and then went into the computer's trash bin to retrieve it. Matt wasn't the most eloquent man on paper, but Davon knew he had a good heart. Glancing at her watch again, she picked up the telephone receiver, "Yes I would like to place a call to the United States, and then I need to speak with someone in accounting regarding my salary." As the phone rang, she wondered what time it was in Boston.

"Hello," said her mother, sleepily.

"Mom, its Davon, sorry to wake you, I don't know what the time difference is."

"Darling, I'm so glad you phoned. Dad and I have been worried about you. It is just after 2:00 am, but we don't care, call us anytime you can. How are you Sweetheart? How is your job going?"

"Great, everything is great. The culture is quite different, but I'm figuring things out. The people are wonderful and kind for the most part, and I met the Prince. He's everything you would expect a Prince to be, good looking, incredible personality, and very rich."

"Hang on your father is getting on the extension. I hope you are not thinking about getting involved with the Prince!"

"Mom, that wouldn't even be possible, plus he already has nineteen wives."

"I read an article about an American who got involved with Iranian royalty and…"

"Mom, don't worry it's not going to happen. How is everyone at home?"

"We're all fine. Matt called the house looking for you. I told him where you were, I hope that was okay?" said her father.

"No problem Dad, he sent me an email. Said he regretted breaking up, and wished I'd come home."

"Are you coming home?" asked her mother.

"No! I signed a contract for one year, and I'm going to fulfill it. I'm making a ton of tax-free money, and when I get home I'll be able to go back to school, or set up a practice. I'm fine; you don't need to be concerned. This is such an amazing place. When I arrived in Dubai, the Prince had the plane stopped on the tarmac, and I was the only passenger allowed to get off. I was put in a limousine, and taken to a helipad where I was flown by private helicopter to the palace." She carefully left out the part of driver being accosted by the military. "And I'm living in the most luxurious apartment you have ever seen, and even have a live-in servant to cook and clean."

"My goodness, it sounds incredible," said her mother.

"It is, the only problem I have is calling, or emailing home. There's only one place in the palace for communication, and unfortunately I have limited access. If you don't hear from me that's the reason. I'll try to call at least once a month. But, now I'm late for clinic and need to go. I love you both tons. Give my love to Meg."

They exchanged goodbyes. The second Davon hung up the phone, it rang again.

"Accounting," said a male voice.

"Hi, this is Dr. Davon Marshall. I have a few questions regarding my salary and the bank account it's being deposited to. Are you the person I should speak with?"

"I may be able to help you Dr. Marshall as I dealt with the internet arrangements of your employment. However, questions or concerns like this usually go directly to Mr. Bedon."

"Oh, I only have two quick questions, hopefully you have an answer. When I accepted the job, I understood my salary would be deposited in an account set up at the Bank of Dubai. But an exception was made for me, and three thousand dollars every month was supposed to be deposited in my Bank of America account in the United States, to pay for my medical student loan. Today, I received an email from the Bank of America, which said my student loan was paid in full. Do you know anything about this?"

"Yes, I was told to pay the loan. It was paid three days after you arrived at the palace… on let me see… February 15th."

"Okay, thank you. So I guess this means I won't get any salary for the next few months because the money went to pay off the loan?"

"The loan payment was a gift from the Prince. On the last day of every month, as per your employment contract, $50,000 US dollars will be deposited to your Dubai account."

A large smile burst onto Davon's face. "Thank you for your help. I don't have any further questions," she said, placing down the receiver. "Unbelievable! This place is unbelievable!"

By the time she caught up with Raja, forty-five minutes had gone by. Although nothing was said, Davon was acutely aware that Raja was annoyed. It was ironic because Davon was feeling exceptionally exuberant. They walked briskly through the common area, Davon now three steps behind Raja. Taking a moment to enjoy the surroundings, Davon looked up at the dome as they passed underneath it. The stain glass windows seemed to be perfectly positioned to reflect light, emulating a clock. It was almost 11:00 am and the light was coming through the window of 11:00 o'clock. As Davon paused to examine this phenomenon, she was reminded of the Pantheon's dome in Rome, Italy. She remembered reading in Matt's Architectural Design magazine something about the sundial effect of the Pantheon's oculus. She wanted to ask Raja about this, but hesitated. It probably wasn't the right moment for touristy questions.

As Davon expected, Memen had made a complete recovery from his asthmatic attack. When they arrived at the suite he was rough-housing with his younger brother, and without even examining him, Davon knew he was okay. Kids were really amazing, if they were sick, they were very sick, there seemed to be no in-between. His quick recovery, she presumed, had to do with the end of the sand storm, but she gave him another dose of the corticosteroid, just to be sure. Both lungs were clear and she could hear no wheezing, or whistling. Getting Raja to translate, Davon informed the mother that she would like to do a few tests at the clinic.

Looking at her watch, she was surprised it was already lunch time. "Raja, thanks for assisting me this morning. I think I'll grab some lunch at the suite. If you have something else to do, I can make my own way to the clinic after I eat," said Davon, cheerfully trying to make amends.

"As you wish," replied Raja. Turning quickly, she abandoned Davon in the hallway.

Wow, she really is mad, thought Davon. I guess it's my fault, though I don't understand why she keeps saying there's a problem at the communications department. It seems to be a simple process to put through a call. As she walked briskly down the hallway, she suddenly became aware that the area had been cleaned. The dusty smell in the air was replaced with a hint of lavender, and the small piles of red sand that had gathered yesterday in the cracks and corners of the doorways were gone. Davon hummed softly to herself. She still couldn't believe the Prince had paid off her student loan.

CHAPTER EIGHT

When she finished eating more than she had planned, she yawned. Normally Davon only drank coffee at breakfast, but today she asked for a cup to accompany her to the clinic. Going into the kitchen to get a larger cup to use as a travel mug, her thoughts turned to Bin's tiny room beside the pantry. It was going to be very awkward addressing Bin's living situation with Raja, especially now. She reflected on her courses in Psychology, and one particular lecture on marital power struggles. The power in a marriage was directly related to earnings and social status. Davon was positive she was making more money than Raja, but the social status of a female physician in the Middle East had to be low, lower than that of a translator. Suddenly the pager in her pocket began to vibrate, and Davon jumped almost spilling her coffee. Placing the cup on the counter, she ran for the phone.

"Dr. Marshall here."

"You have nine patients waiting at the clinic," Raja said, in a rather cool fashion.

"I'll be right there," replied Davon, hanging up the receiver. She had almost apologized for being tardy when she caught herself, remembering that the secret in winning a power struggle is to never ever appear subservient.

The shutters had been removed from the medical clinic windows, and bright sunlight streamed into the full waiting room of beautifully clothed women and children. Davon greeted everyone as she sailed through the door. She noted with relief that Raja was no longer among the group. Pulling on her lab coat and placing her stethoscope around her neck, Davon went to get her first patient. By 4:20 pm she had seen fourteen routine cases, and was finishing up some paperwork when someone knocked on the partially open office door.

"Come in," said Davon, very confused when a woman clothed in a full black burka entered.

"So you are the famous Davon Marshall," said a deep male voice, with eyes that leered.

"And you are?" Davon asked, not impressed with the game playing.

"I am Hepbet, Prince Abdul's eldest son." He quickly laughed at his announcement, and then threw off the costume. "One day all this will belong to me," he added, gesturing towards the palace and its grounds.

He was a handsome boy, slim, about 5'10" with dark curly hair and black eyes exactly like his father's. He sat assertively down in the chair beside the wall, and slid it towards the desk trying to look menacing. Looking Davon in the eye, he then said, "Well, how do you like it here, my dear?"

Davon struggled to keep a straight face. She leaned back in her chair, and drummed her fingers on the wooden arm. "I love it here, Hepbet. But you know very well you're not supposed to be in my office, or in the women's quarters for that matter!"

"Of course I know. Do you think I would dress like this unless it was critically important for me to meet you?"

"And the critically important reason is?" inquired Davon, assuming the boy was pulling a prank or doing this on a dare.

"Aren't you going to offer me tea?"

"No Hepbet. If you get caught in my office there will be consequences for both of us. What have you come to see me about?" asked Davon, jumping up to close the office door.

Hepbet slumped forward and placed his head in his hands, and Davon fought the urge to console him. After all he was just a boy of seventeen.

"My father likes you very much. He said he respects you."

"And I like and respect your father."

"I want to go to university in the United States. My father says it's too dangerous. He won't even let me go to Europe, even though he went to university in France," Hepbet muttered quickly, his initial confidence deflated. "I want you to persuade him to let me go to your country." He looked up at her as if to beg.

Sighing, Davon returned to her seat and looked at him. "I wish I could help, but honestly I hardly know your father. I've only met him once, and I really don't think a suggestion from me of where you should go to school would change his decision."

"Please try to talk with him. You have to understand, my father is overprotective! Ever since my brother, the real heir died, he smothers me. You went to school in the United States and so you know what it's like. He will listen to you. I'll give you this money for your help." He held out five one hundred dollar American bills.

Davon pushed his hand away and patted it. "I don't want your money. This obviously means a great deal to you and I'll gladly do what I can, the problem is I rarely see your father. I don't know when I will see him again, and I'm not sure how I would ever have the opportunity to bring up the subject of your schooling."

Hepbet smiled, and became quite animated, "You will see him again, I know. And you promise to tell him I should go to university in the United States, please promise me! I'll give you a present, anything you want. What do you want?"

Davon laughed. Hepbet was a very likable kid. "Alright, I promise to help if I ever meet your father again. However, realize it's a long-shot, or risk, that it may not happen. Now, if you're serious about wanting to do something for me, there is a little problem I'm having," said Davon, gazing into his beautiful brown eyes, "Tell me, do you have any access to furniture?"

It was after 6:00 pm and dusk was slowly settling in as Davon made her way home. She had agreed to give Hepbet forty-five minutes to remove himself from the women's quarters before she left the office. The last thing she wanted was to get caught talking with the young heir, especially since she had been specifically warned to have no contact with the older male children of the harem. It didn't help when Hepbet assured her getting caught wasn't a problem because his father and Mr. Bedon were traveling, she had an uncanny sense that Raja was lurking somewhere in the looming shadows, watching. Unconsciously she turned around and took one last glance at the clinic. It was as if she somehow expected to see Raja standing on the porch surveying her movements. A fresh, salty sea breeze gently brushed her cheek. She paused, and then turned back to take in the view of the lonely bay just seconds before the sun dipped quickly below the horizon.

The dim solar lights along the pathway suddenly became brighter, and Davon feeling foolish about her fears, chastised herself. Taking a deep breath, she started again on her way laughing about Hepbet's getup. It's a wonder that he thinks he's invisible when it's forty degrees outside, and every other woman in the harem is in light summer clothing! In better spirits, Davon jogged up the outside staircase and down the hallway to her suite. Yanking open the door, she flew into the apartment and collided with a single bed and overstuffed armchair.

Over the next few months, the number of patients coming each day to the clinic increased. There were always the usual ailments, childhood diseases, colds and flu, however now Davon had the added issue of social calls. Many of the women--most from the belly dancing class, came to the clinic not for medical attention, but to gab. Davon not only felt this was inappropriate for a medical facility, she found it very difficult to stop in the middle of her day to enjoy this unusual aspect of the culture. The dead giveaway was when the ladies arrived dressed to the nines carrying picnic baskets. The typical contents were thermoses of tea, sandwiches and desserts. Davon was expected to immediately stop what she was doing, sit down, and entertain. When the social calls started to increase to two or more a day, her work hours, mainly home visits, were pushed into the evening. She was grateful the women of the harem had accepted her, but her days were becoming longer, and she was getting tired and gaining weight. All of the women were extremely kind and considerate, yet they didn't seem to understand Davon was being paid to do a job. This was probably due to the fact that none of them had ever done a day's work in their lives. For them, every day was fun and games, indulging in beauty treatments, and gossiping. Although the children were pampered by their mothers, even the unpleasant task of child-rearing was taken care of by carefully selected servants.

Davon stared at the calendar and noted the date. It was August 30th and Matt's twenty-eighth birthday. She circled the number with her finger and whispered, "Happy birthday my love," before turning to grab her stethoscope. It had taken three months for her to cool down and finally reply to Matt's emails, nine in total. But it had been too late. They had just started politely communicating when Davon received an email from her sister saying she had seen Matt with another woman. Not just with another woman, kissing one. Perhaps it's for the best, Davon thought, recognizing her contract at the palace was for another five and a half months. If Matt and I were really supposed to be together, I wouldn't be here! She looked at her list of appointments, and tried to concentrate on her work schedule. She could push Matt out of her mind, yet she couldn't quite obliterate how amazing their relationship had been. Beyond the anger and pain, she really loved him. When she took the stethoscope from her bag, the sleeve of the starched white lab coat caught on her diamond bracelet. Carefully pulling at the thread, she exhaled loudly, her day was going to be busy and if one picnic basket showed up, she was going to lose it! She didn't understand how the harem women expected her to relax and drink tea for hours while patients lined up in circles around the clinic? It was a complete mystery, because even the waiting patients didn't complain. Up until now, she had faked enjoyment since she was trying to make friends, but no more! Her work was piling up and there was absolutely zero time to do what she wanted to do, like swim or go to the gym. She was working too many hours, and barely had enough energy to attend the weekly dance class.

Her bracelet caught in the morning sunlight and Davon playfully twisted her wrist to watch the reflecting light dance on the wall. It had been a gift from Prince Abdul for the diagnosis and safe surgery of his daughter Anish. Although Davon knew she shouldn't accept another present for doing her job, she did so because she didn't want to insult the Prince, and because she truly loved the gift. It was the simplicity of the piece, which Davon found so attractive, forty diamonds set in white gold with claws so tiny you almost thought the diamonds had been glued one next to the other. The moment she received the bracelet she had refused to take it off, totally abandoning her strict rule about not wearing jewelry to work.

Opening the office door Davon walked into the waiting room to see the chairs full, and six patients standing. She recognized most of the faces and forced a smile. Then she noticed Lamna, looking gorgeous, decked out in a turquoise low cut silk dress with matching stilettos. She was sitting near the door with a picnic basket, and large shopping bag. Oh great, Davon thought. It has to be Lamna, the nicest, funniest woman in the harem.

"Davon," yelled Lamna getting up, "I've got some great news. We're going to Dubai tomorrow. Here's your burka. I've checked with Raja and it's all set. We leave at 7:00 am. I brought you tea and scones, but I can't stay and have it with you. Do you think I'm horrible?" Lamna asked with a comical pout.

Davon couldn't help but smile as she breathed a sigh of relief. "Of course not, I'm actually too busy to stop for tea today anyway. Thanks for thinking of me, but I can't go to Dubai tomorrow, I'm way too far behind in my work."

"Yes you can, Raja said it was okay. We'll just let everyone know you are taking a day off," whispered Lamna, leaning forward.

"I'm surprised Raja agreed to let me go," said Davon, whispering back.

"She had to say yes because I wrote a note to Abdul."

"You what?" asked Davon, completely shocked.

"I wrote a note to Abdul and told him you're working too hard. You haven't had a day off since forever, and you're so exhausted at dance class, I'm surprised you make it through the session. You look drained, and have bags under your eyes! Believe me, you need a day off. I don't care how busy you are, you're coming to Dubai," Lamna said. Turning around to face the waiting patients, she spoke rapidly in Arabic. "I just told them you won't be here tomorrow."

"Well then, I guess I'm going to Dubai," said Davon, grinning as she took the basket and bag.

The burka felt surprisingly comfortable over her light summer dress. Bin had helped her put it on making sure all of her blond hair was tucked under the head covering. When she got into the car, the other women giggled. Davon wasn't sure of the reason since they were all wearing the same get-up, but nonetheless her face reddened.

Lamna came to her rescue. "With your tan, you really look like one of us Davon. The minute we get on our way, you can take off the head covering. We'll slip it back on just before we arrive."

When the vehicle started to move, Davon copied Lamna and removed the head piece letting it fall to her shoulders. The other women in the car did the same. There were ten women on route to Dubai in two identical black limousines. Two uniformed bodyguards followed closely behind in a white jeep. Only one held a machine gun, the other Davon noticed had a holstered gun on his belt. She eyed them carefully when she slipped into the back seat, wondering why the women needed such protection. Managing to get a window seat, she was pleased that she would have the opportunity to enjoy the scenery. They were on a newly paved road heading into the middle of the desert with a bright blue sky that smoothly converged with the flat golden-red sand. It looked totally unreal. As she scanned the environment, she found there wasn't one sign of life, so instead she focused on the heat waves curling upward. Today was going to be a scorcher, she thought, wondering how she was going to cope in a black burka.

When the other women made small talk in Arabic, Davon tuned them out, searching for occasional glimpses of the coastline. Suddenly she heard her name. "Davon, are you with us?" asked Lamna waving her hand at her.

"Sorry, I was looking at the scenery. I didn't hear what you said."

"What are you planning to buy in Dubai?" asked Sepida, one of the older women.

"I'm not sure. I need some clothes, and maybe a pair of shoes," she replied. The women burst out laughing, and Davon looked perplexed.

"You're not going to find western clothing where we shop Davon," said Lamna, "shoes yes, but not clothes. Any clothing we get comes from a catalogue, and that includes bathing suits. The shopping area we go to sells jewelry, ornaments and carpets. Gorgeous carpets, you should buy one of those."

"What about the tourist sites? I'd like to see the manmade ski hill?" said Davon, glancing at each face in the car.

"We never go to those places," replied Sepida. Two of the other women nodded in agreement.

"Why can't we?" Lamna piped in. "We could tell the driver to take us to the ski hill for lunch. I have only seen the building, but I'd love to go inside and see the snow. It could be fun. Besides, I know Abdul contributed to the construction of the hill," she added.

Davon watched the women shake their heads as Lamna nattered on, and when the conversation switched back to Arabic, she turned to look out the window. If they didn't want to go to the ski hill, she'd make arrangements to go on her own. She had no problem exploring solo. She glanced periodically at the group, and noticed that the discussion was suddenly becoming heated. Lamna was talking loudly, perched on the edge of her seat, and pointing at Davon. "Oh please," whispered Davon, wanting to interject. She didn't want to be responsible for an argument. But just as she was about to let them know she would gladly go to the ski hill on her own, Lamna suddenly announced in English that they would be going there for lunch.

The second after Lamna blurted out the news, there was a change in the mood of the other three women. They became distant, and Davon noticed increasing tension in the air while Lamna naively blabbed on about bravely volunteering to inform the driver of their decision. The women seemed to be nervous, and Davon questioned whether the suggested adventure might result in horrible repercussions.

They drove in uncomfortable silence the rest of the way. Finally, they started to approach the city center, and Lamna leaned over to help Davon with her head covering. "The five of us stick together to shop. The bodyguards wait outside of the store when we go in. One guard is for us, the other guard is assigned to the second limousine. All of the shopkeepers know who we are, and there's a credit system already set up. If you find something you want, just sign for it. It will be delivered to the palace. We don't carry any purchases because it's not proper," confided Lamna, as the car pulled into the parking space. "And don't say anything to the ladies in the other vehicle about where we are eating lunch, it's a secret."

Davon nodded. "I have money to pay for anything I want Lamna. You just need to tell me how much it costs."

"Don't be ridiculous, you don't pay for anything. Buy what you want and don't worry," she replied getting out of the car.

The first stop was gold heaven. A hundred or so individual gold shops stood side by side, partitioned from neighbors by plate glass. Floor to ceiling windows flanked the four sides of each stall, regardless of size. The effect was an illusion of one large store, and as Davon surveyed the area, she felt intimidated by the miles and miles of exquisite, handmade jewelry dangling in the glass display cabinets. There was twenty-four carat gold everything, including gold bars.

She tagged along behind Lamna and watched her select and try on several pieces. Davon didn't wear much jewelry at the best of times, and never would have worn the type of earrings and necklaces Lamna was looking at. At the sixth shop they entered, Davon finally saw something she liked. It was a ring, with a wide gold band and three sapphires embedded in the face. She nudged Lamna and asked if she could try it on, waiting while the shopkeeper unlocked the cabinet to remove it. The ring fit her perfectly, and she told Lamna she wanted to buy it.

"Davon this ring is for a child, you should get something with much larger stones. Something like this," she said pointing to a two carat diamond with small rubies surrounding it.

"But I love it. I like the way the stones are positioned in the band. And because there's no high edge, I could even wear the ring when I 'm working."

"Okay, if it's what you want, I'll sign for it," said Lamna, shrugging.

By the time they finished shopping in the gold district it was 2:00 pm. Lamna rolled down the privacy partition once they were all settled in the back of the car, and informed the driver that they were to be taken to the ski hill restaurant for lunch. The driver softly replied something, and although Davon couldn't understand what was being said, the tone of the Lamna's response was not pretty. In the end, Lamna yelled and closed the partition. The driver pulled quickly away from the curb, and Davon watched the confused bodyguards, who were waiting for the women in the second limousine, wave their arms dramatically. She then turned to look at Lamna.

"No problem," Lamna said, winking as she leaned back into her seat. "Because we won't have a bodyguard, it's really important that we stay together. I don't think the guards or the chauffeur are too happy!" she added, with a light laugh. There was no reply from anyone else, so Davon took it upon herself to thank Lamna for dealing with the driver.

The minute they arrived at the restaurant Lamna took charge again, summoning the manager. She demanded the best table and arranged for the cost of the luncheon to be billed to the palace. Davon couldn't help but admire her new friend. Even the three moody companions started to brighten up once they had a look at the opulent five star dining room. They were seated at a round glass table with an elaborate gold, wrought iron bottom. It was adorned with exquisite gold place settings, set on crisp gold colored linens. Three glass vases with exotic flowers had been pushed together in the center, forming a riot of color. Because the table was situated next to the large plate glass window, there was a deluxe view of the snow covered hill. They could see a ski instructor giving pointers to first-time skiers at the top, who nervously tried to make it down the run. Since none of the women besides Davon had seen snow, it was fun to watch their animated excitement as they stood with their noses almost pressed against the pane.

"Okay, after lunch we can go down and touch the snow, but you're not dressed to try to ski. Pipa, look at what those people are wearing? They have ski clothes on," said Lamna, laughing. They were speaking in English for Davon's benefit.

"Maybe I can buy an outfit," replied Pipa.

"There's no time for you to buy ski clothes and ski today, it will have to wait," interjected Sepida rolling her eyes.

"It probably won't take long to do one run, and besides it doesn't look that cold, I can ski in this," answered Pipa.

"You actually might be surprised at how cold it is in the ski area. Remember it needs to be below zero degrees Celsius to snow, so the room will be at that temperature. Any warmer and the man-made snow will melt," said Davon, smiling. She was glad everyone was enjoying the outing.

"Have you actually seen real snow Davon?" asked Sepida.

"Yes, in fact it snows a lot in the winter where I'm from. Sometimes we have four, five feet of snow on the ground. It usually starts snowing in November and lasts until March."

"Having always lived here, that's hard to imagine," said Lamna, just as her cell phone started to ring. After speaking to the caller, she shut the phone and translated for Davon, "The other women are extremely jealous," she giggled, "We're supposed to meet them at the rendezvous point at 5:00 pm, to start on our way home. We won't have any more time to shop, is that okay?" In unison, Pipa, Sepida and Frane agreed they'd rather experience the snow than shop. Lamna turned to Davon and grinned. "Your idea was a good one Davon, thanks."

CHAPTER NINE

One morning, Raja was extremely elusive and quiet on the walk to the medical clinic. So Davon was quite taken aback when they arrived on the porch, and she suddenly said, "I have an invitation for you, and was asked to wait for a response." She politely held out a fancy envelope and diverted her gaze.

Perplexed at the sudden change in Raja's demeanor, Davon cautiously accepted the envelope. Turning her back, she slid her finger carefully across the seal so as not to rip the edge. Removing the hand written card, she was at first surprised, then uncertain, and then confused. She tried to remain calm because there was no way she wanted Raja to know she was feeling anxious. Her heart began to pound. Turning slowly around, she nonchalantly said, "That's fine Raja, you can tell him I accept."

"Thank you, Dr. Marshall. The car will pick you up at 7:00 pm."

Davon nodded, but did not reply, and Raja realizing that she had been dismissed, left.

After briefly greeting the four waiting patients, Davon dashed through the reception area into her office, and shut the door. She clasped her hand over her mouth and whispered, "The Prince has invited me to dinner! Me! I can't believe it!"

Her initial feelings of excitement quickly became feelings of guilt. What am I thinking, she asked herself, plopping down in the chair. I can't go on a date with the Prince, and give medical attention to his nineteen wives and children! Oh My God, I should have said no! Why did I say yes? She hung her head in embarrassment, and listened to the thumping of her heart. It's probably not a date, she quietly rationalized. He most likely wants to talk about my work. He probably does this with all his employees. She grinned and bit her lip. All she could think about was his unbelievable sexy brown eyes as she put on her lab coat and proceeded to get her first patient.

Somehow, she managed to make it through the workday. Glancing at her watch for the fiftieth time, she grabbed her medical bag, jogged across the courtyard and up the stairs to her suite. She had just over an hour to get ready. As she lathered her hair in the shower, it suddenly hit her! She had nothing appropriate to wear. She had brought several dresses, but only two were semi-formal, and neither suitable for dinner with a Prince. By reminding herself it was a business meeting, not a dinner, she reduced her panic to uneasiness. The dress she settled on was a below-the-knee, red, v-necked knit with mid-length sleeves. At home Davon usually wore this dress with black boots, for a sort of business-casual look. Today, she slipped on her thin-strapped, black high-heel sandals, and placed a three string white pearl necklace around her neck. She stood in front of the long gilded wall mirror, and cringed. The outfit looked absolutely ridiculous. The material was too wintery, the skirt was too long for sandals, and the fake pearls made her look like a grandma. It was 6:15 and she had no choice but to cancel!

Completely depressed, Davon slumped onto the bed and momentarily glanced at the black crepe hanging at the very back of the closet. It was a stunning sleeveless creation she had thrown in at the last minute. She knew she looked terrific in the dress; the issue was that it was completely inappropriate. She got up, removed the knit and pearls, and wiggled into the crepe. It was a simple, but dramatic design, and looked fantastic with her sandals. However, her bare arms and shoulders were a problem. Yanking out every sweater and jacket she had, she contemplated: too heavy, too long or too stupid. She even thought about wearing a black long-sleeved shirt under the dress, and then laughed at the absurdity. Eyeing the white silk scarf Raja had given her when she arrived; she placed it over her shoulders knotting it at the front. By using the scarf as a shawl, the dress was passable, still a bit short, but passable.

Now the last concern was her hair. A second scarf would look ludicrous. She had left her hair down, but wondered if she should pull it back into a funky knot, drape the white scarf loosely around her head, and let it cover her hair as well as part of her shoulders. Sighing, she thought about the Prince's comment that westerners were not expected to cover their hair. If he wasn't concerned, then why should she be? Gritting her teeth, she prayed Raja wouldn't be accompanying her to the car.

At exactly 7:00 pm when no one came to the suite to assist her, Davon nervously walked to the side courtyard on her own. There she saw a chauffeur, standing beside the passenger door of a steel gray limousine. As she approached, he opened the door making no eye contact, closed the door when she got inside, and then got into the front passenger seat. Because the engine of the car immediately roared, Davon realized there was someone else at the wheel. She had half expected the Prince to meet her at the car and wondered if he was driving because she had heard from his wives that he was quite a prankster.

Thinking about Hepbet and his get-up, and that the apple doesn't fall far from the tree, Davon laughed. She had a feeling she was going to enjoy her time with the Prince. They sailed quickly past the indoor swimming pool and stables, and then the car came to a sudden halt beside the helipad. When the rear door was opened, Davon saw her date standing stiffly beside the royal helicopter. He was dressed in a suave black suit and had his hands tightly clenched in front of him, as though he was nervous. But the second he saw her exiting the vehicle he appeared to relax, his hands falling naturally to his sides.

Smiling warmly, he walked over to greet her. "Davon, you look breathtaking. Thank you for coming. Let me assist you," he said, indicating that she should take his arm.

"You look very nice yourself Abdul," she replied, feeling a tad awkward calling him by his first name. "Where are we off too?"

"That's the surprise. I hope you will like it."

The helicopter blades started up as the Prince helped Davon settle into a comfortable leather bucket seat, one of two in the roomy back. The royal helicopter was much more deluxe than the one that had brought her to the palace. Offering her ear protection, Abdul showed her how to put the headset on. She was surprised when she heard his voice as they lifted off.

"Davon, look out your window at the reflection of the moon on the lake."

She did as she was told, and saw an incredibly romantic scene. The image of the oversized, almost full moon surrounded by tall shadowy palms, was truly magical. Nothing she had ever seen before could compare. Although she would have loved to enjoy the view for a few minutes longer, the pilot banked turning the copter towards the desert.

"Can you hear me Abdul?" asked Davon, not sure if she had a microphone in her headset.

"Yes, of course," he replied.

"The moon on the lake was absolutely gorgeous. Thank you for pointing it out."

"The lake was my grandfather's pride and joy. He was the architect, the one who designed it."

"Really?" said Davon, her thoughts turning to Matt.

"Architecture was what he took at university. The lake and palace were just a few of the many things he designed and built. But one of the most difficult, because the plot of land he chose to build the palace on once looked like this," he said, pointing out the window to the desert, "waterless sand."

"I can't imagine how hard it must have been. How long did it take to build?"

"Five years, constructed by over nine hundred craftsmen imported for their skills."

Davon was so enthralled with the history of the palace, the hour long flight seemed to take only minutes. In the distance she could see twinkling lights. They were above the city preparing to land on the top of a tall skyscraper. It wasn't the tallest building Davon realized, but it was near the water, and when they stepped out onto the roof she was enthralled with the spectacular view of the bay.

"This way Davon," said the Prince gently taking her arm.

Together they walked towards an archway, down six stairs and into a very large completely empty restaurant. It was grand; the type of high-class restaurant that Davon knew would not have prices on the menu. The maître d greeted them at the door and Davon noticed at least ten waiters standing at attention against the wall. The friendly conversation between the maître d and the Prince, which completely excluded Davon, made her feel uncomfortable. Although they spoke in English perhaps for her benefit discussing the weather and the latest sand storm, no questions were directed to her, and the maître d acted as though she was not there at all. Finally, the small talk came to an end and they were shown to a square table set with exquisite crystal, gold dishes and gold cutlery. Cut flowers and seven candles floated in a low glass bowl in the middle of the table and when Davon sat down she saw exotic fish swimming among them. Instead of sitting across from her, Abdul had his chair moved beside hers, so that they both faced the amazing view.

"Is this suitable?" he asked smiling.

"It's unbelievable. There doesn't seem to be anyone else here," said Davon, looking around at the empty tables.

"I reserved the restaurant because I wanted you to taste the most delicious ethnic food in the country. This is to thank you for taking such good care of my little Anish."

"Abdul, please don't feel that you have to reward me for doing a job I love. You've paid my student loan, and you have given me this watch, and bracelet. It's too much…"

"I enjoy giving things to people who are good to me," he answered, briefly touching her shoulder.

Two waiters appeared and began to discretely place drinks and food in front of them. The conversation halted. When the waiters retreated, Abdul continued. "I am totally fascinated by you Davon Marshall and I would like to get to know you much, much better." His voice was deep with only traces of a Middle Eastern accent. Davon found it extremely sexy and had a hard time concentrating on what he was saying.

He looked into her eyes, and Davon against her better judgment melted. He was powerful, rich, kind, very handsome, and he wanted her. She found herself smiling, and being pulled into the dream. He asked her questions about her childhood, her family and why she chose to be a physician. He was engaging, enthusiastic, and entertaining, and Davon was having the most wonderful time. It was easy to forget that he was not only her employer, but very, very married!

Between courses they somehow got onto the topic of young people, and Davon thought of Zatum.

"Abdul, there is something I would like to discuss with you, but I hesitate because I'm afraid you'll say it's none of my business."

"I would never say that to you. You can talk with me about anything," he said, with a reassuring smile.

"Although, it's probably not the best time to bring it up, I do so because I'm not sure when I'll see you again. It is about Zatum."

"What about her?"

"She is extremely depressed Abdul, and I'm worried about her. Something needs to be done."

"What has she to be depressed about? She has everything," he said calmly, putting down his fork.

"Yes, she does have everything, but she's young, too young to be in the harem and should be returned to her parents."

"Impossible, you ask the impossible," he said, waving an approaching waiter away. "If I returned her to her parents, they would be humiliated. You don't understand our culture, Davon."

"Maybe I don't, but I understand depression, and this is not going to go away. The only way Zatum will get better is to be with her family. You have no idea how homesick she is. Please, do this for me."

"I would do anything for you Davon, but sending Zatum away is not possible. Let's not spoil the evening with talk about this."

Davon sighed, and changed the subject. At least she could tell Zatum she tried. She asked him about his university education, with thoughts of her promise to Hepbet, and nodded pleasantly in response, but she wasn't really listening. All she could think about was how Zatum was a time bomb waiting to go off. She had to find a way to get Abdul to agree to remove her from the harem, but how?

The meal was out-of-this-world, and Davon was thoroughly enjoying Abdul's company up until she stupidly brought up the subject of his young fiancé. Slowly, the "Prince Charming" fantasy started to fade. Abdul was wonderful, but he had nineteen wives, and a relationship with him would be preposterous. She had gotten lost in the moment. Besides, she still loved Matt and her infatuation with Abdul had to be plain rebound.

"…and that is why I am asking you to come with me," he said, toying with his dessert.

"Pardon, I'm sorry I didn't hear what you said?"

"I'm going to Cairo for business and I would like you to come. You said in my office that Cairo was a place you dreamt of visiting."

Davon laughed. "Cairo? Thank you for thinking of me, but talk about impossible. I have a job to do, Abdul. There's no way I would be able to leave the palace for several days. I'm starting to get quite busy at the clinic."

"You work for me, Davon. I'll arrange it," he said, stroking her hand.

"No, I'm sorry. I can't come, it wouldn't be right," replied Davon, shaking her head.

Now, Abdul laughed. "If you are concerned about sleeping arrangements, you don't need to be. You'll be given your own suite, my dear. It will be very proper."

Davon shook her head again. "Thank you, but no."

"I see," said Abdul chuckling, "maybe you do understand our culture. Are you bargaining with me Davon Marshall? Humm, if I give you what you want and return Zatum to her parents, will you come to Cairo with me?"

Davon grinned. Bargaining, had not even been on her mind when she had instinctively said no to Cairo. But Cairo was a place she had always wanted to see, a place she had dreamt about visiting since a grade four field trip to the Washington D. C. King Tut exhibit, and if it meant that Zatum could leave...

"What are you thinking?" he asked, smiling sweetly.

"If you promise on your honor that Zatum will be returned to her parents in a way that will not cause them to lose face, I will go to Cairo with you. However, I want to be clear that I'm accompanying you to Cairo as a friend, not as a mis…" She couldn't even say the word.

"I understand. Then we have an agreement. We leave for Cairo in three days," he replied, with a twinkle in his eye.

CHAPTER TEN

Davon was filled with anticipation, as she pressed her forehead against the window of the private Lear jet hoping for a glimpse of the Pyramids. They had begun their descent, and she could now clearly see the River Nile and small towns dotted along its banks. Most of the buildings looked primitive, and closely knit. They were one storey structures with red brick or clay walls, and tin roofs. She even saw a fenced-in herd of camels. But what she found most interesting was a distinctive line of about one-half mile, which marked the fertile land along both sides of the river. Beyond that point there was nothing but desert, nothing but rock and red sand. Now, she understood why the Nile was called the 'River of Life'. Within minutes they were over the outskirts of Cairo. She could see a definite increase in the number of low and high rise buildings. The plane turned and veered away from the river heading inland, and just as Davon thought she had misjudged their position, she saw them, the Pyramids of Giza. Unexpectedly she became emotional and tears trickled down her cheeks.

"I felt like that too, the first time I saw them," said Abdul, squeezing her hand. "I remember thinking that no matter what I would be able to accomplish in my lifetime, it would never compare to what the pharaoh must have felt when he saw the completion of the Great Pyramid, his final resting place."

"Will you come with me to Giza?" asked Davon, dabbing her eyes. She was pleased to see that Abdul had a sensitive side.

"Unfortunately I have important business to attend to, but I told Bedon to organize a tour guide to show you the all the highlights of the city. However, on Thursday night I'm attending a formal charity event at the Sphinx, and I'd like you to accompany me. It will be as you Americans call it "stuffy" but it should be entertaining."

The steward asked them to fasten their seatbelts for landing, and as

Davon did so she frowned. "The Sphinx event, you said it was formal, how formal? I really don't have anything to wear to a formal affair."

"I'll be wearing a tux, so buy something. Clothing is Bedon's department," replied Abdul, as the plane touched down.

They were staying at the beautiful historic Hilton on the Nile, a hotel which held a permanent suite at all times for the Prince. When the two limousines drove up the covered ramp-way and stopped at the entrance to the lobby, Davon noticed hotel staff lined up on both sides of the door waiting to greet them. The owner of the hotel stepped forward as the doormen opened the car's rear doors and enthusiastically welcomed Abdul, but seemed to ignore Davon, who exited the vehicle after him. Davon, becoming used to this type of behavior from the male population was aware, but unconcerned. Although, she felt as though no one really noticed any female in this part of the world, quite the opposite was actually true. The owner, the staff, and all the guests had to fight to not stare at the stunning blond accompanying the Prince.

The impeccable Mr. Bedon, who had arrived in the second limousine, immediately began yelling orders at the six bellmen who attempted to assist with the luggage. Guests, who were stopped from driving up the last portion of the ramp-way until the Prince entered the hotel, honked their horns and argued with security. The heat, the smells, and the noise at the hotel, which blended in with the street racket below them, created bedlam, yet instead of irritating her it suspended Davon in a world of her own. Drifting towards the side of the massive glass lobby doors she watched the pandemonium and thought, this is everything I knew Egypt would be.

"Dr. Marshall?" asked a young woman with glasses.

"Yes."

"I am Lani Tecke, your Egyptologist. Welcome to Egypt. I have been hired to show you the treasures of Cairo."

Davon smiled and reached out to shake her hand, "I can hardly wait. I have wanted to come to Egypt my whole life. I saw the Pyramids when we flew in. They were so spectacular. I can't tell you how excited I am to be able to actually stand in front of them."

Lani returned her smile. "I thought we would go to see them tomorrow. Sunrise at Giza is something everyone should see. Would 5:00 am be too early to start?" asked Lani, cautiously.

Davon giggled. "As a physician I'm used to early hours. I'll be in the lobby at 4:45 am."

Lani laughed with her, "Fantastic. If I could suggest that you wear pants, I thought it would be fun to explore the Pyramids on camels, unless you oppose that idea?"

"Oh I can hardly wait! I don't know if I will be able to sleep tonight.

Lani grinned showing the most beautiful white teeth. "We will be at Giza for most of the morning, and then I plan to bring you back to the hotel for lunch. We usually go to the Egyptian Museum in the afternoon because it is air conditioned, but we can leave that for Thursday morning, whichever you prefer."

"There's an event we're going to Thursday night. I may have to get back to you," said Davon, turning her head when she heard another woman calling her name. "It looks like they are ready to take us to our rooms. Thanks for coming to meet me Lani, I'll see you tomorrow."

Davon walked over to the woman who had politely called out to her. She was dressed in a hotel uniform--a below the knee navy skirt and matching jacket with red piping.

"I'm sorry to interrupt Dr. Marshall, but I'm sure you are ready to get out of this heat. I'm Ranit and will be showing you to your room."

Men, thought Davon looking over her shoulder at Abdul, who was still talking with the owner, and Mr. Bedon, who was arguing with the bellmen. Oh well, at least I'm already organized for tomorrow and on my way to my air conditioned room.

The lobby she entered was immense with forty foot ceilings, exquisite moldings, and white marble flooring. Around the top perimeter of the room was a black wrought iron railing and Davon could see several guests looking down, watching her, watching them. Obviously not locals, she thought, noting the women with uncovered hair. She skirted around a group of full-sized palm trees growing in the center of the room with fanning fronds that almost touched the ceiling. Antique rattan furniture had been placed invitingly beneath. Given no time to explore, Davon was ushered into a private elevator and whisked to the penthouse. When the elevator door opened, she was in the living room of her suite overlooking the city and the Nile.

"Your luggage will be here shortly. Is there anything else you require, Dr. Marshall?"

"Nothing I can think of, thank you," said Davon calmly, bursting inside. "This is amazing!" she yelled the minute she was alone. Running out to the balcony, which ran the whole length of her suite, she leaned against the railing taking in the view.

When the phone rang Davon darted back into the sitting area. "Hello Abdul?" she said happily.

"This is Mr. Bedon. I have been asked to inform you that the Prince is detained the whole evening. He thought you may enjoy some beauty treatments. Shall I arrange something?" he asked, in his usual flat tone.

Davon was disappointed. "No, I'll make my own arrangements." Mr. Bedon was the last person she wanted involved in her beauty treatments.

"As you wish. I understand you've met your Egyptologist. I've told her to take you shopping tomorrow afternoon. Purchase something appropriate for the charity event. It will be very formal and the Prince is not to be embarrassed by your common attire."

The voice in Davon's head screamed. Did he talk to everyone like this or was it just her? How dare he speak to her like she was trash, dressed in rags! Clean yourself up and buy a nice dress so the Prince is not embarrassed! "Of course," she said politely, before slamming down the phone. "I can't figure it out. I can't! Why is everyone so nice, but Raja and Mr. Bedon? What have I done to them? What? Is it a power thing or just me, a foreigner?" she asked the phone, unconsciously sitting down on the arm of the antique couch. Something wasn't right! It was almost as if Mr. Bedon called the shots, not the Prince. "Whatever! I'm not going to let Mr. Bedon get to me and spoil my life-long dream of coming to Egypt," she told herself. "I'm going to enjoy having me time tonight, and then have a fantastic day tomorrow! I can't expect Abdul to entertain me, and I don't want him to anyway. Nothing is going to happen between us, that's for sure!" Picking up the phone she asked the operator to connect her to the spa.

By 10:00 pm she had had a Red Sea mud bath, manicure, and pedicure, and was snuggled in her king-sized bed reading Margaret George's book *Cleopatra*. Meg had given her the novel as a going away gift. "Promise me you will go to Egypt on the way home," she had said, knowing about her sister's secret dream, "and if I can, I'll join you."

Davon wished Meg was here now. She suddenly felt very homesick and lonely. Had she made a mistake leaving Boston? She realized that running away from your problems didn't really solve anything, but it had helped. She'd almost forgiven Matt, and although she wasn't quite ready to go home and face the issues yet, she felt ready to move on. But why had she agreed to come to Cairo with a married man? She rationalized it was because of Zatum; however she had to admit that it really was because she wanted to be with Abdul. He made her feel welcome and special, and went out of his way to be kind to her, the same way Matt always did. Davon sighed, and thought about Matt in his dirty construction clothes, leaning against his black truck, holding a single red rose while he waited for her to finish her shift at the hospital. He was gorgeous, strong, loving and faithful, and had always been there for her until that day…. Her heart sank at the memory.

"But he broke up with me! How can I ever go home and trust him again? No, a bird in the hand is worth two in the bush, and I'm going to see what happens with Abdul," she said out loud, turning off the bedside light.

As her thoughts wandered, Davon questioned whether she was

subconsciously replacing Matt with Abdul. Did Abdul really have Matt's amazing qualities, or was she imagining it because she desperately wanted it to be that way? Davon laughed as she snuggled under the covers, if her mother found out she was in Egypt with the Prince, there would be hell to pay.

The unpleasant high-pitched sound of the alarm woke her from a deep sleep. With only thirty-five minutes to shower, dress, and eat, Davon quickly switched into doctor emergency mode, her superman get-ready trick where she could even wash her hair, and still be out the door in less than nine minutes. The breakfast cart had been delivered when she was in the bathroom, and Davon impressed with the punctuality of the room-service, snacked on coffee and toast while she pulled on her trousers. By 4:40 am looking smart in a long-sleeved tan shirt, brown cotton pants and walking sandals, she made her way to the lobby.

She had pulled her hair back into a tight ponytail, which exaggerated her flawless skin and large blue eyes. Her junk-free diet, compliments of Bin and daily exercise routine at the palace had sculpted Davon muscles, and as she marched towards the entranceway full of energy, every male in the vicinity noticed the slim gorgeous blond. Over her left shoulder was slung a worn beige leather bag that looked like something an archeologist would carry. It had been a gift from her Canadian grandfather when he had discovered her interest in King Tut, and once was filled with treasure maps, books on the Pharaohs, the Pyramids, and the novel *Aladdin*. For eighteen years, Davon had lugged the bag around with her joking it was her good luck charm--insurance that she would one day visit Egypt. And now here she was, in Cairo on her way to Giza with her famous bag. For some reason she had thrown the old attaché case into her suitcase instead of into the storage locker, and although she remembered feeling silly about bringing it to Dubai, today she was glad she did. Having the bag on her arm completed her dream.

"Dr. Marshall!" said Lani, as she approached her. "Are you ready for an adventure?"

"Good morning. Yes, I'm very excited," replied Davon, sporting a huge grin.

"Great, then we are all set to go. Giza is a twenty minute drive out of the city."

Davon noticed a definite thump when the SUV moved off the pavement onto the hard packed sand. There was hardly enough early morning light, but she could see they were in a valley bottom approaching a windy road that ran to the top of one of the smaller dunes. The sand was golden, a soft yellow, so different from the brownish red sand surrounding the palace. The area was extremely dry, and the car left a long dust trail as it wound its way up to the top.

"Look," said Lani, directing Davon's gaze towards the horizon as they exited the vehicle.

Below them several miles away stood the three Pyramids, side by side on the desert plateau. Davon could see nothing else around the Pyramids, no buildings, no trees, no shrubs. Only three enormous monstrosities built in the middle of nowhere on a flat piece of wasteland. Why, thought Davon, would the Egyptians select this particular site to build their funerary temples, a bleak desert plain miles from the Nile? And yet, as she stood there mesmerized by the sight, she realized the inhospitableness of the barren desert only amplified the effect of the glorious Pyramids, they were absolute grandeur against a simple back-drop.

Suddenly the sun broke free of the horizon. The Pyramids were instantly flooded with blazing red light and seemed to be on fire. "Oh….it's magnificent! Please, could you take a picture of me Lani before it's too late," cried Davon, anxiously reaching for her camera while refusing to take her eyes off the amazing sight.

Within seconds the sunbeams quickly advanced up the sides of the rock structures. The intensity of the sun made it difficult to watch. Shielding her eyes, Davon looked away for what seemed to be only a moment, but when she looked back the experience was over. The sun had risen and now danced in the clear blue sky.

"Thank you," said Davon, dabbing her eyes with a Kleenex. "I'll never forget this as long as I live."

"I'm so glad you enjoyed it. Sunrise at the Pyramids is a favorite part of my workday," said Lani, handing Davon back her camera. "Take as many pictures as you like, and when you are ready the guide is here with our camels."

Davon smelt the camels before she saw them. It was a distinctive dusty, musky, old mat smell, not unpleasant, but noticeably strong. The guide was a small boy in native dress with short cropped coal black hair, and a big smile. He held the reins of three good-sized camels, all with colorful woven saddles, and beckoned Davon to approach him.

"Missy, I have best camel for you. If you let him kiss you, he will be your friend," the boy said, grinning from ear to ear.

"Well I'm not sure, does he bite?" asked Davon, as she cautiously walked towards her ride.

"No, no, Fen will not bite. He is good camel. Put your face here Missy, and Fen will kiss you."

Although Davon did as she was told, the minute she saw the huge furry head coming near her face, she closed her eyes and prepared for the worst. She was surprised at the softness of the large lips as they gently brushed across her cheek, and the tenderness of the animal offering the affection.

"He likes you and will give you good ride. You important lady, only tourist today," said the boy, as he instructed Fen to kneel so that Davon could mount. "Hold on here very tight," he added, pointing to the large saddle horn near the hump.

Offering her the hemp reins, the boy made a clicking sound and the beast began to stand. Fen was six and a half feet, the tallest of the three camels. As Davon shifted her weight to determine the best way to maintain balance, she assessed the situation. The girth of the camel was rounder and bigger than a horse, and although she was sitting as she would on a horse, it was uncomfortable. Her legs dangled on either side. There were no stirrups, and the saddle although well padded, felt wobbly.

Fen was patient and stood unmoving behind the guide's smaller camel, while Davon adjusted her position. Each time Davon jiggled about, she patted Fen's neck to comfort him. His short caramel brown fur was course to the touch and smelt dusty. She caught herself saying "That's a good boy," and then laughed. Fen most likely only understood Arabic.

When she heard the guide's clicking sound, she turned to see Lani's camel rising to a standing position, and then noticed that Lani had one leg wrapped over and around the horn of her saddle. "I see you have one leg around the horn, Lani. Should I try to do that? I don't feel entirely balanced with my legs on either side of Fen."

"There's no right or wrong way to ride a camel, but I find having one leg wrapped around the horn gives me a sense of security. You should try it."

Davon gripped the horn and lifted her right leg over Fen's neck, copying Lani's stance. Although she did feel more comfortable and was less likely to fall, it still felt awkward. With the guide on his camel at the front of the caravan they started on their way down the steep dune. The motion took on a natural rhythm, and Davon let herself relax. Instead of fighting the feeling of falling forward, she tried to sway with the beast as best she could.

The camel's feet sunk into the sand, kicking up dust. It added to the haze and the whole "caravan" experience. It was wonderful. Davon reached into her bag unconcerned about the dirt accumulating on her face and clothes, and pulled out her hat and sunglasses. She let herself drift back in time trying to imagine living in the Egyptian civilization 4600 years ago.

"The three pyramids Dr. Marshall were built for Kings of the Fourth Dynasty: Khufu, Khafre and Menkaure. The largest, the Great Pyramid was build for Khufu and took 23 years to construct. It is made of more than two million blocks of stone, and rises 454 feet towards the heavens."

These were facts that Davon was aware of having read the history of the Pyramids many times. "Interesting, tell me Lani, why were the Pyramids constructed here, so far from the Nile?"

"Ancient Egyptians believed that burial must be in the west, just as the sun journeys across the sky to end its day in the west, so must the human spirit finish its journey in the west. We don't know why this site was chosen, but it was prepared and flattened so that no rock would ever move. The funerary temple was meant to last an eternity, and perhaps this area was picked because they knew the pharaoh's final resting place would be unaffected by the floodwaters of the River Nile."

Lani, having completed a degree in Egyptology was wealth of information. She continued to tell Davon details about the workings of ancient Egyptian culture, and the struggles of everyday life.

It was hot by the time they arrived at the base of the largest Pyramid. When Davon slipped off the back of Fen, she felt relief, but also sadness. She had become attached to the gentle giant. As the camel stood he turned his head towards her, bowed his head, and tenderly kissed her cheek."

"He really like you Missy," said the boy.

"And I like Fen too. He is a very nice camel, and you are lucky to have him. This is for you, thank you for being a good guide," replied Davon, giving the boy fifty US dollars.

"That is not necessary, Dr. Marshall. The Prince has taken care of all the costs, and paid a lot of money for you to have this experience without any other tourists," said Lani, telling the boy in Arabic to give the money back.

"No," said Davon, insisting, "I want the boy to have the money for himself. Please tell him he can keep it." Now Davon understood what the boy had meant when he had said she was "important". She was his only tourist this morning. What had Abdul paid? She felt a little guilty because oblivious to this fact, she had been wishing Matt was here experiencing the tour with her. As an almost architect with a minor in archeology, he would have loved it!

They explored the grounds on foot, and Davon had the opportunity to go inside the inner chambers of the Great Pyramid. By the time she exited the narrow passageway, there was a long line up of people waiting to enter, and hundreds of tourists milling about the site.

"Dr. Marshall, it is noon and I have been told to take you back to the hotel for lunch, and then shopping for a gown. Are there any other photographs you would like to take?" asked Lani.

"No, not here, but we haven't seen the Sphinx."

"Oh I'm sorry, I was told you would be visiting it with the Prince," replied Lani nervously.

Davon immediately understood that Lani had been instructed not to take her to the Sphinx. She wasn't about to push the idea of touring the site and get Lani in trouble with Mr. Bedon. "Oh, I guess I'll be seeing it at the charity event. Thank you for such a wonderful morning."

CHAPTER ELEVEN

It was 2:30 pm and Davon suddenly felt very tired. She had arrived at the hotel, showered, and had lunch, and was now on her way to the shopping district. She leaned back on the leather headrest and thought how wonderful it would be to close her eyes for a few minutes. Covering her mouth, she yawned. The day had started a tad too early. But just as she started to doze, the limousine came to a halt. Opening her eyes, she noticed they were parked in front of an attractive store called 'Cheri's Creations'.

Davon was buzzed into the dress shop. It was fairly large, two levels, and empty of customers. The older woman who came to assist her was impeccably dressed, and Davon felt a little embarrassed wearing her thirty-nine dollar summer special. Straightening out a small crease in the front of the dress, she tried to shift the emphasis to her shoes. Thank goodness she had worn her gaudy, golden sandals.

"It's a formal affair, at the Sphinx. My date will be wearing a tuxedo," said Davon, when the sales woman Cheri asked what she was looking for.

"Yes, I'm familiar with the event. There will be international diplomats, and movie stars. Do you have a particular style or a color in mind Madame?" Cheri questioned.

"Not yet, I'll have to see what you have, but of course I want something that will be appropriate for the occasion. Is that a French accent I detect?"

"Oui, I'm from France. The store I buy from is in Paris. The collection however is from all over Europe. This shop is fortunate to have the best selection of gowns in Cairo. If you would like to come with me to the upper level, I have a beautiful gown in mind."

"Does it come in a size four?" asked Davon, as she followed her up the stairs excited that she might find something unique.

"Of course Madame."

The whole upper level was an array of evening gowns, hundreds of exquisitely made dresses in every imaginable color. Cheri began to rapidly select gowns from the many racks placing them on a giant hook in the large change room. She obviously was an expert in her field.

"Please if you would undress we can begin," she said, tapping her cheek as she analyzed Davon's coloring. "The gown you select must be stunning, and yet simple. You must wear your hair in an upsweep, and shoes….what type do you have to wear with the gown?"

"Well…would these work?" Davon asked, holding out one foot.

"But no Madame, the shoes must never outshine the gown. I will call my friend to bring a selection of sandals. Size?"

"Seven," said Davon, deflated that Cheri thought her gold sandals weren't suitable.

The first gown Cheri showed her was an unusual color, strapless and made from a silky, satiny fabric. It wasn't Davon at all.

"No, it's not really me," said Davon, shaking her head. "I don't think the color works."

"Alright," said Cheri, "I still would like to see you try this gown on later, you may be surprised."

The first dress she actually tried on, picking it from the group for the color, was a light blue empire waist with bell sleeves.

"Too young," said Cheri, immediately unzipping her before she could look at herself in the full-length mirror. "You are a beautiful woman, and I will not have you dressed in anything but perfection."

Brother… thought Davon, feeling intimidated about her next choice. She went with another blue, darker in tone, short capped sleeves, regular waist line, and gathered at the bust. It certainly accented her blue eyes, and in her mind looked quite sophisticated. As she turned back and forth in the full-length mirror she noticed the intense look on Cheri's face.

"Better," Cheri said, "but not dramatic enough. You must be the jewel of the night."

The next dress was yellow, a very light, creamy color that Davon could only wear when she had a tan. It had two wide bands of fabric which crisscrossed each shoulder and flowed over her breasts leaving part of her back exposed. The fabric was chiffon and the skirt was full. She could imagine it on the runway in Paris, but it was a little too wild for her. The only saving grace was it looked fantastic with her gold sandals; at least that was what she thought.

"No," said Cheri, unzipping her.

She tried on gowns in black, white, red and even purple. The one she liked the best, a black crepe, which had wonderful simple lines and small rhinestones on the neckline was immediately vetoed by Cheri based on color. It was not the season for black, or so she said.

"Are you ready to try on the first gown I selected Madame?"

"I can Cheri, but I do like the black gown. Honestly, does it really matter about the season? I thought black was appropriate for any function. In the States people are even wearing black to weddings."

"Black is a color which is regal, but also formal and stiff. It is a fall-back color women choose when they can't find anything else. I guarantee there will be many women dressed in black tomorrow night, but I doubt there will be anyone in this color," she replied, holding up the first gown Davon had been shown.

When Davon stepped towards the full-length mirror she was amazed. It was as if the dress had been made for her. The color was unique, a shimmery silvery taupe satin or "champagne" as the label called it. But it suited her. It emphasized her slimness giving her a slightly hourglass look. She appeared radiant, elegant, and yet unpretentious. The gown was strapless, with a tightly fitted bodice covered with tiny folds that fell gently to her waistline. The skirt was loose, and hung dramatically in layers, which pooled delicately on the floor.

"This is the gown you must buy. You look stunning. Now for the appropriate shoes," Cheri said as if the decision had already been made.

"Wait a minute, I admit you were right, this dress does look fantastic, but is it suitable being strapless? Aren't there cultural taboos here?"

"In some ways yes, however you are a tourist and because it is an international event, the gown is entirely suitable. This is the matching wrap, which should be worn like this." Cheri scrunched the shawl into a two inch band, and flung it around Davon's neck letting the ends cascade down her back. The effect was dazzling.

Before she knew what had happened, she was at the cashier desk with the gown, wrap, matching shoes, and bag, ones Cheri had also selected. Davon played with her Visa card, and fretted about her $5000.00 limit. Noticing a jewelry display on the counter, she picked out an unusual silver brooch.

"I'll take this too," she said.

"No Madame, it is not suitable," said Cheri, looking up from the register.

"I'm not wearing it with my gown, it's for a friend," replied Davon, feeling incompetent about her purchasing abilities.

"I see," said Cheri, giving her a funny look.

Unable to read the sales slip Cheri placed in front of her, she bit her lip and asked, "What is the total cost in American dollars?"

"Considering the gown just arrived yesterday, it is very reasonable, $8,134.00 US dollars, including the shoes, purse and…" she paused, "brooch."

"What?" exclaimed Davon, trying to hide the fact she was freaking out.

"Oh, I'm afraid I have a limit on my Visa. I'm going to have to make a quick phone call to arrange the rest of the payment."

Cheri smiled politely, "It has been taken care of by a Mr. Bedon; you just need to sign here. If you require my services to help you dress tomorrow, I'm available. The number to call is on the card."

Davon quickly scribbled her signature on the bill of sale. "Thank you Cheri, I'll be in touch," she said, as she left the shop. When she got in the back seat of the waiting limousine she let out a huge sigh of relief. "This is one time I'm glad for Mr. Bedon. I would have been terribly embarrassed if I had to call Visa." She patted the box noting it was the most expensive piece of clothing she had ever owned.

Leaning into the air conditioner and enjoying the cool air on her face, she felt ecstatic. Cheri was absolutely right about the dress, and her hair. She'd make a hair appointment the minute she got back to the hotel. Opening the bag containing her new sandals and clutch purse, Davon laughed, they were exactly the same color as her dress. Cheri definitely had an eye for fashion.

Maybe I should hire her as a personal shopper, she contemplated. Buying clothes was certainly not one of Davon's favorite pastimes. She always had trouble finding her size, and never really knew her colors. In Boston, she knew many women who had assistants, really personal shoppers, but they were women with old Boston money. Could she afford to do something like that? Of course she could, fifty thousand dollars a month was a lot of money. The problem was she still didn't believe she was actually making that much, and hadn't even checked the balance in her Dubai bank account. Typically Davon was a saver not a spender; however she could use some new clothes.

In the private elevator going up to her suite, Davon thought about tomorrow's schedule. Lani was picking her up at 8:30 am for the trip to the Egyptian Museum. The gala event started at 8:00 pm and Davon figured she would need at least four hours to get ready. That meant she needed to be back to the hotel by 4:00 pm, which didn't leave much time to see a museum one can spend days exploring.

A massive bouquet of long stemmed pink roses sat on the corner of the dining room table with a note. Davon read the beautifully hand-written message and wondered if Abdul had written it himself. Of course it said he was tied-up with a business meeting again tonight. He begged her for forgiveness. Davon let out a sigh. When they had been on the way to the dress shop, she had told the limousine driver to drop Lani at home because she found out they were driving right by her apartment. Although it had seemed like a good idea at the time, she now regretted the decision. For one thing, she knew Mr. Bedon wouldn't have approved of giving Lani the afternoon off, and now that Abdul was unable to see her this evening, she could have used the time to go sightseeing in Cairo.

"There's no way I'm calling Mr. Bedon to reach Lani," she muttered, as she rummaged in her pocket for Cheri's card. Picking up the phone, she dialed the number. "Cheri, it's Davon Marshall, I was just in your shop. No, there's nothing wrong with the gown, actually I'm so happy with it I was wondering if you have access to regular, everyday clothes? When I came from Boston, I only brought two suitcases, and since I'm working here for a while, I really should buy a few things."

"I sell every type of clothing, including exquisite lingerie. I also have many clients who don't live in Cairo. With those customers, I select pieces and send the clothing to them wherever they may be."

"Would it be too much to ask you to bring some outfits to the hotel, or should I return to the shop? I'm only available this afternoon and evening."

"I'm more than willing to come to the hotel, but we'll have better success if you could possibly return."

"Yes, you're probably right. I'll grab a taxi and will be there within the hour."

"Very good Dr. Marshall, I'll pull out everything suitable in a size four."

By 9:00 pm Davon had twelve gorgeous outfits, two pairs of jeans, five cotton shirts and four pairs of Italian shoes. She felt very lucky to have been introduced to Cheri and to have the money to afford these expensive, but unbelievable pieces of clothing, which fit her figure so beautifully. With all the purchases she had made, Cheri suggested she order a large suitcase from the shop next door. Arrangements were made for the shop owner to wrap and send everything to the hotel.

"So we're all set?" Davon asked, pleased with herself. "The minute I return to the palace, I'll pay off my Visa in full, and you can then put the rest of the charges onto the card. And thanks for doing this Cheri. Now, you have my address here, and in the States, my phone number, my email address, and if you can email me the pictures of the lilac jacket when it comes into the store, I'll most likely buy it too. Are you sure it won't be difficult to mail a coat to the palace?"

"Not at all, as I told you I have forty or more clients I send things to on a regular basis."

"Well thanks again Cheri," Davon said, looking at her watch. "Oh my goodness, it's late, and you must be exhausted! Could I possibly take you for dinner? Please say yes, I'd love the company."

They went to a quaint French restaurant around the corner from the shop. It was dark, smoky and filled to the brim with customers, mostly male. Although they had to wait twenty minutes for a table, it was well worth it. The food when it came was simply mouth-watering. The lightly grilled fish melted on the palette, and the steamed vegetables floating in a delicious cream sauce tasted like heaven. Davon hadn't realized she was so hungry.

They were seated at the back of the restaurant close to the kitchen, at a tiny table. Red and white checkered tablecloths and napkins enhanced the atmosphere. The ambiance of the place was certainly European. However, Davon thought it appeared to be a little more Italian looking than French. It was extremely noisy, and conversations in many different languages could be heard.

Davon practiced her French with Cheri, who was surprised at her complete fluency. Davon explained about her heritage, and French minor at university. She then asked Cheri how she had ended up with a clothing business in Cairo of all places. Cheri looked down at her plate, and suddenly became quiet. Worried that she had insulted her, Davon was just about to change the subject when Cheri looked up.

"It's hard to believe it was thirty years ago that I came to Egypt as a young bride. I married the most wonderful Arab business man. He was the one who ran the store. He sold locally, but also exported burkas, shawls and carpets to other countries, as well as to France, and that was how I met him. When I moved to Cairo, I helped set up a very small importing business, expanding the store to include some of the latest European fashions. I was surprised at the demand for western clothing. We were married only two years, when he was killed in an automobile accident. I never remarried. Because my Arabic was so poor when my husband died, I let go of the exporting business, and focused only on importing European fashions. It's been a very successful business venture."

"Oh Cheri, how sad, but you must be really proud of yourself for continuing your business in such a male dominated society. It must have been difficult being here on your own. Did you ever think of returning to France?"

"Yes, many times. But I loved Cairo and as the business got busier and busier, the time just seemed to pass. However, I do go to Paris twice a year on buying trips, and to visit family."

Davon nodded. "I understand your love for Cairo. This is the first time I've been to the city, and yet I feel as though I belong here. It gives one a mystical, magical feeling! It'll be extremely hard to leave on Friday."

"Well Dr. Marshall, if you ever return, you're more than welcome to be my guest. I have a small but rather nice house overlooking the Nile."

"Thank you, I'd like that very much," said Davon, smiling warmly.

When the flaming meringue dessert was placed on the table, Davon moved her chair back a few inches to avoid the heat. Suddenly she noticed Mr. Bedon standing in the doorway of the restaurant. He had his hands behind his back, and his legs in a wide military stance as though he had been there for quite some time. The edges of his lips, which were at first pressed tightly together, turned instantly downward as they made eye contact through the smoky haze.

"Just a minute, Cheri," said Davon, reverting back to English, "I think the man over at the door is looking for me. He's Prince Abdul's second in command."

Getting up, Davon walked confidently towards him. "Hello Mr. Bedon, what a coincidence. Are you here for dinner?" she asked, knowing full well he was not.

"The limousine is outside ready to take you back to the hotel when you are finished, Dr. Marshall," he said curtly, ignoring her question.

"Thank you, but I was planning on taking a taxi. I'm very capable of taking care of myself, you know. How did you find me anyway?" she asked, annoyed with his tone.

"It's my business to know your whereabouts, and although you may believe that Cairo is a safe city for a single female to roam, it's not! The limousine driver has been given explicit instructions to wait for you," replied Mr. Bedon, rudely. He then spun on his heels leaving Davon alone and perplexed.

Returning to the table Davon laughed, "I guess I'm in a little bit of trouble for going off on my own. I have to go Cheri. Let me get the bill."

The morning was already hot by the time they arrived at the Egyptian museum. When Davon entered the enormous courtyard, she skirted quickly around the long rectangular reflection pool, drawn towards a statue of the Sphinx. It appeared to be carved from grey granite and had evidence of facial damage.

"It's an exact replica of the original, except on a smaller scale of course," said Lani, "Tonight, you will be seeing the real thing. This is granite; the real Sphinx has a head and body carved from solid rock with legs and paws made from limestone blocks. Some think it was built to be the guardian of Giza, carved on the plateau in perfect alignment with the rising sun."

"The body of a lion with a human head," muttered Davon. "What's the story about the nose?"

"There are many theories, the most popular is that the nose was blown off by a cannonball fired by Napoleon's soldiers, however historians believe it was purposely maimed in 1378 AD by a Muslim when he discovered the locals worshiping the Sphinx as a God," replied Lani, smiling. "This way Dr. Marshall, we should be going into the museum as we have a lot to see and only six hours."

There was a dramatic change in air temperature inside the museum, so cool compared with the heat outside, Davon reached for her jacket. She stood for a few minutes in the lobby's entranceway taking in the experience of being in a museum she had only dreamt of visiting. The lobby was immense. The walls were white plaster, the floors were white marble, and the ceiling was at least twenty to thirty feet high. It was a gigantic room, and yet she could see it was filled to the brim with statues and artifacts.

"Where do we start?" she asked Lani enthusiastically.

"If you would like to come this way, we will begin with the Rosetta Stone. The black granite stone was found in the city of Rosetta in 1799 by the French. This is a copy. The original is in the British Museum in London."

"The key to hieroglyphics," whispered Davon, leaning forward to see a two by three foot chiseled piece of rock suspended in glass.

"That is correct, it bears three inscriptions: Egyptian hieroglyphs, Egyptian demotic script and ancient Greek. The Rosetta Stone is the key to hieroglyphics, but also gives us understanding of ancient Egyptian civilization and literature."

Davon took her time examining the stone. However, Lani soon coaxed her away, reminding her of their time restraints. They walked from room to room on the first floor looking at a vast collection of sculptures, coffins and sarcophagi. It was overwhelming. Not only was the collection large, most of the pieces were in good condition, some perfect. Davon found it hard to imagine these amazing artifacts predated the birth of Christ.

"Tell me Lani, is there actually a difference between a coffin and sarcophagus?"

"Yes there is a difference," answered Lani, "however people often confuse the two. A sarcophagus, usually made from limestone, is just a stone container, a box, a burial container. A coffin or anthropoid, is human shaped, and can be decorative. When we go up to the second floor to see the King Tutankhamen exhibit, we will look at three nested coffins, two in gilded wood, and the last made of solid gold."

They had already spent three hours at the museum and had one more room to see on the main floor. Lani asked Davon if she'd like to stop for lunch. "No!" replied Davon, adding that she didn't want to waste any precious time. By 12:45 pm they were on their way upstairs to the King Tut exhibit, and Davon could feel her heart beginning to pound in anticipation.

Although the collection on the first floor was absolutely fantastic, she found it didn't come close to the stunning and priceless King Tut exhibit. Discovered in 1922 by Howard Carter, King Tut's tomb had been found intact, the only one ever to be found this way. In spite of the fact that Tutankhamen was only a minor Egyptian King, the collection was vast and impressive. Four gilded shrines nested one inside of another, three coffins, jewelry, furniture, weapons, games and the famous gold death mask, all unbelievably exquisite and in perfect condition. She went through the exhibit twice, and didn't want to leave.

"Why don't we go through the rest of the second floor quickly, I'll try to focus on the most important pieces, and then if you like we can return to the King Tut exhibit before we leave? There are a few more discoveries I want to show you," said Lani, extremely happy Davon was enjoying the museum.

It was with great sadness when Davon stepped into the waiting limousine. She desperately wished she had had more time at the museum, and promised herself she would come back one day. Her hair appointment was in twenty minutes, and if it hadn't been for that and the gala affair in the evening, she would have refused to leave the museum until closing.

On the way back to the hotel, the traffic was horrendous. In both directions the lanes were plugged with bumper to bumper cars puffing out thick black smoke. Frustrated drivers shook their fists, and lay on their horns creating unnerving racket. Not only was the road congested with vehicles, both sidewalks were overflowing with pedestrians. It seemed as though the whole population of Cairo was on the street today. It was total chaos, but Davon calmly ignored the noise as the limousine inched its way along, and looked out the window trying to appreciate the size of a city housing fourteen million people. When the limousine finally pulled up the ramp-way to the hotel, Davon checked her watch. She was seventeen minutes late for her appointment.

CHAPTER TWELVE

The first thing Davon saw when the elevator doors opened was her evening gown. It was hanging from the glass chandelier in the living room. Cheri, kneeling beneath it was inspecting the hem.

"I hope you don't mind Dr. Marshall, I had to get the gown from the bedroom to steam press it," said Cheri looking up.

"I'm glad you found it. Did you have any problems getting into the suite? I did remember to tell the desk clerk you'd be coming."

"The bellman brought me right up. But I was beginning to get worried about you. It's almost six o'clock."

"I know, I was late getting back from the museum and had to run to my hair appointment. I should have called you. It's been a crazy, but wonderful day!" replied Davon, smiling. "I still need to have a bath, and I think I should eat something before I dress because I'm absolutely starving. Can I order you something from room service?" she asked, picking up the phone.

"If you insist, a small salad would be nice. At these fund raisers they only have a midnight buffet. If you are hungry, you would be smart to fill up now."

Davon had bathed, eaten, and was just stepping into her dress with Cheri's assistance when the phone rang. Cheri grabbed the hands free and handed it to her.

"The car is here? I'll be down in five...no make that ten minutes," said Davon, when Cheri flashed her ten fingers. Handing the phone back to Cheri she exclaimed, "Oh no, I feel like my hair is falling down at the back. I'm not going to be ready in ten minutes."

"You'll be in the lobby on time. Stay still Davon, I'll pinup the curl that's fallen after I finish doing up your gown. There, you're zipped and your hair's fixed, now let me help you into your sandals," replied Cheri, noting the perfect neutral color of Davon's toe nail polish. "Here's your evening bag. You still need to transfer your things. Where is your purse?"

"I threw my attaché case by the elevator door. I only want my stethoscope--I never go anywhere without that, my camera, and a Kleenex. I don't think I'll need my wallet."

When Davon turned around Cheri nodded with appreciation and smiled, "You look absolutely gorgeous."

Davon caught her reflection in the gilded mirror above the buffet. She not only looked beautiful, she looked as though she had money, lots of money, "Wow, you were right Cheri, I almost don't recognize myself. Thank you so much for insisting I try on this gown, and for coming tonight to help me dress. You are really, really good at what you do!"

Two minutes later, Davon was on her way down the elevator with Cheri, her matching scarf casually covering her bare shoulders. Cheri had encouraged her to wear the scarf around her neck letting the ends fall dramatically down her back, however Davon felt too exposed, and argued she was in Cairo not Boston. She had agreed though, to reposition the scarf at the event if she saw other women in strapless gowns.

When she walked through the lobby towards Abdul, who was waiting near the enormous glass doors, Cheri held back. "You look like a goddess, Davon. The gown, I have never seen a more beautiful one!" exclaimed Abdul, taking her hand. He was dressed in a smart black tuxedo, crisp white shirt and black tie. Together they made a handsome couple. "Let me help you to the car. Bedon the door!"

In the limousine Abdul could not take his eyes off her. He apologized over and over for leaving her on her own on Tuesday night and Wednesday explaining that there had been complications with his business dealings in Cairo. Because entertaining and business went hand in hand in his culture, it was of the utmost importance that he socialized with his male business partners at night. He gently lifted her hand to his lips and kissed it. "Do you forgive me for abandoning you?"

"Of course I do Abdul. Just make sure you show me a good time tonight," she replied laughing lightly.

Abdul threw back his head and joined in the merriment. "I promise tonight will be unlike any other!"

It was dark when they arrived at the event. As she exited the car, Davon saw the illuminated Sphinx. Much larger than she expected, she paused noticing how it dominated the landscape making the three pyramids on the rise above and behind it look smaller than they actually were. The shadows created by the spotlights on its human face gave it a sinister, haunting feel, and she shuddered as though someone had walked over her grave. The shattered nose, the headdress and unforgettable carved eyes, were exactly as she remembered from her Giza history book.

"Davon, this way," said Abdul, gently guiding her towards an open courtyard.

The elegantly treed brick courtyard was filled with men in tuxedos, women in fabulous gowns of every color, and sheiks in immaculate white robes and head dresses. Tiny lights delicately hung from the branches of the palm trees creating a romantic ambiance. It was comfortably warm. A cacophony of conversations could be heard drifting from the thirty or more small groups of people speaking in a variety of languages, and although Davon had no idea what they were talking about, everyone appeared to be having a great time. It was a scene of opulence and money, and Davon was grateful Cheri had insisted on this gown. Even if she didn't feel like she belonged at an event like this, Davon certainly looked as though she did.

Abdul nodded and smiled to some of the guests as they casually strolled towards the center of the courtyard. He didn't stop to converse with any of them, instead he directed Davon to the side where rows of white chairs had been organized for the charity portion of the night. As she turned around after placing her wrap on one of the two chairs Abdul had selected, she noticed a very large Victorian mansion directly across from them. Several waiters holding trays of refreshments and appetizers served the mingling crowd on the wraparound porch.

Davon instantly fell in love with the gorgeous house so totally out of place next to the Sphinx. "What a beautiful setting Abdul," she said enthusiastically.

"Yes, it's nice," he replied, obviously not as impressed. "Would you like something to drink?" he asked, eyeing a group of men on the porch.

"No thanks," said Davon. She noticed that one of the men was trying to get Abdul's attention. "If you'd like to go and talk with your friends Abdul, I'm happy just looking around."

"Absolutely not, I promised you one hundred percent of my time! But the event will be starting soon, and I think I'll get a beverage. Are you sure you don't want anything?"

"No I'm fine," said Davon, as he drifted towards a waiter holding glasses filled with punch.

Davon watched him leave. He wasn't as tall as Matt, but he was gorgeous all the same. Her eyes followed him to the steps of the house where he paused to speak to an older gentleman.

"American I presume?"

Davon turned to see an attractive bleached blond dressed in a light blue silk gown that exposed a little too much cleavage. She was dripping in diamonds--diamond earrings, necklace, bracelet and at least a three carat rock on her wedding finger.

"Yes, I'm Davon Marshall from Boston."

"Amelia Tucker. Originally from Dallas, but now I live in Jordan with my husband. Pleased to meet you," she said, with a smile that was on the border of a smirk. "Your hair color is a dead give-away. So, I see you're with Prince Abdul...how yummy!"

"Well actually it's not like that," said Davon. The woman's leer was making her feel extremely uncomfortable. "I work for Prince Abdul, and came to the event as his guest."

"My dear it's always like 'that' in this part of the world. You may not be aware of it, but believe me it's true. I'm married to an American. However, I've lived here long enough to know women in this part of the world are considered to be objects, toys. You were hired purely for your looks and age. I'm sure when you applied for the job, they asked for a picture?"

"Well yes, but…"

"But nothing, this is the Middle East. What did you say you do anyway?"

"I'm the personal physician to the harem," answered Davon, gritting her teeth.

"My, a doctor and so beautiful, just make sure you don't become part of the harem," exclaimed Amelia, clicking her tongue. "My husband's done business with Abdul several times, and he actually said the Prince is a nice guy, however they all are the same when it comes to..."

"And what type of business is your husband in?" interjected Davon, wishing Amelia Tucker would go away.

"Oil of course, the only business," she replied, with a wink.

Abdul suddenly appeared. "Davon the event is about to start."

"Amelia Tucker I'd like to introduce Prince Abdul," said Davon, turning towards him. "Amelia said you know her husband."

"Yes I've had dealings with him. I didn't see Spencer when we arrived," remarked Abdul, not looking at Amelia, but at Davon.

Amelia gestured to the general sitting area where her husband was socializing with a group of men. Abdul politely nodded and then took Davon's arm. He guided her around Amelia towards their seats. Annoyed, Amelia leaned towards Davon when she passed and loudly whispered, "See what I mean."

The auction portion began with a woodwind quintet playing light classical music. It had a delightful Middle Eastern sound that suited the ambiance of the evening. When Davon closed her eyes she imagined herself among a group of Bedouin nomads, camped beneath the great Sphinx with tents, carpets, flutes, and dancing girls. Four unique pieces were played, and from the enthusiastic applause, it appeared that everyone enjoyed the performance.

As the musicians cleared the stage, the master of ceremonies walked flamboyantly onto it. He shielded his eyes with a hand to avoid the glare of the lights, peered at the crowd, and then dramatically acknowledged a few of the patrons, including Abdul. He was an attractive man dressed in a designer white tux. However, his flashy entrance was the antithesis of his speech. He spoke impeccable English, but basically launched right into a boring power point presentation. Then without warning, the bidding started. Davon was confused by the sudden flurry of activity with literally everyone in the audience raising and lowering their paddles. Paddles were going up and down so quickly, Abdul's included, that it was impossible to know who was getting the bid. The gavel would loudly bang, the auctioneer would yell, and the paddles would come down for less than a minute before the whole process would repeat itself. People were on the edge of their seats trying to beat out one another. Finally, a break was called.

"We have fifteen minutes until the next session. Why don't we stretch our legs?" suggested Abdul, gently patting Davon's hand as he stood.

"Abdul, what exactly are you bidding on? I understand it's for charity, but there are so many paddles going up and down, I don't have any idea who is winning what."

"This is an event where the rich give to the poor. Organizations are named, and we bid to be the main contributor for the year. If you really listen, you can hear the auctioneer calling out the winning number. The auction lasts about three hours and then we'll have dinner. Come on, let's walk around."

Davon followed him and stood to the side when he stopped to chat to a group of sheiks. They spoke in Arabic, ignoring her as usual while she smiled and drifted into her own world. She stared at the Sphinx, and pondered the theories about when it was built, and how some historians thought the face had the likeness of King Khafra. It was a magnificent piece, and she wished she could get closer to examine it. She noticed the area surrounding the Sphinx was completely roped off, however she wondered...

"Davon, do you need anything? They have just rung the bell, we have five more minutes."

Davon was so lost in her thoughts that she hadn't seen the sheiks leave. "Maybe I should make a quick trip to the ladies room," she said quietly. "Do you know where it is?"

"I'm not sure, but Bedon can help you find it. Where is he?" asked Abdul, looking towards the direction of the parking lot.

Davon shook her head, "Honestly, I don't need Mr. Bedon. It's probably in the house, excuse me," she said, walking towards the Victorian mansion.

She gazed up at the enormous verandah that skirted the perimeter of the house, the large shuttered windows, exquisite stained glass, and gorgeous wicker fans, which were whirling rapidly and giving off a refreshing breeze. It was definitely a British design, and Davon assumed it had been built by them when they occupied Cairo. Lifting her skirt, she made her way up the wide outer staircase. As she entered the massive entrance hall, she was forced to inch her way around exiting guests, who were already starting to make their way back to the bidding area. Flagging down a waiter, she asked for the washroom. He looked perplexed seemingly embarrassed by the question, and after pointing upstairs quickly rushed away.

Grabbing the hem of her gown, Davon made her way up the gorgeous oak staircase to the second level, enjoying the dark heavy wall paneling, thick spindles, curled newel posts, and hand-carved banister. As she reached the last stair, she noticed a woman dressed in a flaming red sari coming out of a room near the end of the hallway. Presuming it was a restroom she headed that way. As they passed, they exchanged courteous smiles.

The room she discovered was indeed a bathroom, probably original. It was a good size, with double crown molding, expensive gold and navy striped wallpaper, and an amazing antique slipper claw legged bathtub situated under the window. The large white pedestal wash basin had been placed atop an antique dresser and boasted delicately embossed gold faucets. The whole room was absolutely exquisite. After she locked the door, Davon took her camera out of her bag and snapped pictures. This was the bathroom of her dreams, a bathroom similar to the one Matt had once promised to design for her.

As she washed her hands her thoughts again turned to Matt, and a brief moment of sadness assaulted her. She missed him. "Why does everything remind me of Matt?" she asked the reflection in the mirror. Sighing, she turned off the tap. That was when she heard a muffled, but obviously angry exchange. It was coming from the adjacent room. Turning her head sideways, she leaned into the wall and listened. The men were speaking in French and Davon, although at first thinking it was crazy, thought one of the voices belonged to Mr. Bedon. Even though she had never heard him speak French before, he had an unforgettable arrogant way of talking, and she was positive she could hear the unusual raspy tone, and the creepy way he lowered his voice at the end of each sentence. Pulling her stethoscope out of her purse, she put the ear plugs in, and placing the end to the wall, she laughed at her image in the mirror.

"Take that James Bond," she said softly. Her eyes widening as she listened.

"No more excuses. It must be done tonight. He's sitting in his usual seat at the end of the row and will be an easy target. But it must be fatal!" said the voice Davon was positive came from Mr. Bedon.

"You were to bring all of the money, the total amount. How will I be paid if I have to leave Cairo right away?" the second male roughly questioned.

"I have given you half, the rest will be forwarded. You'll get your money, however honor should be enough for being chosen to complete this task. Now do as you have been told. I must get back to the limousine before I'm missed," said the first voice.

Davon heard a door open and close. She quickly unlocked her door, opening it a crack. Placing one eye to the small gap, she broke into a cold sweat. There was Mr. Bedon hurrying down the hallway towards the staircase. She tasted bile at the back of her throat, and felt like she might vomit. Of course they had been talking about Abdul, but even if he wasn't the target, someone was going to be killed very soon. Carefully, trying to not make the slightest sound, she re-bolted the door and leaned her forehead against it. She knew she needed to act quickly, but couldn't think clearly enough to formulate a plan.

Gathering her wits, she rushed to the window, and scanned the sitting area for the event, which was directly across the courtyard. She could see that the auction had started. If Abdul was the target, and she assumed he was, the hit man was in a perfect position. She watched Mr. Bedon go down the outer staircase and steal his way towards the parking area. A shiver passed through her. Davon pressed her face against the side of the pane, and looked for the barrel of a gun poking out the window next door. She couldn't see anything, but noted the assassin's window was on a bit of an angle. She considered opening her window to scream a warning to Abdul and the policing personnel in the area, but promptly decided against it. Over the noise of the auction, no one would hear her calls except the hit man who could easily turn his gun on her through the lath and plaster wall. Her only option as far as she could determine, was to interrupt the killer. It was a far-fetched idea, but she had to do something.

Moving into position she stood frozen with her hand on the bathroom door knob. I can do this, she told herself, trying to calm her nervous tremors. Unlocking the knob and taking a deep breath, she quietly left her refuge and rapped on the door beside hers with authority. "Excuse me, room service," she said in perfect French, twisting the locked door knob while listening for any movement or noise. "Excuse me, I'm here to clean the room," she repeated in French, knocking loudly again. She could hear no sound. Again, the horrible taste of bile regurgitated in her throat. Suddenly panic replaced her initial feelings of terror. What was she going to do if he yanked the door open? Should she try and rush him? Oh My God what am I thinking? He's a hit man with a gun!

Now afraid the assassin might come to the door, Davon decided to flee. Turning and gathering the hem of her gown into a ball, she bolted down the hallway and stairs. Red faced and breathless, she reached the porch.

Allowing her dress to fall naturally to the ground, she hesitated for a moment examining her surroundings. The sound of her pounding heart echoed loudly in her ears, and that with the annoying voice of the auctioneer made her anxiety level climb. She could plainly see Abdul attentively listening to the bid, raising and lowering his paddle. There were no security men in sight, only waiters setting tables for the evening meal. Pretending to enjoy the architecture of the mansion, Davon ran her hand along the porch railing and looked up. The assassin's window was slightly to the side, blocked from her view. She had to get to Abdul. Quickly determining the best route to interfere with the assassin's view of his target, she strolled down the stairs and into the courtyard. She fought the urge to look back, not wanting the assassin to associate her with the woman at his door.

The moment she reached the Prince, Davon used her body as a shield and leaned over. "Abdul, I need to speak with you. It's of the utmost importance!"

"Davon not now, I'm bidding. Sit down," replied Abdul, standing up so that she could move in front of him.

"Please Abdul, it's urgent, we have to leave…"

Abdul glared and whispered, "Don't embarrass me! Please move to your seat!"

A Caucasian gentleman behind them tapped Abdul on the arm. "Prince Abdul, could you please sit down. I can't see." He was obviously annoyed with the interruption.

Placing a hand on either shoulder, Abdul physically began to assist Davon to the seat beside him. "Wait!" demanded Davon pulling away.

"What's the matter with you? Sit now!" said Abdul, moving out from the row so that Davon could return to her seat. "People are staring!"

Davon moved over and sank into her chair hoping he would listen once she was seated. The second Abdul sat down, she turned. "There's a plot to kill someone! I think it's you. We have to get out of here!" she whispered urgently. Trying to get his full attention, she roughly grabbed onto his arm and knocked the bidding paddle he was holding to the ground. Frowning, Abdul leaned over to retrieve the paddle. "You must believe me! Something happened in the bathroom…" She never completed the sentence. A muffled whiz was the only indication that the gunman had fired. Abdul sat slowly upright and then slumped back in his chair. The paddle slipped again from his fingers. Out of her seat in a flash, Davon stood over him in exactly the same place where she had been only moments before.

"I'm okay, don't say a word and stop looking alarmed. No one must know. We have to get to the car," said Abdul, breathing heavily.

As Abdul stood, Davon mentally assessed his injury. At least he was moving. She could see a blood stain quickly spreading down the black sleeve of his tuxedo and knew it would only be moments before it began to show on the white cuff of his shirt. Remembering Bedon's word 'fatal' she worried about a second attempt. But not wanting to make a scene, she let Abdul make his own way out of the row. She watched the other guests raise and lower their paddles in coordination with the annoying banging of the gavel, totally oblivious to the shooting, all except the man behind them, who shook his head in dismay at the second disruption.   Abdul glanced at him and said, "Must get back to the palace tonight Henry, good to see you."

Although she felt like yelling a safety warning to everyone in attendance, Davon did as Abdul requested, and acted as though there was nothing wrong. When he turned towards her, he winced in pain, and she became concerned. Carefully cradling his left arm in hers, she applied pressure to the bloody area, and slowly direct him to the parking lot, all the while maintaining her position between him and the mansion. As they slowly, but steadily made their way towards the parked limousines, the noise level of the event began to dim, and Davon heard a change in Abdul's breathing pattern. Fearful that the bullet had gone through the arm and lodged somewhere in the chest wall, she pulled him towards a clump of palm trees.

"You need to go to a hospital," she stated with authority. Removing her shawl, she wrapped it tightly around his arm.

"I can't because the press will be all over it. Just stay with me, and try not to let on that something happened. The limo drivers are already gawking. Look for Bedon. We have to find Bedon!"

"No! Listen to me, Bedon is not to be trusted. He was involved in the shooting," exclaimed Davon, doing a quick check of the area around them. She glanced to both sides, behind them, and then towards the limousine drivers who were at their vehicles. Some were polishing, some leaning, some gabbing, and now some were watching.

"Don't be ridiculous, Bedon has been with me since I was a child. There he is! Bedon get the car!" yelled Abdul, leaning more of his weight onto Davon.

"Abdul I beg you, things are not what you think."

"My Prince, what is it?" cried Bedon, jogging towards them with the limousine driving closely behind.

"I need to get back to the hotel!" called Abdul, trying his best to act and sound normal.

Bedon waved the car to a stop, and opened the door for the Prince. Davon looked at Bedon's face and struggled to read his thoughts as she went around to the opposite passenger door, pulling open and slamming shut the door on her own.

Once they were all inside, Bedon lowered the partition between the front and back of the limousine, feigning concern. "I see you have injured your arm, My Prince. Shall I call Dr. Rahish to come from Dubai?"

"My medical bag is at the hotel. I'll look at him as soon as we get back," said Davon, completely revolted at his pretense.

"That's not necessary Dr. Marshall, the Prince has his own physician," stated Bedon, avoiding eye contact with her.

"I'm afraid it is Mr. Bedon. The Prince has been shot, and needs immediate medical attention. He can't wait for a doctor to fly in from Dubai!" said Davon rudely, while she pulled paper napkins out of the snack bin. "You worry about us getting back to the hotel, and I'll worry about his arm!"

Davon pushed down the button to close the partition, and then looked at Abdul who was leaning against the door frame with his eyes closed. When she pressed the white napkins against his arm, they immediately became soaked with blood. "I really think we should go to the hospital, you're bleeding a lot, and I'm concerned about your breathing. You need a chest x-ray."

"No Davon, I want to go to the hotel. If you think I need hospitalization, I'll fly to Dubai tonight."

"Okay, hang in there. We should be at the hotel in ten minutes."

The limo pulled up to the back door of the hotel, and the Prince was discretely assisted by the bodyguards and Mr. Bedon through a small hallway to his private elevator with Davon walking sideways so that she could continually put pressure on his wound. As the group made its way through the suite to Abdul's bedroom, Mr. Bedon blocked Davon's way. The bloody napkins flipped onto the floor.

"That will be all Dr. Marshall, thank you for your help. I'll take over from here."

"Let me pass! Abdul help me!" yelled Davon, wanting to strike the treasonous assistant.

"Bedon, Dr. Marshall is here as a physician. I want you to leave!" commanded Abdul, flopping onto the bed in pain.

Bedon glared, but allowed Davon to walk around him. Rushing to Abdul's side, she lifted his legs onto the bed. "I need towels Abdul. I'm going to get some from the bathroom."

In the bathroom, Davon saw that she had blood on her hands and down the front of her beautiful gown. Washing her hands with soap and hot water, she ignored the stain on her dress, and wet two washcloths. Grabbing towels, she returned to her patient. The two guards and Mr. Bedon had left, closing the bedroom door. Thank goodness, she thought as she removed the ruined scarf from Abdul's arm and took off his jacket. The blood had started to coagulate and the shirt sleeve was stuck to the wound. She needed scissors.

Picking up the phone Davon called the front desk. "Yes, this is Dr.

Marshall. Could you please have someone go to my suite, and get my black medical bag? It's sitting on the tall dresser in the bedroom. Bring it to Prince Abdul's suite right away. Thank you."

Davon wasn't about to take the chance of getting her bag herself, for all she knew Bedon was outside waiting to kill her. She continued applying pressure to the wound on the arm and did a visual examination of his chest. There was a six inch long gash, gaping more at the top of the wound with a large blue bruise forming along the side. It looked as though the bullet went through the fleshy part of the arm and skimmed along the rib. How lucky was that? The offending bullet was probably in the back of the auction chair.

"Abdul, why weren't your bodyguards at the event tonight?"

"I stupidly told them to stay at the hotel! I didn't want them hovering around us, interfering in what I thought would be a romantic evening." He looked at her and groaned. "Was any part of it romantic?"

"Well let's put it this way, its one date I'm never going to forget!" said Davon, with a brief smile.

Her concern for her patient was paramount, and when the doorbell rang Davon wrapped a towel firmly around Abdul's arm, and then ran into the living room. The elevator for the suite opened into an executive foyer with a set of massive wooden double doors leading into the apartment. Looking through the tiny peep hole she saw a young bellman standing at attention and holding her bag. Convinced he was legitimate she unlocked the door. As the boy fully expected to bring the bag into the suite, he was caught off guard when Davon in her blood soaked dress reached for it. They wrestled for a moment on the stoop, Davon pulling in one direction, and he in the other. It wasn't until she firmly and loudly asked him to let go, that he did, causing her to almost lose her balance. Without saying another word, Davon shut the door, locked the deadbolt, and left the confused and tipless bellman on the other side.

When she returned to Abdul, she was dismayed to find fresh blood on the white towel. He was moaning. "Abdul, I'm going to give you something for pain. Are you allergic to anything?"

"No," cried Abdul, lying as still as possible with his eyes closed.

"I'll give it by needle in your good arm so it will work faster," said Davon, as she adjusted her gown to climb onto the bed. Removing the right arm from the sleeve of his shirt, Davon administered the subcutaneous needle. "That should start working in a few minutes. Okay, now I have to clean the wound. I'm going to try to be gentle, but it'll be a bit uncomfortable because your shirt is stuck to it, so bear with me."

Davon efficiently sliced the shirt sleeve in half cutting right up to the collar so that the bulk of the garment completely fell away. She then worked on the portion of the shirt glued to the wound, alternately wetting, and pulling. She applied pressure when it started to bleed. Expertly she inched the material up and away from the skin, and firmly pulled one last small thread from the wound. She then cleaned around the wound with the damp washcloths, and then the wound itself with sterilized swabs. She could see a definite entrance, and ragged exit wound, but without an x-ray couldn't tell whether or not the arm bone was compromised.

"How are you doing?" she asked, glancing up at her patient.

"Better, I can hardly feel a thing," Abdul replied, opening his eyes. "How does it look?"

"I'm going to have to put in a few stitches. It seems the bullet went through the inner fleshy side of your arm, exited, and slid across your chest wall. It probably ended up in the back of your chair. You were lucky, Abdul. I guarantee the assassin was aiming for your heart. If you hadn't dropped the paddle you might not be here," said Davon, shaking her head.

"It was your doing that I dropped the paddle. I'll never be able to repay you for saving my life." He chuckled, and then gripped his side with his good arm. "Oh, that hurts!"

"You're not going to be able to laugh for a while, that's for sure. Okay just a little prick. I'm freezing the area before I sew. I'm afraid you'll have a couple of scars," said Davon, totally focused on her work. "Can you straighten your arm this way? Great, now hold still."

Davon began to stitch the entrance wound carefully pulling the sides together with medical cat gut thread. She used the flap technique and slightly overlapped one side so that when it healed it would fall evenly flat. The entrance wound needed seven stitches, and the exit wound because of its ragged edges, required ten. Although the top of the chest wound didn't really need sutures, she chose to put in three small stitches instead of using butterfly bandage because of the flight home tomorrow. Once she finished her handiwork, she dressed the wounds, and removed the soiled linen from the bed.

"When we get home you'll have to have an x-ray of the arm just to be certain there isn't any bone or bullet fragments," said Davon, pulling out her stethoscope. She paused to examine a mole on Abdul's face. "You know, you have a very black mole on the side of your chin. It should be removed."

"No way, the mole was the only way my parents could tell my brother and me apart when we were little," joshed Abdul.

"Well, I'm sure they can tell you apart now. A mole like that could be malignant! Has it changed, become larger or darker as you've gotten older?" she questioned professionally, peering closer.

"Maybe, I don't know. Do you find it tantalizing?" asked Abdul gazing at her.

Picking up on his sexual innuendo, Davon shook a finger at him. "No, and you should have a dermatologist look at it! I want to have a quick listen to your lungs. Can you sit up?"

Deflated, Abdul asked, "Why did you bring your medical bag to Cairo?" He reached out with his good arm for assistance, and smiled sweetly at Davon as she helped him, holding on to her for a touch longer than was proper.

"I take it wherever I go. And my stethoscope is always on my person. I know it sounds weird, but it's just something I do. I even had my stethoscope in my evening bag tonight," she told him, inserting the ear pieces. "Now take the deepest breath you can. It's going to hurt a little." Davon listened to his breath sounds on both sides. "Okay, let me help you lay back down." She put two large pillows behind his head, and pulled up the covers noticing how beautifully developed his chest and upper arm muscles were. His black chest hair, which curled slightly at the ends, was quite appealing and sexy. Looking into his eyes, Davon felt a warm tingling sensation run down her spine. She shook herself mentally. Even if they desired each other, it would never work. He had nineteen wives for heaven's sake! She looked away, and kneeling down on the floor started to repack her medical bag. Abdul's eyes followed her every move.

Davon pushed a stray curl away from her face, and stared at him soberly. "You may not want to hear this, but I want to tell you what happened during the break at the event. I heard men arguing in the next room, the room beside the bathroom I was in. They were arguing in French. I took out my stethoscope and listened at the wall," she explained, determined to tell the whole story whether or not he wanted to listen. She noticed Abdul's look of surprise. "Don't look at me like that, it's not something I routinely do, but..."

"You speak French?"

"Yes, my grandparents were French Canadian. Anyway, I heard Mr. Bedon tell another man to kill you!" She rocked back on her heels, and stared at him with concern in her eyes.

"Davon, I'm living proof you heard something, but I can't believe Bedon was part of it. Besides, this is something a woman shouldn't have to worry about." Abdul pushed himself up on the pillow, and smiled. "Your gown is ruined. I'm going to buy you another one."

Davon felt the heat rising in her cheeks. "Do you hear yourself? This is something a woman shouldn't have to worry about? I'm a physician. My job is to save lives! I'm not some fluffy female who only cares about clothes and being beautiful. When I heard Bedon ordering the assassin to shoot you and make the shot fatal, I was frantic! That's why I wouldn't sit down when I came back to the auction. I also know Bedon is involved because I saw him leaving the room, and you have the audacity to tell me I shouldn't have to worry about it! I'm scared, scared for you and totally scared for my own life. However, that didn't stop me from trying to abort the attempt on you tonight. And considering I could have been killed..." Tears formed, and ran down her face. She tried very hard to control herself, but found her emotions getting the better of her. "I should go to my own room."

"No, come here Davon. Come and lie down beside me," said Abdul, his voice deep, masculine, and soothing. He reached out to her.

She brushed his arm away. "I'm your doctor. It wouldn't be right."

"You're not my doctor. You're a dear friend, who put herself in danger for me. You even fixed me up when I needed help. Come here and we can talk, honestly talk about the whole situation. I'm sorry for implying you're fluffy," Abdul said seriously. "I'm only treating you the way I'm used to treating women in our culture. I'm trying to protect you from the cruelties of life."

Davon took a tissue from the nightstand, and sat on the edge of the bed. "That's something I don't get. The women in your harem are smart, and highly educated. Why do you treat them as bimbos?"

"Ah," said Abdul wincing, "do you mind moving to the other side?"

"Sorry," said Davon, sliding over to the right side of the bed. She lowered herself on the soft downy pillows.

"It's hard to explain. Most of the men in this part of the world were raised to put women on a pedestal. Conversations between the genders are more often than not superficial. There are certain subjects women are too delicate to handle, like assassination attempts." Abdul took her hand, and gently stroked the underside with his thumb.

"Well, I definitely don't want to be on a pedestal, and I'm not delicate!" She pulled her hand away. His touch was just too damned distracting!

Abdul turned to look at her. "I'll tell you a secret Davon. You're the first woman I've ever chosen to go out with."

"Really? You have nineteen wives and I'm the first? I find that hard to believe, you seem like quite a Casanova." She smiled, and then added, "I do mean that as a compliment by the way."

Abdul returned the smile. "I guess a thank you is in order then. All of my wives were chosen for me, my mother, my father, my uncle...it's the way we do things. But you, I find you so fascinating, so stunningly beautiful, and so different!"

"If you are trying to melt my heart, you're succeeding, but don't change the subject. I want to talk about the assassination attempt. Why would Bedon want you dead?"

"Only one reason... money."

"And who would be paying him?" demanded Davon.

"It could be anyone. A man in my position has many enemies. It might be someone in my own family. A cousin, uncle, step-brother, one of my wives, and even... "

"Someone in your family?" interrupted Davon, feeling shocked and saddened.

Abdul sighed, and began to explain. "It could even my twin brother, who was born nine minutes after me. Because I was the first born, I inherited everything. Of course he has a lovely palace in Morocco and more money than he could ever spend in a lifetime, but if I die before my eldest son becomes of age, Adin gets everything."

"God help us, your brother would have you murdered because he wants more money?"

"Not just money Davon, the palace my grandfather built, and three others in neighboring states, numerous oil wells, hotels, racing tracks, the list goes on and on, however its more than the things, it's the power and prestige that goes with the title," groaned Abdul, "Yet, Adin and I are close and the only children of my father's first wife. I don't believe he would ever harm me."

"You mentioned your wives. You don't honestly suspect one of them!"

"How can I explain to you?" he asked looking at her, his eyes filled with sorrow. "Can you ever really trust anyone in your life? A woman you meet for the first time on your wedding day? I don't mean to sound bitter, but I feel as though I've been alone my whole life."

Davon took his hand. "I'm sorry Abdul, I didn't understand." There was a moment of silence before she turned to him and asked, "When will Hepbet come of age?" She thought of the boy and her promise to him. The discussion about university in the States would have to wait.

"Have you heard of Hepbet?" Abdul looked totally surprised.

"I met him," she replied, nonchalantly. "He came to the medical clinic once. He really is a sweet young man."

"A young man who'll have to be disciplined, he knows better than to go into the women's quarters!" Abdul shook his head and laughed. "He does get into mischief! Hepbet will be eighteen in seven months and once he comes of age all of my assets automatically transfer to my heirs, my sons. Hopefully after that there will be no trouble."

Davon put on her sleuth hat. "Okay, let's presume someone else is behind this, why would Bedon help them if he has been with you for years? Doesn't he have any loyalty?"

"I have no idea. I'm completely mystified." Abdul thought for a moment. "When you saw Bedon leaving the room beside the bathroom, do you think he saw you?"

Davon shook her head. "No, I'm positive he didn't. But I was worried because I thought he might notice I wasn't in my seat."

Abdul was quiet for a few seconds and then pulled her hand towards his lips. He gently kissed it. "As much as it hurts, I have no choice but to send you back to America. You'll go directly home from Cairo tomorrow. I'll pay you for the full year of work."

"And I don't have a say in this?" exclaimed Davon, sitting bolt upright. She was shocked at his command. "You're doing it again Abdul! I admit I'm afraid of Bedon, but don't protect me by making me go home to America. Get rid of him!"

Abdul slowly nodded contemplating her suggestion. Gently wrapping his arm around her shoulder, he pulled her towards him. Davon let herself succumb. He simply held her. Breathing in his musky masculine smell, Davon realized how much she desperately missed intimacy.

"Stay with me tonight," murmured Abdul, gently stroking her arm.

She was dumb struck for a moment. Although she had fantasized about having a relationship with the Prince, she hadn't anticipated that she would actually end up in his bed. She became unusually sober, "You're a wonderful person Abdul, but we live in totally different worlds. You have nineteen wives and I'm not about to become your mistress. You see, I can't share the man I'm involved with, it's just not who I am."

"What if I asked you to marry me?" Davon stared at him in amazement. "Let me finish," he said, as she started to wrench away. "I would make you my first wife. You would be the most important woman in the harem, and I would promise to never sleep with any of the others again. Although it's common to do, I've never promoted one of my wives to first wife. I don't know why, probably because I never selected any of them myself. I like all of them well enough, but I have to admit I don't truly love one of them. I've never told that to anyone." Abdul spoke quietly, and turning to look into her eyes, he continued, "And that's just it! I can talk with you, really talk with you. I feel you understand me, that we belong together. You're absolutely wonderful and would be the partner I've always dreamt of. Please, say you'll marry me!"

Davon kissed him softly on the neck and then sat upright. "This is insane Abdul! We live in the twenty-first century. I can't believe we're even having this conversation. I like you, but we don't really know each other. And if by some crazy chance..." She waved her hands in the air. "I did agree to marry you, my whole life would change! You probably wouldn't let me continue working as a doctor, and my career has just begun."

Abdul laughed. "Think about it Davon, I'm offering you an amazing life. You'll have everything you've ever wanted and more!" He groaned when he tried to reposition his arm.

Carefully sliding off the bed, Davon said, "I'm going to give you another shot for pain and help you get ready to go to sleep, and then I'm going to my suite. I really need to get out of this dress."

"I'd feel better if you stayed here for the night, only because I know you'll be safer with me," said Abdul, grimacing as she injected the morphine into his arm.

"And that is because?" asked Davon, suppressing a smile.

"What? Are you suggesting that I can't protect you?"

"No, I'm suggesting I may need protection from you," she replied, laughing.

Abdul laughed with her. "Under normal circumstances you may be right, but tonight you don't have to worry, I'll be a proper gentleman. However, my suite unlike yours has two bodyguards at the base of the elevator, and I'm just not up to making arrangements to have your suite covered, especially because I can't pick up the phone and tell Bedon to do it!" He wasn't used to Davon's direct and honest approach, the way she spoke to him as though he was a regular guy not Prince Abdul, but he liked it. "By the way, you realize if Bedon finds out you know he was involved, your life could be in danger." Abdul tried to soften the statement by using the word 'could' instead of 'is'.

"Now, you are scaring me! I'm already afraid of that man. But, I'm positive he doesn't know I heard and saw him. For one thing, he doesn't even know I speak French." She looked up from the dressing she was reinforcing. "Aren't you going to have him arrested, Abdul?"

"You don't seem to understand, this isn't the United States, and I'm not in my own country. I'll deal with him, but we have to get back to the palace," he replied, as she pressed another piece of tape over the gauze dressing, "If you refuse to fly home to Boston, I think you should fly back to the palace in the morning. I'll stay in Cairo, and then Bedon will be forced to stay here with me. It will give me time to make a few phone calls and organize a reception party for him the minute we get off the plane in Dubai."

Davon looked frightened. "You aren't going to kill him are you? Wait, don't say anything, I'm not sure if I want to hear an answer to that question."

"This is precisely why men don't really talk to women," Abdul said, as he closed his eyes. "If you want to get out of your gown, there's a robe behind the bathroom door. I'm beginning to feel very, very sleepy..."

Davon tidied up, dimmed the lighting, and then made her way to the enormous bathroom all the time whispering the pros and cons of spending the night in the Prince's suite. Staying here may not be the best idea, she rationalized, but I'll never sleep if I'm alone, especially now that Abdul has suggested I could be in danger.

In front of the wall to wall bathroom mirror she examined her gown, the most expensive piece of clothing she had ever owned. It was ruined. The stain, now dried was almost perfectly centered under her right breast. Perhaps, she thought, she could get it out with a bit of soap and water. Undoing the covered buttons with one hand, she let the expensive material slide off and pool on the cool marble floor. She stepped out of it as she filled the sink, and catching her reflection in the mirror, she unconsciously fingered the delicate lace of the strapless teddy Cheri had insisted she purchase. Could she even consider marrying Abdul? Could she leave her family, everything she had ever known, for what, a life in a harem? She was crazy to consider it. And then there was Matt. "I'll always love you Matt," she said, "but I need to do what's best for me. Abdul's a great guy and a life with him would be amazing! I know I lust for him, but is it love?" She tilted her head to one side and then to the other. "Too much stress, my neck and shoulders are killing me!" She began to massage them, and then giggled wickedly. "Yep, I could use a little sex about now. It'd be sooo relaxing!"

As she picked the gown up from the floor, she went quietly to the door and peeked in on her patient. Abdul was asleep and breathing peacefully. Damn, I shouldn't have given him so much morphine, she thought, fantasying about a sexual relationship. Returning to the sink, she sighed and plunged the stain underneath the water generously rubbing liquid soap over the surface. The water instantly began to discolor and the stain appeared to fade. She was pleased as she rung out the excess moisture, thinking she had saved her beautiful gown until she noticed the dry clean only instruction tag. Discouraged, Davon grabbed the phone on the wall.

"Yes, this is Dr. Marshall. I've spilt something on my evening gown. Do you have dry cleaning services during the night? You do? Could you send someone up to get the dress? Would it also be possible to go to my suite first, and bring me the black and gold suitcase on the floor in the bedroom?"

Putting on the blue full-length silk bathrobe she found hanging at the back of the door, Davon gathered up the gown and tip-toed past her sleeping patient into the living room. She was thankful she had thought to ask room service to bring the black and gold suitcase containing her newly purchased clothes from Cheri's. At least she wouldn't have to wear the housecoat back to her room in the morning.

As Davon stood at the window admiring the spectacular night view of Cairo, she recalled the last two days filled with such excitement, and now this! She couldn't seem to wrap her head around the fact that she was contemplating marrying a man whose life was in danger. A cold shiver ran through her. Wrapping her arms around herself, she rubbed them vigorously, wondering if there would be another assassination attempt. Bedon didn't seem to be the type of person to give up after one foiled endeavor! It was interesting though, she thought, that Bedon's involvement had been such a surprise to Abdul. Instinctively, she had known Bedon was a major creep the very first time she met him. She bit the inside of her cheek. Compared to the routine she had left in Boston, it was unsettling being thrust into the middle of a plot to assassinate her employer, now possible husband. Working in Emergency, she had given medical treatment to countless gunshot victims and had witnessed many gang related DOA's. But because she had never personally known any of the injured or dead, it hadn't seemed to affect her. It was just part of the job. She had learned early on in her career that emotions could wreak havoc with a doctor's skill set, which was why all physicians were discouraged from treating family members.

A brisk knock made her jump, and she found herself coming back to the present. Cautiously looking through the peephole Davon saw the same porter, the one who had brought up her medical bag, appearing nervous. Slowly unbolting the door and opening it, she smiled. "Hi, let's exchange goods here, you give me the suitcase and I'll give you the dress."

Without hesitation he carefully placed the suitcase on the floor beside her and stuck out his arms. Davon lay the gown over his outstretched limbs and put a note on top, which asked the hotel to give him a twenty dollar tip and charge it to the room. She smiled again, but noticed he was avoiding eye contact. Probably because I'm in a bathrobe, she thought.

"Whatever," she whispered, quickly relocking the door and jamming an extremely valuable antique chair under the knob.

Returning quietly to the bathroom she removed the pins from her hair. Her hair fell softly around her shoulders, a mass of gorgeous curls. Slipping out of her teddy, she walked into the shower and turned on the water. She inhaled the heavenly scented lavender shampoo, and began to wash her hair. Suddenly, she realized she had forgotten to lock the door. Davon imagined Abdul sliding into the shower behind her, massaging her tight shoulders, and then slowly, oh so very slowing moving lower...her body ached for him. Why does he have to be married? And why do his wives have to be so damn nice, she asked herself? The fantasy quickly evaporated with the thought of Lamna, Nisha, Sepida, and Pipa.

Finishing up, she donned the bathrobe, brushed her teeth with her finger, and switched off the bathroom light. Abdul's suite was twice the size of Davon's, but only had one huge bedroom attached to an enormous living and receiving room. It was a suite probably used more for entertaining then sleeping. In the silk robe with a white towel wrapped tightly around her hair, she walked back into the living space. She went from sofa to sofa looking for one with extra softness and comfort. Finally, after sitting on all of them, she selected a comfortable, over-stuffed couch to sleep on. Turning her attention to finding a blanket and pillow, she opened every cupboard and closet in the place. The only bedding she was able to find was a couple of plastic wrapped pillows perch on one of the highest shelves.

"That was a waste of time!" she exclaimed angrily.

Exhausted and not willing to sleep without a blanket, Davon wandered back into the bedroom pausing to gaze at Abdul. He was sleeping on his back, his breathing easy and regular. She resisted the urge to reach out and push back the sheet, letting out a soft sigh at the sheer beauty of his features. She was more than attracted to him, she enjoyed being with him. Clutching the dressing gown, she watched him sleep, and that was when Amelia Tucker's parting words flew into her thoughts, "Just make sure you don't become part of the harem!" Davon pondered the statement. It was hard to believe Amelia had Davon's best interest at heart. She was probably being nasty because she was jealous…or was the woman actually speaking the truth from her vast experience of living in the Middle East?

Removing the towel from her almost dry hair, she moved to the other side of the enormous king-sized bed, and carefully slipped under the covers. The Egyptian cotton sheets were incredibly soft, and she nuzzled in, comfortably knowing she was at least six feet away from him. She wouldn't think about anything else, she was tired, unbelievably tired.

There had been some sort of disaster, an earthquake, a fire. Every stretcher was filled with a mangled, bloody body, and yet the paramedics kept bringing more. The line of patients stretched down the corridor and into the street, and there seemed to be no end to the string of desperate faces calling, pleading for medical attention. "We can't take care of all these people! Divert to another hospital," yelled Davon, as she inserted the needle into the vein, starting the IV. She looked up when there was no response, and suddenly realized there were no other medical personnel. She was by herself, the only individual standing in a sea of injured, dying people calling for her.

Opening her eyes, Davon was instantly out of bed. The moaning was coming from Abdul. Grabbing her medical bag, she withdrew the last of the injectable morphine from the vial. "Abdul, it's alright, I'm giving you something for pain. Sorry, I should've set the alarm to get up during the night." She gave him the needle.

"Ouch! What time is it?"

"Ten to seven, how did you sleep?"

"Okay, until I tried to move a moment ago. You look gorgeous this morning. Please don't tell me you slept in my bed last night," he groaned.

Davon smiled, pulling up the collar of the robe which had fallen off one shoulder. "I would have slept on the couch if I'd been able to find a blanket. Anyway, we were miles away from one another in this gigantic bed."

"Come here," said Abdul reaching out to her with his good arm.

"No Abdul, none of that until I make my decision. Right now I need to check your dressings. Lift up so I can untangle the sheet."

Abdul did as he was told. "And have you made a decision?" he asked, wincing.

"No," replied Davon, trying to concentrate on the removal of his arm dressings. There had been some bleeding from the wound during the night.

"How does it look?" asked Abdul, peeking down.

"Good. This may sting a little because I'm using antiseptic to remove the crusty bits around the sutures." Davon paused in the middle of what she was doing and looked at him. "You're going to need a dressing change again tonight, and something for pain. I really don't think I should go back to the palace and leave you here."

"I'll be fine Davon, and I promise to be there tomorrow, at lunchtime. Pad up the dressing, or do something so it can wait until then," said Abdul, reassuringly.

"And what about your pain? The only pain pills I have are Tylenol #3's, which are just Tylenol and a small dose of codeine. I'm not sure they will be strong enough."

"I'll manage. Anyway, the needles make me groggy, and I have to have my wits about me to deal with Bedon."

Davon let out a big sigh, "Are you really sure this is the best way?"

"Trust me," said Abdul softly, "I want to spend the rest of my life with you, and I won't do anything to jeopardize it. Now Bedon will be arriving with my breakfast at precisely seven-thirty, and as much as I hate saying this, I don't think he should find you in my suite."

Moving quickly Davon began to pack up her medical supplies. "I do trust you. However, it's difficult to leave you with Bedon, the person, who I know wants you dead!"

"Thank you for caring, but again, I can handle the situation. So future wife, will you do me the honor of giving me one kiss before you go?"

"You sound extremely confident I'm going to marry you, Prince Abdul, even though I haven't said yes," replied Davon, grinning. She stood up, holding her bag, and stopped to look at the gorgeous, half-naked man asking for her hand and a kiss. Her heart began to pound rapidly. How could she refuse him anything? He was absolutely perfect for her!

Slowly, leaning towards him Davon had a second thought, "Abdul!" she cried, her lips parting slightly.

"Don't say anything, just kiss me."

Their lips met. Abdul reached up and tenderly pulled her head towards him. He played with her hair, twirling a piece around his finger as he gently nibbled at her lower lip. Davon felt a cascading warmness, a wonderful tingling sensation, which encompassed her. Although the kiss lasted only seconds, it was so sensual, she had trouble pulling away. There was chemistry between them, strong chemistry, and Davon knew she would enjoy a physical relationship with him.

As she carefully tucked the covers about him she wondered about the trick of fate, offering her another man with family obligations. Glancing at the digital clock, she frowned. "I've got to get dressed and out of here. Promise me you will be back at the palace tomorrow."

"Don't worry Davon, I'll be there."

"Here are the pain pills. You can take one or two every four hours," she said, placing a pill container on the bedside table. "I'll be at your suite tomorrow afternoon, right after I finish seeing patients at the medical clinic. If you need me before that time, call for me, promise..."

"I will my love," answered Abdul, blowing her a kiss.

CHAPTER THIRTEEN

The hotel limousine whisked Davon directly to the airport terminal where the private jets were held. When they stopped on the tarmac in front of the plane she was to take back to Dubai, she could see the Prince's larger more luxurious jet parked beside it. The middle aged man, who had sat with the driver on the way to the airport, opened her door and without saying anything, directed her with a small gesture to the plane and the portable stairs, which were already in position. She didn't recognize either of the men accompanying her, and felt they were suspicious looking. They wore black suits and ties, but their clothing was untidy, slightly grimy. The driver looked like an over-sized body builder, who watched her like a hawk out of the corner of his eye, and the assistant was plump, and balding with pock-marks on his face. They had the total semblance of criminals, and she wondered if they worked for Bedon. As she moved towards the plane, she noticed they were leering at her, and then sneering at one another. It gave her a bad feeling, and made her anxious about the flight. She thought of Bedon's involvement in the assassination, and his utter hate for her. It would be easy to throw a passenger out of a plane over the Red Sea, she thought, pausing for a moment at the bottom of the stairs. Did Bedon know she knew? Reassuring herself that he didn't, she made her way up the steps and ducked to enter the air conditioned cabin.

The door to the cockpit was open and the two pilots, who seemed extremely professional, nodded politely. However, unlike most of the men she had encountered in the Middle East, they continued to stare at her for an uncomfortable few minutes. As Davon settled in her seat, she stared back, analyzing them. She wasn't about to let them intimidate her. One of them eventually got up and closed the cockpit door. Davon shook her head as she did up her seatbelt. "Good grief!" she whispered under her breath. She watched the ground crew shut and lock the main door of the jet, and remove the portable stairs. If she was going to get off the plane, she had to do it now. Rooted to her seat, she admitted she was afraid of Bedon, but reminded herself that Abdul had promised he would take care of him. She had to have faith.

Looking out the window as the plane moved towards the busy runway, Davon nervously smoothed out a small crease in her pant leg. She had worn her new cream colored pant suit and a dark red v-necked, silk shirt-- one Cheri had selected. The matching red silk scarf to cover her hair upon arrival at the palace had been folded and placed in her bag. Today, her hair was in a French braid, which accented her high cheek bones, making her already large blue eyes seem even bigger.

Hoping to get an aerial view of the Pyramids, she pulled out her camera, and tried to shake off the horrible feeling in the pit of her stomach. The jet taxied quickly on to the runway, butting in front of several larger planes, and within minutes they were in the air. Unlike the flight to Cairo, there was no steward to serve drinks or food. She was alone in a deluxe four seat passenger jet. Removing her seatbelt, she opened the mini-fridge and helped herself to a soda. The flight back to Dubai she assumed would be similar to the one to Cairo, just over two and a half hours.

Settling back into the leather seat, she snapped a few pictures, and then watched the Pyramids disappear into the distance. Cairo was a city rich in history, full of mystery, conspiracy, and secrets--the perfect place for murder. Her thoughts lingered on Abdul, the assassination attempt, his proposal, and then on Mr. Bedon. Why couldn't she get Bedon out of her head? His ugly face always seemed to be hovering somewhere in the back of her mind. She hoped Abdul was planning to have him arrested, and reflected on their conversation last night. He wouldn't kill Bedon, would he? The phrase, 'an eye for an eye' came to mind, and made Davon feel extremely uneasy.

Two hours and forty-five minutes later Davon saw the buildings of Dubai coming into view. They flew over the airport and landed directly beside the helipad. This was one benefit of flying on a small jet. Within fifteen minutes she was out of the plane, into the helicopter and on her way to the palace.

The helicopter pilots were the same ones from her original flight. They still didn't help or speak to her, but she did see a brief smile of recognition when she propelled herself into the back of the copter grabbing the ear protectors on the way. Doing up her seatbelt, she grinned. It felt good to be going home.

As they approached the landing pad, Davon took in the view. The lake dazzled in the morning sunshine, and everything seemed peacefully calm. Squinting, she shielded her eyes and looked more closely. Along the path, which skirted the lake, she thought she saw someone on horseback. They were riding in and among the grove of palm trees. "How wonderful," muttered Davon, thinking she would ask Abdul to take her out riding. The helicopter banked, and Davon quickly lost sight of the lake, but then noticed Raja waiting in the golf cart beside the helipad. This could be awkward she thought, pulling the red scarf out of her bag.

"Dr. Marshall, welcome back, I hope you had a nice time in Cairo," Raja yelled over the sound of the revolving helicopter blades.

"Yes I did. Thanks for asking," replied Davon, getting into the cart as though she owned the place. She sensed a slight change in Raja's demeanor. It seemed a touch more respectful, or was it just her imagination? Refusing to chitchat about the trip, Davon said nothing else, and so they traveled in silence until they reached the women's quarters.

"Will you be going to the medical clinic today, Dr. Marshall?"

"I will. Have there been any problems?"

"Not really, one of the boys had an asthma attack during a mild dust storm two days ago, but he settled down when the mother gave him his puffer."

"Memen?"

"Yes."

"Please ask his mother to bring him to the clinic this afternoon," ordered Davon, as she picked up her medical bag and jogged up the stairs to her suite. "Bin! I'm home," she yelled at the front door kicking off her shoes.

Hurrying from the kitchen Bin reached up to hug her. "Meece you," she said with a thick accent.

"I missed you too, and I brought you something," Reaching into her pocket, Davon took out the silver brooch she had bought at Cheri's and pinned it to her uniform. She hadn't expected Bin to burst into tears.

"Formee?"

"Yes for you. Do you like it?" asked Davon, now becoming emotional as Bin nodded and hugged her closer. Her thoughts turned to Bin's past and the little she knew about it. Bin was a widow, and although she had had three children, none of them were alive. As far as Davon knew Bin was alone, with no living relatives. Davon never asked what happened to her family. The horrible, painful look on Bin's face when they briefly talked about it was enough to make Davon tread carefully. From that moment on, Davon secretly vowed to help her. She even contemplated taking Bin back to the States when her contract was finished.

Taking Davon's hand the way she always did, Bin pulled her towards the dining room and directed her to sit down. On the table were six of her favorite dishes.

It was hotter at the palace than it had been in Cairo, so Davon changed into a cotton summer dress before she started off to the clinic. On route, she noted the accumulation of sand in the garden beds and around the walkways, and wondered how bad the sand storm had been. The waiting room was empty when she entered, and totally unconcerned, she went straight to her office to put on her lab coat. She yanked the recently washed and starched white coat off the hook behind the door, turning to see a florescent yellow envelope lying atop her neatly stacked journals. Moving to the desk, she picked it up, and examined the 'Dr. Marshall' scribbled on the front. The package was bulky and heavier than one would expect for its size. Opening it, Davon smiled. She fingered two exquisite gold hoop earrings, ones she recognized. They were accompanied with the words 'thank you', printed in large letters on a piece of yellow paper, but there was no signature.

"So," she said out loud, as she leaned dreamily against her desk. "Zatum has gone back to her parents. What a wonderful man Abdul is!"

This was precisely why she was falling for him. He was kind, loving and kept his promises. Feeling ecstatic, and full of energy, Davon took her medical bag to the supply room, and restocked it with dressings, pain drugs, antibiotics and extra gauze. She wanted to be completely organized and ready for Abdul's arrival tomorrow. Just as she was almost done, Davon heard the front bell tinkling. Peeking around the door frame she saw Lamna.

"Where have you been? You take off and leave a sign on the door saying you will be away for a few days? Raja wouldn't say a word, and the only reason I knew you were back is because I heard the helicopter come in and saw you in the golf cart with her. So….?"

Davon blanched. "I was in Cairo."

"Cairo? What were you doing there?" asked Lamna, obviously surprised.

Davon was unsure of how much to tell her. Lamna was a friend, but she was also now a rival. "It's kind of a long story. My whole life I've always wanted to go to Cairo to see the Pyramids and the Sphinx, and well the opportunity came up and so I took it."

"I guess being the doctor here you're not under the same regulations as the harem. How lucky are you! Did you have fun?"

"It was great! The history…and the Egyptian museum is utterly fantastic. I definitely want to go back. What's been happening here?" she asked, noticing a sparkle in Lamna's eye.

"I think I'm pregnant!" she exclaimed, beaming.

Davon managed to hide her distress. "Isn't that exciting? I'll grab a pregnancy test kit from the back room."

When the word 'pregnant' appeared on the stick, Davon took a deep calming breath. She had asked Lamna to wait in the reception area while she checked the results because she knew if Lamna was indeed pregnant, she would need a few minutes to compose herself. Damn it! This is exactly the type of thing I'm worried about, she thought. She wasn't the type of person to share the love of her life, and more importantly she didn't want to! Wearing a pressed on smile, Davon left the utility room and called for Lamna to meet her in the office. "Congratulations Lamna, you are pregnant. Now, let's find out when you're due."

Lying in bed Davon glanced at the clock, another thirty minutes had passed and she still couldn't fall asleep. She was lonely, frustrated, angry, sad, in love, out of love, and she wasn't sure what her next step should be. There were too many unanswered questions, and no one to discuss her options with. Her practical side told her the idea of marrying Abdul was ridiculous, but her free-spirit said this was a once in a lifetime opportunity. Could she throw all practicality to the wind? Although she cared about Abdul and was certainly attracted to him, she realized she didn't love him like she loved Matt. Of course she had dated Matt for years and knew him like the back of her hand. They were soul-mates, or was that something only she had felt? Nothing was real anymore. It seemed like forever since she had laid eyes on Matt, and she was beginning to have trouble formulating his image in her mind. Would you, could you, forget someone you had loved to the depths of your heart?

Davon punched her pillow. Oh, who was she kidding? Matt was dating someone else. He had moved on, and so should she. Besides, Matt was the one who always said she needed to loosen up and take a risk. But marry Abdul? Could she give up everything she had ever known and become part of a harem? Yet, when she really thought about it, there had to be a reason she had ended up here when she had planned out her entire life in Boston. It was fate, and who was she to deny fate? She needed to say yes!

The next morning, Davon awoke feeling quite jubilant. She could hardly wait to see Abdul and tell him about her decision. It was Saturday and normally her sort-of day off, sort-of because she was supposed to have every Friday and Saturday off, but never seemed to. Taking extra care as she put on her makeup and did her hair, she decided to wear one of Cheri's picks--a light blue linen skirt and matching jacket. Davon wanted to look absolutely smashing when she walked into Abdul's chambers and agreed to marry him.

Too excited to eat, Davon downed a glass of juice, and headed out of the suite almost knocking over Raja, who was just about to knock on the door. "Didn't expect you Raja, are you okay?"

"It's eight-thirty, Dr. Marshall," replied Raja, with a scowl.

"Of course," agreed Davon happily. No one not even Raja was going to put her into a foul mood.

Humming to herself, Davon walked quickly aware Raja was trailing somewhere behind. As they approached the clinic, she could see a line of patients already forming. "What's going on?" asked Davon, turning around to look at the interpreter. Raja seemed just as surprised. Stopping in midstride, Raja mumbled something, and then she abruptly turned back towards the palace. "Forget something?" yelled Davon, watching her retreat. Davon threw her arms in the air. "Great! The one time I'll probably need you and you take off!"

The first five patients she examined all had the same thing, a bad case of the flu. They were related, a two and four year old, their mother Tischi-- wife of Abdul, grandmother and great grandmother. Davon saw all of them together in the largest of the examining rooms, a nine by nine space, but including their servants, there were twelve people jammed in a room meant for no more than four. It was chaotic to say the least, and as Davon weaved in and about the group checking vital signs and patient breath sounds, she became concerned at the possibility of an epidemic. Even one of the servants seemed to be in the early stages of the disease.

There was also growing pandemonium in the waiting room. Every time Davon removed her stethoscope's ear pieces, the racket on the other side of the wall seemed to be getting louder. Trying to ignore the outside noise, she informed Tischi that all of them should go home to bed. "Everyone home to bed, except your grandmother who must remain here, she needs further assessment, possible hospitalization," explained Davon.

"I can stay with Momma Ba to translate," said Tischi, resting her head in her hands as she told the head servant in Farsi to take the children and her mother home.

"No, you need go to bed too Tischi, or you may end up in hospital. I can speak a little Farsi, and Raja will come and help me," she replied, wondering where in the hell Raja was. "Leave one of the servants to assist with Momma Ba, and go home. I'll come to the apartment tomorrow to check on you."

With little argument, Tischi, and her family left once Momma Ba was positioned comfortably on the examination table. After quickly scanning the full waiting room, Davon gave the grandmother a thorough going over. Reaching for the portable oxygen tank and moving it next to the stretcher, Davon placed the mask over Momma Ba's nose and mouth. She was going to have to send the elderly woman to the hospital in Dubai.

Davon dashed into her office and picked up the phone. "Raja, please make arrangements to transfer Momma Ba to the Dubai Hospital. I'll fly with her once I've checked out the rest of the patients in the clinic. And by the way, I could use a little help!" said Davon, as she hung up the receiver.

It wasn't more than five minutes before Raja burst into her office.

"You'll have to take care of Momma Ba here. There are no flights going out today."

"Well, arrange something! She needs IV antibiotics, monitoring, and her lungs are filling up with fluid. She's very sick," stated Davon, moving towards the door.

"You have to take care of her! That's what you're being paid for!" answered Raja, raising her voice.

"Look Raja, I am taking care of her. And I'm telling you for the last time, she needs immediate hospitalization. Make the arrangements to send her to Dubai."

They glared at each other for a few minutes, neither one of them willing to give in.

"The only way Momma Ba can get to Dubai today is by car! You'll have to take her!"

"No, absolutely not! Momma Ba couldn't survive a four hour car trip! And have you looked at the waiting room? There are other patients that need to be seen before we go. We have to go by helicopter. Why can't you arrange a helicopter?" asked Davon, tapping her foot on the floor.

"Because," said Raja hesitating…because both of our helicopters are in Dubai. I can order a third if it's a true emergency, but it better be, Dr. Marshall!"

Davon narrowed her eyes. "Please don't threaten me or imply I don't know what I'm doing! Order the helicopter now, and inform the hospital we will be landing on their helipad!"

Skirting Raja, Davon stormed out of the office. As she returned to the room where Momma Ba lay struggling for breath, she made another quick visual of the people filling the waiting room. None of them seemed quite as sick as the little lady in room two. Davon organized the equipment to start an IV because she knew it was imperative to have an open line for emergency IV drugs when transporting a patient. She also wanted to give a small dose of IV Lasix, a diuretic to help eliminate some of the fluid building up in Momma Ba's lungs before they left. Smiling at her patient, she explained the procedure in Farsi the best she could prior to inserting the needle into the woman's vein.

Momma Ba was seventy-six but looked much older, a tiny weathered female no taller than four feet. Her thick white hair was pulled into a bun on the top of her head, exposing the many wrinkles on her face and neck. Grinning, she chuckled at Davon's explanation. Davon figured she had probably misinterpreted some of the words. Taping the needle and tubing into position, she gave the Lasix, adjusted the IV rate and oxygen mask, and then headed into the reception area. Raja was nowhere to be seen.

"Everyone, could I please get your attention. Momma Ba has a very bad case of the flu and I need to take her to the hospital in Dubai. If you are here because you also have bad symptoms of cold, cough, fever and or headache, stay in the reception area and I will have a look at you before I leave. If you have anything else that can wait until tomorrow, please leave, and come back then. Thank you."

Twenty-four of the twenty-six patients immediately stood, quickly departing the clinic. Surprised, Davon watched them as she unconsciously pulled her stethoscope out of her pocket to examine the two people left. "I guess it's not a flu epidemic," she said, looking at Memen's mother and his younger brother Pheely. "Hello Tagette, how can I help?"

"Pheely has same breathing problem of Memen, he need a puffer too."

"Let's have a look," said Davon, feeling the boy's forehead.

He was warm to the touch, and his nose was runny, but when she listened to his chest the breath sounds were good.

"Have you heard him wheeze, like Memen?" Davon asked.

"No, but he coughs and says head hurts."

Davon sat down beside them, "I think he has a cold, or the beginning of the flu. But asthma can run in families, so it's good you brought him in. Take him home, put him to bed, and give him lots of fluid. If he gets worse in the night call me," she said slowly. "Because he is contagious, which means others can catch his cough, you need to keep him away from the rest of the family, especially Memen. I will come to your suite tomorrow morning to check on Pheely. Do you understand Tagette, or would you like me to get Raja to translate?"

"I understand," she said, helping her son to the door just as Raja entered.

"The helicopter will be here in fifteen minutes, and there's a limousine outside waiting to drive you to it. I called the hospital from the communications department, and they're expecting you and Momma Ba, but they want a report from you," said Raja, nervously twitching.

"Fine," answered Davon, wondering why Raja was so uptight and weird. The woman definitely had mood swings.

Raja watched Davon wash her hands. She then followed her into Momma Ba's room, as if to assess the patient. Although Momma Ba's breathing difficulties had improved, her color was still very poor. Davon turned up the oxygen, and debated whether or not to give her another small dose of Lasix as she checked her vital signs. "Raja, can you ask Momma Ba if she's having chest pain?" When the answer was affirmative, Davon wasn't surprised. The problem was figuring out if it was from the pneumonia, congested heart failure, or both. "Please explain that I'm taking her to the hospital."

The servant helped Momma Ba off the bed while Davon held the IV bag high above the patient's head. Momma Ba could barely stand, and almost slipped to the floor. "This isn't going to work," said Davon, quickly grabbing her under the other arm. Sitting Momma Ba in a chair, Davon turned to Raja. "Get the limo driver Raja; he'll have to carry her to the car."

Raja, although Davon hated to admit it, was an excellent organizer. Her arrangements always seemed to fall together like clockwork. When they arrived at the helipad, the helicopter was in the process of landing, and it literally took only minutes with Raja yelling orders for the driver and the lone pilot to get Momma Ba boosted into the passenger seat. As Davon hung the IV bag on one of the seatbelt hooks, she realized there was no place for her to sit.

"If you are planning to come, you'll have to sit up here with me," yelled the pilot over the whirl of the blades. He pointed to the co-pilot's seat when he saw Davon settling by Momma Ba's feet. "You can't sit on the floor."

"How am I going to take care of her?" yelled Davon back.

"Your seat spins around. Get in and I'll show you."

Davon strapped herself in and put on the ear protectors the pilot handed her. She could now hear his voice clearly explaining how to unlock her chair. "Thanks, I understand. I won't disengage the seat until we are on our way."

"Hang on," he said, as they became instantly air borne.

It gave Davon a whole new perspective sitting in the co-pilot's seat. The curved glass went to the floor, and the panoramic view although amazing, was also unnerving because it felt as though there was nothing to stop her from falling to the ground. For the first few minutes she took the pilot's advice and hung on to the shoulder straps as tightly as she could.

"You American?" he asked, as he steered the helicopter into the desert.

"Yes, from Boston."

"Me too!"

"You're from Boston?" questioned Davon, turning to look at him.

"No, I'm American, well half American. My dad's from here, but my mom's from the States."

Davon took a sudden interest. "How did they meet?"

"At university in California."

"And they married and came here to live?"

"Yup, five kids later and they're still here."

"Wow," said Davon thinking about her situation with Abdul, I guess we're not an isolated case. She looked back and visually checked Momma Ba. "Do you go to the States often?"

"Never been, but I do plan to go."

Interesting, thought Davon. She wondered if his mother ever went back home to California, but figured it would be weird to ask. "Is it alright if I check on my patient now?"

"Just give me a second to level out."

Davon pulled the pin and turned her seat around. She felt a click. Her seat was now locked facing backwards. Feeling for Momma Ba's pulse rate, she grabbed her stethoscope, and then realized she wouldn't be able to hear over the noise of the blades. Momma Ba didn't look good, but there wasn't much more Davon could do in the small confines of the helicopter.

"I don't assume you can go any faster?" she asked the pilot.

"I'll do what I can, but it's going to be at least another twenty-five minutes until we get there."

She was glad she had insisted on flying to Dubai because the flight seemed to be taking forever. She couldn't imagine trying to take care of such an ill person on a four hour road trip. Glancing at her watch, she thought about Abdul. It was two forty-two. She had said she would be at his suite at three o'clock. Sighing, she looked out the window and scanned the horizon for the royal helicopter. They'd probably pass each other in flight. She berated herself for not thinking to write him a note. Reaching out to check her patient's pulse rate again, she was surprised when Momma Ba took her hand and held onto it. Her palm was cold and sweaty, which was not a good sign. Gently rubbing it, Davon attempted to reassure her. "We will be at the hospital soon. Try to relax," she said in English. Not knowing the word in Farsi, she demonstrated the universal sign for sleep.

She had given Momma Ba a bronchodilator to dilate her airways before they left the clinic, but she could tell it hadn't helped much by the way her patient was laboriously breathing. Davon turned and called to the pilot, "How much longer? If it's more than ten minutes I need to give her another dose of medicine."

"Just notified the hospital we're ready to land," he answered.

As they began their descent hovering over the helipad, Davon could see a stretcher and a medical team of about ten people. When she felt the thump of the copter setting down, she took her seatbelt off, stood up and removed the IV bag from its hook. The door was immediately yanked open by two men in white uniforms, who came aboard to lift Momma Ba onto the stretcher. Giving the IV bag to one of the assistants, she watched as they rushed the patient inside the building. Davon stepped out of the helicopter and pulled out her roughly written report, waiting patiently while four of the team members conversed. Finally, one of them approached her.

"Dr. Marshall, I presume? I'm Dr. Veenn."

They shook hands and Davon handed him the paperwork. "I apologize for the brief history on the patient, but I don't speak Arabic. She's a seventy-six year old female who's developed pneumonia from the flu. She might also have some mild congestive heart failure. Her pulse is 120 and thready, BP is 165/90, and she has fluid in both lower lobes. I gave her IV Lasix and Ventolin approximately fifty-five minutes ago at the palace. I think she needs another dose of Lasix stat."

"I'm on my way to the ICU to assess her. Would you like to come and see the unit?"

"Alright," said Davon with reservation because she knew she should be getting back to the palace. "But just to make sure Momma Ba's settled. It's unfortunate, because the rest of her family has the same flu, so no family member was able to accompany her." Davon glanced back at the helicopter. "If you can give me a second, I'll grab my bag, and ask the pilot to wait for me."

When the automatic sliding glass doors opened, Davon was astonished at the architecture. The hospital appeared to be completely made of polished chrome and glass. They were standing on the top floor of one of the towers looking down seven stories upon a massive open courtyard. It had a vaulted glass ceiling suspended by a single curved steel beam, which was so thin, it was almost invisible. Natural light flooded the terrace below, and Davon could see thirty or so people milling about and sitting on leather couches positioned around potted flowers and trees.

"What a unique building," she said.

"Yes, very modern, but I like it. This way please," replied Dr. Veenn, directing her towards an elevator. He was all business and appeared content to look at the wall as they waited.

"Dr. Veenn, can I ask if you've seen any flu cases recently?" She followed him through the elevator doors when they opened.

"In the last month I've treated a dozen cases, two deaths," he said, in a matter of fact way, as though he was speaking about the weather.

"Really?" exclaimed Davon, "Do they think it is related to the HN strain?"

"We are working on identifying the virus," he replied, and then added, "During the world-wide outbreak of H1N1, we chose not to immunize."

Davon thought it was a strange thing to mention, but just as she was about to comment, they arrived at their destination. They stepped out of the elevator into a state-of-the-art intensive care unit. It was every doctor's dream. Wow, would I ever love to work here, thought Davon, focusing on the newness, neatness and calm. As they approached the ultra modern nursing station, she saw that it boasted shiny black granite counters with computer terminals built into the backdrop. The station was open on three sides, with a fully stocked drug and equipment room at the back. Medical staff, all male, appeared to be busy, however, as she watched them go about their duties, it was in an orderly fashion. She hadn't covered her hair with the scarf, which hung clumsily about her neck, and although she felt self-conscious when she noticed sideways glances from the men, she refused to embarrass herself further by doing it now. Ignoring them, Davon focused on Dr. Veenn, and his tour of the unit.

"How many beds did you say you have?" she asked politely, amazed at how quiet the unit appeared to be.

"Capacity is fifty patients and we are pretty close to being full," he answered, stopping in front of room twenty-seven. "Your patient is in this room, Doctor Marshall. Shall we go in?"

By the time she got back to the helicopter it was almost four-thirty. When she yanked opened the door, she startled the pilot. Hopping in, she settled into the co-pilot's seat, which had been turned back to face the front. Fastening her seat belt, she glanced at him and said, "I'm really sorry, thanks for waiting."

"Please don't apologize. This is what I get paid to do." He smiled shyly. "Before we head back, how would you like a city tour?"

Davon winced, if only he had been her pilot when she had arrived in Dubai. "Believe me, if I had time I'd say yes, but I'm still working today and have patients I need to see at the palace. This emergency put me way behind."

The pilot didn't comment, but started up the helicopter and began flying back the way they had come. He stared straight ahead focusing on his instruments. Davon was sure she had offended him. "I noticed you speak English very well, even thought I heard a bit of slang. I guess your mom taught you," she said, trying to make amends.

"Yeah, we speak English instead of Arabic at home."

"I haven't attempted to learn Arabic, but I've learned a few words in Farsi since I've been here."

"Tell me the words you know," he said, jokingly.

Feeling a bit embarrassed, Davon spoke some Farsi to him.

"Not bad, not bad at all."

He corrected some of her pronunciation and helped her learn a few new words. The whole flight ended up being a language lesson, and Davon was thrilled. She could hardly wait to try out some of the phrases on Bin. It was bitter sweet when she saw the lights of the palace coming into view. Because two helicopters already occupied the helipad, the pilot was forced to land on the lawn. He manipulated the machine skillfully, and put it down well away from a grove of palm trees. Davon removed her seat belt and stuck out her hand.

"Thanks for getting me back safely, and for the language tips. I don't even know your name."

"Jack, Jack Haseme."

"Pleased to know you Jack, and thanks again."

Jumping to the ground with her bag in tow, Davon waved goodbye. She watched the helicopter lift off and suddenly felt very alone. There was no one there to meet her, and it was unusually dark. She basically knew her way home, all she had to do was follow the paved pathway to the women's quarters. "Follow the yellow brick road," she said laughing, as she raced along the side of the trickling stream. She could hardly wait to see Abdul. It must be love, she thought, reminiscing about Cairo. As she jogged around the corner, she suddenly realized she had taken a wrong turn. Instead of being at the side of the building, she faced the main entrance to the palace. Its lights blared and beckoned her to enter. She stopped walking and contemplated. Because she was already late for her appointment with Abdul, it might just be better to go home as planned, freshen up, and eat something before going to his suite. She was starving, and positive she looked horribly ragged.

Undecided, she just stood looking up the outside stairs into the empty foyer. She was almost three hours late, and Abdul was in need of medical attention. There was no point in going home first, she could freshen up in his chambers and eat with him after she had changed his dressing.

The glass door reflected her image as she approached it, and Davon paused before she pulled on the large brass ring, taking a moment to run her fingers through her hair. She looked through the glass at the beautiful mosaic tiles, and thought of Matt. Would he be upset about her marrying Abdul? She considered it for a moment and then said, "He had his chance!" under her breath, as she wrenched the door open letting it close on its own with a bang. The echo bounced off the far wall, and Davon looked around to see if she had disturbed anyone. The whole place was uncomfortably devoid of life, so unlike the couple of times she had been there in the past. Instinctively, her senses jumped into overdrive. "Hello, anybody here?" she called out, cautiously.

As she scanned the area, she felt the foyer looked larger. There were too many bright lights blaring in the entranceway, and none near the grand staircase. She felt a bit frightened to go up the poorly lit stairs. This is crazy, she told herself, there are bodyguards here somewhere! Crossing the lobby to the marble staircase, she held her medical bag to her chest, feeling more like a burglar than the future wife of Prince Abdul. As she crept up the stairs, she listened, and watched for security. Reaching the top of the landing, she encountered no one. Since the hallway sconces were for some reason unlit, she had to walk along the hall in semi-darkness. How could Abdul be so careless, especially after being shot, she asked herself?

The door to his suite looked uninviting in the half shadows, but Davon ignored the fact and pushed the doorbell. Her initial trepidation was replaced with excitement. She was finally going to see Abdul! She could hear approaching footsteps, turning of the doorknob, and then…

"May I help you?" said a heavily accented elderly gentleman dressed in a three-piece suit.

"Yes, I'm here to see the Prince," replied Davon, with a huge smile.

"I'm not…one moment please," said the man, squinting at her.

Davon could smell the most delicious aroma floating towards her. Thank goodness everything worked out. I have to learn to be more trusting, she said to herself, as she leaned against the doorframe. The doorman must be Bedon's replacement. I'm so glad he's finally gone. Life will certainly be much easier!

She now heard hurried footsteps, and stood up straight, wondering if Abdul was coming to greet her. Dark brown leather slippers, and stripped lounging pajama bottoms could be seen moving beneath the foyer's curtain. The material panels suddenly parted, and Davon's smile faded.

"Dr. Marshall, how dare you come here!"

"I--I--the Prince asked me to come tonight to change his dressing," she said, feeling the blood drain from her face.

"Something wrong Doctor?"

"No, Mr. Bedon, everything is just fine. If I could come in and take care of the Prince's dressing, I'll get it done and be on my way. It has been a rather long day," she said, mustering as much professionalism as she could.

"Humm," he replied, staring at her with disgust. "As I have told you in the past the Prince has his own physician. He does not want or require anything from you. Go back to the women's quarters!"

The door was immediately shut, and Davon unable to move gripped the wall beside her. Biting at her lip, she felt strangely indifferent, as though the incident hadn't really occurred. This can't be happening, she thought, Abdul promised he would take care of Bedon in Dubai. He said Bedon wouldn't be coming back to the palace. And yet here he is, dressed casually in pajamas. "Oh dear God," she whispered, "What if the pajamas belong to Abdul?"

The energy she had embraced minutes before vanished, and she walked in an almost hypnotic state retracing her steps. She was totally unaware of her surroundings. Her bag felt unbearably heavy and her stomach queasy. She tried to understand what had happened, and began to map out every possible scenario, including the one that hurt the most, that the Prince had lied about caring for her.

As she descended the stairs into the lobby she realized there were only two possible explanations: either Abdul had not believed one word she had told him about Bedon and the assassination plot, or Abdul was dead. It was as simple as that. Davon swallowed hard and seized the hand rail to steady herself. Then panic began to set in. If Abdul was dead, her life could be in jeopardy. She knew she was powerless against Bedon, and there was absolutely no one she could turn to for help. Raja, Abdul's wives, none of them would help an interloper? This realization depressed Davon more than anything else.

The foyer she had once adored with its dome ceiling and exquisite mosaic tiles appeared bleak and threatening. She stepped off the last stair and into a dimly lit edge on her way to the women's entrance, and then cautiously turned around to see if someone was following. She couldn't see anyone, yet she had an uncanny feeling that someone was watching her. Pulling the door open, she was just about to go through the doorway, when she stopped. Turning around, she let the door carefully close, and glancing up the staircase once more, she swiftly walked across the foyer to the communications center. Although she was trying to be quiet, her shoes made a scratchy eerie sound, which echoed off the marble tiles. Reaching the other side, she took a deep breath and slipped into the shadow of the office alcove. Once hidden, she surveyed the foyer again before entering the room where she made phone calls.

Shutting the door, she locked it. Trenk wouldn't be working, and Davon prayed she would be able to convince the night receptionist to place her call. "Yes this is Dr. Marshall. Would you please place a call to this number?" She entered her parent's phone number on the keyboard, and when there was no response from the receptionist, Davon was just about to say the call was urgent when she heard a ring tone and her mother answer.

"Mom, it's Davon."

"Oh Sweetie, I'm so glad you called. Is everything okay?"

"Yes, Mom I was wondering if Dad is around."

"No honey, he's out playing golf this morning, but there is someone else here."

Davon heard giggling as the phone exchanging hands.

"Davon, how are you?"

The second she heard his voice, her eyes became moist. "I'm good Matt, really good."

"I popped in to check on your folks today. Your mom and I were talking about you, and you call. How weird is that?"

"Pretty weird," said Davon, choking back the tears. "You sound great, how are you?"

"Okay, except you're not here," he whispered.

"Matt, I…"

"It was me, Davon. I was the one who made a big mistake."

Suddenly the call was disconnected. Cursing, Davon hung up then pressed the button for the receptionist. "I lost my call. Could you please put the number through again?" she asked, with a sob.

"I am sorry Doctor, a storm is affecting the lines and I can't reconnect. The system will most likely be down until morning."

"Alright, thanks," she said, getting up slowly from the chair.

Although she hated to admit it, hearing Matt's voice was comforting.

Before she talked with him, she was sure she had finally come to terms with their relationship being over. "I'm such a basket case!" she sighed, rubbing the moisture from her eyes. She still cared for Matt, but there was no going back. She had decided on a future with Abdul. And now, she would just have to figure out why Abdul wouldn't or couldn't see her.

Sitting down again, Davon picked up the lone gold pen, which straddled a pad of paper. Matt would have to be at her parent's house when she called! He breaks my heart and admits it was a mistake. Well tough luck for you Matt, I'm not about to let your remorse affect my decision! She took a deep breath, emptied her mind, and decided to rationally map out her options. If only her father had been home, he would have helped. With his military training and work at the Pentagon, Davon knew he would've steered her in the right direction. But then, when she really thought about what he would have said, she became even more depressed. Her father would have told her to get out, to leave the palace immediately. There was no way he would have been sympathetic to her concerns about Abdul's safety, and if she brought up the proposal…well he most likely would have gone berserk. No, she was going to have to figure this one out on her own.

The fact she didn't want to face, a horrible terrifying reality, which made her physically sick, was that she was in a foreign country with no allies. Yes, she had Bin and possibly…Lamna, Abdul's ninth or tenth wife. But she couldn't involve Bin, and Lamna…how could she even think of going to one of Abdul's wives and confess what really happened in Cairo. The acid churned in Davon's stomach as she recalled her interactions with the wives of Prince Abdul. The reason she wasn't close to any of them was because she had always maintained a doctor-patient relationship.

Davon drew circles on the paper and wondered if Lamna had access to Abdul's private cell number. To get it, she'd have to tell a huge whopper. Maybe, she thought, she could makeup an illness about…Davon scratched off that idea. She could be evasive, but she wasn't a liar. However, she might be able to encourage Lamna to call Abdul about her pregnancy. She would tell Lamna she needed to speak with Abdul because the pregnancy was…nothing came to her.

She wasn't naturally devious, but Abdul's life was in danger and so was her own! If she could only hear Abdul's voice, know he was okay, she would be satisfied Bedon wasn't holding him hostage or preventing him from getting the medical attention he needed. She wondered what lies Bedon had told him about Cairo, what Bedon had said to get back in his good graces. He could have told Abdul anything, even spun a story that she was involved in the assassination attempt. "That's what I'd do if I was Bedon," she said out loud, "I'd blame the American."

Amelia Tucker's words suddenly flashed a giant neon warning sign in her head.   Abdul, as nice as he was, had most likely led her on, and the more she thought about it, the more Davon was sure this was the answer. She usually had a strong gut feeling about people, and really felt Abdul was an honest and good guy. "But I guess I called him wrong," said Davon, standing up.

Feeling miserable, but in more control of the situation, she left the communications department and began to make her way to her suite. She tip-toed back across the dark lobby still jittery about the whole encounter with Bedon, and entered the silent hall of the women's section. The last forty-eight hours kept replaying in her head, and she was getting a headache.

Finally home, she twisted the door knob to her suite. It was locked. Davon rolled her eyes, and slamming her bag onto the floor, she searched for her key, swearing. When she finally got the door open, she discovered the apartment was in complete darkness. She was exhausted, hungry and dejected, and Bin was out! Of all the days for her not to be home! Blocking the door open with her bag so that she could get light from the outer hallway, she felt her way to the storage room and flicked the master switch. The lights blared on.

Retrieving her bag, she stomped towards the bedroom with thoughts of taking a shower. "Bin must be attending some social event," she said, trying to calm down. But in the back of her mind she was worried. It was after eight o'clock, and this was the first time Bin hadn't been home waiting for her. Davon tried to recall if Bin had mentioned anything that morning. Kicking her clothes to the side, she stepped into the shower, and under the soothing hot water she let the pounding pressure massage her tense shoulder muscles. She struggled to relax, but found it next to impossible. She was a control freak, and not knowing the whereabouts of Abdul, and now Bin was killing her.

In her dressing gown with her damp hair hanging loose, she made her way to the kitchen. There were leftovers in the fridge, but she bypassed them knowing her unsettled stomach wouldn't be able to handle the spicy food.   Plopping a large dollop of yogurt in a bowl, she sliced two bananas on top, and grabbed a spoon from the drawer. Instead of sitting at the large, recently polished dining room table, Davon steered towards the living room sofa, which gave her a bird's eye view of the front door. Settling down to engulf the creamy sauce, she glanced up every few seconds and listened.

The howling wind outside harshly contrasted the empty silence of the suite, and every time one of the window shutters rattled, Davon tensed. "I'll give her thirty minutes and if she is not home, I'm calling Raja," she whispered, unsure of the working regulations for servants at the palace. She figured Bin was supposed to have some time off, and felt bad that she hadn't ever asked her about it. Chewing on her thumb nail, she tried not to worry.

When the door opened fifteen minutes later, Davon was instantly on her feet. "Bin, I missed you!" she cried, giving her a hug.

"I sorry," said Bin. She explained she thought Davon was spending the night at the hospital in Dubai. "I make food."

"No food," she answered in Farsi, "just tea and then I need to go to bed."

Everything will be okay, Davon repeated to herself as she went into the bedroom to retrieve her computer and patient notes. I have to smarten up, and stop being so paranoid. I'll figure out some way to get in touch with Abdul. This time only to make sure his wounds are healing and sutures are taken out. I think the romance part is over. It's too darn stressful being in love with a prince.

CHAPTER FOURTEEN

The next morning while eating breakfast, Davon came up with a way to find out if Abdul was at the palace. She'd get Bin to nonchalantly ask the other servants. It was a great plan because the question would be assumed to be idle gossip, and no one would trace the query to her. Although she tried to wipe the last few days from her mind, not knowing the whereabouts of Abdul was driving her insane. She had slept poorly worrying about him, and it showed through the dark circles under her eyes.

At eight-thirty when Raja hadn't come to escort her, Davon started off to the office on her own. It was a beautiful day with little evidence of the storm. Davon took in the fresh air and walked leisurely along the path, stopping when she saw the large crowd gathering on the clinic porch. "Two days in a row," she whispered, pursing her lips. "Something's very wrong!" Increasing her pace, she jogged up the porch stairs, and grimaced when she made her way through the group to see every chair in the reception area filled.

Grabbing her lab coat she immediately went to work seeing the sickest patients first. Everyone had the identical symptoms of Momma Ba. There were coughs, fevers, and runny noses. The only saving grace was that no one was as sick as the little lady Davon had flown to Dubai hospital. It took all morning and part of the afternoon to examine everyone. Finally, during a brief lull, Davon was able to open the windows. She got on the phone and asked Raja to get the cleaning women to disinfect the rooms of the clinic. Picking up her file folders, Davon added twenty-three cases of influenza to the six from yesterday.

Instead of doing house calls before she left the palace, Davon had reversed her usual routine, coming to the clinic first. Her initial thought was not to contaminate the office with flu germs, but now she realized the attempt had been futile. She'd have to tell Raja to get the word out that anyone with symptoms of the flu must stay at home in bed, she would go to them.

Davon grabbed several masks and put them in her bag as she set off to check on the condition of the flu victims from yesterday. It took her two hours to see the four patients, and would have taken longer if Davon hadn't refused to stop for tea. Momma Ba's family showed no improvement, in fact one of the children's cough was now so severe Davon ordered a humidifier for the bedroom. By the time Davon returned to her own suite for lunch it was almost five o'clock. She knew Bin had been to the food center to get groceries and was anxious to hear if she had learned anything.

Bin ushered her into the dining room the minute she came home, and Davon being incredibly famished, sat down and ate two bowls of lentils and rice before saying a word. As Bin served the coffee Davon looked up and asked if she'd found out if Abdul was back at the palace.

"People see Bedon, no Prince."

"So does that mean they think the Prince is here because Bedon is here?" asked Davon, in half Farsi and half English.

Bin shrugged and shook her head, "Maybe, no maybe."

"Thank you for trying to find out for me," said Davon, none the wiser.

Davon had heard rumors when she had first arrived that Bedon never left the Prince's side. Bedon was the Prince's male handmaiden, his personal assistant. He seemed relatively intelligent, understood etiquette and fashion, and was fluent in several languages, at least four that she knew of. But what was his driving force? What made him tick? And why did he want Abdul dead?

As she mumbled incoherently to herself, Davon grabbed a scarf from her bedroom and headed towards the door. "I'm going to the communications department to call the hospital about Momma Ba. I'll be back in an hour," she called out to Bin, when she passed the kitchen.

The grand foyer was buzzing with activity. Davon ignored the bustle, and quickly made her way to the room she always used. Although it was Sunday, Sundays were like Mondays, and most people worked. Davon picked up the phone hoping to hear Trenk's cheerful voice.

"Dr. Marshall, what can I do for you today?"

"Trenk it's good to hear your voice, how are you?"

"I'm well Dr. Marshall, and you?"

"I'm good. Could you place a call to Dubai Hospital, intensive care unit, please?"

"Of course, right away," he answered.

Davon was quickly connected to the ICU and Dr. Veenn, who reported that Momma Ba was still in critical condition. "Dr. Veenn, I now have twenty-nine cases of this flu, most likely this year's influenza. None are as severe as Momma Ba's thank goodness, and I'm attempting to limit the spread, but I think I should vaccinate everyone at the palace. I would like you to order some flu vaccine for me."

There was a long pause, "Well, I can order the vaccine, but we aren't sure this is influenza, Dr. Marshall."

"Have you tested Momma Ba to see what the culprit is?"

"Not yet."

Davon shook her head. "If you would test her, it would be very helpful. And could you let me know the results," she asked, upset that Dr. Veenn hadn't thought to do the blood work. By the end of the conversation Davon convinced him to order and send three hundred and fifty doses of this year's flu vaccine. She had decided to immunize everyone at the palace.

Just as she was about to leave the communications room she picked up the phone again. "Me again Trenk, is it possible to get Prince Abdul on the phone?" She held her breath.

"Let me try for you, Dr. Marshall."

She heard the ring tone, and wondered why she hadn't thought of this before as she waited nervously for him to answer.

"Yes."

"Abdul?" inquired Davon.

"Dr. Marshall?" asked the person on the line.

Davon cringed. "Mr. Bedon, it's imperative that I speak with the Prince right away."

"You say it is imperative! You fail to understand your place, Dr. Marshall. I can't imagine who you think you are!"

"I would like to speak with Prince Abdul!" yelled Davon, interrupting him.

"Your request is denied!"

Davon fumed. "Let the Prince know there's a major outbreak of flu in the palace, twenty-nine people are very sick, and one person is in critical condition at the hospital in Dubai…and…and that I'm resigning from my position!" she suddenly added, not really knowing where the last statement came from. "I'll make my own travel arrangements. And I want my passport. Have Raja bring it to my suite!" She slammed down the receiver.

Sitting rigidly in the chair, she stared at the phone breathing heavily. It felt as though she had run a marathon. Bedon was such a horrible man! But what had she done! She gripped the sides of the table and tried to calm down. "I don't care," she said, "I refuse to work under a murderer! And that's what he is. It doesn't matter that he didn't pull the trigger, he organized the whole thing, I know it!" The room was cool, yet beads of perspiration formed on her forehead. Her first instinct was to call her parents, but Davon figured it would be better to compose herself, get her passport, and have her itinerary ready before she let them know she was coming home. Getting up, she left the room on shaky legs.

The congestion in the lobby had decreased as it was near the end of the work day. Davon glanced at the window and noticed it was getting dark outside. She needed air. Pushing open the large plate glass door she jogged down the stairs towards the paved garden path, her bag swinging wildly behind her. Her scarf, which had fallen to her shoulders caught in the wind almost blowing away before Davon reached for it and stuffed it into her jacket pocket. She walked with purpose, stamping her feet into the paving stones angry her whole world was upside down. She hated to fail, and being unable to complete her contract made her feel like a failure. She was letting people down because her patients needed her now more than ever, but she had quit, and there was no way she was going to give Bedon the satisfaction of changing her mind. But, how could she leave in the middle of an epidemic? How could she leave Bin?

Davon had always planned to find a way to bring Bin to the United States, if only for a visit and now she berated herself for not looking into the paperwork beforehand. She wasn't even aware if Bin had a passport. Probably not, she thought, attempting to calm herself by taking in a deep inhalation of the salty sea breeze.

When she stopped at the staircase to the women's quarters, she squinted and looked out to sea. She would give the usual two weeks' notice, and hope that that would be enough time to complete the vaccinations. The harem had always functioned without a live-in physician before she had come, and so they would again, until she was replaced. What was the big deal? Unable to control herself, she started to cry. Leaning her head against the dusty stone wall at the bottom of the stairs, Davon sobbed into the sleeve of her dress, trying to muffle the sound. It was getting dark, and she pushed herself into the shadows so that the workmen in the area wouldn't see her. What she needed was a friend, a sounding board, someone who was on her side. Although she desperately tried to think, she could recall no one that would jeopardize their livelihood by standing up to Mr. Bedon. Except Abdul--he was the only person who could make things right. "Where are you, Abdul? I just know you wouldn't leave me like this. I'm trying to be strong, but I'm so afraid," she whispered.

"Dr. Marshall, is that you?" asked a female voice.

"Raja… yes… sorry did you need me?" replied Davon, quickly wiping her eyes, and hoping the darkness hid her tear-stained face.

"I've been looking for you. A Dr. Veenn telephoned to say he is sending two nurses with vials of vaccine tomorrow morning by helicopter. I paged you four times, and when you didn't call me, I went to the medical clinic, and was just now on my way to your suite."

"I must have left the pager at the clinic. Sorry, the last few days have been extremely exhausting. It won't happen again," said Davon, avoiding eye contact.

"Why wasn't I told you were planning to vaccinate everyone at the palace?" asked Raja curtly, "Where do you expect to give the male employees their inoculations? They can't go to the medical clinic in the women's quarters! I suppose you expect me to work all night setting up some sort of work station for you? Well do you?"

"Raja please, I've had a trying day. All you need to set up in the main foyer is a table with two chairs. It'll take two or three minutes per patient to give the shot. I'll vaccinate all of the women and children at the clinic. However, you will need to tell everyone if they have any symptoms of the flu or have had the flu, they are not to be inoculated," replied Davon, sighing quietly.

"Very well, but I need to be informed about these types of situations, and I expect to be the first one vaccinated!"

"I agree Raja, you have a very important role at the palace, and you are in contact with so many people, you need to be the first to get the vaccine."

Raja moved back slightly, and her voice softened. "Why thank you, Dr. Marshall. I'll let you get back to whatever you were doing." With that statement Raja turned, and walked up the stairs leaving Davon alone with her thoughts.

Davon hung her head, she was being sarcastic, but Raja hadn't noticed. So this was what Raja needed, confirmation of her importance! How ironic, she thought, I finally figure out how to get along with her when I'm leaving the job. Picking her bag up, she made her way slowly up the stairs dragging her feet. When she reached the landing, she paused to watch the lights coming on in the garden. They illuminated the beautiful flower beds between the palace and the bay. She remembered the turtle she saw months ago, and wondered how many of her eggs had hatched. It had been months since Davon had gone down to the beach. She hadn't even been swimming in the harem's swimming pools since experiencing the wonderful, warm, translucent ocean waters. She reminisced about the day she had arrived; it was hard to believe almost seven and a half months had gone by. She was torn, she wanted to leave and she didn't. Maybe her parents were right; she had been foolish to come. But she enjoyed her work, all the women in the harem were wonderful, and she'd found Abdul. Her heart was heavy as she opened the door to her suite. How would she ever explain to Bin?

The night was long and Davon spent most of her time watching the clock change numbers. She was exhausted when the alarm finally went off. Although breakfast looked delicious, she hardly ate anything, drinking four cups of coffee instead of her usual one. Bin fussed about her like a mother hen, and even though Davon tried to put on a good face, she knew Bin was picking up on her bad vibes.

"Today I must give you a needle, Bin. Stay in the suite until I come back. I'll be about one or two hours."

She had planned to meet the nurses at the helipad, escort them back to the foyer where they would work, and return to the women's quarters to start her share of the inoculations. Davon would make a detour to the suite to inoculate Bin on the way to the clinic.

The nurses arrived exactly on time. They stepped out of the helicopter, both wearing matching white hospital scrubs, and carrying small white coolers. When Davon saw they were both male, she tightened her head scarf and turned to Raja. "What's the procedure to take them to the palace? Do we each take one or should they ride together?" she asked politely, already knowing the answer.

"They should use your golf cart. You can ride with me," replied Raja, as she walked over to greet them.

They traveled back to the palace as a mini caravan, the men in Davon's cart following Raja's. As they walked into the foyer, Raja actually smiled when the nurses excitedly talked while making their way through the lobby to the workstation. Davon had no idea what was said, but guessed it had something to do with the beauty of the place. By using Raja as an interpreter, Davon organized the nurses, and then took the vaccine, syringes, and needles she required. She ushered Raja into the communications room to deliver her injection as promised, and then started off to the medical clinic with one quick stop at home to vaccinate Bin.

There was a line already forming on the clinic's porch when Davon arrived, and she secretly applauded Raja for doing a good job at getting the word out about the inoculations. Jogging up the stairs, Davon looked around for someone to assist her. "Lamna, could you possibly help me?" she asked, "The kids need to be organized by age and weight because they get a smaller dose, and I don't want to make any mistake with the language barrier."

"Sure, tell me what you want me to do," said Lamna, walking over with her little girl.

"Ask the ladies to stand on one side and have their children on the other. And could you tell them I'm going to give the mother her shot first to reduce the anxiety of her child. The kids will probably still cry, but it'll help," said Davon, getting her equipment ready. "I also need to know the weight of each little one. There are scales in the first examination room."

Lamna brought the scales to the front of the line, and started weighing the children. The process began smoothly, and ended with a good deal of screaming and howling. But Davon was prepared, and calmed the scene by having the procession move quickly outside after the injections were given. Lamna was responsible for writing down the name and suite number of each patient as Davon administered the vaccination. Because many of the women had sisters, mothers, cousins, and grandmothers living with them there needed to be an accurate record of who got what.

Davon saw that one segment of the harem was missing. "Lamna, I noticed there aren't any servants in the line. Everyone needs to get the vaccine unless they have had the flu," said Davon, as she drew up another dose.

Lamna looked guilty. "I'm not sure Raja would agree. When she told us to come today, she said no servants were to be vaccinated."

"And does Raja plan to take care of all of you when the servants get sick? She's being ridiculous. Could you please run outside and tell everyone to have their servants report to the clinic as soon as possible. I'll wait for you to make the announcement," she said, quickly adding, "It's a good thing I have you Lamna, thanks for your help!"

Within the hour, seventy-two women were standing at the back of the line. Davon had no idea there were this many servants in the women's quarters. She needed more vaccine. "I'm going to be short twenty-one doses," she exclaimed, visibly counting the women at the end of the line. "Lamna, is there someone you would trust to go to the main foyer and pick up the supplies I need?"

"No one is supposed to go into the main foyer uninvited," Lamna said, grimacing, "But I'll go for you, I don't care if Raja yells at me"

"You're a doll! I have enough for ten more people; if you could write down the names of the next ten women in line, I can carry on until you get back."

"I hope you have a dose of the medicine for yourself," said Lamna.

Davon laughed, "I had my vaccination in Boston before I came, which is precisely why I'm sure it's an outbreak of the flu since I didn't get sick!"

She recognized only some of the servants. They were all petite, older, sweet-looking women, who appeared to be very shy to have a needle. Although Davon attempted to explain the procedure in Farsi before she gave each dose, several of the women shook their heads when she rolled up their sleeves. Davon hoped they weren't passively refusing the shot. She gave her last dose and invited the remaining servants to sit down until Lamna returned. No one took her up on the offer.

When Lamna sailed through the door with a cooler, Davon walked over to meet her, "Thank goodness you're back. I had a few problems explaining why they needed to have a needle. How did it go on your end?"

"I managed to get everything you asked for. At first the nurses didn't want to give me the extra vaccine until I yelled, and told them who I was," said Lamna, breaking into a grin. "It was hilarious though because I had just taken the vaccine and walked to the entrance of the women's quarters, and there was Raja flying through the front door! She didn't see me." Lamna laughed again.

"Good work!" chuckled Davon, emptying the supplies from the cooler. "Did the nurses mention how many men they vaccinated?"

"No, but they said they didn't have much medicine left."

"Humm. Do you know if the Prince and Mr. Bedon had an injection?" inquired Davon, trying to make the question sound as though it was asked out of medical interest.

"They're not at the palace. I wish Abdul was home because I still haven't told him about you know what," she said, patting her stomach.

Davon swallowed, "Can't you call him on your cell phone to let him know?"

Lamna leaned over and whispered, "Nisha is the only one who has a cell phone with international privileges. I snuck into her bedroom last week and used it to call Abdul. But don't say anything because she doesn't know."

"Of course I won't," replied Davon, feeling her heart begin to race. "Were you able to speak with him?"

"Only for a minute, he was in a meeting and promised to call me back, but he didn't!"

"Oh," said Davon casually, as she drew up the vaccine into the syringe, "I'm sure he'll call soon."

Davon motioned for the next patient to come and sit in the chair. She felt her hand shaking as she swabbed the injection site. It had to have been Wednesday or Thursday when Lamna called him, when they had been in Cairo. If Lamna thought Abdul was away, there was definitely something wrong. She couldn't have known that Bedon was at the palace. As Davon injected the serum into the servant's arm, she considered mentioning that she had seen Bedon at Abdul's suite, but suddenly changed her mind.

Taking a breath, she reminded herself to take things slowly. Her father had once told her that you need to gather as much information as possible before reacting, and more importantly be one hundred and ten percent sure of the loyalty of person watching your back. She glanced at Lamna concentrating on writing the servant's names in order on the sheet, and wondered if she could confide in her. It wasn't necessarily a trust issue; it was more the subject matter. Could Lamna handle the fact that Abdul had taken her to Cairo, and had narrowly escaped an assassination attempt? The whole situation was overwhelming, and Davon closed her eyes for a moment as the next woman settled in the chair. She needed to calm down so that she could think clearly. Panic added no value. Turning her full attention to the job at hand, she finished the last inoculation, and started tidying up. "Thanks so much Lamna, I couldn't have gotten through all these patients without your help."

"I enjoyed helping you. If we're done though, I should get home to Ismil. Are you coming to belly dancing this week?"

Davon shrugged, "There are so many people with the flu I'll have to see how it goes." The reality was Davon was worn out, she hadn't been sleeping or eating properly for days, and although exercise would have probably done her good, she didn't have time to spend three hours flitting about the dance studio.

It was after three, and Davon still had house calls to make. She felt miserable as she left the clinic, and wished she could stop worrying about Abdul. The circumstances were weird and complicated, and she didn't want to be in the middle of any of it. Yet, she had an awful feeling something really bad had happened to him. Her stomach growled as she started up the outside stairs, and deciding that she needed sustenance to carry on with her day, Davon jogged down the hallway to her suite instead of to her planned home visit. Tired and hungry, she opened the door looking forward to the scent of some exotic dish.

"Bin I'm home," she called, to no answer. "Bin where are you? I haven't much time."

Circling through the apartment it became quite clear Bin was out. Davon noticed the bedroom and bathroom had been cleaned, and the kitchen had been tidied from breakfast, yet there was no evidence of any luncheon meal. Hungry, and in a hurry to start her patient visits, she opened the fridge to see what she could eat, and then stopped dead in her tracks. The door to Bin's room was open! In the seven months Davon had lived in the suite, she had never seen Bin's door ajar. Dashing towards it, Davon called out. Her first instinct was that Bin had reacted to the flu vaccine.

"Oh My God!" she said in total shock, looking into the room. "I think she's gone!"

The tiny space had been emptied of all personal belongings. The bed was stripped. Two blankets lay neatly folded on the small bedside table. Davon stared in disbelief, and then marched to the phone grabbing it roughly out of its cradle.

"Raja, Bin wasn't here when I came home for lunch! It looks like she's packed up and left! What is going on?"

"Ah yes, I meant to let you know earlier, but with the vaccinations…"

"What's going on?" yelled Davon, into the receiver.

"Bin had to return to her village, some sort of family emergency," replied Raja.

"I find that hard to believe! Bin told me she had no family. They're all dead," growled Davon, ready to kill someone.

Raja ignored the comment, "You'll get a replacement tomorrow."

"I don't want a replacement! I want to know what is going on!" cried Davon.

"As I said, there was a family emergency."

"I bet there was!" yelled Davon, slamming down the receiver. Rocking nervously back and forth on her heels, she wanted to scream. What in hell was happening? Was she being punished by Bedon because he knew she wasn't afraid of him, because she challenged his authority? Bedon hated her, she understood that, but would he sink so low and take away the one person she cared about in this foreign land? It had to be his doing, she thought, there's no way it's a coincidence. Davon sank to the floor in defeat, her hands covering her face.

She lay there for a while thinking about nothing in particular running her fingers back and forth along the pattern in the Persian carpet. Her fighting spirit had left her. She was empty, broken, and so very tired. Someone else would have to attend to her patients. She couldn't help anyone anymore!

The room was dark when she woke. Getting up, she turned on the lights and looked at the clock, surprised that she had slept on the floor for an hour and a half. She felt somewhat rested, but still wanted to go to bed and sleep some more. There was still time for her home visits, but Davon wasn't interested. She would only see medical emergencies until she left the palace. In the bathroom, she brushed her teeth robotically, and for the first time since Cairo, looked at her reflection in the mirror. She was haggard. "Who cares?" she frowned, "If Bedon a mere servant can get away with an assassination attempt, and run this place as though it's his kingdom, I guess evil has won. I give up. I just want to go home."

She gazed at her reflection once more, and although the hunger pains had left her, she knew she better eat something. Even through medical school with the long shifts and sleepless nights, she had never looked so horribly worn out. Returning to the kitchen, Davon foraged through the fridge finding leftover stew, and warming it up in the microwave she ate in the living room with her feet up on the glass coffee table, tasting nothing. She would never sit in the dining room again! The memory of Bin hovering around her with platefuls of food was incredibly painful.

When she was finished, Davon went back into the bathroom and brushed her teeth once more. Pulling an Ativan bottle from the medicine cabinet she popped one of the tiny pills under her tongue. She needed something to help her fall asleep, not wanting a repeat of last night. The thought of the sleeping aid knocking her out so that she might not hear the phone ring if there was an emergency, gave her some concern, but she dismissed it knowing Raja had a key to her suite. "I've got to worry about my own health," she said, getting into her pajamas, "so I have enough energy to get the hell out of here." Sliding the pillow off the bed to fluff it, she noticed a rumpled piece of paper that had been neatly tucked beneath the upper and lower sheet. The edge of the paper was ragged as though the leaf had been hastily pulled from a notebook. Picking it up, Davon burst into tears. In her hand she held a child-like drawing of a tall stick figure with long hair, linked by a line to a heart. From the other side of the heart, the line continued to a small chubby figure. Bin, in all her anxiety of being discharged had found a way to let Davon know she loved her by using the method they developed when Davon was learning Farsi.

Davon sat down on the edge of the bed. She felt extremely sad. Bin had come to work at the palace with nothing but the clothes on her back, and yet she had been so excited because she earned about ten cents a day, had a roof over her head, and food. Davon remembered feeling guilty about all the money she was earning, and offered to pay Bin a salary, however she had been informed by Raja that this was not permitted. Not wanting to get Bin into trouble, she had let the matter drop, and now she regretted the decision. Bin was elderly and had crippling arthritis in her hands and feet. How was she ever going to survive? Carefully folding the note, Davon placed it inside her wallet. She knew it was her fault that Bin had been let go.

"I'll try to find her before I leave the country," she whispered, promising herself she would pay whatever it cost. As she slipped into bed she reminisced about how secure and safe her life had been in Boston, totally unlike this place where a wave of a hand can change your destiny.

The Ativan was beginning to make her sleepy, and as she drifted off she thought about Matt. He would know what to do. Davon had always teased him saying he should have been a detective. He was a closet sleuth who loved to solve mysteries, and spent hours talking to her father about espionage and hero stories from the war. Closing her eyes, Davon wished she was snuggled up against him now.

CHAPTER FIFTEEN

When the doorbell rang Davon put down her bowl of yogurt, and went to answer it. "Please come in," she said politely to Raja, who was accompanied by a miniature version of Bin.

"This is Pona, your new servant. Is there anything in particular you would like her to do today, Dr. Marshall?" asked Raja sternly, obviously still smarting from Davon's phone call.

"If she could concentrate mostly on cooking, that would be helpful," said Davon, in a matter of fact way.

Raja turned to Pona giving rapid instructions. The servant hung her head, and made no eye contact. She appeared to be in her forties or fifties, and was very thin. Her off-white cotton uniform, most likely one of Bin's, hung off her shoulders and fell below her ankles almost sweeping the floor. She looked like a tiny waif, who was in need of a good meal. Davon felt immediately protective over the new addition to her household. When Raja finished her lecture, she shoved Pona towards the kitchen. Davon stood silently watching and said nothing, knowing better than to interfere. The noise of moving dishes and pans quickly began to penetrate the apartment, and it sounded as though Pona was starting her job by cleaning out the cupboards.

"I won't be going to the medical clinic today, Raja. If there are any problems or emergencies, please call me here." Raja gave her a quizzical look. "Also, I'm expecting something from Mr. Bedon. Did he give you a package for me?" inquired Davon, sweetly.

"No, I've received nothing from him. Is there anything else?" she asked sharply, walking towards the door.

Davon found it curious that Raja didn't ask why she was getting a package. Clearly, she was still upset about yesterday evening. "Yes, I want to apologize for my comments. I was really upset about Bin losing her job, but I shouldn't have taken it out on you. I'm sorry."

"I see," she snapped.

Davon cleared her throat, and decided to go for it. "Raja speaking of jobs, can I confide in you?" Raja turned back, and stared. "I want to let you know I've resigned. I informed Mr. Bedon, and of course I'll be giving the usual two weeks' notice. I've asked him for my passport because I need to make travel arrangements and…" Davon paused because Raja was looking at her in total disbelief.

"Mr. Bedon agreed to this?" she questioned, with a snarl.

"Well not exactly, but none the less I'm leaving in two weeks."

"Dr. Marshall, I'm not sure how things work in America, but here the employee cannot resign." She said the word 'resign' as though it was a dirty word. "You were hired for a specific period of time, and you will finish the contract. You'll get your passport back, if and when Mr. Bedon decides to let you go back to America. He may want you to continue your work here for another year."

Davon stood up feeling hysterical. "I'm not from here! I'm an American citizen, and my contract is with Prince Abdul not Mr. Bedon. Believe me Raja I've enjoyed working with you, and I care about the women and children of the harem. If it wasn't because of some unfortunate circumstance that I find myself in, I would stay. But regrettably I can't, and therefore I'm letting you know I will be leaving in two weeks time!"

"It's not possible, and I would advise you not to speak about this again, especially to Mr. Bedon," said Raja, raising her voice.

"I'm asking for your help Raja because you know the ins and outs of what goes on here." Raja shook her head, and raised her hand indicating for Davon to say no more. "Well then, what if I gave you money to help me?" murmured Davon. She felt extremely anxious offering a bribe.

"So you think for a few dollars I'll risk my future to help you, when you have always treated me with such contempt?" snorted Raja.

"No…you've got the wrong idea!" Davon felt a rush of unease as the reality of her predicament sunk in. "If you could just steer me in the right direction, assist me in getting my passport back, I'll do the rest. I don't want to get you into any trouble."

"What you ask is impossible, Dr. Marshall," she said, flinging the door open as she stepped into the hall.

The door closed. Shaking, Davon lay down on the sofa and covered her head with her arms. The situation with Raja couldn't have gone any worse! And the scary thing was Davon had no clue if Raja was more upset about the fact she was planning to leave the palace, or because she had been offered a bribe. If it was true that Bedon could make her stay another year when she didn't want to, then she really was in trouble! But why, why would Bedon care if she left the palace? He definitely hated her, so one would think he would want her gone. Was it a game he played, making other people's lives as miserable as his own? Or was it revenge? The circumstances of her arrangement had dramatically changed beyond her control. She had come to the palace in good faith to work as a physician, and had somehow landed in the middle of a diabolical plot. If that wasn't reason enough to end her contract, then what was? She would give Bedon two days to come up with her passport, and if he didn't produce it, she was going to the American Embassy to plead her case.

The banging of pots and pans in the kitchen jolted her back into the present, and suddenly she noticed the luscious smell of curry floating gently past. Pona was starting the luncheon meal. Yet, for whatever reason, the routine noise and smell made Davon extremely irritated. It took a great effort not to stand up and tell the new servant to shut up! Blocking out the clatter, she focused on her list. She needed her passport, money for a one-way ticket home, and cash for bribes.

The phone rang, and Pona poked her head out of the kitchen. "I'll get it," said Davon, gruffly picking up the receiver.

"Hey Davon, I'm calling to let you know belly dancing is cancelled. Too many sick people," said Lamna.

"That's actually good because it takes several days for the vaccinations to give a protective effect. We don't need any more flu victims," answered Davon, hiding her recent upset by switching to her doctor voice.

"Have you heard about Hepbet?"

"No, what about him?" asked Davon, imagining he had been caught sneaking into the women's quarters.

"He's very, very ill. They sent for the doctor from Dubai, but it will take a while for the doctor to get to the palace," said Lamna, in a gossipy way that Davon found repulsive.

"Should I go and see him," asked Davon, suddenly concerned for Abdul's son.

"He's seventeen, and the heir to Abdul's kingdom, you wouldn't be allowed to touch him with your baby finger," answered Lamna.

"I understand, but if he is really sick…"

"He is. His mother is trying to keep it quiet, but I found out he's throwing up, has headaches, and his hair is falling out! Sounds awful, I hope it's not contagious."

"Has Prince Abdul been called?"

"That's how I found out. Everyone is looking for Abdul. Apparently even Bedon's not answering the telephone."

Davon squirmed, "Tell Sashic if she wants, I'll come and see him. It sounds like Hepbet should be on his way to Dubai Hospital, not waiting for a doctor to come to him!"

Extremely worried Davon hung up. Maybe Lamna was misinformed. She had only taken four steps towards her bedroom when the phone rang again.

"Yes Sashic, calm down and tell me what's wrong."

"Hepbet is very sick. For three weeks he's not been well, but over the last four days he's become really ill. I talked with Bedon three days ago and told him to get the doctor and he said he would, but nothing was done, and now…I think it is too late." Sashic began to sob.

"Would you like me to come and see him?" asked Davon, understanding that if she didn't get permission there was nothing she could do.

"Yes come. Raja called Dr. Rahish and he is on his way, but I'm afraid Hepbet is going to die before he gets here."

"I'm leaving my suite now. Have one of your servants meet me at the entrance to the women's quarters."

Davon adjusted her mask and tightened the strings hugging the back of her head. The scent of sickness permeated the room. Not only wearing a mask, but gloves and a disposable gown, she picked up her bag and entered the room leaving Sashic hovering by the door. The lighting was dim, and although there were two large sets of windows, they were closed, the heavy drapes which adorned them drawn. As Davon approached the bed and looked down at the boy upon it, she felt a sense of hopelessness overtake her. Hepbet lay on his back with his eyes closed. A heavy white comforter had been pulled up and tucked under his neck, leaving only his head and right arm exposed. His dark thick hair was matted. Random bald spots were apparent where clumps of hair had fallen out. Strands littered the pillow case and sheets. His once flawless complexion was now taut and shiny. Blemishes covered his cheeks, and the tone of his skin had a sickly yellow cast.

"Hepbet, can you hear me? It's Dr. Marshall."

"Yes, but I can't talk, I'm sick," said Hepbet, barely able to form the words.

"That's why I'm here, to figure out what's wrong, and help you get better. But you have to help me Hepbet. I'm going to ask you a few questions. If the answer is yes hold up one finger, if the answer is no hold up two fingers. Can you do that?" she asked softly.

He held up one finger.

"Your mom told me you have been sick for three weeks, is that correct?"

Hepbet held up two fingers.

"So, you have been sick longer. Four weeks?"

Two fingers.

"Have you been sick for five weeks?"

One finger.

"Was the reason you didn't tell anyone you were sick until three weeks ago because the symptoms weren't too troublesome in the beginning?"

One finger.

"I know you have nausea and vomiting. Do you also have diarrhea?"

One finger.

"Are you having abdominal pain?"

One finger.

"Do you have a headache?"

One finger.

"A constant headache?"

One finger.

"Are you having trouble with your vision? For example if there are bright lights, is it painful?"

One finger.

"Now you have had some hair loss, when did this start? Was it at the beginning of your illness?"

Two fingers.

"Did your hair loss start when you became really sick four days ago?"

One finger.

"Do you remember having a temperature or getting very hot when you got sick?"

Two fingers.

Davon wanted to check his vital signs including his temperature, but hesitated. "I can see you've been scratching your arm. Does your skin feel itchy all over your body?"

One finger.

"Hepbet you're doing a great job answering my questions. One last thing, if you could open your mouth, I'd like to have a quick look to see if you have white spots on your mucous membranes. But, I need to use a flashlight so keep your eyes closed."

The inside of his mouth was flaming red and his tongue cracked. He had symptoms of oral inflammation and dehydration, and Davon could see the lymph nodes on either side of his neck were swollen. She wished she could to do a full examination of his abdomen and lower limbs, but knew it would be a risk with possible repercussions. As a female doctor she had been warned not to give treatment to any male outside the women's quarters.

Davon left the bedside and walked over to Sashic who was nervously waiting. "Being respectful of his age, I didn't do a physical examination. But from my observations and the symptoms he said he has, Hepbet needs to be transferred to the hospital right away. We'll have to do tests, but it's possible he could have hepatitis or cholera. I'm going to start an intravenous drip because his body desperately needs fluid."

They heard a commotion downstairs. "Dr. Rahish is here!" said Sashic, panicking. "You must leave Davon before they see you! Hide in here." Sashic ushered her towards a small storage room and motioned for her to be silent as she closed the door.

After the door shut, launching her into semi-darkness, Davon slid quietly down the wall into a sitting position. She could see moving shadows through the gap between the bottom of the door and the floor. There were two, possibly three people in the room. Taking off her mask, she placed it upside down and pushed it as far away from her body as she could. Worried Hepbet was contagious, but afraid of making noise and drawing attention to herself, she left her disposable gown on, but slowly removed her gloves. Turning them inside out, she threw them on top of her mask.

Davon could hear Arabic being spoken, and listened to the male voices carrying on a long winded discussion. "You're wasting time, Dr. Rahish. Hepbet needs to get to the hospital right away!" she whispered, feeling frustrated. She was sitting with her knees bent, one arm leaning on her medical bag, and although she wasn't too cramped, she wasn't exactly comfortable. Trying to pass the time she closed her eyes, and recalled Hepbet's symptoms matching them with the symptoms associated with her possible diagnoses. Hepatitis had symptoms of nausea, vomiting, diarrhea, jaundice, itchy skin and abdominal pain. Cholera had symptoms of nausea, vomiting, diarrhea, severe dehydration, drowsiness and coma. Neither one of the diseases were associated with vision problems, or hair loss. Could it be possible that Hepbet had some other underlying condition? Headaches were often a result of dehydration, and Hepbet was dehydrated, so Davon put aside that symptom. But vision issues, she ran through the possibilities in her head...causes of vision problems are bacterial eye infections, tumors, stroke. Causes of excessive hair loss are stress, lupus, diabetes, and hormonal imbalance. As Davon mentally ran through the lists, she suddenly realized the talking in Hepbet's room had ceased.

Leaning closer towards the door, she could hear movement. It sounded as though they were transferring Hepbet from the bed to a stretcher. Thank God, she said to herself, hoping they had started an intravenous. She wished desperately to be part of Hepbet's medical team, to discuss Dr. Rahish's diagnosis, and found it difficult to remain silent and hidden in the small compartment.

At least another fifteen minutes passed before the door was finally yanked open. "I'm so sorry, Davon. I hope you weren't uncomfortable," said Sashic, "They're moving Hepbet to the hospital, and then the helicopter is returning to the palace for me. Thank you so much for coming to see my son, if there is anything I can ever do for you..."

"I was glad to help," said Davon, as she stood up, exiting the closet. Removing the disposable gown she added, "Sashic, is there anyone else with the same symptoms as Hepbet?"

"Not that I know of, and I feel fine even though I've been helping to take care of him for the last week," answered Sashic.

"That's interesting," said Davon, "Please Sashic, let me know what they find out in Dubai. I wish Hepbet and you well."

When Davon returned to her suite she showered, and then booted up her computer. It had been almost two months since she had even turned it on. With no printer and limited internet access, and only at the communications department, there seemed to be no point. In the clinic, she had had no choice but to move away from the computer age back to hand-written patient reports. When the desktop came alive, Davon clicked on Medical Diagnosis, a piece of really cool software that she had shelled out megabucks for after graduation. It was an amazing program where symptoms were matched with possible diagnoses, and accompanied by percentage of probability. Used mainly by hospitals, the program was extremely helpful when physicians were stumped by an unusual or rare condition. Typing in Hepbet's symptoms, Davon pushed enter. Only one diagnosis flashed on the screen. "Can't be!" she said, reentering the information carefully. When the same diagnosis appeared for a second time with a probability of ninety-eight percent, Davon panicked. She had to talk to Sashic before she left for Dubai.

Glancing at the time, Davon figured she had only twenty minutes. Jumping up, she threw on a sweatshirt, and jeans. Quickly toweling off her hair, she pulled it into a ponytail. As she jogged towards the front door, she stopped and turned back to grab her computer. Sashic was a nice woman, but Davon didn't know her well. She'd need proof to be convincing!

As she dashed down the hallway of the women's quarters, she remembered she had left her scarf on the bed. Hepbet's suite was on the second floor in the main part of the palace opposite Abdul's, which meant she had to cross the lobby. It was close to noon and she knew the area would be busy. Leaving the confines of the women's quarters, Davon entered the foyer. It was full of staff, but for the most part people seemed to be indifferent as she hurried by them wet hair and all. She took the stairs two at a time and when she arrived at Hepbet's apartment she was panting. Knocking loudly she waited, praying Sashic would still be there.

"Please I must see Sashic," Davon said in Farsi to the servant who answered the door.

Within minutes Sashic was down the stairs. "Davon what is it?" she asked, concerned when she saw Davon's intense expression and appearance.

"I know you're in a hurry, but I need three minutes of your time. Is there somewhere we can talk in complete privacy?"

"Of course, come into my personal living area," she replied, showing Davon a beautifully decorated intimate space. Closing the door, Sashic waited for Davon's explanation.

Davon opened the computer and spoke quietly, "I have a sophisticated computer program called Medical Diagnosis, which helps a doctor pinpoint a diagnosis when the patient's symptoms are unusual or odd. Because two of Hepbet's symptoms were peculiar, I used it. When I put in his symptoms this is what came up." Davon let Sashic see the results, and waited a moment for the information to sink in.

"I don't understand. The computer is saying Hepbet has arsenic poisoning?"

"Yes and the probability of him having it is ninety-eight percent. Sashic, it looks as though someone has been poisoning him."

Sashic sat suddenly and put her hands over her eyes. "Who would want to hurt my Hepbet?" she asked, exceedingly distressed.

Davon touched her shoulder. "I don't know," she said quietly. "Sashic, you have to ask Dr. Rahish to take a hair sample from Hepbet, and have it checked for arsenic. The faster we find out what's wrong with him, the faster he can get treatment."

"Do you really believe the computer?" asked Sashic looking up, her face tear streaked.

"I do," answered Davon. "There is a treatment for arsenic poisoning, but he has to get it immediately." Davon knelt down and looked into her eyes. "Sashic, the minute you get to the hospital, find Dr. Rahish and ask him to do the test. And don't share this information with anyone, but the Prince. If Hepbet does have arsenic poisoning, it won't be safe for him to return to the palace."

"Yes, I understand. I have a sister in Dubai, we'll go there. I must speak with Abdul," she said, recovering slightly when she heard a knock at the door. "Raja is here. Thank you again my dear, Dr. Davon." Standing up, she gave Davon a hug.

As Sashic headed towards the door, Davon moved back. "Is it alright if I wait here until you have gone? I don't want Raja to see me in your suite."

"Of course, I should have thought... please make yourself at home and stay as long as you like," replied Sashic as she slipped out of the room.

Davon settled down on an antique loveseat somewhat relieved. Unintentionally she had opened a huge Pandora's Box. Hepbet's poisoning had to be connected to Abdul's assassination attempt! Someone was trying to clear the path by getting rid of ruler and heir, and she had disrupted both murderous attempts! Thinking about the ramifications, she let out an anxious, inappropriate laugh. The situation was becoming dangerously complicated, and Davon was being pulled into the conspiracy, as an unwilling participant. Fearful for her own safety, she realized she had to tell someone. Her stomach lurched, as she tried to strategize. She felt absolutely ill. Nervously biting her fingernail, she recalled her conversation with Sashic. She had been very clear when she had said to only tell Abdul about the arsenic poisoning, hadn't she? The exact words she used were muddled. What if unable to get a hold of Abdul, Sashic told Bedon about her discovery? Davon trembled at the thought, and wrapped her arms around herself, suddenly feeling cold. Why hadn't she considered that possibility? Bedon didn't know about Cairo, or so she hoped, but if he found out she had suggested the arsenic testing...

She had to get a hold of herself! Getting up from the sofa, she tip-toed to the door and opened it a crack. There was no one downstairs, and she could hear a vacuum cleaner buzzing noisily on the floor above her. Being adjacent to the front door, it was easy for her to reach it unnoticed. Quietly, she exited the suite, and made her way down the empty hallway to the lobby, feeling apprehensive about her involvement. When she reached the bottom of the staircase, Davon headed straight into the communications room. She had heard from two sources that Bedon had left the area, and knew Raja was at the helipad sending off Sashic. There was only a slim chance of being caught in the off-limits zone.

When she picked up the phone, she was happy to hear the familiar voice on the other end of the line. "Trenk, its Davon Marshall, I need the internet, and could you please place a call to my parents, the number is…"

"One moment, Dr. Marshall," he said seriously.

Davon anxiously waited, tapping her foot on the floor. When the seconds turned into minutes, she positioned her computer on the table with hopes of getting a connection. She needed to get an email to the American Embassy in Dubai explaining her passport predicament.

She heard a click, and then Trenk came back on the line. "I'm sorry to have to tell you this Dr. Marshall, but your communication privileges are suspended."

"Suspended, what does that mean?" asked Davon, annoyed.

"You are prohibited from using the phone or internet," replied Trenk, nervously.

Davon was mystified. "My friend, I'm not sure why this has happened, but it's unacceptable. I would just like to call my parents. You've put my calls through before. Can't you help me out?"

A brief moment of silence followed. "Dr. Marshall, there are records. I can't place a long distance call. Please…"

Davon tried to control her anger. "Of course I wouldn't want to cause you any grief," she said sarcastically, not really blaming Trenk. "Would it be possible to call the hospital in Dubai and check on a patient?"

"I'm not sure…"

"Yesterday, you probably had a flu shot. Did you have one?" she asked, rudely snapping the question.

"Yes, I did," answered Trenk.

"Well, I arranged for the nurses to vaccinate everyone at the palace because there is a woman, my patient in Dubai Hospital, who is deathly ill from that exact flu! I'd like to check on her condition. Is that possible?" demanded Davon, gripping the telephone receiver angrily in her hand.

I'll put the call through," replied Trenk, his voice shaky.

When Dr. Veenn came on the line, Davon took a breath and flipped into doctor mode. "Morning Dr. Veenn, it's Dr. Marshall. I'm calling to check on Momma Ba and inquire about the results of her blood work."

"Yes, yes, I meant to call you. Your patient has been moved out of ICU, and her condition is stable. She seems to have overcome the flu, but we are having problems controlling her congestive heart failure."

"I see, so she does have congestive heart failure," commented Davon, "which is probably the reason she ran into trouble."

"Yes," agreed Dr. Veenn. "Regardless, she'll be with us until we get her medications sorted out."

"And was it influenza?" asked Davon.

"Her blood test was positive for influenza. How did the vaccination program go?" he asked.

"Very well, I think we managed to get to everyone in the palace. Thank you for sending the vaccine and for the help! The nurses were a bonus," replied Davon, thinking how fortunate it was that she had insisted on the vaccinations. When Dr. Veenn's beeper went off, the call ended.

The second Davon hung up the receiver, she quickly unplugged the telephone cord and plugged it into to her computer, hoping the line would still be active. But it wasn't. Trenk had anticipated the move. "Damn it!" she yelled, wanting to call him back and demand internet access. She smashed her fist into the desk, and then slumped back in her seat fuming! "You bastard Bedon!" she cried. She knew the order had come from him. She felt like she was in prison, a caged puppet with no free will. If she didn't conform, Bedon would take away her every liberty! "So what's next, you giant SOB BASTARD! You're afraid of me because I'm smarter than you. Well, I've got news! I'm a fighter and you aren't going to take me down!"

Standing up, she rushed to the door and opened it with a jerk, shutting it hard. A loud bang drew attention to her presence. Daring anyone to challenge her, she stomped across the foyer to the women's entrance. When the second door closed, the cool silence of the hallway calmed her somewhat, and she released a long drawn out sigh. She had to outsmart him to survive, there was no other choice!

Her first challenge was to find a phone to the outside world, next she had to get to a bank. She wished she hadn't racked up the charges at Cheri's boutique because her credit card was at its maximum. But what did that matter? The only benefit in having a clean Visa would be to pre-buy her plane ticket online, and now she couldn't even get on the internet!

Davon looked at her watch. It was getting late, and she had flu patients to check on. Suddenly, she felt awful. Many of them were really ill and in need of medical attention, and here she was wasting time worrying about herself. As a physician, she had pledged to put her patient's needs first. She pushed a strand of blond hair behind her ear, and hitched the leather strap of her bag higher on her shoulder. Listening to her blue jeans swish as she marched along, she became aware that they were wrinkled. It was a frivolous observation, but it bothered her. Smoothing down one crease she increased her gait while making a mental list of the patients she urgently needed to see. Memen was at the top of the list.

When Memen had shown up at the flu clinic with his mother yesterday, Davon had been concerned. Not only had his asthma flared up again, but he had developed a cough. After listening to his chest, she had given him the vaccination with reservations, unsure if it was too late for the serum to be effective. Thinking about this, she halted in front of his apartment and knocked.

"Docta!" cried Memen, when he looked up from his game and saw her. Jumping up, he ran to greet her. He'd been playing marbles with his brother on the floor and breathlessly raced towards her with outstretched arms. Skidding to a stop about three feet away, he looked up shyly, waiting for approval.

Davon laughed and wiggled her index finger. He approached slowly and looked up once more before gently wrapping his arms around her waist, wishing her welcome in Arabic. As she tousled his hair, she watched the younger brother dancing and twirling behind him, waiting for his turn to say hello. There was a six year difference between the two, and yet other than size they were equals. Davon wondered whether Memen's mother had been told, or had come to the realization that her eldest son was mentally challenged. Davon wasn't positive what the cause for the mental slowness was, and hadn't broached the subject because it was an extremely sensitive matter, especially because Memen was the second son, and next in line to inherit the kingdom after Hepbet. For a brief second her thoughts lingered on Hepbet, and the impact it would have on Memen, if he didn't survive. No, she reassured herself feeling protective, there's no way Bedon will hurt this little guy if he becomes the heir.

She looked down at Memen, who clung to her as though she was a possession. He was affectionate and so sweet. Davon really cared for the child. She hugged him for a few minutes and then gently pried him from her leg reaching into her bag to retrieve her stethoscope. The younger brother immediately took advantage of the three inch gap created, and squeezed in to hug the same leg. Davon rubbed his head with one hand, while she helped Memen remove his shirt with the other.

"Welcome, please, I sorry, I busy," said Tagette, running down the stairs.

"Don't worry Tagette, the boys have been entertaining me," replied Davon, enunciating her words carefully because she knew Tagette's English skills were poor. "Memen seems a bit congested. Has he had his puffer today?"

"No, tomorrow," said Tagette, pulling her youngest towards her as Davon placed the stethoscope on Memen's back.

"Memen must have his puffer every day. If you can bring the medicine to me, I will give him a dose right now," said Davon, lifting her eyebrows in frustration.

Kneeling down to listen to Memen's breath sounds, Davon was concerned. She had specifically told Tagette to give him his puffer twice a day, and to keep him away from his sick brother! Lamna had even translated so there was no excuse for her not to understand. It looked as though she was going to have to go through every step again, and explain the consequences of the boy not getting his medication. She could hear congestion in both lower lobes, yet he appeared quite happy, and twice tried to run back to where the colorful marbles lay on the floor. By the time Tagette returned with the puffer, and the younger son in tow, Memen was sitting on the carpet shooting marbles across the terra cotta tiles to Davon.

Davon took the inhaler, administered a dose, and looked up. "Tagette, for five days Memen must have his puffer two times a day. You must give the puffer twice a day, for five days, then once a day," explained Davon, holding up fingers as she spoke. "Two times a day. I will get Raja to translate."

"I understand. Two times, five days, yes?" she replied, smiling.

"That is correct. Then after five days, once per day."

"Okay," said Tagette.

"I'd like to listen to Pheely's chest, even though he looks much better," said Davon, walking towards the five year old. "How is he doing?"

"Sometimes hot, but he wants to play," answered Tagette.

His forehead was cool to the touch, and his color was good. She listened to his chest, while she watched Memen lie down on the floor and roll around. "Pheely is doing well. It looks like he has recovered from the flu. However, still keep him indoors for the rest of the week." It was too late to remind Tagette to separate the boys, so she didn't bother. "I will ask Raja to come and translate later today," she said, as she waved goodbye to the boys.

After doing four other home visits, and seeing nine patients, Davon took a side hallway to Lamna's apartment. She rehearsed the conversation she wanted to have in her head. Somehow, she had to convince Lamna to help her get to Dubai.

"Davon come in," cried Lamna, "have you had lunch?"

"Not yet, but I didn't come for food, just to ask you something," answered Davon, as Lamna ushered her into the living room.

"Don't be crazy. You have to eat, and we only finished a few minutes ago. Come and sit, I'll get you something."

Lamna turned towards the kitchen and yelled in rapid Farsi. Two servants immediately appeared with cups of tea, and platefuls of chicken, vegetables, flatbread and fruit. The oddly shaped light pink china cups and plates were asymmetrical, which gave the illusion they were on the verge of tipping over.

"Unusual looking china Lamna, I love it! And the food smells delicious, thank you," said Davon, actually feeling hungry.

"So eat, eat! You got here at a perfect time, my mother just left for the pool with Ismil, and so we can gossip!" laughed Lamna, "What happened with Hepbet? Did you see him?"

"Sashic called and I did go to his suite," she hesitated for a moment, "thanks by the way for telling her I was willing to see Hepbet," she added between mouthfuls.

"And…what did he have?" Lamna asked, leaning forward.

"I don't know. I barely got there and Dr. Rahish arrived and took Hepbet to Dubai. We'll have to wait and see," said Davon, trying to be evasive. "Anyway Lamna the reason I'm here is because I was wondering if the women went to Dubai last Thursday?"

"No, although it was the last Thursday of the month, people were getting sick, you were away, and no one really felt like going."

"Do you think it might be possible to organize a trip for next week?" asked Davon, crossing her fingers.

"Possible, but I'm not sure because the limousines are usually only available to us one day a month on…"

"I know the last Thursday of the month!" interjected Davon, "But since you didn't go last week don't you think you could ask about driving there next Tuesday, Wednesday or Thursday? The reason I'm asking is because I know the next four or five days are going to be exhausting. I've seen eleven flu patients this morning, and have seventeen more to see this afternoon, and then it will be paper work until the wee hours of the morning. I guarantee when next week rolls around, I'm going to need a break. What do you think?"

"Why don't I call the service right now, and see if there is a car available? If we can't get a car there's no point in even talking about it.

Stay here and eat. The phone is in the bedroom," yelled Lamna, dashing out of the room.

Davon smiled and congratulated herself, if anyone could get her to Dubai, it would be Lamna. But getting there was just part of the problem. The main issue was to find a way to the American Embassy. She ate another forkful of potato, and swirled it around in her mouth trying to identify the spice. Bin always made rice and vegetables with curry sauce, and lentils with chili pepper and cinnamon, but Lamna's cook had added something unusual, which gave the vegetable a totally unique flavor. Bringing the dish to her nose she inhaled deeply, the scent was pleasant, but different. Davon had no clue what the seasoning was, and was positive she had never tasted or smelt it before.

Drifting back to the cacophony of Cairo and the delicious smells of the spice market, she thought about Abdul. If only she could go back in time and alter the outcome of the trip. She should have never left him in Cairo with Bedon! The image of Abdul was so clear, it was almost frightening. She could see him lying bare-chested on the king-sized bed trying to be brave, as she meticulously sutured his wounds. His wicked, seductive smile pulled at her heart strings even now. Would she ever see him again? Feeling tears forming in the corners of her eyes, she shook her head. Fretting about Abdul and Bin and every bad thing that was happening was clouding her assessment of what she had to accomplish to get out of the country. She needed to be proactive, not melancholy! Yet, try as she might to switch to doctor mode, where nothing in her private, emotional life mattered, she began to spiral into a deep despair.

A shiver suddenly encompassed her, and almost spilling her food, Davon placed her plate on the coffee table. "The arsenic was put in Hepbet's food! It had to be," she whispered, envisioning the plot. The strong flavors the people enjoy in this part of the world would be a natural cover for the deadly toxin, and a small daily dose would bump someone off in a short period of time! It would have been very easy for Bedon to plant someone in Hepbet's household to do the dirty work, most likely someone new, someone desperate and evil enough to poison an innocent seventeen year old! She trembled again. Yet somehow, she couldn't imagine any of the servants she knew participating in such a horrible deed…but she was getting ahead of herself, she rationalized, the diagnosis of poisoning hadn't yet been confirmed. She tried to calm herself, and then thought of Pona. The new servant hired by Bedon. "Stop it!" she cried, "You're just being paranoid!"

"Whose paranoid?" asked Lamna, coming back into the living room.

"I was just talking to myself," said Davon, forcing a laugh, "How did it go with the car?"

"I was able to get one limo, and one bodyguard for next Wednesday, which means only five of us, can go. I'll call around tomorrow, and see who wants to come," she answered, sitting down beside Davon. "What are you looking for in Dubai?"

Davon was caught off-guard. "Presents for my family," she said, fibbing. "My contract will soon be up and I was thinking there might not be many more opportunities to shop." She stood and moved her plate to the hand carved tray. "Thanks for lunch, and for organizing the trip. I'm looking forward to next week."

"Oh, don't go yet, you haven't had dessert!" cried Lamna.

"I wish I could stay, but I need to finish up my home visits," replied Davon. She felt guilty that she hadn't brought up the pregnancy. She wanted to ask, really she did, but the fact was Davon wasn't ready to talk about Lamna having Abdul's child, even from a medical point of view. Giving Lamna a quick hug, Davon jogged down the hall towards the neighboring apartment.

After spending the first two months getting lost in the maze of the harem's quarters, she was now quite comfortable finding her way around. She had been in almost every apartment on the women's side, and all of the suites were exquisite. However, there was a notable difference between the apartments of the favored wives, and those that were not. Davon contemplated which suite she would have been given if she married Abdul. "Don't even go there," she said to herself, "it's not a possibility anymore!"

By the time she completed her house calls, restocked her medical bag at the clinic, and returned to her suite it was past nine o'clock. She felt tired. After politely greeting Pona at the door, she went immediately into her bedroom, stripped and headed to the shower. The warm water from the powerful jets hit her neck and shoulders, and she stood there for twenty minutes enjoying the pounding sensation. There were so many things to sort out, and while she considered her next move, she found herself again getting depressed. If she could only speak to Abdul! There had been no word, not even a note. And as far as she knew, he hadn't been in contact with any of his wives either. Although Abdul traveled frequently, he kept in touch with his favorite wives on a daily basis, or so Davon had heard, therefore one would think she'd be included in the daily phone calls. After all, he had asked her to marry him. Twice now, Lamna had mentioned in casual conversation that she hadn't been able to reach Abdul to let him know she was pregnant, and Sashic had been close to hysteria this morning, when she'd said Abdul hadn't returned her calls regarding Hepbet. Davon remembered Abdul's sincere concern for Anish when she had needed emergency surgery, and knew without question if he had been able, he would have immediately come back to the palace for Hepbet. No, she wasn't imagining things! Abdul was either dead, or a hostage in some God forsaken place!

Wandering in a zombie-like fashion past the food laden dining room table, Davon plopped down on the plush living room sofa totally lost in thought. Different scenarios played out in her mind, and she methodically worked out every pro and con before trashing each one of her plans. Every idea she came up with needed another person, an inside man. She recognized it would be impossible to get out of the country without help. Of course the logical person was Raja, she knew the palace, was in charge of organizing transportation, knew the schedules of the Prince and Bedon, and spoke the local languages, yet before she had even heard the reason why Davon had resigned and wanted to go home, she'd rebuffed her request for aid. Davon thought back on the conversation, and contemplated what she could have said or done differently.

As she stared into oblivion she unconsciously picked at the fluff on her housecoat throwing each little ball onto the recently vacuumed carpet. Raja disliked her, and there was probably nothing she could do to rectify the situation. She dropped her head to her chest in silent defeat, and racked her brains. Who else could help? Suddenly, five plates of food on a bright green placemat came into focus. Pona had moved her dinner onto the glass coffee table, and she hadn't even noticed. Turning her head towards the kitchen, she saw her servant standing at attention by the dining room door. Davon felt terrible as she looked at the pitiful sight. "Thank you Pona," she said, nicely in Farsi, "You go and have your dinner. I won't need anything else tonight." She didn't feel the least bit hungry. She was tired and discouraged. Reaching for two bananas, Davon picked up her medical bag and the patient files she had left beside the sofa. She'd catch up on her reports and read about arsenic poisoning in bed.

CHAPTER SIXTEEN

The following days were busy, and three nights in a row, she was woken to tend to youngsters with congestive, croupy coughs and raging fevers. She had to prescribe antibiotics, order humidifiers from Dubai, and bring in a nurse to take care of one of the toddlers. But all in all, most of the flu victims were on the mend. Just as her workload peaked, it rapidly tapered off, and before she realized, a week had flown by. Tomorrow was the trip to Dubai.

Unexpectedly, sleep came easily that night, and when she awoke the next morning she felt well rested. Slipping her black burka over her cotton dress, she rushed to the limousine, which was parked beside the last set of stairs to the women's quarters.

"You're late!" giggled Lamna, "We've been waiting for ten minutes!"

"Sorry," muttered Davon, as she bent over and got into the car. "I over-slept for the first time in my life. It was almost as if I had been drugged!"

The comment made the women chuckle, but Davon blanched when she thought of Hepbet. Considering she was worried about herself, Abdul, Bin, and her patients, it did seem a bit strange how deeply she had slept. Leaning back in the luxurious leather seat, she casually opened her bag and felt around the right-hand bottom for the jewelry she had stashed before going to bed. Touching the coolness of the metal, she gave a small sigh of relief as she half listened to the women nattering in Arabic. Sometimes they would throw in an English word for her benefit, but other than smiling whenever she heard her name, Davon tried to ignore the conversation. She had to focus on her plan to separate from the group.

"So the Gold Warehouse…where would you like to go, Davon? Davon?" Lamna tapped her on the shoulder.

"I was thinking about Carpet Store, the huge place, with the big yellow sign. It's the one we drive by just before the shopping district," she said, pleasantly. Davon knew there was a bank beside the store.

Lamna looked at her and smirked, "I've never been in that place, and I don't know how good it is. If you want a carpet, we should go to Carpet Baggers."

"We can go there too. But please, I really have my heart set on the store with the big welcoming yellow sign," insisted Davon, her eyes almost begging.

Lamna turned to the others. There was no objection. "I don't know why you want to go there, but alright!" she exclaimed, cheerfully.

Davon grinned. Taking a sip of bottled water, she strategized how to get from Carpet Store into the bank. The hard and fast rule was that the women always had to stay together. So, she'd have to make the decision to go into the bank sound random. It was just a coincidence that the bank, her bank, was besides the carpet warehouse-- that's what she would say. Then, she would have to act quickly before one of them grabbed onto her. There would be no sense in trying to explain, because they wouldn't understand why she needed to check on her money. None of them, Davon bet, had ever handled a dollar bill, let alone a coin. Looking out the window at the heat waves rising off the sand, she felt skeptical of the plan.

It was early October and still very hot. The car pulled slowly up to the curb, and parked under the shade of an over-sized date palm. Davon glanced out the window at their first stop, before following the lead of the others in covering her hair. The wide and immaculately maintained boulevard lined with exclusive shops was exquisite. Healthy, fully-grown trees, pots of magnificent exotic flowers, hand-carved wooden benches, and colorful, uniformed doormen adorned every entranceway.

Flinging her bulky bag over her head and to one side, Davon trailed behind the others into a modern, very large air conditioned shop. There seemed to be no end to the glass display cases filled with necklaces, earrings, rings, bracelets, and anklets, all perfectly made in twenty-four carat gold. Behind each display case stood a salesman ready to show his wares. Davon stood to the side watching as the rest of her group enthusiastically began to try on the expensive trinkets.

"Come and see this, Davon," called Lamna, wanting to include her in the excitement. "What do you think of this necklace?" she asked, dangling a gold chain with a dazzling five diamond pendent.

Davon walked over and examined the piece. "It's lovely."

"Maybe...the diamonds should be larger," said Lamna, putting the necklace around Davon's neck to view it.

"If the diamonds were bigger it might be too much. They say simple is better. However, I guess that depends on what you're looking for."

"I'm going to get it. Why don't you look for something?" she suggested, switching from English to Arabic as she turned to speak with the merchant.

"I'm not much of a jewelry person. Besides, I'm saving my money for a carpet."

"Don't be silly, you won't have to pay for the jewelry. What about this ring, it reminds me of you?"

The merchant removed the ring from the case and offered it to Davon. It was a two carat emerald embedded in a wide band. "Oh, this is really beautiful," she commented, trying it on her finger.

"Good! I'm buying it for you! Now let's find the girls and go to your carpet place." Lamna laughed, and nudged her towards the group.

When the limo parked in front of the gigantic, tacky, yellow sign with large orange Arabic symbols and the words Carpet Store in green, Davon strained to see if they were at the right place. The sign, which sagged to the left, made it appear as though the billboard was holding up the crumbling exterior. Davon opened the passenger door, and looked first at the dilapidated carpet store, and then at the neighboring Dubai Bank, whose elegant frontage dramatically contrasted the warehouse they had come to visit. The bank, built of immaculate red and gray brick with recently painted black trim around each of the tall arched windows, and two healthy cedar trees in black ceramic pots on either side of the door, beckoned one to enter. Davon mentally prepared herself.

"Oh look," she said, speaking rapidly as she pretended to just notice, "That's my bank, what a coincidence. I think I should go in and check on my account. I'll meet you guys in the carpet shop." She didn't wait for consent, but hurried quickly towards the embossed brass doors ignoring the several loud gasps.

"Davon hang on," yelled Lamna, "we're supposed to stick together! Wait!"

Disregarding the warning, she yanked the bank's door open and entered. The interior held a uniquely intimate, yet opulent appeal with an abundance of light streaming through the over-sized window panes. Gray marble pillars, white granite floors and solid granite counter tops seemed just a touch over the top. The lobby, almost empty, had a handful of male, well-dressed customers milling about. Yet, when Davon approached the counter, the lone male teller took no notice of her until she cleared her throat several times. He only glanced up briefly and then back down, pursing his lips as though she was annoying him. Upset, but trying to be patient, Davon waited, and when he looked up once again because the main door banged shut for a second time, she took advantage of the eye contact and asked, "Do you speak English?"

"I do," he answered, returning to his work.

"Excuse me, I have a lot of money at your bank and I want to withdraw some of it! Are you going to help me, or do I have to demand to see the manager?" she asked brusquely, as he continued to act as though she wasn't there.

"Davon," called Lamna softly from the entranceway, where she stood huddled with the other women.

Davon waved her hand behind her back to indicate she was in control of the situation. "You think you are embarrassed at having me come into your bank, well you haven't see anything! You better get up from your seat and get your supervisor mister, or I'm going to start yelling for assistance!"

The teller did not reply, but left his stool and proceeded into one of the back rooms. He returned a moment later with a gentleman in a dark suit.

"May I help you?" asked a kind face.

"Yes, thank you. I have a large sum of money at your bank, and I would like to withdraw some of it," said Davon, faking a smile.

"I see, perhaps we could discuss this in my office," he replied, taking a sideways glance at the customers watching them. "This way please."

He opened and held the small gate for Davon, but before she followed him she called to the girls. "You go to the carpet store. I'll catch up with you there."

They proceeded into an office which was richly furnished, cozy but not huge. He indicated a brown leather chair, pulled close to one of the over-filled bookcases, and made himself comfortable behind a massive carved wooden desk. Taking off his glasses, he took a long hard look at her getup, before he said, "So, you were saying you have a sum of money in the bank that you would like to withdraw."

"Yes," declared Davon, "I don't understand what the issue is. Your teller completely ignored me until I threatened to make a fuss."

"I apologize, Miss?"

"Dr. Davon Marshall."

"If you could give me your account number and passport, I will look into the details," he said, robotically.

"Here is my account number," answered Davon, pushing a piece of paper towards him. "I don't presently have my passport, but I have a driver's license and birth certificate. Is that sufficient?"

He stood, frowned, and began to sweep the documents into his hand. "One moment," he replied, leaving her alone.

Davon twisted the emerald ring around her finger unconsciously. She would take out five thousand in US dollars, send one thousand to Bin, buy a plane ticket for around two, and the rest she would keep for bribes. In retrospect she realized she should have looked into how much the plane ticket cost but...

"Dr. Marshall," he said.

"Yes."

"I have the information about your account." He resettled in his seat and slid her ID and account number across the desk towards her. "You have three hundred and fifty thousand dollars at our bank, however…"

"Good, I'd like to withdraw six thousand in US bills if possible," she said, interrupting. She suddenly had changed her mind about the initial figure of five in case the plane ticket cost more.

The manager sniffled, "As I was saying, you have three hundred and fifty thousand dollars in the account. However, you cannot access the money because it is in a special type of account, a holding account."

"What! You've got to be kidding!" exclaimed Davon, digging her nails into the soft leather cushion.

"I'm afraid not. Your employer has deposited fifty thousand dollars for the last seven months in an account with specific instructions. The money is held there, and will be transferred to a Bank of America, presumably to your account," he looked down at his sheet, "on February second of next year. So if there is nothing else," he murmured, standing up.

"Actually there is. I don't understand. It's my money, you've verified this and frankly I need some cash. There must be something you can do, like change the account from holding to regular. I'll sign for it, and pay any service charges."

"This can't be done, however if you would like to use the ATM machine to access your account in America, the teller will be more than happy to assist you." He moved towards the door to show her out.

She squirmed in her seat. "Are you positive? I only need six thousand dollars. It's not that much."

"Quite positive. Now if you please, Dr. Marshall," he answered, opening the door.

"Wait, I have a valuable Rolex watch that I'm willing to sell." She nervously pulled it out of her bag and offered it to him. "Or you could accept it as collateral for a loan," she added, thinking the watch had to be worth at least fifteen thousand. When she saw him recoil in abhorrence, her face fell.

"Dr. Marshall, there are money lenders in the back alleyways. I suggest you take your watch to them. Good day!" he said, sharply.

Distraught Davon walked passed him, through the gate, and up to the teller. Pulling her Bank of America card out of her wallet, she quietly said, "I'd like to withdraw nine hundred from this account, and get it in US funds."

The teller swiped her card, and offered her the hand-held machine to enter her pin number. She hesitated for a moment because she realized the withdrawal would leave her with a balance of less than one hundred dollars. It wasn't fair. The three hundred and fifty thousand was hers. She hated Bedon and his tactics! He was a cunning bastard, and had purposely set up the account this way to trap her, to keep her under his thumb until he was ready to release her! Without access to her money, she was putty in his murderous hands!

Without making eye contact, the teller left his stool and returned, laying nine, one hundred brand new US bills on the counter. Davon snatched the money and turned, surprised to see the women standing together in exactly the same place franticly whispering. Plastering on a smile she approached. "Thanks for waiting, but you didn't have too."

"Yes, we did Davon, because we are supposed to stay together! We only have one bodyguard today, and he can't be in two places," exclaimed Lamna.

Davon bit her lip, "Sorry, it was important for me to check on my account."

"Never mind, I liked coming into the bank. This is the first time I have ever been in one," said Pipa.

"Me too," said Frane. The others nodded.

"Well, I guess it's a first for all of us. Is your money safe?" inquired Lamna, giggling.

"It's not funny when you are responsible for your own welfare, Lamna." replied Davon briskly, yanking the door open.

"Why don't you get married?" asked Pipa.

"In the Western world women usually work, even if they are married, and even if they have children." They walked over to the carpet store, and Davon paused in front feeling completely deflated. "We don't have to look at carpets. I spent a lot of time in the bank, and its past lunchtime. We should go to the restaurant."

"But I'm looking for a new carpet for my bedroom," whined Lamna, "Come on, we're already here."

The plywood door creaked and a small bell tinkled when they opened it. Following the others, Davon slipped through the unsafe entranceway into a colossal warehouse filled with mounds of carpets of every imaginable size. They were beautiful, thick rugs made of wool and silk blends, hundreds of colors and patterns, and piled in groups according to length and width.

The bell must have alerted the owner because within milliseconds he was at their side promoting his most expensive wares. He spoke rapidly, smiling and gesturing towards several groups of carpets, and although Davon couldn't understand a word, she recognized the samples he was showing them were of very high quality. As the bodyguard hovered at the doorway, the women worked their way around the room, pointing at carpets. Numerous attendants who had suddenly appeared from the back, hauled out the selected ones, from the top, middle, or bottom of the heap.

Davon hung back as she had done in the jewelry shop, but this time trembling with rage. Although she had managed to get to the bank, she was still without enough money to get home. She needed an ally, a collaborator, someone she could borrow money from. She mentally ran through the list of everyone she had met since she had arrived in the country as possible candidates, including Cheri and Amelia Tucker. All were women except for Abdul, Hepbet, Jack the helicopter pilot, and of course Mr. Bedon. As far as she was concerned, the harem women were powerless, there was no way to contact Cheri or Amelia, and she had blown it with Raja. Her thoughts lingered for a moment on Hepbet and his mother. Davon had gone out on a limb explaining her suspicion of poison to Sashic in an effort to save Hepbet's life. Because Sashic was the first women Abdul had married, she was more mature than any of women Davon was here with today, and she owed Davon a favor. If Davon found some way to get a hold of her, would she help? As she stood overwhelmed by racing thoughts, Davon ran her hand back and forth across a white, red and blue carpet flung atop a large heap in front of her.

"The boy's saying there is a matching one that's a bit smaller. Do you want to see it Davon?" called Lamna.

Suddenly coming back into the world, Davon looked at Lamna and at the little boy trying to get her attention. He was no older than five years of age. Skinny and dressed in an over-sized white cotton shirt with both sleeves rolled up at least three times, he was jumping up and down waving at her from the other side of the pile.

Davon laughed. "Tell him I'll look at it." The child was so adorable and enthusiastically trying to get her attention, she didn't have the heart to hurt his feelings.

Both carpets the youngster proudly displayed were wool, one approximately nine by twelve, the other five by seven. They had white backgrounds boasting red and blue flowers. When Davon actually examined them, she realized how wonderful they would look with her most prized possession, her grandmother's antique sofa. She figured the boy was telling her what a good price he would give her, and Davon couldn't help but laugh at his determination. "A born salesman", she sighed, "if things were different I'd buy the carpet, but right now I have much bigger issues! How can I explain that to you?"

"I can't believe it! I've found the exact carpet I want!" said Lamna, coming over to where Davon was standing. "If it wasn't for you, I never would have come into this dumpy store! They have an unbelievable stash of gorgeous carpets. Are you getting those?" Lamna glanced at the carpets the boy was displaying.

Davon shrugged.

"Pipa and I are getting our carpets sent to the palace, but if you want those two," she said, pointing at the new addition the young child was dragging on top of the bigger one, "then I suggest you have them sent to the States. All you have to do is write down your address in Boston, and I'll give it to the owner."

"But…"

Lamna rolled her eyes. "Don't even mention the price, it's taken care of! I just have to explain to the owner what we want him to do. Write down your address at the desk over there," she said, leaving Davon as she hurried to the dusty counter in the middle of the warehouse.

"You take?" the boy asked in Farsi.

"Yes, I take," replied Davon, returning his dazzling smile.

They dined at the same restaurant where Abdul had taken Davon on their first date. Being there with four of his wives made Davon feel uneasy and she was glad that Lamna dominated the conversation, cheerfully telling the others about the unusual luncheon at the Dubai ski hill.

"Speaking of interesting places in Dubai, do any of you know where the American Embassy is?" interjected Davon.

"I think it's on the opposite side of the city, why?" asked Pipa.

Davon flushed, cringing inside. "I thought it might be nice to see it before I leave. Maybe we could drive by."

Her suggestion was met with silence.

Finally, Lamna said something. "We're not American Davon, and it wouldn't be right for us to go to the American Embassy. People recognize us, even if we are in burkas, and they recognize the car. It's one thing to go to a tourist attraction, but completely different to go to an embassy."

"I'm sorry, I didn't understand," answered Davon, hopelessly discouraged. "Maybe I could grab a taxi and rendezvous with you at the next shopping spot… I don't mind going on my own."

Lamna reached out and grabbed her arm. "It wouldn't be safe for you to go alone. Women here travel in groups. You'll have to stay with us. Only one more stop, and we'll be on our way home anyway," she said with compassion, when she noticed Davon was upset.

The journey home seemed to take forever. All of her companions nodded off while Davon pressed her forehead into the window feeling nothing but disappointment and bitterness. There had been two opportunities where she could have gotten away, one at the restaurant when she had exited the washroom ahead of everyone else, and the second at a fabric shop, where she could have slipped out an open side door. However, like a fool she had hesitated, and both opportunities had been lost.

By the time they reached the palace it was dark. Lamna linked arms with Davon and walked her to her suite, humming as they made their way up the stairs. "Are you alright?" she asked, once they were alone.

"I'm fine," said Davon. "I'm mainly tired and upset about losing Bin.

Does Bedon do this to you; send your servant away for no reason?"

Lamna gripped both of her shoulders firmly. "Bin was only a servant, why are you so upset? Did you not get a replacement?"

"I did get a replacement and she seems nice, but I want Bin. You have to understand it's been hard for me to learn the way things are done here. I miss my family and I'm lonely. Bin was like a mother," muttered Davon, starting to tear. "Don't get me wrong, I'm grateful for you Lamna, you've been wonderful to me, but I want to go home…"

"You only have a few more months to go, you'll get through it," replied Lamna, hugging her.

"Lamna, could I ask you to give something to Bin? I want to give her money," said Davon, pulling the nine hundred dollars from her bag. "Can you get this to her?"

"Oh, I can only do my best," answered Lamna, pausing for a moment. "You realize some of it will have to be used for bribes."

"That's okay, as long as most of the money gets to her."

Lamna hugged her again. "You're a thoughtful person, Davon. Don't forget we're friends. You're not alone, I'm here for you!"

"I know," whispered Davon, wishing she could come clean about the real problem she was facing.

At precisely eight-thirty the next morning Raja appeared at her door, noticeably distressed. "Dr Marshall," she said, the second she saw her. "You went to Dubai yesterday without permission."

"I didn't realize I needed permission. It's never been required before."

"You're not to leave the palace grounds again, without asking."

"Why, did something happen? Did someone need medical treatment?" inquired Davon, angrily.

Raja refused to answer the questions, "Your excursions have been cancelled by Mr. Bedon, and he won't be happy to learn you went to Dubai with the harem."

"So, Mr. Bedon is here, at the palace?" Davon was fishing for information.

"The Prince and Mr. Bedon are out of the country."

"Well then, Mr. Bedon doesn't need to know I went to Dubai," she exclaimed, pushing her way around the interpreter into the hall. She felt upset with the reminder that Abdul was out of the country, yet was glad Bedon was gone.

"Wait!" called Raja, "I've been asked to tell you something else."

Davon stopped and turned back. "What is it?" she said sternly, feeling quite incensed at Raja and the rules.

"I'm not sure why Sashic wants you to know, but Hepbet the heir has died." She choked on the words and then hung her head. Davon thought she heard a sob.

Instantly at her side, Davon cried out, "No! Tell me what happened!"

"I cannot. Please say nothing about this to anyone!" commanded Raja, quickly gaining control of her emotions. Spinning on her heels, she left, abandoning Davon to deal with the news on her own.

Poor Sashic, Davon thought, as she unconsciously leaned against the wall. She stood motionless, feeling completely overcome with sadness. Her bag slipped from her shoulder, and fell to the floor, and she let it go, staring straight ahead at the wall, but seeing nothing. Bits of information regarding Sashic's deceased sons floated through her mind. Tilly, Abdul's firstborn and older brother to Hepbet, had died at age sixteen in a riding accident. She had heard the boy had been riding one of his father's most valuable, but jittery stallions, and had fallen when the horse suddenly reared. The boy had died instantly at the scene from a broken neck. Abdul, totally distraught had ordered the horse to be killed, a stallion he had purchased for three million dollars. Davon compared Tilly's death with Hepbet's, questioning whether the fall had been an accident. Horses like people could be given stimulants, and a jumpy horse? That would certainly add fuel to the flame, causing an already anxious animal to become completely out of control! She clenched her fists and grimaced, it couldn't be a coincidence that Tilly and Hepbet, both heirs to the kingdom, passed away at approximately the same age, it just couldn't.

Now more than ever, Davon was convinced Hepbet had been poisoned. Usually, her instincts were correct in regards to medical diagnoses, but somehow she had to get in touch with Sashic to confirm, find out if it was poison, and then maybe….maybe what? Her thoughts raced in a million directions. Finding out the truth wouldn't bring Hepbet back, and if she dug deeper or implied that Bedon was involved, and he found out, she was sure he wouldn't hesitate to kill her! She trembled involuntarily. Two murders, possibly three, if Abdul didn't turn up, and this might only be the tip of the iceberg. Who else had Bedon bumped off in his quest for money and power? She shook her head and tried to get a grip on the reality of the situation. She was treading in unknown waters in a sinking dinghy, and the cloak and dagger secrets she kept stumbling upon were things that would eventually drag her down. Grabbing at her stomach, Davon felt the acid churning. She had a terrible feeling that something else, something more horrendous was about to happen.

A door down the hall creaked open, and she jumped. Tensing, she held her breath and listened for the direction of the footsteps. The sound moved away, dissipating, and Davon relaxed. She wasn't prepared to chitchat and act as though it was just another day. She needed time to prepare herself. Reviewing the facts again, Davon came to the conclusion that Raja definitely had to suspect something. When she had sputtered out the news about Hepbet, she had seemed truly upset, but also nervous. Her breathing had become hard, and she had trembled, wringing her scarf with both hands as though she was trying to wipe them clean. She had looked at the floor, not at Davon, and hurried swiftly away after spilling the news, as if she was hiding some truth. Davon wondered if Raja was involved.

Unsure of what to do, Davon realized she had to be smart and not tip her hand too soon. Like detective stories, the culprit is always the person you least suspect. It was totally possible that Raja was in cahoots with Bedon, since they definitely had similar personalities and both craved power. Yet, for some reason Davon didn't think Bedon would include a woman in his scheme. He was a misogynist, and had no need of the weaker sex. Her thoughts then swung in another direction. If they weren't working together, then perhaps Raja had accidently stumbled on Bedon's diabolical plan, had ignored the evidence, and now that Hepbet was dead, she felt guilt ridden.

Davon waffled back and forth for some time, but in the end decided to not tell a living soul what she had uncovered. Her safety was now in jeopardy, and the best scenario would be to wait and watch for at least another week. As painful as it would be, she'd have to carry-on business as usual, gathering information and proof until she was prepared to make her move. Feeling more decisive, Davon forced herself to remain calm, and make her way to her first home visit. She assumed the women in the harem would be told, maybe even today, about the death of Hepbet, and she intended to critically examine each and every reaction. As she walked, she thought about the women. Although it was highly unlikely that any of them were involved in the poisoning, anyone with a male child had to be a suspect! Now that Hepbet was dead, that made eleven year old Memen the heir. His mother Tagette was quiet, inept and not exactly the type of person to plan a murder. But one never knew! Davon walked on auto-pilot, deep in contemplation.

All of a sudden, she was at the door of the apartment she was planning to visit. Pressing the doorbell, she smiled. "Morning, I'm here to see the babies." The servant nodded and directed her towards the luxurious staircase.

The first object Davon noticed when she reached the top of the stairs was a dozen or so long-stemmed red roses in a beautiful hand cut crystal vase. They had been placed on a side table, which hugged the wall between the children's doorway and another. Very interesting, thought Davon as she walked over to examine them. She recalled the pink roses Abdul had sent her in Cairo when he had bailed on their dinner date. Was it possible that he sent these? Eyeing a hand written note, she picked it up and scanned it. It was written in Arabic. "Damn it," she said under her breath, suddenly aware the servant was watching her. Trying to cover-up her behavior, she put down the card, and returned to the entrance of the boy's room, exclaiming in half English, half Farsi, how beautiful the roses were. The servant nodded and moved away, and Davon turned into the nursery hoping nothing would be mentioned to Nisha.

She recalled that Nisha had just gotten back to the palace, so maybe these were welcome home flowers. But who had sent them? Although she wanted them to be from Abdul, because that would mean he was safe, she couldn't handle the thought of him sending flowers to one of his wives. Davon felt a twinge of unwanted jealousy. As she entered the room, the gurgling and cooing of one baby could be heard. Davon was glad of the distraction when she looked down upon the infant. She loved children, especially babies. Examining the first born of Nisha's twins, Davon playfully tickled his foot, laughing when the child smiled, and giggled in response. At almost seven months of age he was not only heavier than his brother, teetering on plump, he was also much more alert. She politely addressed the nannies and then walked over to the other cradle, comparing the eldest to the second born. Her thoughts returned to Memen and his mental insufficiency. Could it be genetic? While it was still too early to tell, she had a strong inkling there was something wrong with the second little boy she gazed upon.

The twins looked identical. Facial features and coloring were the same, and they were similar in length, which indicated they were growing at a comparable pace. Yet, unlike his brother, the second born was two pounds lighter. He remained almost placid when she tickled his foot, and when she examined him, he didn't return her smile. As she listened to the musical murmurings of the first, she continued to observe the silent second twin, all the time running through the DNA tests she'd like to order.

"How wonderful to see you, you're terribly efficient, we only got back yesterday. So how are my boys?" asked Nisha, noticing Davon's blank, serious look.

"Oh Nisha, I didn't hear you come in." She mustered a smile. "They're very handsome children," she answered, knowing it wouldn't be prudent to tell Nisha about her concerns. "I hope I haven't come too early, I wanted to call on my healthy patients before I see my patients with the flu. How was your trip?"

"Good, my parents were very happy to see the children. It wasn't too hot, so we spent a lot of time outdoors. It was just nice to be home. I miss my mother particularly, and would have stayed longer if it wasn't for…" Davon held her breath waiting for Nisha to say something about Abdul or Hepbet, but it didn't happen. "…my parents having to go off on a trip to see my brother! Apparently they had planned the vacation a long time ago, but had forgotten to tell me."

"Humm," said Davon, interested to understand why Nisha seemed to have so much more freedom than the other women. "Where do your parents live?"

"They have a small palace not far from Dubai. But when I visit, the helicopter takes me directly there, so the trip is relatively easy."

"That's fantastic, especially when you have to travel with these two little guys," she paused before adding, "Do you always go on your own, or does the Prince go with you?" Not looking directly at Nisha, she walked over to pick up Kal, the first born, who suddenly started fussing.

"He has," replied Nisha, guardedly.

The nanny approached and took the child from her, and Davon feeling the coolness of Nisha's response, decided to change the subject. "When you were away everyone in the palace got a flu vaccination. I imagine you have heard how sick some people were, and that Momma Ba had to be hospitalized."

"Yes, that was part of the reason I went home. But everyone is better now, are they not?"

"Much better, yet it's still important for anyone who has not had the flu, to be inoculated. I've brought flu vaccine to give to your family, and servants today, if it's alright with you."

"Whatever you think, Davon. Let me call the servants," answered Nisha, appearing very concerned. "Where would you like to do the procedure?"

"The living area would be a fine. I only need a small table and one chair. And Nisha don't worry, it's really a simple thing," answered Davon, reassuringly.

Thirty minutes later Davon completed the inoculations. As she tidied up her work station, she dwelt on her conversation with Nisha. It was obvious Nisha didn't know about Hepbet, her behavior indicated she probably wasn't even aware of his hospitalization. Considering she was a favored wife it could only mean one thing--she hadn't been in contact with Abdul. Davon lifted the small drop leaf table and placed it against the wall, pausing for a moment to look up the staircase to see if Nisha was still nearby. There was a favor she wanted to ask.

Suddenly, she caught a glimpse of Nisha on the landing, and before completely thinking about the ramifications, Davon called out. "Nisha, could I speak with you for a moment?" Nisha paused on the top stair delicately stroking the carved banister, listening. "I don't know if you've heard, but Mr. Bedon has cancelled my telephone privileges, and although I want to call my parents in the States, I can't. I hate to ask, but is there any way I could use your cell phone?"

"I'm sorry my cell phone range doesn't include North America."

"Oh," answered Davon, frowning. "I haven't been able to contact my parents for such a long time, and when you started talking about your folks, well it made me think of them."

Nisha's rigid stance softened. "Why don't we phone your parents from here? I'll tell the communications department to put the call through, just write down the number for me so I don't mess it up."

"You can do that? You can make a long-distance call from your suite?"

"Of course, come with me," said Nisha, directing her to the bedroom.

"Raja is such a jerk," said Davon under her breath, as she bolted up the stairs. Why would she lead me to believe long distance calls had to be made at the communications center? With a sense of urgency, she ran behind Nisha into the bedroom.

Because it was very possible the call would be monitored, Davon realized she would have to be careful how she told her parents she was in trouble. She quickly planned what she would say as Nisha ordered the call to be put through. The best idea she had to communicate her problem was "cabbage". This was a secret family word, which meant "high alert". Davon's father, who had worked in the military, had created the word when she and Meg were little. It was a word that immediately initiated action, if said by parents or children. Davon had used it only once when she had been seven years old. She had been playing at a friend's house when the girl's nine year old brother grabbed her, and kissed her on the mouth. Terrified, Davon ran to the phone, called home, and yelled the word cabbage several times when her mother answered. Within minutes, her Dad was at the house to rescue her. Davon felt emotional as she relived the event. She knew her father wouldn't physically be able to come and save her this time, after all, he was almost seventy-five.

As she listened to Nisha argue with the communications department, she rethought her plan. Maybe it was a mistake to inform her parents. She didn't want to cause them grief, but her father was the only person in the world who would understand the meaning of the message she was trying to convey, and if this was her only chance to let someone know she was in danger...

She still hadn't decided what she was going to do when the receiver was thrust into her hand. "Mom, it's Davon, sorry to wake you."

"Honey, I'm glad you called. Dad and I were talking about you last night. Three and a half months and you'll be coming home," said Davon's mother, cheerfully.

"That's why I'm calling," Davon paused for a moment. "I might be staying another year."

"You can't be serious? Just a minute, I want to get your father on the phone. Pete, its Davon, she wants to stay and do another year."

On the extension, Davon's father who was slightly deaf yelled, "Davon Marshall, you better think this out clearly, I thought you were coming home to complete your studies in Pediatrics? You shouldn't postpone it for another year."

"That was the plan Dad, but things have kind of changed," said Davon, sadly.

"What do you mean Sweetheart?" asked her father, lightening his tone.

"Well, I have an amazing opportunity here to make money, even though I really miss everything at home, especially both of you, and Meg, and food like cabbage."

"Cabbage?" said her mother, quickly exchanging a serious look with her husband.

"Yes, you know how much I love cabbage, and I don't think it grows here. I miss cabbage so much it's scary."

"When you get home I'll serve you a big plate of cabbage," said her mother, emphasizing the word. "In the mean time, if you can't come home, then maybe Dad and I will come for a visit."

"I wish you could, but they don't allow visitors at the palace, and I'm not sure if I could meet you in Dubai for a holiday because I am usually on call here 24/7. Not that I'm working all the time, but I have to be available for emergencies. The only time I get away is the last Thursday of every month. The other women and I go to the shopping district of Dubai for the afternoon. If there is something that you would like Mom, I'll buy it and send it to you."

"Let me think about it, Davon."

"How can we get a hold of you? Do you have a private number where we can call, or leave a message?" asked Pete.

"Not really, the palace is way out in the desert. It's like I told you before, I can only call you through the communications department. The call is monitored and totally organized for me. I guess you could say I'm quite pampered. Anyway, I have to go, but I'll try and call again soon. Please eat some cabbage and think of me," said Davon, fighting the urge to cry.

When she hung up the phone, Davon heard a second click. The call had been recorded. She turned to Nisha feeling embarrassed at the tears welling in her eyes. "They're doing well. I get a little homesick when I hear their voices. Thanks so much Nisha for getting the communications department to put through the call."

"Anytime. I don't understand why you can't call from your room. I'll speak to Abdul about it, when I finally get a hold of him! Did I hear your parents may come for a visit?" she asked.

"They mentioned something about coming, but my Dad is in his seventies and suffers badly from arthritis, and honestly I think it's too long of a trip for him. Mom is quite a bit younger. However, she would never come without him. And the other problem is I'm really on call every day.

I'd have zero time to spend with them." Davon had perked up at Nisha's slip of information about Abdul. She was dying to ask when she last spoke to him. Instead, they made small talk about the weather as they walked side by side down the stairs towards the hall door. Nisha seemed talkative, a touch more friendly. When Davon put her hand on the doorknob, she turned back. "It was such a surprise to find out you can make long distance calls from your room, is there any chance you can also hook up to the internet?"

"I don't think so. It was nice to see you Davon, next time let's have tea," said Nisha.

CHAPTER SEVENTEEN

"Something is not right, Pete. She used the word cabbage four times. We have to fly there immediately," said Anne, pacing back and forth. "I can book tickets, and we'll need to get the passports from the safety deposit box…."

"Hold on Anne, we need to think this out. Davon was trying to tell us what the problem is. It seems to me that for some reason, she's not being allowed to leave the country. Maybe she tried to quit, and they wouldn't let her. I find it a bit odd that she would call, and say she might stay another year with only three months and a bit left in her contract, and interlaced the conversation with the word cabbage," said Pete, sinking into a large wing-back chair by the bed. "She was warning us not to try and come to the palace. She also let it slip that the phone calls are monitored, therefore the reason for the cryptic message. She's is allowed to go to Dubai on the last Thursday of every month, so that gives us two weeks before she is back in Dubai, where there's an American Embassy. Smart girl, she gave us a lot of information, which to an eavesdropper would seem upbeat and normal."

"You got all of that out of the conversation?"

"What did you think I did for a living?" Pete asked good naturedly, but with a look of concern for their daughter. "You forget decoding was a big part of my work. That's exactly what Davon was telling us. Before we book any flights, let me call some people at the Pentagon."

"I know you had a top secret job, even though you tried to keep it from me Pete, but do you still have connections at the Pentagon? I mean, it's been ten years and the people you worked with are mostly likely retired too," said Anne, feeling distressed.

"Not everyone. Remember David Whiting? He was brilliant, young, and about twenty-five when he was my assistant. I recently read in the paper that he has been appointed ambassador to Britain."

"Britain is a long way from your daughter!"

"To a civilian maybe, but in our world there are no boundaries. Let me give him a call before we panic. In hind sight, I should have phoned David before Davon left! You call Meg on the cell, and tell her we need to have an emergency family meeting today."

A huge weight felt as though it had been lifted off her shoulders. Her parents had definitely gotten the message that something was wrong, and just knowing they knew she was in trouble made her feel better. As she scurried down the hallway towards Momma Ba's apartment she rehashed the conversation and hoped her parents weren't overly excited. Her father would be fine; it was her mother she was concerned about. Anne was a classic worrier.

The servant led her towards the end of the hall, and knocked gently on the bedroom door before opening it. Momma Ba lay in the middle of a double bed propped up on pillows with flashy magazines and leather bound books surrounding her. Her face looked thinner and slightly haggard, yet her cheeks were pink and her eyes appeared bright and lively.

Davon greeted her in Farsi as she approached the bed, and Momma Ba smiled and stretched out both her arms in welcome. Her hands shook when Davon reached for them, and although there was strength in her grasp, Davon noticed the tremors lasted for several minutes. Taking her stethoscope out of her bag she indicated with hand gestures that she needed Momma Ba to lean forward. Momma Ba giggled, and slowly, but awkwardly did as she was asked. Rubbing the end of the stethoscope to warm it, Davon slipped the hub down the neck-line of the night dress, and had just started to listen when Momma Ba's daughter burst into the room.

"Sorry, I was not here to greet you, Dr. Marshall," said Zata.

Davon held up a finger requesting for her to wait a moment while she completed the examination. "Thanks, I was in the middle of checking your mother's breathing and missed what you said."

"I said I would have been here to greet you if I had known what time you were coming. I apologize. How is she?"

"She's doing well. However, there is still a bit of congestion in her right lung so it's important to get her to move around and cough up the mucus. Is she getting out of bed?" asked Davon, feeling for Momma Ba's pulse.

"She can get up to go to the bathroom, but needs help."

"I would suggest she gets up for fifteen minutes, three times a day. She can sit in a chair here or in the living room, and have her meals. As she gets stronger we'll increase the amount of time. I'm going to give her some medicine for the congestion. Can you tell her I'm very happy with her progress?"

Zata translated and Momma Ba produced a huge grin, talking and pointing at the night stand. Walking over to it, Zata pulled opened the dark mahogany drawer and took out a flat purple velvet box. She handed it to Davon. "This is for you from Momma Ba."

"Oh my goodness," exclaimed Davon, opening the box to see a three inch thick, embossed, gold bracelet embedded with precious stones.

"It belonged to my grandmother and is over one hundred years old. You saved my mother's life and we are both grateful," said Zata, as she removed the bracelet, released the clasp, and placed it on Davon's wrist.

"I'm speechless, thank you," said Davon, squeezing Momma Ba's hand politely. She actually felt quite awful taking the priceless antique away from the family, but knew better than to refuse the gift. "Let me check her blood pressure and then I'd like to see how she does standing. Would it be possible for you to arrange for the servants to get her up please, Zata?" The bracelet felt heavy as she wrapped the blood pressure cuff around Momma Ba's upper arm.

"Never off," said Momma Ba, patting Davon's arm, "Okay?"

"So you do speak English, Momma Ba," said Davon, laughing.

"No Anglish," she giggled, "Never off." Momma Ba pointed to the bracelet.

"I understand. I won't take off the bracelet, unless it's absolutely necessary, okay?"

"Okay," echoed Momma Ba, looking pleased.

Just as she finished taking the blood pressure, three servants appeared with Zata. "Are you ready to watch Momma Ba get out of bed?"

"Yes, I'm ready. Are you ready Momma Ba?" Davon teased, moving to the bottom of the bed.

With a huge smile, Momma Ba waved away the servants. Swinging her legs over the edge of the bed, she sat. The exertion was taxing and her breathing immediately became labored, however pushing away from the bed, she managed to stand on her own.

"Good work, Momma Ba! Please tell her she's amazing Zata, but I don't want her to overdo it. Baby steps, a little more each day and within ten days, I guarantee she will be back to her usual routine. How is everyone else in the family?"

"We are all fine. Little Bini's cough is finally gone. I think the antibiotics did the trick. Do you want to see the grandchildren?" asked Zata.

"Not today, I'll be back tomorrow to see everyone. Please thank Momma Ba again for the bracelet, and tell her I'll treasure it forever!" Davon exhaled deeply as she left the suite. It was these people she would miss, so warm, caring and generous, they almost made-up for the horrible Bedon. Jiggling the bracelet, she held up her arm to really examine it. Diamonds, emeralds and rubies, some very large, were embedded in the engraved gold. It had to be worth a fortune.

The next few days Davon threw herself into her work. She did home visits in the morning, going back to her suite at noon for a quick shower, change of clothes and lunch, then she'd leave for the medical clinic where she would attend to the typical walk-in type of ailments until dinner time. Life had settled back into a rhythm. The flu victims dramatically improved, and the unbearable hot weather, and the accompanying unladylike sweating, abated. If Davon could have forgotten the tragic events of the previous weeks, she would have been happy.   But she couldn't allow herself the luxury of becoming lax, lulled by the daily routines. The stress of constantly watching, observing, and planning was starting to have its toll. No one mentioned Hepbet's death, and Davon wondered why the harem hadn't been informed. There certainly had to be some type of funeral, or mourning period. She found the whole incident very disturbing.

Yet, it wasn't the only bizarre occurrence. Raja had stopped coming by in the morning to escort her to the clinic, and hadn't paged or called her. Although occasionally Raja missed a day, she had never missed a week. At first Davon was pleased because she was tired of the chastisements. But by the sixth day, she was worried that Raja too had disappeared! What added to her anxiety was the phone call she had made to Raja that afternoon from the medical clinic. There had been no answer. Raja always picked up on the first ring. She finally decided she had no choice, but to go to Lamna.

Davon had just placed her medical bag down in her bedroom, and was concocting a story to tell Lamna, when her pager went off. Before Davon even had a chance to get to the phone in the living room, it started to ring. She picked up the receiver, and immediately rolled her eyes wondering why she had been so concerned. "Slow down Raja, I can't understand a word you're saying. What?"

"It's an emergency!   I'm coming to get you now!" yelled Raja, talking so quickly she was slurring her words together.

Davon had just pulled the receiver away from her ear when she heard the loud click of it being slammed down. Jogging back into her bedroom, she grabbed her medical bag, and had barely returned to the living room when she heard a desperate pounding at the door.

"I'll get it Pona," she called, when the servant appeared.

She opened the door, and Raja yelled two words. "Follow me!"

Davon did follow, her bag swinging wildly as they ran down a flight of stairs, crisscrossed hallways, and down a second flight of stairs to a covered courtyard, a place where she had never been.   Tiny beads of sweat glistened on her forehead, and she felt her palms becoming sticky. The door, which they stood before looked exactly like the door to her suite, nevertheless Davon was nervous. Something wasn't quite right. Raja was acting completely out of character. She was anxious, jittery, and kept taking sideway glances at Davon as she fumbled her keys trying to open the door. Was this a trap? Was Raja luring her here to lock her in the basement? Davon took two steps back toward the staircase while she cautiously eyed Raja struggling to work the lock. Sensing movement, Raja abruptly turned and faced her.

It was noon. Pete sat in the leather wing-backed chair drumming his fingers on the coffee table reading his notes.

"Dad what is it? What's the problem?" asked Meg, raising her voice when she noticed him getting his glazed over look, the look he got when he was deep in thought. She figured he had forgotten she and Matt were sitting on the love seat waiting to hear the reason for the emergency meeting.

"Oh, yes, when your mother gets back," Pete replied, not looking up.

"Mom, get in here!" yelled Meg. "I have to get back to work, and I'm sure Matt does too. What is going on Dad? Is Davon okay?" She glanced at Matt sitting beside her in his work clothes. He looked great in his manly checked flannel shirt, jeans and work boots. She still didn't understand why he had broken up with Davon.

Anne scurried into the living room carrying a wooden tray with drinks and a plate of sandwiches. "Sorry dear, I wanted to make lunch for you and Matt since I figured you wouldn't have time to get something before going back to work."

"Thanks," they chimed together, reaching for sandwiches as Anne made herself comfortable on the sofa.

"Alright, to answer your question Meg, Davon does appear to be in some sort of trouble," said Pete, launching into the story of the early morning phone call. "I was able to get a hold of one of my Pentagon assistants, David Whiting, who is now the chief of staff at the embassy in London, England. Luckily for us, he took my call. He gave me the name of a guy at the Dubai embassy that may be able to help. I called, but wasn't able to get a hold of him yet. In the meantime, my friend recommends that someone fly to Dubai," Pete paused, and looked from Meg to Matt.

"If you are suggesting I make the trip Pete, count me in. But how do I find Davon?" asked Matt, leaning forward.

"I'm willing to go Dad, there is no way I'm letting you or Mom make the trip," added Meg, putting her half-eaten sandwich down on the table.

"I thought I would...."

"Pete! Don't even go there. We discussed this and you're not going! Your father won't admit that he is old, and riddled with arthritis," Anne turned and looked at him lovingly. "Honey, think about it. When you were at the Pentagon you never would have sent an old, arthritic agent into the field. You'll stiffen up on the flight, and won't be able to walk for a week!"

"I know Anne; stop throwing my arthritis in my face!"

"Dad, this is about Davon!" Megan nervously shoved a piece of blond hair behind her ear. "I'll go, I'm her sister. It should be me."

"I'll go with you Meg," said Matt, patting her hand in an attempt to calm the situation down. "Pete, how about if Meg and I fly to Dubai to do the ground work, and you stay put in the States as the contact, go-to person?"

Davon tensed, locking eyes with Raja and held her bulky bag close to her chest as though it was a shield.

"Please, Dr. Marshall I need help, it's my mother!" cried Raja, her bossy self completely deflated.

The door sprung open as she spoke, and beyond Raja Davon saw a spacious living room tastefully furnished. An anxious servant hovered by the wall. Giving a small sigh of relief, Davon let down her guard, the emergency she'd been called to was legitimate. She followed Raja into the suite, and down a hallway towards a bedroom. When they entered, she noticed three servants surrounding the queen-sized bed. Raja briskly ordered them away, and motioned for Davon to come to the bedside. As she looked down, she saw someone who looked familiar, a woman probably in her early fifties, notably disorientated, and picking at her bed sheets. Her flawless skin was very dry. She had cracked lips, and slightly labored breathing. Davon felt her forehead--no fever. "Give me some background, what happened? How long has she been like this?" she asked, grabbing her stethoscope from her bag.

"It's the same thing Hepbet had? She's going to die?" said Raja, tearfully.

Davon paused and looked at Raja feeling no pity. "Get a grip Raja! I need some history. What happened?"

"She was fine, maybe a little more tired, I don't know. She complained of stomach pain and wasn't eating much. She said she was more thirsty than hungry. I told her to go see you, but she wouldn't, and then tonight her servant found her like this!" Raja let out a loud sob.

"Ask the servant if she's been peeing more than usual? Having to get up several times in the night?" Davon checked her blood pressure and pulse rate, ignoring the banter in the background.

"Yes," said Raja. "The servant said Mother was getting up almost every hour to urinate."

Davon pulled a little apparatus out of her bag. "I'm going to poke your mother's finger because I need a blood sample. Please hold her hand for me like this, and don't let her pull away."

Expertly poking the patient's baby finger, Davon turned the hand over smearing a drop of blood onto a cartridge, which she then inserted into a small machine. The glucometer muttered for a few seconds, and then buzzed loudly flashing a number.

"Your mother is diabetic, Raja. Is there anyone else in your family who has diabetes?" asked Davon.

Raja appeared surprised. "Her mother did, I think, but she died a long time ago. So you're saying it's definitely not what Hepbet had?"

"I'm positive. Right now your mom's blood sugar is extremely high, and that's causing the confusion. She needs some insulin immediately, but it's in the fridge at the clinic," explained Davon, "I'll run and get it." Repacking her medical bag and slinging it over her shoulder, she jogged out of the room.

The US Embassy was in an exclusive part of Dubai built on a man-made finger of land extending out into the Persian Gulf. Although they sat facing an amazing view, neither one of them noticed. Jet-lagged and blurry-eyed, Megan and Matt sat in matching chairs, in front of the diplomat's desk while he searched for Davon's file. He was about fifty years of age and balding, but he had a genuine smile, and his green eyes sparkled when he spoke.

"I didn't expect you so soon. Just talked with your father a couple of days ago, and as I told him..." Ted slapped a pink file folder on his desk. "there's not much in the file. I actually have no record of your sister, Davon Laura Marshall, entering the country."

Meg grimaced. "I'm not sure I understand why the American Embassy would have a record of that."

"We share information, it's a courtesy. Tomorrow morning I'll have your name and Matt... What's your last name?"

"Weatherby," said Matt.

"...and Matt Weatherby on the list here," he replied, waving a piece of paper, "saying you've cleared customs. But that being said, it doesn't mean she isn't here. Your father said she's been working for Prince Abdul for about eight and a half months, correct?"

"Yes, as a physician to the harem," replied Meg.

"Great gig!" Ted whistled. "Prince Abdul is the richest man in the country, probably the entire Middle East. So to continue, Davon called home to say she's in trouble and told your parents the Prince won't let her leave her position, or the country?"

"Not exactly," said Matt, squirming.

"Let me explain Matt," interrupted Meg. "It might sound a bit weird, but because Dad worked at the Pentagon we had a code word to let our folks know if we were ever in trouble. Last week when Davon called home she used the code word four times. We're positive something's wrong."

"I see," said Ted, closing the file folder. "So you and Matt have flown half way around the world because Davon used a code word four times in a conversation? What was the word?"

"Cabbage."

"Davon said the word cabbage four times, in a row?" asked Ted, finding it difficult not to laugh.

"Look Ted, this isn't a joke. Davon's in trouble. She's a professional who came over here to do a job. She works hard, and doesn't goof around, ever!" said Matt, raising his voice. "The last time she called, she interlaced the word cabbage by saying things like she missed everyone and eating cabbage, that she didn't think they grew cabbage here, etc. She was also able to let Pete know the phone calls are tapped, and that the only time she is allowed out of the palace is on the last Thursday of the month."

Ted leaned forward, and looked from Meg to Matt. "Okay, why don't you tell me the whole story, everything she said, word for word?"

CHAPTER EIGHTEEN

Davon walked briskly from the palace to the clinic taking deep inhalations of the salty sea air. She could feel a headache developing as she marched towards the clinic's illuminated porch lights, two beacons in an otherwise unlit landscape. The night seemed unusually dark, and Davon found herself straining to see if she was still on the path. Solar tea lights stationed along the walkway gave inadequate light. It was a more romantic lighting, than functional. She was in a foul mood, and took no notice of the refreshing breeze, pleasant temperature, or amorous surroundings-- things she would have normally enjoyed. Jogging up the stairs to the clinic, she opened the door and flicked on the interior lights moving quickly to the storage room fridge. She had four bottles of insulin, one fast acting and three slow, thanks to another diabetic at the palace. The woman, Marana, a cousin to one of the wives had developed diabetes as a child. For some reason she had started living in the harem's quarters about three months ago. Although she was a big know-it-all, demanding this and demanding that, Davon had to admit she was well versed on her disease and treatment.

She recalled the first time she met Marana. The young woman had told the doctor no one could possibly understand how hard her life was. She was nineteen, drop-dead gorgeous, and living on Abdul's dime because according to her, no man would marry a diabetic. Maybe that was true in this part of the world, Davon had told her, but in most countries a gorgeous, well-educated and wealthy woman could have her pick of any man. At the time Marana had brushed the comment off, but Davon had seen the girl's side-ways grin, and knew she'd taken the information to heart. Perhaps, Marana could assist with Raja's mother's diabetic teaching? At the diabetic clinic in Boston they always used seasoned diabetics to help out with the newly diagnosed, a system which seemed to alleviate some of the stress of discovering you had developed a life-long disease.

Davon removed the documentation and order sheet for medications that hung on a hook beside the fridge, and began entering the insulin vial numbers and codes. She checked her watch for the date and time. It was Monday, the last week of October. Pausing in mid pen stroke, she took a dramatic breath, exhaling loudly. Thursday, the harem would be going to Dubai. She had to find some way to go with them!

As she hurried back to Raja's suite, she contemplated strategies. She hesitated to ask Raja if she could go to Dubai, because she was afraid she'd be refused. But, if she left without permission, it would be just her luck that one of the wives would mention it.

When she returned to the bedroom, she found Raja in exactly the same position, by the bedside clenching her mother's hand, and Davon looked at her, wondering what she should do. Organizing a work station, Davon poked a needle into the vial's stopper. By pulling back on the plunger she withdrew insulin into the syringe. Swabbing the site, Davon inserted the needle in the fleshy part of Jasmine's arm. "I've given her insulin, which will bring down her blood sugar. She needs two types: fast-acting insulin, which reduces very high blood sugar quickly, and slow-acting insulin, which will help maintain her sugar at normal levels over a twenty-four hour period. I'll be starting diabetic teaching with her tomorrow, and I expect you to take part." As Davon began tidying up, she noticed Jasmine watching. "Welcome back. How are you feeling Jasmine?"

"Funny," she replied, licking her lips. "What am I doing here?"

When Raja began to speak to her mother in Arabic, Davon shifted her gaze, allowing them to have a moment. Repacking her medical bag, she placed it on the floor.

Their conversation ended and Davon spoke. "Jasmine, you're probably going to feel funny for the rest of the night, and that's normal, but I guarantee in two days you'll feel better than you have been feeling lately. You've developed diabetes. And to get to the stage where you were tonight, takes a long time, sometimes months." Davon offered her a sip of water. "I understand your mother was a diabetic."

"She was in her eighties when she acquired the condition. I'm only fifty-six," groaned Jasmine.

"Children can get diabetes. It's a disease with no age discrimination. But don't worry about this tonight," said Davon, patting her hand. "I'm going to teach you everything you need to know over the next few days." Jasmine looked discouraged. "I'll be back at ten tonight to check her blood sugar again, Raja. If she starts to have any problems, call me right away.

Raja merely nodded.

Twenty-four hours later, almost exactly to the minute, Meg and Matt waited at the entrance of their hotel for the resident limousine, admiring the decadent surroundings. The two thousand room hotel, like many others, had been built in less than a year. Endless, manicured lawns bordered by colorful flower beds, met a world class golf course on one side, and a warm, turquoise ocean on the other. While Meg stooped to examine the flowers of a delicate burgundy orchid, Matt focused on the lines of the impressive, ultra-modern buildings. The architecture was sleek, incorporating five towers turned at thirty degree angles so that every room had an amazing view.

When the dark grey Lexus drove under the covered walkway, the concierge motioned to Matt, and opened the door to the vehicle. Meg slid in first, fingering the soft grey leather seat as she moved towards the window. "I could get used to this," she said quietly to Matt, as he got in beside her. "The whole place is breath-taking! Funny, I didn't notice yesterday."

"Well, we were both pretty tired from the flight. The only thing I noticed was how comfortable my bed was, and that was only for a second before I fell asleep," replied Matt, just as the car started to move.

"Does he know where to take us?" Meg asked, looking out the window.

"I hope so. The car was arranged by the concierge. I didn't want a repeat of yesterday, a twenty minute drive taking an hour and a half. We were totally ripped off by the taxi driver."

"I'm just glad we made it to the embassy."

When the car dropped them at the black wrought iron gate, Matt pressed the intercom. "We have an appointment with Ted Whily."

They were buzzed through the gate and into the building. After checking in and getting visitor badges, like the day before at the reception desk, they were directed towards the elevators. Ted was waiting for them when the doors opened. "Hello again, Meg, Matt," he said, shaking their hands. "Come on down to my office. I've got good news. We were very lucky, most of the information we were looking for I was able to get from my contact early this morning." They walked into his office and he motioned them towards the same chairs they sat in yesterday. "On the last Thursday of the month, the harem does in fact go to the exclusive shopping district of Dubai, two limousines with seven to ten women, and two bodyguards. They have certain stores they seem to go to on a regular basis. I asked my guy to verify it. He spoke with some of the store owners, and the store owners after a few bribes, admitted that it is usually the same wives who come shopping each month. One problem we have though..." He looked at the two of them. "How do we know Davon will be with the harem this Thursday?"

Meg bit her lip. "I guess we don't."

"It's irrelevant. We can't possibly know because we can't get a hold of her. All we can do is go to the shopping area on Thursday and look for her," said Matt, pulling a small pad of hotel paper and a pen out of his pocket. "So Ted, how do you recommend we proceed?"

Ted looked down at the file folder and drummed his fingers on the desk. "There's something we should talk about right now before we get into the nitty-gritty. Anything the US Embassy helps you with is strictly off the record. And I mean strictly. You can never ever tell anyone about our involvement, here, or in America. Do you understand?"

"Of course Ted, Dad already warned us. We completely understand," replied Meg. Matt nodded in agreement.

"Good, so we're totally clear. Now, I've come up with a scenario, which I'll run by you. However, you need to understand that you have to do the job alone. And you'll probably only have one chance to snatch Davon, one chance," said Ted, emphasizing his point by holding up his index finger, "so, you better make it good."

"And what if we blow it? We're not mercenaries! I'm sorry Ted. I'm not comfortable with this set-up." Meg shook her head. "Dad said you'd organize professionals to abduct her." Megan looked to Matt for support.

"Let's just hear the man out. Talk to us Ted."

At precisely 8:30 am Tuesday morning Davon was at Jasmine's door. She brought several teaching pamphlets, two books on diabetes, and Jasmine's next dose of insulin. Ushered into the living room she was surprised to see Jasmine dressed and relaxing on a chaise lounge reading a book.

"Dr. Marshall, thank you for coming again. I apologize for not being a proper host yesterday. May I offer you tea?" she asked.

"Tea would be great," said Davon, placing the instructional material on the glass coffee table. I hope you haven't eaten yet Jasmine because I'd like to check your blood sugar again. I want to see how you've responded to the medicine. How are you feeling this morning?"

Jasmine called for a servant to bring the tea and food, and then turned to Davon. "I feel like my old self again. I've been in such a fog these last few weeks, just didn't know what was wrong with me. Imagine one needle and I'm completely better! I can't thank you enough!"

Davon cringed. The first teaching session was always the worst. "Is Raja coming?" she inquired, pulling out the glucometer.

"No, I told her it wasn't necessary. She's extremely busy running the whole palace because Mr. Bedon is still away with Prince Abdul. As if Raja doesn't already have enough to do! When Mr. Bedon is gone her work-load triples," said Jasmine, over-dramatizing her point. "Thank goodness they'll be home tomorrow. And to answer your question, I haven't eaten. I did remember you telling me last night to wait until you came this morning. "

"Perfect," replied Davon, trying to mask her excitement at what Jasmine had blurted out. Abdul was coming home tomorrow! Maybe, she had been freaking out about nothing. "You've made a splendid recovery, I'm pleased. Do you remember how I tested your blood sugar by getting a drop of blood from your finger?" Jasmine nodded, offering her the same finger. "It's important to alternate sites. So let's poke the baby finger on your other hand today."

Squeezing the tip of the finger, Davon forced a drop of blood onto the cartridge, and placed it in the machine. Seconds later, the blood sugar reading was flashing on the screen. "Okay, the good news is your blood sugar is better than yesterday, but the bad news is you need another needle, which I'm going to give you right now." Davon prepared the injection while she launched into a teaching moment. "A person develops diabetes when their pancreas decreases or stops producing a hormone called insulin. Insulin is necessary to keep your blood sugar within a certain range." Davon looked up and saw Jasmine listening intently. "Depending on the severity of the disease, some people need needles every day of their lives, and others only need to take a pill once or twice a day. I'm afraid that you need the needles." Davon inserted it into Jasmine's upper arm. She didn't flinch.

"But I feel so good. Can't I take pills? My mother did."

"Overtime if your blood sugar stabilizes, I might be able to switch you to pills, but I don't want you to get your hopes up. I'll teach you to give yourself the injections. It's really very simple, and once you learn how to control your diabetes, you'll live a perfectly normal life." Davon pushed the tray of food closer to her. "Diet plays a big role, and it's important to eat a healthy meal, especially after taking insulin. You should eat something now." Jasmine selected a bowl of yogurt and fruit. "I took the liberty of bringing some pamphlets and books on the disease. I'd like you to read the booklets, and then we can sit down and discuss the issues. You speak English well, can you read it?"

Jasmine smiled. "Of course, I was born in Britain, Raja grew up there!"

"I thought I detected a slight British accent. What brought you here?" Davon disposed of the syringe and sat down on the sofa.

"My husband died many years ago in London after struggling with a long illness. He left me with a faltering fruit and vegetable business, which I sold, almost gave away, and although the money situation wasn't great, we could've managed. However Raja had other ideas. She had just graduated from university and wanted employment overseas. That's when my sister, Sashic's mother got her the position here."

"Wait, are we talking about Sashic, Prince Abdul's wife? She's your niece?" questioned Davon, quite taken aback.

"Yes, Raja's cousin. I'm surprised you didn't notice how much they look alike. Sashic is thirteen years older, but the resemblance is uncanny." The tea arrived and Jasmine indicated for the servant to pour.

Davon gave a mischievous smile. She had uncovered an inside source of information. What else did Jasmine know? "Well actually, now that you mention it, I do see the resemblance. They're both extremely beautiful," said Davon, cheerfully exaggerating. She leaned forward. "So that would make you Hepbet's great aunt. Do you happen to know how he's doing?" She instantly regretted the question. What if Raja had told her mother Davon knew about his death?

Jasmine shifted her position and took a sip of tea. "As far as I've heard, he's still in the hospital. I wanted to go and see him, if only to support Sashic, but Raja forbid it. He has a contagious disease you know, and in my weakened condition Raja thought I'd acquire it. She's such a good daughter and worries about me all the time." Her facial expression showed great sadness. "But it's my duty as the senior member of the family to go. Raja just doesn't understand. I'm going to insist Raja order a helicopter for me. I need to be in Dubai with Sashic. Thank you for reminding me, as I said I've been in a bit of a fog lately."

Breathing a sigh of relief, Davon spoke in a gentle tone. "I understand your responsibility to Sashic. However, I have to agree with Raja. You really should stay put until we get your diabetes under control." Jasmine immediately became upset and closed her eyes. Davon thought she heard a small cry. "That being said if Mr. Bedon is coming back tomorrow, and if Raja could accompany you, then maybe I could call the hospital in Dubai and arrange for you to go to the diabetic clinic there for your insulin, and blood sugar tests. What do you think?"

Jasmine perked up a little. "I'll talk it over with Raja, and see what she says."

Davon felt her palms becoming sweaty. Raja would flip if her mother told her about their actual conversation. "Could I make a suggestion, Jasmine?" Davon paused, and when there was no response she continued. "Knowing how stressed out Raja is, especially with running the palace and everything, it might be better if you don't mention having this conversation with me. I wouldn't dream of giving Raja the impression that we were conspiring. Why don't you just ask Raja about Hepbet? Tell her since you're feeling less foggy in the head, you suddenly remembered he was in the hospital."

"Good idea," said Jasmine, brightening. "I'm so glad Raja has you, such a good friend. The other women don't like her much and I don't understand why. Raja should be the one to dislike them. She's given up her whole life to serve, while they're pampered...well, I won't say anymore."

"What about Sashic?" asked Davon, feeling a touch guilty about the deception.

"Sashie's wonderful to us, but Raja needs a friend her own age. I'm glad she has you. I always felt badly about not giving Raja a brother or sister."

"Well, there's not much you can do about that now," laughed Davon. Jasmine giggled with her. "If you do end up flying to Dubai, let me know because I'll have to phone the hospital and make the arrangements for you. I'll be speaking with Raja later today about your diabetes, but I promise not to mention anything else we talked about. It should be our little secret, okay?"

"I promise," said Jasmine, with a wink. "Will I be seeing you this evening?"

"Only if you're not feeling well," said Davon, standing up. "I'll be here tomorrow morning at the same time. "One of the most important things about diabetes is diet. You need to eat three good meals a day with two or three healthy snacks." Davon picked up one of the books and scanned through it. "Have a look at this section, and call me if you have any questions. And please Jasmine, eat more breakfast!"

Taking a sip of tea, Davon grabbed her bag and said goodbye. As she proceeded outside, she thanked her lucky stars Jasmine hadn't been told about Hepbet's death. "That was close!" she whispered. "I don't know what I was thinking!" She hummed a little as she went back up the outside stairs to her next home visit. Could Abdul really be coming home tomorrow? The thought of seeing him excited her, but would it change anything? The world he lived in was so different from hers, and she knew she could never conform, knew she could never fit in. She had made her decision to leave and wouldn't alter her plans unless...

CHAPTER NINETEEN

It was late afternoon when Davon ran up the stairs, two at a time, to the medical clinic. She had gotten tied up at her last home visit because Momma Ba had insisted she have lunch. Usually she managed to get out of the ritual pleading a heavy workday. But today Momma Ba wouldn't listen. Oh well, Davon thought, at least I don't have to waste more time going home for a meal. When she opened the door to the clinic, there were five patients waiting in the reception room: Marana, decked out in a black slinky dress and silver stilettos looking bored, Pipa playing with her precious eighteen month old daughter, and Tagette clinging anxiously to Memen.

"Marana, I see you got my note. I'm going to see Tagette and Pipa first, do you want to come back in about forty minutes?"

"Just give me my insulin, and I'm gone," yawned Marana, uncrossing her legs. "I don't need anything else from you."

Davon stared her down. "Well I need something from you. Either wait, or come back. Did you take your insulin this morning?"

"What? Do you think I'm stupid?" snarled Marana, standing up.

Pipa turned to her in horror. "How dare you speak to the doctor like that? I'm telling Salli!" she said in English, adding a second comment in Arabic.

Tagette looked the other way, and clutched Memen tighter, trying to avoid the confrontation.

"Enough! Come back in thirty minutes Marana and I'll see you and give you your insulin." Davon walked over and escorted her to the door. Shutting it, she looked from Pipa to Tagette. "Who was here first?"

"I was," said Pipa, "but I'm only here for Lindle's vaccination. If you need to see Tagette and Memen..."

Davon took two large steps, pulled out her stethoscope and listened to Memen's chest. She chuckled as he quietly lifted his hand to stroke the underside of her arm. Memen was such a gentle soul. "He's okay, Tagette. Let me give Lindle her vaccination and then I'll take you in the office." Tagette nodded in agreement, but Davon again wondered how much she really understood.

Reaching for Lindle, Davon cradled her in her arms. The beautiful little girl with jet black curly hair and big brown eyes smiled contently, and cooed as Davon carried her from the waiting room, to the office for her chart, and then into the examination room. "You have a gorgeous little girl, Pipa," said Davon, placing the child in the mother's arms. She opened the medicine cupboard and began to prepare the inoculation. "Lindle needs one needle today. She'll probably be a bit fussy tonight. If it gets bad, call me and I'll give her something." Davon swabbed the cubby arm and inserted the needle. The child let out a wail, and a second later Memen rushed through the door.

"It's alright, Memen. Give her this." Davon removed the plastic covering from a red sucker and offered it to him. "Give the sucker to Lindle, and you can have this one," she said, motioning for him to hand the lollipop to the baby in order to get one for himself.

Although he tried, Lindle continued to squirm and yell. She wanted nothing to do with the peace offering until Pipa took it and rubbed the sweet over her lips. Within seconds the wailing stopped. Sitting quietly on Pipa's lap, Lindle was now totally focused on the red candy her mother occasionally swiped over her tongue. Memen protectively watched her, sweetly caressing the baby's face between his licks.

When a servant arrived at the clinic to assist Pipa home, Davon ushered them out with instructions. She then turned to Memen's mother. "Come into the examination room, Tagette."

The woman stood slowly at the sound of her name, and timidly approached the doorway. She was obviously distressed, and took several small gulping breaths before she made eye contact with Davon. She was Abdul's most beautiful wife. With perfect features and eyes that sparkled with flecks of gold, flawless skin and thick auburn hair, she made the other wives look dull. Gently touching her shoulder, Davon assisted her to a chair and closed the door. "How can I help you, Tagette?" she asked tenderly, sitting on a stool beside her.

"I do not know if I can tell. Please help me!" she cried, tears forming in her beautiful almond eyes.

"I will help you if I can Tagette, but you have to tell me what's wrong."

"You will not tell others?" She reached out to grab Davon's hand.

"I will not tell others," said Davon, trying to remain calm. She instinctively turned to look at Memen wondering if she should remove him from the room, but changed her mind when she saw him contently playing with the stick from his sucker.

"It is Memen!" his mother whispered, pleadingly.

"Memen's breathing is fine today. You have nothing to worry about," said Davon, reassuringly.

"No! You do not understand. They are taking him! They told me to get him ready." Tagette squeezed Davon's fingers so tightly they were starting to hurt.

"Slow down, who is taking him?" asked Davon, gently prying open Tagette's grip. Memen hearing his mother's distressed outburst, came to stand beside her.

"Bedon, he say Abdul wants Memen in Dubai tomorrow. Not truth! Abdul would never take him away from Tagette. Please help, I have no one!"

Davon blanched and suddenly felt ill. What was Bedon up to now? Get rid of Hepbet, and go after the next boy who's supposed to inherit the kingdom? A sweet, mentally challenged child who could never ever hurt anyone! What a sick bastard! Standing up she gave Tagette a big hug, that Memen took part in. Her mind flew in a million directions.

"Do you have any family in the area, anyone you can go to?"

"I do not know. I have no one to help."

"Tagette, listen to me!" Davon felt her heart beating ferociously. She was beginning to understand. Abdul wasn't coming home tomorrow, Jasmine had it wrong. Bedon was coming to get Memen! "Tell me where your parents live? Do you have brothers or sisters?" questioned Davon, slowing down her speech so Tagette could comprehend what she was asking.

"Parents live far, near Dubai," she sobbed, hugging Memen who also started to weep.

Far, near, oh brother, thought Davon. "I can help you, but you must stop crying. It's upsetting Memen." Davon rubbed the boy's back and he turned to hug her. "Now, what I can do is send you, Memen and Pheely to the Dubai hospital this afternoon. I'll tell Raja Memen is having trouble breathing, and needs tests at the hospital right away. Once you are in Dubai, you telephone your parents, and get them to come and get you and the boys. You will go to your parent's house, and will not come back to the palace."

"Raja will not say yes, and Bedon is coming..." she said, looking dreadfully frightened.

"Let me worry about that! Go to your suite, and pack a bag for you and the boys, and meet me at the bottom of the outside stairs in twenty minutes. I will order a limousine to take us to the helipad."

The instant they left, Davon picked up the phone and paged Raja. "I don't care if someone has plans for the boy! He just had a dreadful asthma attack, and needs to get to the hospital today for testing, testing I've put off for too long. No, he can't wait until tomorrow. A second attack during the night could be fatal! You've seen the boy during an attack, and you know how bad it can be! Believe me Raja, Prince Abdul will not be happy if he loses another son," said Davon angrily. She hoped the last statement would launch Raja into action.

"A two passenger helicopter is the only one available. And it won't be able to bring you home tonight," stuttered Raja.

"That's fine. I want him to stay overnight anyway. Tagette should go with him because he's quite distressed. I've already given him his medication, so he'll manage the flight. If you can order a car to take them to the helipad, I'll go with them and get them on board. Oh and Raja, I'll need to call the hospital." Davon hung up and smiled. She hated Bedon!

The door to the clinic opened, and she peeked around her desk to see Marana strutting in. Davon had completely forgotten she was coming back. "Come on in Marana," she yelled. "I'll get your insulin from the fridge." Davon dashed into the storage room and pulled out the last two vials. She had ordered more insulin, but it hadn't yet arrived. Returning to the office she asked Marana to sit. "You should be really proud of yourself. You do a fantastic job of taking care of your diabetes." Marana grinned, and Davon continued to talk as she glanced at her watch. "We have a new diabetic at the palace, and I was wondering if you'd be interested in getting involved with her teaching?"

The grin quickly turned sour. "And why would I want to do that?" she asked, crossing her arms and legs.

"In America we have thousands of clinics where diabetics work alongside nurses to teach newly diagnosed patients. It's one thing for a non-diabetic nurse or doctor to educate a person who's recently acquired the disease, and it's another for someone who's lived with the disease. I wouldn't be asking you if you weren't so amazing at taking care of yourself. Besides, if you ever came to the States, it might even turn into a job." Davon saw her eyes brighten.

"Well...I guess...if you need my help."

"Thanks Marana. I'll check with the patient, and see if it is okay with her, and then I'll send you a note. How would you feel about teaching her injection techniques?"

"Fine," she replied, looking more interested.

"Then we've got a deal. Here's your insulin. I've ordered more, which should be here later today. You know where the syringes are in the storage area, and I'll write out her dose and injection times for you. Our new diabetic's blood sugar is still fluctuating, but it should settle down over the next couple of days. I've got her reading a book on the diabetic diet, and that's something else you could go over. I can't tell you how much I appreciate this," said Davon, talking rapidly and moving towards the door.

"You're really helping me out!"

They left the clinic together and chatted pleasantly on the way back to the palace. Davon was introduced to a whole different side of Marana. The young woman was interesting, agreeable and even bordered on jovial as they discussed science, disease and schooling in America. "Have you ever considered going into medicine?" Davon asked.

"They wouldn't take a diabetic!" replied Marana, bitterly. She looked at Davon as though she was crazy.

"Marana that's not true. You get into medicine based on grades. You're a smart person. Think about it, you could specialize in diabetes, change the way we treat it! Consider medicine," she called out, as they parted.

Marana headed into the palace, and Davon scooted around the outside wall towards the waiting limousine. She paused for a moment at the side of the wall to take in the picture, perfect bay. The water was calm, and the azure sky seemed to fall into the ocean without a beginning or end. Tugging at the silk scarf knotted around the strap of her bag, she thought about the bizarre events of the last few weeks. No one at home would ever believe what she had witnessed.

Taking the scarf she placed it over her hair, and stepped out into the open. Children's laughter could be heard in the distance, and Davon looked up to see Tagette hurrying the two boys along the outer corridor with a servant in tow. Arriving at the car ahead of them, Davon pulled the back door open, beating the limo driver by five seconds. The driver ignored the incident, and moved back to the front of the vehicle averting his eyes. Memen, spotting Davon ran to her with his arms outstretched. She hugged him, ruffled his hair, and then encouraged him to get into the back seat of the car. Pheely of course copied his brother, and Davon went through the same hugging procedure, before Tagette arrived with a servant dragging a large suitcase.

"The helicopter taking you to the hospital is only a two passenger," explained Davon, holding up two fingers. "You won't be able to take your servant. As it is, Pheely will have to sit on your lap," she added, taking the suitcase from the helper. None of the women of the harem could live without their servants, and Davon expected an argument. She was surprised when Tagette casually shrugged and ordered the servant to leave. Although Tagette wasn't upset, the servant was, and it was rather evident when the woman scowled and stomped back in the direction of the palace without even saying goodbye. Unfazed by the incident, Tagette made her way into the limousine. And Davon more than impressed by Tagette's attitude, followed her.

The helicopter was idling, its blades whirling, when they pulled up next to it. The driver took responsibility for the suitcase, while the co-pilot helped the boys into the back of the copter. Memen and Pheely were all smiles. Davon nudged Tagette, and requested one last word. "Listen carefully Tagette, I will order breathing tests for Memen at the hospital. Let him have the tests before you go to your parents, so it doesn't look suspicious. I wish you and the boys well, take care of yourself." Davon said, feeling emotional when Tagette came to embrace her.

"Thank you, Davon. You are my friend. I never forget you," replied Tagette, turning to leave.

When the helicopter took to the air the boys waved, and Davon waved back, letting her tears fall freely. The warmth of the day was beginning to wane, and Davon wrapped her arms about herself and circled around to the footpath to return to the palace. She had told the limousine driver not to wait because she wanted to be alone. She wanted time to think, to plan how she was going to leave. Why hadn't she forced Raja to order the larger helicopter so that she could have gone with Tagette and the boys? It was almost as if she was unconsciously sabotaging her own escape. Stupid! She was making stupid mistakes!

She thought about Jasmine's and Tagette's comment about Bedon returning to the palace tomorrow. A part of her wanted to believe Abdul was coming home, and that everything would be alright. She longed for the wonderful feeling of being in love, cherished, and wanted. But, did she truly love him? Or was it the lost love of Matt she was desperately trying to recapture? Davon began to question her sanity. "Stop it," she said out loud. She quickly looked around to see if anyone had heard her. She was standing alone atop the stone bridge watching the crystal clear water trickle beneath it, and a small goldfish reflecting the last rays of the setting sun. Stop berating yourself! You're a good person Davon Marshall and sometimes bad things happen to good people! Fingering an American penny she found lodged at the bottom of her pocket, she took out the coin. Tapping it three times on the side of the stone railing, she wished for home, and tossed it into the water.

Jogging up the outer stairs, Davon went directly to the communications room, and picked up the phone. The call to the hospital had been prearranged by Raja and was put through immediately.

"Good evening Dr. Marshall," said Dr. Veenn. "I presume you are calling about the helicopter you've sent to us?"

"Yes, it can't be there already!"

"No, no, it should arrive in thirty minutes or so, the pilot radioed us."

"I see," said Davon, breathing a sigh of relief. She knew she had dawdled back to the palace, but didn't think she had wasted that much time. "Prince Abdul's son, Memen is on the flight with his mother and brother. The boy has asthma and has had several severe attacks since I've been at the palace, including one this morning." Davon squirmed at the lie. "He needs a workup and I was hoping you could get him into the asthma clinic today. I've sent his inhalers with him."

"Of course, I will be at the helipad to meet them."

"Thanks," said Davon, hesitating for a moment. "Dr. Veenn, there is one other thing I'd like to ask off the record if I could."

"Yes?"

"Prince Abdul's other son Hepbet was hospitalized last week, and I was wondering if you knew how he was doing?" Davon could hear heavy breathing.

"I'm afraid he wasn't my patient. Is there anything else?"

"No, thank you," said Davon, slowly hanging up the receiver. The words 'he wasn't my patient' indicated that Dr. Veenn knew about Hepbet's death. It was too bad he couldn't have shared the information with her. She desperately wanted to know the cause of death.

Davon sat in the chair and rolled a strand of hair between her fingers. The person who had connected the call was new. She wondered if he knew about her telephone privileges being suspended. Picking up the receiver she listened to the drawn-out ring tone. "Hello, could you please connect me to the American Embassy."

"Hold the line please," said the same male voice. Davon held her breath. He finally came back on the line. "Dr. Marshall, you have no clearance to put through the call. Please try again at a later date." A click quickly followed.

Davon slammed down the receiver and swore loudly. "What does that mean, you ass? Try again at a later date...it means don't bother me because I'm too scared to help you!" She held her head in her hands and stared at the phone. Remorse slowly began to replace the anger. "I know how you feel whoever you are because I don't want to stand up to Bedon either. But we can't let him win, we just can't!"

CHAPTER TWENTY

The alarm on her iPod beeped at the usual time, but instead of feeling well rested, Davon awoke thinking she might vomit. Not only did she have trouble falling asleep, she'd slept poorly. Dragging herself out of bed, she showered and dressed, and forced herself to eat some breakfast. She needed coffee this morning, lots of coffee, and couldn't tolerate it without food in her gut. Selecting her light blue linen pant suit and matching shoes, she blocked her premonition about Abdul, and prayed he was in fact safe and coming home. Regardless of what happened though, she promised herself she would leave tomorrow. She'd go to Dubai with the harem, and hail a cab, steal a car, or do whatever she had to do to get to the embassy. Grabbing her bag from the bedroom, she waved at Pona, and headed off to Jasmine's apartment.

Davon was taken aback when Raja opened the door. "Morning Raja, I'm here to check on your mother. You missed our appointment yesterday," Davon said, nonchalantly walking into the living room. "Ah, there you are Jasmine. I need to check your sugar level." She proceeded to assemble her equipment and made chitchat with the patient when Raja came to stand beside her.

"I completely forgot about the appointment, Dr. Marshall. I've been extremely busy," replied Raja, anxiously.

"Raja is working day and night! I thought I mentioned it yesterday, Davon," said Jasmine, grimacing as her finger was poked.

"Yes you did, but Raja needs to be a part of your diabetic teaching in case something goes wrong. For example, if your sugars get exceedingly high again, you'll have the same symptoms of three days ago. However, if you accidently take too much insulin, or don't eat enough after taking your usual dose, you will end up with extremely low blood sugar, which is another medical emergency. Raja needs to be able to recognize the symptoms, and know what to do if medical attention isn't near."

"I apologize, can we reschedule?" asked Raja, appearing worried.

Davon stopped drawing up the insulin and looked at her. "Today, I have time right now. In fact, why don't you give the injection? It's something you need to learn anyway. Get an orange from the kitchen and you can practice a couple of times."

The teaching session went well, and both Raja and Jasmine learned proper injection technique. Raja nervously injected the insulin into her mother's arm. "That wasn't bad!" she exclaimed, feeling pleased with herself.

"You did a great job, you too, Jasmine. I know it's initially scary when you're learning, but trust me it will soon become just another thing you've got to do in the morning. Now, there's another diabetic in the palace, Salli's cousin, Marana. She has been a diabetic for nine years and is very well versed in the disease. I've asked her to come and talk with you, help you understand what it means to be a diabetic. What do you think?" Jasmine agreed whole heartedly, but Raja vetoed the idea. "In the States this is done all the time, where seasoned diabetics help the newly diagnosed. Your mother needs the help Raja, and you need to be supportive. Let the two of them meet, and if it doesn't work out, then so be it." Finally convinced, Raja agreed to organize the meeting with Marana. Pleased, Davon turned the discussion to the role of the pancreas, normal blood sugar readings, and the diabetic diet, while she enjoyed a second breakfast. After a solid hour of talking, Davon stood. "It's a lot to take in, so I think we'll stop there. I'll say goodbye to you, Jasmine." Walking towards the door, Davon beckoned, "Raja, could I have a private word."

Raja joined her. "Yes, what is it?"

"Is there any possible way I could go to Dubai tomorrow with the harem?" Davon bit the inside of her cheek as she opened the door and started to step outside.

"I...I don't know what to say," said Raja, caught completely off guard. "The Prince and Bedon will be home today, and I'm not sure if the harem will even go." Anxiously, she brushed a strand of hair away from her face. "I told you Bedon cancelled your excursions."

"Can't you make an exception? Please Raja do this for me."

"You've got no idea the predicament you're putting me in!" She thought for a moment and shook her head. "I really can't help you, Dr. Marshall, and I'm sorry because you've done so much for my mother. Have a good day." With that she attempted to close the door.

Davon placed her foot between the frame and the door, and whispered. "Is Hepbet really dead? Why don't the others know?" She bit her tongue because she wanted to continue, blurt out everything--the attempt on Abdul's life, the suspected arsenic, the plan to take Memen away from his mother--all the evidence which pointed to Bedon.

"It's not your concern. Please do your job, and let me do mine!" Raja glared. "Remove your foot, Dr. Marshall!" The door was promptly shut.

Davon walked away completely discouraged. She had been foolish to think she could trust Raja. Her only option now was to find Lamna, and convince her to help. As she passed the empty swimming pool unconsciously making her way to the medical clinic, she heard the sound of helicopters. Squinting, she shielded her eyes from the sun, and looked back towards the desert. There in the distance were two copters rapidly approaching the helipad.

Abruptly changing direction, Davon sprinted back to the palace, and up the outer staircase. She entered the building hastily, running down the maze of hallways to the main foyer. Carefully opening the door a crack, she spied on three burly male occupants milling about the lobby. Swallowing hard, Davon watched them and tried to control the pounding in her chest. Dual helicopters could only mean one thing--Abdul was home! She sighed, glad that she had been wrong. Of course, that didn't change the events with Hepbet and Memen, but now Abdul could deal with Bedon.

A sound of footsteps broke the silence, echoing loudly into the foyer. Davon pressed her eye to the crack and watched as a party of men entered. "Bingo!" she said, throwing open the door. "Abdul, Prince Abdul, could I speak with you?" she called, walking briskly towards him.

With the exception of Bedon, the whole group of men froze, turning their gaze to the approaching intruder. Bedon instantly slid in front of Abdul, blocking her. "Return at once to the women's quarters, Dr. Marshall!" he bellowed, menacingly.

Davon ignored the command and called out a second time, adjusting her position to make eye contact. "Abdul, please it's urgent."

The Prince met her gaze, and narrowed his eyes scrutinizing the beautiful woman before him. He made no response to her plead, and Davon was perplexed. Suddenly, she became frightened. Is this some kind of joke, she thought, breathing heavily. He asks me to marry him, and then he can't even give me two minutes of his time! "I think you'll want to hear what I have to say, it's about two of your sons, Hepbet and Memen."

Abdul still didn't react, but she eyed Bedon, positive he was about to have a seizure. His face turned to pure hate, and he pumped his fists as though he was preparing to strike. Flicking his head in her direction he made two clicking sounds, and four bodyguards responded by moving towards her.

Davon instantly took several steps backwards, and then turned to run. She yanked the door open and slammed it behind her, bolting it with the dusty latch. Plastering herself against the wall she covered her mouth to mute her own gasps, and listened. She was sure she could hear laughter.

"Sick bastards," she whispered, disgusted with all of them.

The light under the door produced two sets of shoe shadows hovering on the other side of the thick piece of brass covered wood. They'd be waiting for orders, Davon thought, and she glanced at the flimsy lock wondering if it would hold. Not wanting to find out, she tip-toed to the first curve in the hallway and then broke into a sprint. I'll barricade myself in the apartment and get my essentials together. And then what Davon, how are you going to get away? Davon blinked away the moisture forming in her eyes and exhaled. As she flew around the next corner, there was Lamna and Pipa strolling towards her.

Slowing her gait, she gave a hint of a smile, and greeted them. "Looks like you've been swimming?"

"We have," they said together.

Lamna came closer. "You look terrible, Davon. Are you alright?" she asked with great concern.

"Yes, just awfully busy!"

"Well, you need to slow down, and think about yourself for a change. Why don't you come for lunch?"

"Thanks for the offer, but as you can see I'm frantically busy. However, I'd like to go to Dubai with the harem tomorrow. I hope there's still room." Davon took a quick look over her shoulder.

"Sorry my dear, the trip's cancelled. You probably haven't heard, but Abdul is coming home today," she sung the last word sweetly.

"Oh," replied Davon, devastated that her last hope of escape was gone. "I've got to get going. You ladies have a great day."

The women passed each other, and then Lamna spun around. "Davon, I forgot to tell you, I got word, the good wishes you sent Bin were delivered." She winked twice in her direction.

"Thanks Lamna, thanks so much," replied Davon, fighting the urge to burst into tears.

Not only did she lock both deadbolts on the apartment door the second she got in, Davon put a dining room chair under the doorknob. Pona watched, but made no comment, and Davon didn't try to explain. Once that was done, she went and plopped on the living room sofa feeling completely exhausted. Abdul had acted weird, indifferent, and hadn't even flinched when she brought up his sons. What was that all about? Was he drugged or under threat? The man she met this morning certainly wasn't the man she had fallen in love with in Cairo. She still couldn't believe he hadn't come to her defense. Why hadn't he intervened when Bedon ordered her back to the women's quarters? She went over the scene again in her head. Nothing made sense. But she didn't have the energy to care anymore. She had to focus on getting home!

Pona placed some food in front of her and she ate unconsciously as she debated the issues. There had to be a way to get to Dubai on a service truck, or a fishing boat. She thought about the pilot who flew Momma Ba to the hospital...Jack...she couldn't recall his last name. Even if she could remember, how would she get in touch with him? Think Davon! Come on, you're smarter than this! Lamna, she would call and ask her to order a limousine. It was the last Thursday of the month when the harem always went to Dubai to shop, and if Davon just happened to be the only occupant, so what? Would the driver refuse to take her? It'd mean finding a way to get past both Raja and Bedon, and ditching the bodyguard when she got to town, but she could do it! She pressed her finger nails into her hand, and dwelt for a few minutes on the fact that it would be an extremely risky venture being alone in the desert with a driver and guard. These were men who worked for Bedon. But she had to take the chance, there was no other option.

Going into the bedroom, she emptied her medical bag on the bed, and removed all of the drugs and unnecessary supplies. She repacked the jewellery she had been given, to use as bribes, her computer, some of her toiletries and a few basic clothes, which she rolled as tightly as she could. In the side pocket she tried to squish in her runners, but they were too bulky and would have to stay. Chucking the runners back into the closet, Davon took one last look at her beautiful clothes and shoes.

"Dr. Marshall!"

Davon spun around and screamed!

"I'm sorry to interrupt," apologized Raja, "Pona directed me here."

"Never mind, you scared me, that's all. How did you get into the suite?" Davon asked acidly, looking around her visitor for any other unwelcome guests. The small hairs at the back of her neck tingled.

Raja crossed her arms, and her face became stern. "As I said, your servant let me in. We need to talk, Davon."

The whole time she had been at the palace, Raja had never called her by her first name. Davon immediately became guarded. "One moment, I've got to check something." At the entranceway she saw that Pona had replaced the chair and relocked the door. "So much for my barricade," she said quietly, leering at her servant on the way back to the bedroom. "What is it Raja?" she asked, leaning against the doorframe so that she could keep an eye on the front entry.

"I was wrong. You need to leave the palace as soon as possible."

Davon blanched, and suddenly felt light-headed. "What?"

"Bedon is extremely angry with you. I've never seen him in such a state. Memen is missing, and he's blaming you." Raja let out a loud sigh. "I'm afraid for your safety."

Davon slid down the post and sat on the floor. "Can you get me to

Dubai?"

"I don't know if I can help. I've come to warn you. People are being watched. I have just learned that the hall cameras were activated today for the first time since they were installed. They will know every time you leave or enter your suite."

Chewing on the inside of her lip, Davon was instinctively restrained. She refused to trust Raja because Bedon could've sent her. "I need my passport and some money."

Raja squirmed. "I wish I could do something but..."

"I know you can't!" exclaimed Davon, standing up. "You want to, but it would put you in an imposition!"

"Tomorrow, I'll figure out a way tomorrow. In the meantime be careful what you say, and to whom, especially on the phone," replied Raja, avoiding Davon's eyes. She made her way to the door and waited while Pona pulled the chair away to open it. Davon stood where she was, and watched.

Something wasn't right. Raja's bit about being careful to whom she talked with, and about what, was like a badly rehearsed script! The woman was definitely involved or being blackmailed. By using Raja as a go-between, Bedon was conspiring to psychologically trap her. He had already taken away all of her physical liberties, and now he was trying to make her paranoid. Cameras, people being watched, he was worried she'd attempt to leave! The question was why? Could it be he didn't want her to get away before he figured out a way to kill her? Or had she somehow become a piece of the puzzle, a piece so valuable he had to keep her around for a while longer?

"I've got to get out of here before I become one of Bedon's fatalities!" she murmured, promising not to dwell any longer on anything, but getting away.

Noticing Pona was dusting in the living room, Davon snuck into the kitchen, and opened the cutlery draw. She selected a slim, sharp paring knife and returned quickly to her room. Wrapping the blade in tissues, she placed the knife in the side pocket leaving the hub exposed. She had no weapon or martial arts training, but as a physician she did know what parts of the body were the most vulnerable. Sitting cross-legged on the floor, she inspected the barricade at the front door. One way in and one way out, if the hallways were now being monitored then she figured she only had three options. She could create a distraction of fire or smoke, generate some sort of disguise by impersonating a servant or Raja, or locate the camera lens, and obliterate it with felt pen or gum. Lists filtered through her brain at a rapid pace with both the pros and cons. Even if she could get out of the building undetected, she still had to get to Dubai.

It was a quarter to five when the phone rang. Davon glanced at the clock as she grabbed the receiver before Pona, surprised that so much time had passed. She hesitated for a moment before saying hello.

"Davon, it's Lamna, I need something, medicine to calm me down. I'm feeling hysterical!"

"You can't take anything Lamna, you're pregnant," replied Davon, robotically.

"I don't care! Abdul's left already, he wouldn't even see me or Ismil, and he said nothing when I told him we were having another child! I need something, my nerves are shot!"

Davon straighten her stance. "I suggest taking a deep breath. You have to look at the situation from the Prince's view. Did he see any of the other wives?"

"No, that's what's so strange! He only came home for a couple of hours to get...I don't know what!" She began to sob into the phone.

"You realize Hepbet is still very sick in the hospital in Dubai, I bet he left to be with his son," said Davon, feeling terrible about lying. "Of course he cares about you, the baby, and Ismil. Why don't you have the servants make you a cup of herbal tea, and you can sit down and think about what I've said."

"Alright, I guess I'm being rather selfish. Poor Hepbet and Sashic!" sighed Lamna. There was silence for a few seconds. "Do you still want to go to Dubai tomorrow?"

Davon smiled, she had planned on proposing the trip once Lamna had composed herself, but didn't want to mention it too quickly after the upset. "The question is, are you up to it, Lamna? You really have to think about the child you're carrying. Emotional upheavals aren't good in pregnancy." Davon wanted to come across as the caring doctor, especially if the call was being recorded.

"You're so wonderful Davon. I really do feel much better. I'm calling for the limousines the minute we hang up. So will you come?"

"I'd love to, but I'm not feeling well tonight, and I don't know how I'll be tomorrow. What time will you leave?"

"At seven, the usual time we always leave. Shall I come to your suite and bring you some food?"

"No thanks, I'll be fine. You take care of yourself and your little baby, and have fun tomorrow." Davon gently replaced the receiver. "Don't worry, Lamna. I'm going to Dubai tomorrow. I just can't let you know."

Meg stood next to the thick plate glass window on the forty-fifth floor of the hotel looking out at the sprawling desert. It seems to go on forever, she thought, as she pulled the portable phone away from her ear. She was waiting for the operator to connect her collect call to the States, and found the canned music irritatingly loud. Finally, she heard her father agreeing to pay for the charges.

"Dad, its Meg. How are you?"

"Me? How are you? Have you located your sister?"

"Not yet, but we're working on it. We've been to the embassy twice and things are getting organized. I'll know more in a couple of days, but I promised Mom I'd call and..."

Pete interrupted. "What is the plan, run it by me?"

"There's nothing concrete yet," replied Megan, wondering if she had the clearance to tell him. She wasn't positive if Ted was including her father when he had said no one can ever know about the embassy's involvement.

"What's going on? You've been there three days, and you don't have a plan? I'm getting on the next plane!" yelled Pete, anger and worry in his voice.

"For God's sake, Pete," interrupted Anne on the extension. "Give Meg a chance. Hi Sweetie, I want you to know, your father and I have every confidence in you." She walked over to her husband and frowned at him.

"Are you two done?" asked Megan. "Matt and I are going back to the embassy this morning to finalize things. You know how it is Dad, need to know basis. I hope I'll be calling tomorrow afternoon with good news. Talk with you then, love you." Meg hung up without giving them a chance to reply. It had been a mistake to call, because now she was more nervous than ever.

Davon had stayed in her suite all evening, and now fully dressed she lay in bed still contemplating an escape route. There were two staircases to the women's quarters, one near the main entrance of the palace, and the other at the end of the building closer to the sea. She usually utilized the rear stairs because they were right by her apartment and in the vicinity of the clinic, but had noticed she was the only one. The harem always used the front staircase, especially when going to the waiting limousines. Tomorrow, it'd be important to blend in and come from the same direction as everyone else. The guards never questioned, or even went near any of the women from the harem, so if she followed the group she would be able to get to the car unmolested. But, how was she going to get out of her suite and down the four monitored hallways unseen?

Davon considered that Raja may have lied about the cameras being activated, yet she refused to ignore the warning. She had one chance to get out of the palace, and wasn't about to blow it. However, she couldn't seem to come up with a way to get out of the suite without exiting through the halls. Discouraged, she sighed, punched her pillow, and rolled to her side. "Wait a minute," she whispered excitedly. Throwing back the covers she leapt from the bed, and darted to the window to examine the intricately carved floor to ceiling inner wooden shutter. Not only was it a solid piece of carved wood, it was bolted into position. When her attempt to lift it failed, she got on her hands and knees and peered through one of the holes. A very large plate glass window was apparent, approximately four feet away with a side panel, which looked like it opened.

Davon quickly returned to the bed and pulled the paring knife out of her bag. Getting down on her knees, she scrutinized the lower part of the panel, and began to saw, cutting through the individual wooden curvy swirls, one vertical segment at a time. She worked diligently making clean, straight cuts, cognizant that she would have to reattach it later. Once she finished the sides, she worked on the bottom of the panel, and when the lower part of the section swung free, she turned her attention to the top. In less than thirty minutes, she was able to carefully remove a two by one foot rectangular section. Pushing herself through the small space, she stood upright on the other side, opened the window pane, and looked out. Analyzing the height, she wondered if she could jump. The apartment was on the second floor of the palace, approximately twelve to fourteen feet off the ground. Expansive gardens ran alongside the outer wall of the building, and although it was extremely dark, she could just make out a multitude of bushes below. A short false balcony, or French balcony as Matt would have called it, used more for decoration than function, was directly in front of the window.

This created a problem because there was no more than eight inches of space between the window ledge and the stout granite spindles. If she got out onto the ledge there'd be no room to place her feet. She would have to situate them horizontally, one in front of the other, and risk falling. She questioned whether it might be better to scramble out onto the stone balustrade, which was about ten inches thick. This would give her room to squat and set up some sort of line to the ground.

Closing the window, Davon climbed back through the hole in the screen, and scanned the bedroom for some sort of decorative cord or wire. She was willing to jump six or seven feet to the ground, but no more. The chance of a sprain or fractured limb would destroy any hope of escape. She rolled the edging of the bedspread between her fingers and wondered how hard it would be to remove. Discarding the idea, she turned to the top sheet of the bed. By twisting the cotton material on the diagonal, she was able to create a strong ten foot piece of fabric, which could easily be draped around one of the balcony spindles. She estimated that with her height, plus the five feet hanging on either side, she'd only have five, maybe six feet to fall. Placing the rolled sheet carefully on the floor beside her packed bag, Davon went to the bedroom door, and checked again to make sure it was locked. She knew Pona was asleep, but felt nervous about being discovered trashing the place. Returning to the bed, she stuffed several decorative pillows under the covers so it would look as though someone was sleeping, and then getting in bed beside her dummy, set her watch alarm for 4:30 am.

"Matt, how can you sit there and read? We need to run through the plan again, this time with the driver!" said Meg, anxiously. She paced back and forth in front of the chair he was sitting in.

"Trust me everything will be fine," he replied, glancing up from the book. "Why don't you try reading, it might calm you down."

"I don't want to read now! We've got to focus on any possible aspect that could go wrong! Davon may not show up, we might not find the right limousines, the security guards could shoot us! Did you think about that?"

"I didn't realize you were such a pessimist, Meg," he said, "Have a little faith in Ted. Things might go wrong, and if they do, we'll do our best to right them. The driver knows where the harem's limousines park and we'll be parked across the street, directly opposite. We also know that at approximately 11:00 am, there'll be two limos and two jeeps with bodyguards..."

"Who have machine guns!" added Meg.

"Yes, who have machine guns coming to park in that exact location. We'll do our bit exactly as Ted told us, and if Davon's not there, we'll try something else. Maybe, we'll have to wait for another month, I don't know. But we have to be calm and positive," said Matt, returning to his book.

"You're being ridiculous! If the attempt bombs, you're going to sit around here for another month?" asked Meg, glaring at him.

Matt put his book on the table and stood. "Look I was kidding. If things go wrong we'll come up with another plan. Ted will help us. I know you're worried about Davon and I am too, but if we let our fears get the better of us, our plan will fail. You know what you need to do, focus only on that! It's late. Go to your room, and get your gear together, and then go to bed. I'll meet you for breakfast at eight o'clock sharp."

CHAPTER TWENTY-ONE

Davon woke seven minutes before the alarm went off. Jumping out of bed, she ran to the bathroom to wash and dress. She pulled her hair into a tight ponytail, put on her long black yoga pants, a light blue sweater, and her black jersey zip up jacket. Changing her mind about footwear, she jammed her black flats into the side pocket of her bag, and rummaged in the back of her closet for her white runners. She'd need good footing on the railing, and would substitute the runners with the shoes once she was on the ground. The burka was carefully knotted around the strap of her bag so it wouldn't float away when she dropped the sac into the bushes. But in the middle of attaching the bulky garment, Davon suddenly realized she had forgotten something. Doubling back into the bathroom, Davon pulled a pocket mirror out of her cosmetics drawer. All of her hair needed to be covered when she donned the burka on the ground, and blond wisps of hair would be a dead giveaway!

What else had she overlooked? Glancing at the time, Davon sat down on the edge of the bed giving herself a few minutes to systematically go through her entire scheme. She couldn't make a mistake. The plan was elementary, yet dangerous, and if she was caught she had no doubt Bedon would have her killed. Looking at her watch again, she realized she didn't have much time before sunrise. She had to use the dark of the night to get from the balcony to the ground, and was worried about the brightness of the white bed-sheet. Looping the end of the sheet around her wrist she tied a practice knot. She wanted the sheet to fall to the ground with her, and not be left tangled on the spindle marking her trail.

Pushing her goods through the cavity, Davon followed. She positioned herself on the floor and pulled a bottle of wound adhesive out of her pocket. Unscrewing the lid, she used the brush attached to the cap to paint the sticky liquid on the ends of the cut wooden pieces of screen. Carefully replacing the section by lining up the individual bits of cut wood, she held it in place while gently blowing on the glue. She glanced at the door to her bedroom once more. Leaving it locked would give her more time before they'd be able to locate the key and open it. She had fixed the hole in the screen to add to the confusion as to how she had left the suite unnoticed, and hoped it would work. When they discovered she was gone, Bedon would certainly have a look at the camera tapes before he scoured the palace and its grounds.

"Here goes nothing," she whispered softly, letting go of the repaired piece. It stayed in place, and as she stood examining her work, she prayed the front of the screen looked as good as the back. Turning to the window, she opened it, and scanned the garden area for security personnel. It was black as Hades and she couldn't see any moving light from flashlights in the area. Hoisting her bag over the window ledge, she flung it out over the balcony, and heard a rustling thump when it hit the ground. Standing on her tip-toes, she then lifted her right foot onto the window ledge, and by hanging onto the side of the pane heaved herself up so that she was now crouched half in and half out of the window. She could almost distinguish the ground, which appeared more like twenty, instead of fourteen feet away, and hesitated for a moment wondering if she should get a second sheet from the bed to attach to the original. There probably was time, but she decided against it. She couldn't risk breaking the panel piece by removing it again. Concentrating on the railing in front of her, she wiggled her right foot forward and let it dangle between the outer ledge and the spindles. Her foot was several inches above the balcony floor and she was now awkwardly twisted holding onto the metal edge of the window with one hand. She shivered, although the night breeze was warm, and recognizing she was frightened, paused for a moment to take a deep breath before she continued on with her task. Yanking the bed sheet outside, she allowed it to drop onto the balcony. She then moved her left foot into position above the railing.

Davon wasn't afraid of heights, but knew there would be nothing to hang onto once she let go of the window frame. Her only prospect would be to immediately grab and straddle the railing if she was about to bounce off the balcony, and fall. Taking a deep breath, she shifted her weight towards the outer wall and loosened her grip. Hanging on to the ledge of the window until the last moment, Davon let go and slid precariously downward. Her right foot landed painfully crammed between the stone wall and the granite spindles, and her left foot awkwardly hung over the balustrade, her balance off kilter. She clung to a roused section of stone along the wall, struggling for several moments to maintain her balance as she attempted to crouch down. Using her left arm, she pushed against the outer portion of one of the fat spindles and was able to slowly maneuver into a sitting position on the railing.

It was getting lighter, and having obtained a better view on the balustrade, Davon checked again for security personnel. Seeing nothing, she shifted her weight and jiggled the bed-sheet out from under her foot, and then draped it evenly around the bottom of one of the posts. Heaving the ends back towards her, she tied one end to her right wrist with hopes that when she let go with her left hand, the sheet would simply glide around the post and follow her to the ground.

Gripping one of the sheet ends in each hand close to the base of the spindle, Davon straddled the top railing, and eased herself over using her upper body strength. She could feel her biceps straining as she clung desperately to the slippery cotton. Because the balcony was narrow, she dangled close enough to the palace wall to be able to touch it with her feet. Sticking the toes of her runners into mortar cracks, she attempted to redistribute some of her weight, and poured all of her attention to locating stone lips and ledges. To move downward, she had to loosen her grip one hand at a time, and inch her way down the sheet. It was a difficult feat, and every time she loosened her hold, she almost fell. She focused on her breathing, locating cracks, alternating grasps, and nothing else. Pretending she was rock climbing, she envisioned her grade ten gym teacher. "Control Davon, it's about control and physics." Sweat from her forehead dripped into her eyes and she made several faulty attempts to blink them away. She didn't dare look down, but realized she wouldn't be able to hold on much longer. Her hands were beginning to cramp. "Not much further, you can do it, Davon!" she whispered, silently. When her left hand moved again, she found she was gripping the last bit of the sheet. Using every speck of strength she could muster, she paused with her feet still against the wall, and took a peek. The ground was much farther away than she had estimated. Sighing, she pushed away from the wall, swayed, and then plummeted.

Davon landed on her back almost impregnated in the middle of a yew bush. The shrub had cushioned her fall, but snapping twigs and branches had rudely interrupted the peaceful silence. Opening her eyes, Davon did a quick body check before rolling to her side and onto the grass. "Thank God I'm okay!" she said quietly, squatting behind the shrub. Doing double duty, she surveyed the area in case someone had heard the racket, while quickly rolling up the sheet. Although she couldn't see anyone, she stayed low to the ground and ran towards a larger group of bushes that were closer to the wall. Jamming the sheet underneath the middle plant, she sat down and quickly removed her white running shoes, hiding them there as well. She now shifted her attention to locating her bag. It lay almost directly under the balcony, and Davon had to jog back from where she came to retrieve it. Grabbing it, she took one last look up. The balcony was close to twenty-five feet above the ground. It was lucky she hadn't been injured! Moving quietly, she stayed close to the palace wall, and headed towards the front staircase of the women's quarters. She knew there was a small opening under the stairs, and planned to shimmy into it. Once there, Davon shook out her clothes and hair, untied the burka, put it on, and then slipped on her black flats.

The sun was rising swiftly and daylight soon overtook the night. Davon looked at the time and saw it was just minutes before six o'clock. She still had an hour to wait. Dusting off her bag, she placed it against the back wall and sat down. Her back ached, and as she leaned forward to stretch, a terrible pain radiated down her leg, causing her to grimace. Adjusting her position she soothingly rubbed the area, knowing she would have a massive bruise tomorrow. Davon shook her head and groaned. Was this really happening? Was she really in a foreign country, hiding in a cubbyhole? She pressed her eyes shut wishing that when she opened them, it would all be a bad dream. She was tired, so very tired!

The sound of a moving vehicle caught her attention and she froze, one of the limousines had arrived early. Quietly removing her headscarf from her bag, she covered her hair and then reached for the compact mirror she had stashed in the pocket. She was shocked at her reflection. An ugly red abrasion ran down the side of her cheek from her brow to the bottom of her left ear, and the blood, which had dried was pooled under her chin. Taking a tissue from her pocket, she cleaned the scrape as best she could and pulled the scarf forward to cover it. If one of the women noticed, she'd have to make something up. Pushing her back against the wall, she swept off the dust that had settled on the front of her burka. The stone floor was dirty and cold, and she was uncomfortable. Discomfort is good, she though, I need to stay awake.

She strained to listen to the drivers nattering. They were a little too far away, and Davon could only pick out one or two Farsi words. She prayed they wouldn't see her leave her hiding place, because although she tried to locate where their voices were coming from, she was unable. After what seemed like forever, she finally heard some activity above her head. She presumed the women were gathering on the landing. Slowly rising, she hid her bag underneath the burka, and tidied her garments. Right on the stroke of seven, the women started down the staircase making their way to the limousines. Davon snuck out of the alcove into the shadows, and watched them, waiting for the right moment. When the last of the party cleared the bottom stair, she stepped out and joined the end of the line. The women had already split into groups. Five entered the first vehicle and the rest continued on towards the second. Looking straight ahead and mimicking the walk of the woman directly ahead of her, Davon paled when she counted five burkas waiting to get into the second car. She glanced at the driver who was standing at attention near the front of the limo, hoping he hadn't detected she was number six.

"Davon," said Pipa, with surprise. She reached out and blocked Davon's entrance to the back seat. "Lamna said you were sick! We already have ten girls going to Dubai."

"Please, could you fit me in," Davon whispered desperately, thrusting her upper body into the cabin. "I've got my heart set on coming! Please!" She felt as though she couldn't breathe, and looked at each one of them pleadingly.

Pipa sighed, then laughed, and slid away from the window. "Move over girls, I guess we'll be having six today."

The driver closed the rear door, and Davon smiled, feeling conscientious about the scratch on her face. "I can't tell you how much I appreciate it!" she said quietly, adjusting her position on the smooth black leather seat.

"Believe me, we always like you to come, Davon. But five in the car is comfortable, six is cramped," said Mielle. Two of the other women nodded in agreement.

"Sorry Mielle," replied Davon, praying her rich, spoiled seat mates wouldn't make a scene.

The limo started up and the women broke into Arabic. Davon was incredibly grateful to be excluded from the conversation. I know you're talking about me, she said to herself, leaning her head against the window. When they passed the grand entranceway, she noticed Bedon in an impeccable gray suit standing on the top stair, motioning to a guard. Pressing back into the seat so that he wouldn't see her face, she watched him out of the corner of her eye, and wondered what he would do when he discovered she had left the premises. Would he come after her, hunt her down? She tried to think like him, and carefully calculated how much of a head start she would have.

When the vehicle veered to the right, the palace was replaced with the rugged, lifeless desert and Davon stared at the shimmering reddish golden sand extending for as far as she could see.   It was a God forsaken place, and she envisioned Bedon yanking her out of the car and leaving her there to die.

"Davon, Davon! Hello!" said Pipa, looking exasperated. "You are always daydreaming! What are you thinking about?"

Davon looked at the five women staring at her. "I was thinking about work, sorry." She tried to calm her nerves and engage.

"You don't look comfortable, is that your medical bag, the huge bump under the burka?" Pipa asked, pointing to the large bulge on the seat.

Davon smiled, and lightened her voice. "Yes, you all know I never go anywhere without it. Just be happy I have it in case of an accident or injury.

Shopping can be dangerous you know!" The women giggled at her teasing, and the tension in the air eased.

The two storey restaurant was packed. Megan sat at a table overlooking the salt water swimming pools, a decadent display of three oval step pools with two cascading waterfalls. As she played with her coffee cup, she counted the number of guests in line at the breakfast buffet. Most of them were tourists dressed in expensive summer wear. She looked down at her own clothing, and felt embarrassed at the frilly off-white silk blouse and slim-legged navy cotton pants. Why hadn't she thrown in some nicer clothing? She berated herself, and scanned the entranceway to the dining room for a fourth time? Where was Matt? They had agreed on eight o'clock! Taking a sip of coffee, she took a sideways glance at the sheiks the maître d was seating at the next table. Their getup was straight out of the movie *Lawrence of Arabia*, and Meg smiled as she imagined them on camels racing across the desert. They were extremely attractive men, dark-skinned, black eyed, and dressed in pure white robes with white head coverings attached by thick, gold and red cord. On every finger they wore heavy gold rings, and Megan couldn't help but notice their expensive diamond studded watches as they adjusted the sleeves of their robes when they sat. Probably Rolex, she thought, feeling even more out of place. Looking up from her own meager watch, she scanned the room again for Matt. That was when her eyes met with one of the sheiks. They were scary eyes, lustful and degrading.

"Excuse me Miss, are you American?" he asked in perfect English.

The question startled her, and she didn't know if she should lie. Slim and buxom, she was blond and blue-eyed like Davon, but had a rounder face, and smaller nose, which turned up at the tip in a pixy sort of way. Her eyes were luminous, and her long black eyelashes with only a hint of mascara made them breathtaking. She was the epitome of the all American girl. "Ah, yes I am," she answered, breaking eye contact to look for Matt.

"And you're in our beautiful country alone?" his companion inquired, deliberately and suggestively licking his lips.

Here we go, she thought, franticly searching for her travel mate among the guests entering the restaurant. "Matt, over here!" she called, suddenly seeing him.

He strode over to the table and smiled. Tall, dark and exceedingly handsome, he too looked very much American in his cotton dress shirt and jeans. "Morning. Sorry I'm late, but I thought about something when I woke up and called Ted to..." Meg looked at him and moved her eyes anxiously towards the men beside them. Picking up on the clue, he sat down and continued by saying, "Anyway, we can talk about that later. How'd you sleep?"

For a few minutes they made typical chitchat and then got up from the table to go to the buffet. "What's going on?" Matt asked when they were out of earshot.

"Those guys were hitting on me," she whispered, selecting a pumpkin muffin from the pastry table.

"The two sheiks, they looked like decent people," he commented, also helping himself to a muffin as well as a butter croissant.

"Are you kidding? I had an awful feeling that if they wanted me in their harem I'd disappear without a trace!"

Matt laughed. "I promise to stick close, one missing sister is enough."

They went to different stations and packed their plates with food, Megan opting for fruit and yogurt while Matt loaded up on eggs, bacon, sausage and toast. Pausing by a palm tree, Meg waited for him. "What were you going to say about Ted?"

"I called him and changed the size of the limo."

"Why? I thought we agreed to go with the Lexus because it cost less," said Meg.

"I know, but it was the wrong decision. If we have a vehicle identical to the ones the rich people drive around here, our car will be harder to follow." Megan pursed her lips. "Listen, how many stretch limos have we seen in the last couple of days? Hundreds, that's how many. It's worth the extra dough."

"You're probably right Matt, I'm glad I brought my other credit card," replied Meg, moving towards their table.

They talked about the weather, the luxurious hotel, and the marvelous food selection for the rest of the meal, avoiding conversation about the reason they were in Dubai. Ted had warned them that on this side of the world, the walls had ears. At nine-fifteen after a delicious meal, they were in the hotel's state-of-the-art glass elevator zooming up to their rooms with six other guests.

"I'll meet you in the lobby in thirty minutes. The car will arrive at ten," said Matt, as they parted company to get their bags. "And don't forget to pull out the floppy hat, Meg!"

"It's already out Matt, stop mothering me!" she called back, accelerating her gait towards the opposite end of the hall.

For the next three hours Davon somehow managed to maintain her composure. Her back and shoulders throbbed, and although she was uncomfortably squished on a smaller portion of the seat, she refused to stretch, not wanting to inconvenience Mielle in any way. She could deal with the discomfort for another hour and then she'd be free! Free of all ties to the palace, free of Bedon! Discretely, she checked her watch, and eavesdropped on the women's trivial natter about shopping and purchases.

225

They were speaking in English for her benefit, and though Davon was pleased they were including her in the conversation, she really didn't have time to talk because she needed to pour all of her energy into planning a slick escape from the clique, once they arrived in the city. Letting her heavy eyelids droop, she relaxed for a moment, thankful that so far all had gone well. She assumed the ruse of locking her bedroom door, and covering her tracks by repairing the cut screen had given her a little bit of extra time. In the morning, when she didn't show up to give Jasmine her dose of insulin, Raja would certainly go to her suite and discover the locked bedroom door. Would the interpreter be relieved or furious when she realized Davon was gone?

The conversation hushed, and Davon found herself being lulled to sleep by the gentle rocking of the vehicle. She was totally exhausted, and as she made her plans to get away from the harem in Dubai, she found herself fading. Slowly, her head slipped to her chest, and just as she started to dream, a loud cry awoke her! Snapping open her eyes, Davon stared at the shrieking woman across from her, and then followed the eyes of the others to the elongated sunroof. A brown, sun-faded helicopter hovered several meters above the car.

"What's going on!" screamed Pipa, over the growing, deafening sound of the whirling blades. As she fidgeted to find the intercom button to speak with the driver, she looked at Davon and said with defeat, "This could be something very bad."

Davon gritted her teeth and prepared for the worst. She had known he would come after her. She thought of her family, her life and Matt. She loved Matt, and now wished she had stifled her pride and had told him when they had talked. But it was too late for regrets. She was a dead woman. Following the lead of the others, Davon slumped down in the seat and continued to peer out the side window. She felt the limousine driver stepping on the gas, and grabbed onto the door handle to prevent herself from sliding forward.

They had just entered the outskirts of town where rural shacks with wares littered both sides of the highway. Colorfully dressed vendors of the small businesses and open air fruit stands shielded their eyes from the sun, while taking in the drama as the copter swayed dangerously back and forth over the limousines, intimately close to the roofs of the vehicles and the make-shift stalls on the sides of the road. Davon watched in horror as many of the canvas coverings blew off, flying into the barren desert. Stands collapsed and fruit and pottery scattered, and vendors fell to the ground as the tips of the copter's blades came entirely too close.

The limousines recklessly increased speed, and as the helicopter continued in chase, the bodyguard's jeep moved along side of their car, passing it. Davon heard gun fire. "Where are the bodyguards going? Are they abandoning us?" she shouted. She could see the jeep racing along the side of the first limousine.

"The helicopter is trying to head us off, push us off the road and into the sand. The guards are well trained, and know how to stop the helicopter from landing. If it lands and stops us, we will be held, and money will be demanded from Abdul," answered Pipa quietly, her face ashen. Like Davon, Pipa was the only one of the wives sitting up with her eyes open, the others, eyes shut, were slumped on the floor clutching one another.

"Has this happened before?" asked Davon, thinking the attack may not be about her.

"Never," replied Pipa, so softly Davon could barely hear her.

Davon nodded and fell silent. She debated telling her companions the truth, to explain that she was the target. She knew Bedon was hunting her, and she worried that someone else, maybe all of them would be killed in the chase. Should she give herself up? Should she tell Pipa to have the driver stop the car? "Pipa, I..." The words lodged in her throat.

The highway widened into four lanes as the city skyline came into view. Buildings grew denser lining the road. They were nearing the downtown core. Suddenly, the driver took a hard right, separating from lead car. Davon gripped the side of the seat as the vehicle lurched sideways. They race down a narrow exit ramp onto a busy side street, weaving in and out of traffic for a least another ten minutes. Holding her breath, Davon listened for the whirl of the blades. There was no sound of a helicopter. Unexpectedly, the car slowed. They were on the same street, but deep in the mist of residential high-rises, with lofty trees flanking both sides of the avenue. As the women helped each other back onto their seats, they strained to look out the windows and sunroof.

"We've lost it!" cried Mielle. "Wait until Abdul finds out about this! We must call him immediately!"

"We've also lost the first car, and the bodyguards," said Pipa sternly. "We need to first rendezvous with the other women, and discuss what to do as a group. I'm telling the driver to take us to the gold shops," she said, taking charge. Pushing the intercom she switched to Farsi, rapidly giving the driver instructions.

CHAPTER TWENTY-TWO

The black stretch limousine pulled up to the curb and parked directly across the street from the gold venders. The chauffeur rolled down the privacy partition and turned around to look at Matt and Meg. "The harem's vehicles park right there, in the indentation between the potted palms." He pointed to the parking space on the other side of the street. "The space is permanently reserved for them."

"Thanks Amil," said Matt, pulling his ball cap down. "Meg, the second we see the two limos park, you'll have to get into position. We have to act before the guards know what hit them. Remember, we have only seconds to grab Davon, and to get away. Don't give her any time to talk or think! I'll keep my face covered, and will have my back to her when she approaches the car. So be prepared to roll, and protect yourself when I shove her into the back seat." Matt looked back at Amil. "And Amil, the instant I yell go, get us the hell out of here!"

"Got it boss," said the driver.

Meg took in a long deep breath, exhaling slowly. "I just hope she comes," she said, as she put on her sun hat. Two seconds after her comment, a limousine pulled swiftly into the harem's parking space. They watched for a few silent minutes. "Where's the other car?" she questioned.

Matt, Amil, and Meg glanced nervously down the street. There was a lot of traffic going back and forth in both directions, but no other limousines.

"I don't know," replied Matt. "What do you think, Amil?"

"I'm not sure. I was told two limos and a jeep with two or three bodyguards."

As they observed the vehicle the rear door of the limousine opened. Matt instantly followed suit. "Let's do it! If she's not there, she's not there."

Meg quickly positioned herself on the sidewalk alongside the car and placed the brim of her hat overtop of her face. Matt stood beside her, scanning each of the woman dressed in head to toe black exiting the limousine across the street. He counted six, and noticed five of them started gathering in a tightly knitted ring, while one appeared to be slowly backing away from the group.

"One of the women doesn't quite fit in, looks like an outsider from the rest. I'm going to give it a whirl, Meg," he whispered. Then, he proceeded to yell. "Help, someone help!" He pretended to look frantically around. "Is there a doctor here, my wife needs a doctor! Please someone help me!" He watched as several pedestrians looked up towards him, and then saw one of black figures, the one who had inched away from the group, jerk her head in his direction. "Help, please I need a doctor!" he screamed again.

Without thinking, the woman immediately dashed into the oncoming cars. Screeching brakes and loud ear-piercing horns could be heard as she made her way madly across the street. The harem women left behind hysterically waved and hollered, but their antics were drowned in the hectic scene. Matt ducked down, and crouched over Megan. "She's coming, stay where you are!"

"I'm a doctor. What happened?"

Still crouched down, Matt grunted, and waited for Davon to get closer. When she squatted to examine the body beside the car, he jumped up, and grabbing her around her waist, lifted and shoved. Davon flew inside the vehicle face down on the floor of the backseat. She instantly began to wiggle and fight, cursing loudly, totally oblivious to Matt calling her name. Stretching out his foot and placing it on top of her back, Matt held her down. He then leapt inside, leaving Meg to shut his door. As planned, Meg jumped in the front seat beside Amil. "Go!" they screamed together.

Matt loosened his hold, and Davon who was now completely tangled in her burka with her head dress flipped over her face, swore at them. "You bastards, my father will kill you, he works at the Pentagon and you're toast! Do you hear me, you creeps!"

"Davon, its okay my love," Matt said, pulling her up and close to him.

Frantically clearing the scarf from her face, she stared at them in disbelief. "Matt, Meg! Oh My God, you're really here," she cried, bursting into tears.

Cradling her in his arms, Matt pulled off the scarf and gently stroked her head. He could feel her body shaking uncontrollably. "You need to stay down, and unseen until we get to the embassy. Let it out Davon, you're safe now. I'm not going to let anyone harm you."

The drive took less than twenty minutes, and Meg caught up in Davon's grief, wept along with her all the way to the embassy. When the wrought iron gates swung open allowing the car to pass, Meg dried her eyes, and reached through the partition for her sister's hand. "It's all over Sis, you're going to be okay. We're taking you home."

After the car pulled into a spot in the underground parking area, Matt patted Davon's back and said gently, "Come on Sweetheart, we're supposed to meet with the diplomat who made your rescue possible. Do you need a few more minutes?"

"No, I'm okay. I still can't believe you're here! Thank you for coming, thank you," she answered blubbering again. Matt assisted her out of the car and Megan helped her out of the burka.

"Are you alright Davon?" Meg asked. "Because if you need time, if you need a moment..."

"I'm great Meg, really, unbelievably great!" replied Davon, grabbing her little sister for a hug.

Matt slung Davon's medical bag over his shoulder, and after thanking Amil for his help, they took the elevator to the fourth floor. The door opened to a large space filled with at least thirty people in cubicles keyboarding. Davon smiled. She felt as though she was home already.

"This way," said Matt, nudging her towards Ted's office.

When they arrived, the receptionist ushered them in. Ted enthusiastically greeted them. "Have a seat Dr. Marshall, Meg, Matt," he said, pushing a third chair close to his desk. "I just spoke to Amil on the cell, and heard everything went as planned."

"A piece of cake," said Meg, grinning as she sat. "Dad's going to be very proud."

"Yeah," said Ted, sitting also. "Remember our agreement, you can't tell anyone what happened and that my friends, includes your father. He doesn't work for us anymore," he added, leaning forward in his chair to look her in the eye. "I'm serious Meg,"

She glanced at Davon and Matt. "Of course Ted, I understand. I was just making conversation,"

"Good. Now Dr. Marshall..."

"Please Ted, call me Davon, and thank you by the way for your help," she said, settling in the middle chair between Meg and Matt. She crossed her legs and waited.

"You're welcome. Now, I have to complete your paperwork before you can leave, so please bear with me, it's very important and shouldn't take too long," he said earnestly. "First off, can you tell me how you came to be in Dubai?" Ted moved his computer closer and opened the pink file folder in front of him, while picking up his pen.

"Well, I found an advertisement for a female physician for Prince Abdul's wives and children on the internet, applied for the position, and got it."

"I see, and how did you get into the country?" he paused, and looked up at her. "The American government has no record of you going through customs."

Davon gulped, and felt the pressure of Matt's hand squeezing hers. "When the plane I was on landed in Dubai, it was stopped on the tarmac and I was told to get off, which I did. The Prince's man, Mr. Bedon took my passport and work visa, and said he would do the paper work. I was put in a limousine, taken to the heliport, and flown to the palace."

"And then what happened? Please be as specific as you can."

"The palace was incredibly beautiful, right on the ocean with four hundred miles of desert between us and the city. My apartment was luxurious and my medical clinic brand new. For the first month I did nothing, the women weren't used to having a physician on the grounds. And then one morning, I delivered the Prince's first set of twin boys. After that I became so busy, I had little time off." Davon adjusted her seat, and caught an encouraging smile from her sister. Ted rapidly made notes.

"Your family contacted the office last week to say you called home two weeks ago and used a code word, namely cabbage, four times in your conversation, which lead them to believe you were in extreme trouble. Was this the case, Davon?" Ted stopped writing, and made eye contact.

"Yes, I was concerned for my life," replied Davon quietly, biting her lower lip. Matt glanced at her and nodded for her to continue.

"Can you elaborate?" Ted asked, modifying the position of his laptop computer on the dark wood veneer desk.

Meg held up her arm to stop Davon from proceeding. "Is this really necessary, Ted? She's been through enough. Can't she complete the paperwork once we're back in the States?"

"I'm afraid not," he said, sitting back in his chair. "Do you have your passport with you, Davon?"

"No, I wasn't able to get it back."

"Precisely," said Ted, looking at Meg. "And to get a new passport from the American Embassy, so she can board a plane tonight, I have to complete all of the paperwork. Shall I continue?"

"But..." said Meg, determined to argue for Davon's benefit.

Davon put her hand on her sister's knee to silence her, and then continued to talk, losing herself in the story. "Things were fine, I mean the culture was definitely different, but my work was going well until a month ago. In September, Prince Abdul asked me to accompany him to Cairo, a place I had dreamt of going my whole life, and so I agreed," she said, purposely omitting the fact she was smitten with the Prince and he with her. "When we were there, we attended a charity event at the Sphinx, and during the course of the evening there was an assassination attempt. Someone tried to kill the Prince." The room hushed and all eyes turned to Davon. "He received two flesh wounds. Luckily the bullet only grazed his arm and chest. Because Prince Abdul wanted no media attention, he asked me not to call for help, but to assist him to the car. Instead of going to a hospital, I cleaned and sutured the wounds in his suite."

"I never heard anything about this, it happened in Cairo, you say?" Ted asked, furrowing his brow. "So you're saying the assassination attempt on the Prince gave you concern for your own life?"

"In a roundabout way, because I discovered who organized it. It was Mr. Bedon, the Prince's valet."

"Oh My God Davon, why didn't you call me?" exclaimed Matt, shaking his head. "You should have come right home from Cairo!"

Davon smiled at Matt reassuringly. "I told the Prince that night about my suspicions, and he assured me Bedon would be questioned, and wouldn't be allowed to return to the palace. But the next day Bedon did return. It was the Prince who did not. After that things started to deteriorate uncontrollably," she said, licking her dry lips. "Would it be possible to get something to drink?"

The second Ted left the room in search of beverages, Meg turned to her. "I know it must be horrible to relive this Davon, but once you're done with the questioning Ted has promised to get us out on the first available flight tonight. This time tomorrow we'll be home."

Davon stood up, and bent over to embrace her. "Just being here with the two of you makes me feel like I'm already home!" She pulled at her ponytail and ran her fingers through her hair. "I probably look awful. I haven't slept well in weeks."

Matt stood, and pulled her into his arms. "You're absolutely gorgeous, more beautiful than ever." Noticing the angry red scratch running down the side of her face, he held her chin and examined it. "How did you get this deep cut, Davon?"

"I did it myself, but that's another story. I'll tell you on the plane."

Ted returned with three bottled waters and four Cokes, and set them down on his desk. "Help yourself everyone," he said, grabbing a Coke for himself and settling back in his chair. "I'm ready anytime you are, Davon."

Matt opened a bottle of water and handed it to Davon, who took a long drink before she continued. "I wasn't sure if Bedon knew I knew he was involved, but gradually over the course of several weeks every liberty I had, including servants, telephone, internet and travel was taken away. When Abdul still didn't return, I feared the worst, that he had been murdered." She fell silent for a moment, and stared at the pink-beige wall, and the tacky black framed diplomas hanging just behind Ted's head. "I was convinced Bedon had killed the Prince. Then last week, Abdul's seventeen year old son and heir died at the hospital in Dubai." She talked about her interview with Hepbet and her diagnosis, the early death of his brother Tilly, and the planned abduction of Memen. "Is that enough information to get a passport Ted?" she finally asked, meekly.

"Believe me, if what you say is true, you are more than qualify," he replied, reaching into the top drawer of his desk. "One more question," he hesitated briefly. "Did the Prince come back?"

Davon snorted. "Yes he did, and our meeting still haunts me. He acted indifferent, as though he had no idea who I was, what I had done for him. I can't figure it out." She had trouble hiding her anger.

"You will probably never find out, trust me," said Ted, nodding knowingly. "Now Meg and Matt, I need to check over your passports, if you could get them out please." Ted grabbed a stamp and ink pad from the table behind him. When Matt handed him his passport, Ted flipped through it quickly and returned it to him. He took Meg's passport from her, stamped it, and put it in the drawer.

"Hey, give me back my passport!" Meg stood up and held out her hand.

"Settle down Meg," said Matt, as Davon grabbed her arm. "I'm sure there's a good explanation, right Ted?"

Ted sighed at the drama, and pushed two American passports towards the end of his desk. "It's typical for employers in this part of the world to take employee passports, so we knew you would arrive at the embassy without one, Davon. We're also very aware of the far-reaching power, which Prince Abdul's kingdom holds. He may be looking for you, and if so, his first stop will be the airport." Ted handed Davon a passport. "We downloaded your picture on file and created a new document for you. Today, you'll be traveling as Julia Prescott, a registered nurse. If you're asked why you're here, we suggest you tell them you won a trip for two to Dubai. We've changed the day and date of your birth, please memorize the information." Ted then turned and looked up at Meg. "Because traveling under the family name could put you in grave danger Meg, we've also given you a new identity. Your Julia's sister, Melba Prescott."

Meg picked up her passport, looked at it, and smiled. "Melba, that's the best you could do?"

The comment was ignored by Ted and he continued. "You'll see the entry date and time is identical to Matt's. Because customs could have a picture circulating of you Davon, we advise you to travel as a threesome. They will be looking for a lone blond American female. Here are the plane tickets complimentary of Uncle Sam. You leave on the 6:00 pm flight to Cairo. It was the first flight I could get you out on. From there you'll fly to London and then home."

Meg looked up. "Cairo, I've always wanted to go there!"

"Not this time Meg," said Matt, scooping up the tickets.

Meg sighed, and continued to thumb through her new passport.

"What happens when we get to the States, Ted? Do I pretend I'm Julia just back from a sunny vacation?" asked Davon

"Oh yes, I should mention that U. S. Customs will be well aware of what has taken place. This is a technique we use to get Americans home, people like you, who are in trouble in a foreign country. We even have a code word for it," he laughed, awkwardly. "When you get back to the States, you and Meg will be pulled aside, and momentarily detained. The temporary passports will be apprehended." Ted stood and extended his hand. "Feel free to freshen up and use the cafeteria downstairs while you wait to go to the airport. I've organized an unmarked car to take you there at four. Good luck to all of you."

Davon held her breath and gripped Matt's hand as the jumbo jet pulled out of the gate. She was completely worn out, her nerves on end. Going through customs had been absolutely terrifying! And she still wasn't sure how they had pulled it off. She had been caught entirely off guard when the agent had questioned her about her relationship with Matt. She had flushed, stammered, unable to come up with a plausible explanation. The only thought that kept running through her mind was Ted's warning that customs was looking for a lone woman with her description. Thank God Matt had protectively piped up that she was his fiancée. Davon looked at him now, resting, his eyes closed, and his head cocked to one side. Every once in a while he'd let out a cute little snore.

The flight attendant went through the safety drill, and although Davon absent mindedly watched the demonstration, her mind drifted to her time at the palace. They'll be okay, she told herself, Momma Ba, Jasmine, Memen, Sashic, Bin, Lamna--the patients and friends she had abandoned. Would they ever know the truth, the reason she had to leave so abruptly?

"Julia, are you alright? You look as though you've seen a ghost," asked Meg, with a chuckle. She continued to play with her ear phones untangling the wires.

"Maybe I have. I was just thinking about the people I'm leaving behind, some really wonderful people I'll never see again." Davon felt a kick at the back of her chair, and turned to glance at the three passengers behind them. An attractive, but over-weight Caucasian woman sat in the middle seat directly behind her beside a dark skinned, dark haired male, who eyed her suspiciously. In the window seat a young brown haired girl, perhaps their child sat cheerfully playing with a doll. Davon turned back around and swallowed, she knew she was paranoid, but after being yanked off the plane on the tarmac once before, there was no way she'd relax until they were in the air.

She exhaled as the plane accelerated down the runway, and felt the G-forces pushing her back into her seat as it took flight. Closing her eyes she smiled, she was going home. Everything was going to be fine.

Meg nudged Davon's arm. "Here's a set of ear plugs if you want them."

"No thanks, I think I'll snooze," replied Davon, closing her eyes and snuggling closer to Matt. For the first time in weeks, she actually felt at peace. It would take a while to repair the hurt, and time to learn to trust him again. Yet, a tiny part of her wasn't positive if she could go backwards. She knew Matt was an amazing man. After all, he had come halfway around the world to rescue her, and she should be happy, she declared silently. But too much had happened, and she had changed. She wasn't the same Davon Marshall that had left Boston in a huff eight and a half months ago.

"Dav... I mean Julia! Look at this!" said Meg, shaking her sister's arm. "Your Prince Abdul is on the news!"

Davon sat upright and glared at the TV screen, as Meg shared one of her ear plugs. The camera returned to the British reporter who was covering the story. "This is a solemn day for Prince Abdul and his family as they attend memorial services for Prince Hepbet, the seventeen year old heir. The cause of his tragic death is still unknown." The camera scanned a large group of men outside, standing around a cloth covered coffin, and as individual faces slowly came into focus, Davon studied each of them, but recognized no one except Abdul. "I don't get it," she murmured to Meg, unconsciously shaking her head. "His personality changed so dramatically. I thought I knew him."

"Who are you talking about?" mumbled Meg, her eyes glued to the screen.

The camera left the crowd and returned to the Prince. He stood just to the side of the coffin clad in an expensive black Armani suit, his mouth pursed, and his eyes uninterested. He looked apathetic, bored. Davon saw the exact same expression she had witnessed yesterday, a coldness she couldn't place.

As the camera zoomed closer, his face larger than life, Davon slapped her leg. "I figured it out!" she exclaimed, loudly.

"Keep it down," warned Meg, as she turned and smiled at the woman across the aisle.

Matt woke at the disturbance, and leaned closer to Davon, who was now only inches from the TV screen. "What's going on?" he inquired, sleepily.

"Now I understand why I was such a threat to Bedon!" Davon whispered, her voice becoming bitter. She looked at Matt and then back at the TV. "Abdul has a black mole right there," she said, pointing to the face on the screen.

"Where, I don't see a mole," replied Meg.

"Exactly," Davon answered, "That man is not Prince Abdul."

"The reporter said he was. Who do you think he is?" asked Meg, looking questioningly from her sister to Matt.

"He has a twin. I've never seen him before, yet I know it's him impersonating Abdul," said Davon. "I'm one hundred percent positive!"

Matt leaned over top of Davon to have a closer look at the screen. "What are you saying Davon, that his brother got rid of him?"

"Something happened to Abdul in Cairo, that's all I know!" Davon pushed herself back into the seat and closed her eyes. She felt terribly responsible, conflicted. She never should have left Abdul in Cairo with Bedon. All of a sudden the serenity she had felt moments ago vanished. Why was this happening, now of all times? It wasn't her problem, she told herself, she was on her way home, and wanted nothing more than to blank out the total nightmare. The acid in her stomach churned, and she felt the bitter taste of bile at the back of her throat. She was guilty of running, turning her back on Abdul, a man she cared for, and at a time when he needed her most. For some unknown reason, Davon had an unusually strong feeling he was alive and still in Egypt. She had to get off the plane when they landed in Cairo.

"Are you okay, Davon?" asked Meg.

"Let her be Meg, she's been through a lot," said Matt, gazing at Davon protectively.

"It's alright, Matt. I only needed a few minutes to think," said Davon. With a stab of uncertainty, she added, "I don't expect you two to understand, but I'm thinking of getting off the plane in Cairo."

"You can't be serous, Davon!" exclaimed Matt, looking incredulous. "We just went to an incredible length to rescue you."

"I said you wouldn't understand."

"I'll listen to whatever you have to say, but you have to be reasonable. You're exhausted. You admit to not sleeping well over the last few weeks. You've lost weight, and you have dark circles under your eyes. I can't imagine what you are thinking!" Matt tried to take Davon's hand, but she pulled it away.

"I can come to Cairo with you, Davon. I have another seven days of holiday time," piped up Meg.

"Please Megan, you are not helping!" snapped Matt.

Davon sighed, and spoke softly. "It may already be too late. But, I have a strong feeling that Prince Abdul is being held somewhere in Egypt." She stopped talking for a moment and rubbed her forehead, remembering Abdul mentioning that his brother would never harm him. "I was the last person to see the Prince, and I feel a sense of responsibility because no one else at the palace knows what really happened. You see, I never said anything. I was frightened and intimidated by Bedon, and then I started to fear for my own life. I didn't know who I could trust. That's when I made the phone call to Mom and Dad."

Matt put his hand on her arm. "This is not your war, Davon. Listen to me. It's admirable that you want to help, but you're not thinking clearly.

You're totally out of your league. When we get back to the States, we can drive to New York and visit the consulate. You can file a report." Matt looked at her and tried to remain calm. "We need to let the professionals handle this."

"You know Sis, Matt is right. As much as I want to see the Pyramids, we have to stay on the plane in Cairo. It's only a forty-five minute stop before it carries on to London, and this is the last flight going out tonight."

Davon stared at the screen in front of her taking in what they said. Slowly, she came to the realization that her plan to get off the plane was foolish and illogical. She wasn't thinking clearly. She was exhausted, had no money, no clothes, and was traveling on a fake passport. And where would she start looking anyway? No, she'd call Ted the minute she got home, ask for his advice, and file a report as Matt suggested. Her aloneness suddenly felt insurmountable. This wasn't her battle, but no matter what, even if she had to return, she wasn't about to let Bedon win.

THE END

Coming in 2015, the sequel to Dance with the Harem:

"The Riddle of Ra"

Back at her old job in Boston and trying to work things out with Matt, Davon is surprised when a stranger with identification from the CIA asks her to return to Cairo to help search for Abdul. Guilt-ridden at being the last person to see Abdul alive, she's worried about returning to Egypt because the stranger has informed her she can't tell anyone about the mission. As time is of the essence, Davon must quickly decide whether to follow her gut instinct or her heart.

For all titles by D.P. Scott visit www.dpscott.ca

ABOUT THE AUTHOR

DP SCOTT, author of *Dance with the Harem*, *The Christmas Elf*, *Saturna*, *There's a Monster in the Wall!*, and *The Wedding Guidebook*, lives in Kelowna, BC with her husband Roy, and their cocker spaniel, Sophie. She is currently working on two sequels, including *The Riddle of Ra*. Her children's tale set in Ireland, *A Wee Bit of Magic*, will be published in March 2014. For updates and news, visit www.dpscott.ca.